More titles from Kristopher Rufty

Hell Departed: Pillowface Vs. The Lurkers
Anathema
Master of Pain
(written with Wrath James White)
Something Violent
Seven Buried Hill
The Vampire of Plainfield
Bigfoot Beach
The Lurking Season
Jagger
Prank Night
The Skin Show
Proud Parents
Oak Hollow
Pillowface
The Lurkers
Angel Board

Jackpot
(written with Shane McKenzie, Adam Cesare, & David Bernstein)
Last One Alive
A Dark Autumn

Collections:

Bone Chimes

DESOLATION

KRISTOPHER RUFTY

LAZARUS
PRESS

Desolation
Text Copyright © 2016
Second Paperback Edition
Copyright © 2020 by Kristopher Rufty
Cover art copyright © 2020 Lynne Hansen
www.LynneHansenArt.com

DEDICATION

For Dad. Thank you for everything.

ACKNOWLEDGEMENTS

Special thanks go to Kevin Woods, Vanelle, and John Foutz for supporting this story from its humble beginnings. I also have to thank some more great folks—Tod Clark, Ronald Malfi, Jeff Strand, Lynne Hansen, Paul Synuria II, David Bernstein, Sandy A. Shelonchik, Jonathan Janz, Bryan Smith, Steve Beaver, Trent Haaga, Deborah Grace, and so, so many more who have been a part of this story. It has undergone many transitions throughout the years before becoming the book in your hands.

PROLOGUE

Dennis Hinshaw's first thought when he awoke was he'd gone blind.

He tried to blink. A sticky residue lined his eyelids, crusting his eyelashes. Trying again, the dark film thinned, becoming slightly transparent. He realized he hadn't gone blind after all—it was just blood.

His blood.

He had no idea why he was convinced of this, but somehow he knew it to be certain.

Tightness pressed against his chest and stomach. Even his shoulders were restrained. He could hardly move, and when he did, it elicited great jabs of pain all over that made it hard to breathe.

He couldn't think straight, couldn't get his mind moving in the direction he needed it to. Comprehension wasn't clear, like trying to find something through a window frosted in thick layers of icy dust. Sluggishly, he felt around him.

Broken sharp pieces pricked his fingers as his hand crawled around the car.

Glass?

Fragments of a memory began to percolate into extended sequences: two bright orbs rocketed toward him. Lindsey screamed over Josh's reciting the alphabet for the fifth time in a row from the backseat.

A loud crash, the crumpling of metal against metal—he vaguely remembered the car spinning out of control.

Dennis rubbed his hand along his chest, and could feel the safety harness under his bloody fingers. He wanted it off so he could move freely. Following the strap down to the buckle, his finger struggled with the latch as it tried to push the button. Finally, it went in. There was a click. He dropped. He bumped his head on the roof of the car, smearing the blood encrusting his face across its padded softness.

It took a moment for it to register that he'd fallen upward. He contorted his body to see out his window. The glass was cracked, lines snaking in three directions, but he was still able to see the night outside, to hear the dueling chorales of crickets and frogs. He could see heavy barrages of trees, their tips facing down.

So this had to mean he was upside down.

Not just me...

The car was on its roof.

He groped the darkness above him, his fingers brushing the center console separating the two front seats. He reached under the lid and found the button. It dropped open, spilling papers and other various items of debris onto him. Something solid rapped him on the shoulder. And he assumed it was what he was looking for.

Dennis found the aluminum tube, gripped the rotund tip between his fingers and twisted. A bar of light pried through the darkness, illuminating everything caught in the bright spike. He saw the curve of the steering wheel, the radio with the broken CD player and the empty socket that used to hold a cigarette lighter that he couldn't remember when it had been lost.

It was coming back to him stronger now. The two orbs he'd seen was the car in the other lane veering into theirs. Dennis had been driving. Lindsey, in the passenger seat, was telling him the baby was trying to kick her way out of her belly button while their firstborn,

8

Josh, rehearsed the alphabet from the backseat, clapping every time he made it through without messing up. Lindsey had taken Dennis's hand and placed it on her belly. He'd felt their daughter squirming through her clothes.

And it had warmed his heart.

Then he'd looked back to the road and saw the lights bearing down. The windshield had filled with a blinding glare as the car consumed his lane, heading straight for them.

Dennis began to sweat as he recalled the memory. Cold wetness streamed down from his forehead, mixing with the blood and nicks and scrapes on his skin, singeing like someone had put a match to him. He rubbed a finger along his jaw and snatched it back when something punctured it. Shining the light on his index finger, he saw fresh blood seeping from the tip as if it had been pricked at the doctor's office.

He attempted touching his face again, being much more careful this time. His fingers tapped against something thin and sharp. Carefully tracing the edge, he realized a triangular portion of glass had lodged into his face. It seemed to have entered his cheek at an angle, and poked down through the skin at his jaw. He worked his tongue against his cheek, tracing the smooth slant of glass inside.

Knowing it was there caused his face to sizzle with pain. Dennis gripped the shard, about to tear it loose, but quickly stopped himself before doing something so foolish. If he did, he'd not only dislodge the glass, he'd rip half his face off in the process. He took several deep breaths, then carefully pulled the shard, as if removing a splinter. He felt his cheek stretch as the fragment popped free.

Dennis dropped the glass without looking at it. Working his jaw up and down, he felt only minimal pain, but tasted a lot of blood.

They had been driving on Cunningham Road, and had only a few more miles before reaching home. Then it would have been time for the routine of getting Josh's bath ready, and putting him in bed within the hour.

Josh should be in bed right now…

Josh.

He rolled onto his side, screwing his body in such an awkward way that his thighs began to constrict, and sharp pains stabbed his hips. "Juh-Josh…buddy, are you all right?" Though he'd intended to shout, his voice had sounded groggy, as if he'd just woken from a deep sleep. Maybe he had. Dennis had no idea what time it was, so he wasn't sure how long they'd been like this. "Josh?"

A steady chorus of crickets from the surrounding woods answered him.

"Den…nis…?"

Lindsey!

He turned to where his wife was in the passenger seat—sort of. The moonlight netted the car in diamonds of gray, underscoring Lindsey who was lying against her door at an awkward angle. The window behind her had been smashed, which explained the glass everywhere and the large piece in his face.

He crawled along the ceiling on his elbows, keeping his head ducked low so he wouldn't bash it on the seats above him. Lindsey was on the roof as well, her seatbelt dangling above her. He wasn't sure if she'd unhooked herself, or if she hadn't even buckled up. She had a habit of not using her seatbelt and, unless Dennis checked before they drove away, he'd have no idea she hadn't. The fuse that powered an annoying buzz whenever the seatbelts were unconnected had burned out and they'd never replaced it. It was on the long list of things that Dennis planned to do when he had the time.

He reached Lindsey. Her back was against the empty window frame. Her right arm looked to be pinned behind her back. Her belly jutted out in front of her, a small six-month-old hill. Aiming the light at Lindsey, Dennis made sure he kept the beam away from her eyes. Her body was a conundrum of bruises and slashes. She had chosen to wear a white sundress for their day trip to the lake, and now it was saturated in blood.

He'd never seen so *much* blood.

Even as hurt as she was, her beauty still stunned him. As he nuzzled up against her, his elbows splashed in a warm, sticky puddle that he

10

figured was more of her blood. "Lindsey, my God, sweetie, are you all right?" He put his head to hers and could feel pricks from the glass specks in her hair. "Can you move?"

"Dennis?"

"Yeah sweetie…it's me…I'm right here…"

"It hurts…*baaaad*…hurts to breathe…"

He noticed the wheezing of her breaths, the gurgling coming from her chest. Looking at her lips, he found a trail of blood cascading from either corner of her mouth. Her lips moved soundlessly, making a thin murky bubble in her opened mouth.

His wife was drowning in her blood.

He fought to control his emotions. She didn't need to see him panicking, not when she needed to remain calm. "We have to get you out of here. Can you move?"

She shook her head. "Noooo…I'm stuck…"

"Stuck?"

He reached for her shoulder, but she stopped him.

"Don't," she said. "You don't want to see…" By now her voice sounded like she was talking with a mouthful of toothpaste. "My arm is pinned…"

"Behind you?"

She shook her head.

Under the car.

He'd thought her arm was behind her, but it had actually gone through the broken window and the car had rolled on top of it. Crushed underneath, it was keeping her there up to her elbow. There was no way he could move her, not unless he suddenly gained superhero strength and lifted the car.

Or severed her arm at the shoulder.

If he had something he could use to cut off her arm, he'd do it without hesitation.

"Josh…" she muttered. Her throat was so full of blood now that she could have been speaking underwater. "Is he…?"

Before she could finish, Dennis pointed the light where his son's car seat should be. It was there, a flat base with arm rests, and the seatbelt still had it latched in place.

But his son was not in the seat.

The rear window was a jagged mouth of broken glass.

His heart lurched, making his breaths come out in shrill huffs through his nose.

"Is…he okay…?" asked Lindsey, sounding as if it took all of her strength to mutter it.

"Yeah," Dennis lied. "He's just fine."

"Good…give him a hug from Mommy…can you do that?"

Dennis stared at his wife. Her skin had gone so pale she looked like a ghost in the darkness of the car. Her eyes were shadowed depressions, the whites slowly sinking into her skull. The vibrant life she embraced each day with was slowly draining from her, pooling around Dennis rapidly. He knew she wasn't going to make it…there was just no way.

Wanting to cry, Dennis held it in. He didn't want Lindsey to see. "I'm going to see if I can get us some help."

"O-Okay. Be cuh-careful out there."

"I will…"

"Luh-love you…" Her head craned back, her neck unable to support it any longer. She rested it on the cushiony roof. She took a deep breath in, slowly letting it out.

Dennis turned away from her, his back to her gargling rasps. It felt as if boiling water was pumping through his veins as he kicked his window, breaking it the rest of the way. Then he scooted across the roof. His feet went out first, his upper body following. More glass lanced his back as he slid out. He hardly noticed it.

Outside was much cooler, and a lot less cramped. He rolled onto his side. The smell of pine and grass drifted into his nostrils. It was a calm spring night. He couldn't recall what month it was, because his mind was flooding with an urgency of finding their son so what he'd told his wife wouldn't have been a lie.

12

He briefly considered digging through the debris inside the car for his cell phone. Since he kept it in the cubby between the seats, he guessed it was probably lost. He'd waste precious time searching and decided not to bother.

Trying to stand threatened to be impossible. His left knee gave him a fit as he struggled to get on his feet, feeling as if it had been wrapped in duct tape. He couldn't bend or straighten his leg. It was much too swollen.

Finally, even with the pain, he managed to get upright.

He looked around, his eyes narrowed and focused. He swept the light one way, then another.

"Josh!"

He listened as intently as he could. The night played tricks. He thought he'd heard Josh answer more than once, but when he'd stumble over to where the alleged cry had come from, nobody was there.

"*Josh!* Where *are* you? Daddy's here!"

His breaths were becoming shorter and much more haggard. There was a great tugging pain in his chest, and he clamped his hand over his heart. He could feel it sledging inside. The streak of light bounced around, never settling on any one object more than a moment.

Panic tried its best to seize him, tried to hunker him down on the dew-soaked ground and hug his knees, rocking back and forth until help came. He wouldn't allow it, even if his brain acted like it was trying to twist into a cold ball. By this point, he was dragging his hurt leg uselessly behind him as he hunted.

Hands grabbed him.

Although he'd felt them high on his shoulders, he thought it was Josh, but only for a moment. He spun around. A man, much older than Dennis's thirty-four years, stood before him. He had a very concerned, albeit kind face just an inch from his.

Grimacing, the man said, "Sir? Are you all right?" The man's hands felt like two weights that might make him fall. He repeated his question.

Dennis couldn't conjure up an answer no matter how hard he tried. He kept thinking about Lindsey, how she'd been taking her last breaths in front of him. He should be by her side, holding her hand, whispering into her ear so she wouldn't be alone. But he *needed* to find their son. He was out here...somewhere.

The seatbelt hadn't been tight enough, he'd been thrown...

"I'm Jerry! What's your name? Can you talk?"

Dennis felt his words being blocked by his stuttering tongue. They tried to formulate into comprehensive sentences. "Muh-my boy..."

"What?"

Dennis strained as if constipated to get the words out. "Have—to find...my boy!"

"Your boy?" Jerry looked from right then left. "Where is he?"

If he knew that he wouldn't be stumbling around the dark like a fool shouting his name. "I don't know!"

"Okay...calm down. We'll find him. Together." He helped Dennis turn around, keeping his arm like a brace at his back. "Oh boy..."

Dennis followed the path where Jerry's eyes had landed on the car. This was the first time Dennis had taken a moment to survey the damage. It lay on its top, the wheels pointing at the twinkling stars. Plumes of smoke drifted from the undercarriage. The muffler looked dented, and the pipes leading from it had snapped in half. There was a popping sizzle emanating from somewhere in the car, and he could faintly smell anti-freeze.

How did any of us survive?

That question couldn't be answered. He wasn't sure any of them *had* survived.

"Looks like you came down the embankment," said Jerry.

Dennis glanced back, seeing a short ridge that led down from the road.

Jerry began to turn him. "Let's not look at it, okay?" He angled Dennis away from the wreckage.

And that was when he spotted the pale shape a couple yards away.

14

"Oh…God…" was all Dennis could get out before he tore away from Jerry and hobbled like a madman toward the shape.

Toward his son.

He recognized the orange stripes on the jacket, even in the dark. He could see them vividly from way back there, and as he neared him they seemed to glow brighter under the colorless filter of the moon.

Josh lay on his side, facing away from Dennis. He'd lost his shoes at some point, and now only his socks covered his feet.

"Joshy? Buddy?"

Other than strands of his hair waving in the light breeze, his son didn't move. His skin looked so blue, but Dennis hoped it was only the shadows making it appear that way. Dropping to his knees, he growled at the stabbing pain traveling from his right knee into his hip.

"Sir?" he heard Jerry say from somewhere behind him. "Is that…?"

"Go get help."

"Sir…I don't want to leave you alone."

"Go get help!"

"It's already on the way. I saw the man up on the road…got him out of his car. He's going to be okay I think, a little banged up. We called for help."

"Man?"

The other driver, the bright headlights no doubt. *That* man.

"Yes. I called for help. They're on their way." As if to prove him accurate, Dennis began to hear the faint wail of approaching sirens. They steadily grew louder. "Please sir, don't touch him."

Dennis turned around. "What do you mean?"

Jerry's lip quivered. "Just leave him be, it's too late."

Dennis gripped the man's pants. "It's not too late!"

"Sir…please."

Dennis looked back at his son. "Josh!"

"Don't touch him!"

His hand had already brushed his hair. It felt odd, artificial, like crepe hair. As he reached for Josh to roll him over, he felt Jerry's hands grip him under the arms. He was surprised by the amount of strength such an older guy could have. Dennis was hoisted up, but not before his fingers gripped Josh's coat.

Not before his fingers pulled him over.

When Dennis saw his son's face, his eyes opened only to slits, all the fight went out of him in one limp-inducing shutter. His eyes grew so wide they threatened to tear their way right out from behind the lids. A cry, stammering at first, quickly gained drive like a tiny motor being choked into life.

Josh stared inertly at him, a blank, puffy-cheeked hollow shell that held nothing inside.

Then Dennis was screaming, agonizing bellows that never seemed to stop.

CHAPTER ONE

Beth leaned forward in her chair, elbows braced on her knees. Her eyes had been threatening tears all through her story, and now tiny droplets were spilling over, diluting her mascara into clumpy black smears.

Grant Marlowe squirmed in his seat. He felt bad for Beth. He wondered which was tougher for her—telling her story, or just the act of getting up in front of their small group. Probably a little of both, but she really seemed to be a having a tough time.

It'd be hard for anyone.

It was hard for Grant, which was why in the eight months he'd been regularly attending AA meetings at Fresh Hope Alcoholics Anonymous, he hadn't once spoken to the group as she was now. Watching her made him regret saying that he would. He needed to get over the jitters and stage fright, though, because he was next.

Christ Almighty, I'm next.

At least Kara was with him. He looked over to his daughter sitting in the uncomfortable folding chair next to him. She was nearly an exact duplicate of her mother at twenty-one—the same lemon-colored hair, bright eyes, and just as beautiful.

It made his chest feel like bees were swarming around his lungs. She was a woman, a full-grown woman with breasts and all. She was probably even…

Don't think about that. It'll make you crazy again.

He'd found a boy in her room once. She'd snuck him in after Marion had gone to bed, thinking her alcoholic father had already passed out in the den. Almost, but not quite. He'd heard the padding of their footsteps coming from the kitchen as Kara led her then-boyfriend through the back door.

Trey Riggs, the son of one of Grant's friends, had gotten many new bruises for his efforts and Kara had lost her car, credit card and cell phone until she'd started college the following autumn.

And it had taken Kara even longer than her college start date to forgive Grant. Sure, he could have handled it better. Perhaps a call to the police reporting an intruder would have sufficed. Let them carry the jerk out in handcuffs and give Kara a good scare. But Kara probably would've thought Trey looked cool being toted off like that and grown even more attracted to him.

Beth sniffled from her seat. Grant gladly brought his attention back to her anguish if it meant distracting him from his own. He was tired of constantly reminding himself how much he'd screwed up in the past.

"…I was achieving my dream of being an actress, doing bit parts in movies. I fought to get an audition…for a big-budget movie—a small part—but it paid really well. And I…but I…" She looked up, face smeared in black lines. Lips trembling, she shook her head as if saying she was giving up.

"Go on," said Georgia. She sat at the front of the circle, a clipboard propped on her knee. She wore an ankle-length skirt that clung to her, slit up to the top of her thigh with one smooth leg draped over the other. She ran the AA meeting and was one of Grant's oldest friends. They'd grown up together, and his kids even called her their aunt. Being in an AA group that she led made it feel like he was cheating on a test.

"You're surrounded by friends here," she continued. "There's nothing you could say to us that should cause you any embarrassment. For every bad story, there is always at least one that's even worse."

Beth exhaled a quivering sigh, knuckled away the tears in her eyes, and nodded. "Okay…I'll try."

Georgia smiled. "We're here for you."

This seemed to put Beth at ease. "By the time I got to the audition, I was so plastered that I stumbled over my lines and even forgot my name. I was so bad the casting director laughed at me. I was mortified and just ran out of the room. I knew I had an important audition, but I still partied the night before. I just can't *stop* drinking once I start…"

Beth's voice faded away. She hadn't stopped talking. Grant had just stopped hearing her words. He knew what she meant by her last statement because he was the exact same way. The first swallow was always the best, but the others were nearly just as good.

"…and my Mom still hates me."

"She doesn't hate you," said Georgia.

Beth raised her hands. "She was living the life she'd always wanted *through* me. So not only did I blow it for me, I blew it for her. She doesn't talk to me anymore. I can't even look at myself in the mirror, which is why I look like this." She pointed at her face, wiped her eye and brought it back dabbed in crummy blackness. "I bet I look hideous."

"No," said Georgia. "You're beautiful." She looked at the rest of the group, the other ten or so. "Don't you agree?"

Claps, a few whistles. Beth's cheeks flushed.

Grant was one of those who clapped. So was Kara after they shared a glance and a smile. Beth was a very pretty girl but was probably gorgeous before the abuse had given her face puffy cheeks and swollen pink eyes. She had a husky voice thanks to hard liquor scorching her throat on its way down.

Grant wondered how bad he'd looked at his worst. He'd successfully avoided seeing any pictures of himself from back then…from the accident…and trial.

The guy sitting on the other side of him, Grant thought his name was Tony, leaned over. He wore a beanie on his head with long dark hair swathing the sides of his face. He was trying to grow a beard, but it was thicker in certain patches than others. His mouth close to Grant's ear, Tony quietly said, "Would you bang her?"

Grant ignored the question. Eventually, Tony figured out he wasn't going to respond and turned away.

Georgia slipped her ink pen behind her ear. It vanished in the curls of her hair. "I'm proud of you, Beth. You made a great first step by joining our small group and a giant leap when you shared your story. That's the hardest part of the process. And guess what? You've done it. The hard part is *over*. You've admitted that there *is* a problem. Now, as a team, we will work to help you get past it."

"Thank you, Georgia." Beth smiled her first genuine smile in the three or more months she'd been in the group.

"Why don't you take a break? Relax for a bit? One of our regulars is going to speak tonight, much to his chagrin. He's attended these meetings for a long time now."

Oh shit, here it goes.

"And he hasn't trusted us enough to share his story, but today is different. Right, Grant?"

He couldn't find his voice. He felt a gentle elbow nudge from his daughter on his arm.

"Go on, Dad," she whispered.

"I changed my mind," he whispered back.

"You can do this."

"Grant?" called Georgia. "Are you ready?"

"Um…"

"You'll be fine, Dad." Kara smiled. Her hair was pulled back, and she had on glasses today instead of contacts. He liked her looking like this, a little dressed down, even though it did nothing to hide the beauty she'd inherited from her mother.

He sighed. "If you say so."

"I know so. Now go. Be a tough guy."

"Oh, sure. Because I'm so good at that."

Kara made a face.

Georgia called him again. "You didn't have a change of heart, did you?"

"No," said Grant. "Of course not."

The others suddenly applauded. He held up his hand like a politician at a rally, his shoulders hitched up. He kept his hand in the air, trying to wave down the volume of their applause as he leaned forward in the chair. He could feel his hair going even grayer as he got ready to speak.

He scanned the group. It was a small number of people, but he felt as if he faced a crowd of ten thousand. Somehow that made it seem easier.

It was hard to believe at one time Grant could stand in front of a packed courtroom and not miss a beat delivering his proclamations. Now he found it nearly impossible to speak to more than one person at a time.

He took a deep breath. "Hello, everyone."

Everyone in the room greeted him back.

He winced at the loudness of their combined voices. "You know me, but since it's sort of the thing to do when you talk, I'll introduce myself. I'm Grant. And I've been sober for oh…" He looked at the imaginary watch on his wrist. "One year, eight months, one week, and eight hours—but who's counting, right?"

He let out a nervous laugh and was surprised when he got a polite chuckle from the group, including Georgia who was watching him with the same skittishness that he was displaying from his chair. He looked at his daughter. Kara continued to smile. She looked like she was the delighted parent, watching her child give a speech for the first time.

Grant took another deep breath. "Wow." He cleared his throat. "So here I am, finally, and I have no idea where to start. I don't want to do the cliché thing where I talk about my shitty childhood and stuff like that." He noticed the painful expressions spreading through the group. "Whoops… Was it my shitty language?" He smiled.

They did not. Georgia cleared her throat.

To Grant it was like a ruler slapping a desk. "Okay. Sorry. I cuss like an asshole when I get nervous."

This time there was some laughter, but not much.

He started again. "Anyway, I don't want to talk about being a kid. Not because it was an abusive stretch of time, but because it was actually a great childhood to have. So I can't blame my upbringing for how *I* turned out. It just sort of started one day and never stopped. I was at my absolute worst almost two years ago. Dribbling some vodka in my orange juice in the morning, a little bit of scotch with my coffee, a little bit of beer with my scotch. And so on and so on…"

Even though it was December outside, with gunmetal clouds threatening to drop white all over, and their assembly room was an old storage cellar in a church with crappy heat, Grant felt sweat trickling down his sides.

Another deep breath, then he kept going. "I'm sure all of you remember who I used to be. Grant Marlowe, the celebrity lawyer from Leaf Spring. The last ten years or so, there hasn't been a case I haven't won. But that was threatening to change. I was trying to put away a middle school teacher accused of wicked sexual acts with his students…remember that one?"

The group did. He doubted there was anyone who hadn't heard about the case. It had taken a long time to assemble just twelve peers for a jury who hadn't.

"Well, proving everybody wrong I went and won the damn thing. I put that bastard away for a long time. The odds had been stacked against me and I pulled through at the very end. The trial wrapped around ten in the morning and I was celebrating at lunch. Not the fact that I'd put away a bad man, but because I'd proved to everyone that I *could.*"

He could still taste the margaritas, could feel the salt clinging to his lips. He rubbed the back of his hand across his mouth, expecting to find little off-white clumps clinging to his knuckles.

"God, this is hard…" Grant attempted a smile but couldn't get his lips to move.

"Grant," began Georgia, "this is all part of the procedure. You're just warming up. Like swimming, you're dabbing your toes in the water to see if it's warm enough."

A little melodramatic but he supposed he understood. Georgia's first career choice was a poet, but she'd never been published. "Right."

"Just share your story, confront the fear you have so you can overcome it. We will help you along the way."

"You're the boss in here."

Georgia smiled. "That's right. So go for it."

"I'll try." He took another deep breath, looked at Kara's smile and felt a little better. "I was at the bar, my favorite place, Renny's, which was owned by an old friend from high school. Naturally, I got a nice discount there. I used it to my advantage that day and, honestly, I kept using it well into the night. I opened a tab and just kept putting drinks on it. I started putting *everybody's* drinks on it. In the meantime, while I was slamming back shots and margaritas *and* beer, I had completely forgotten about the promise I made to my wife. See, after the trial was over, I called her and told her to meet me at Palm's Bar and Grill so we could celebrate my victory in a much calmer environment."

Grant lowered his head, replaying the night in his mind. He could hear the cheers of his so-called friends urging him to drink another, to have one more for the road. He'd told them he had to go, Marion was waiting. Eventually he forgot all about her and all that mattered was the cheers, the hoots, the good time.

Nobody told him he'd had enough. Nobody offered to take him home. Nobody suggested he should call a cab.

"Nobody took my keys," he said aloud in response to his thoughts. "Not one person. When I finally stopped trying to avoid Marion's phone calls, I answered to a very emotional wife, crying her eyes out. Not so much because I stood her up, but because she knew I was drunk—oh and did I neglect to mention I had been hiding my drinking from her? Had her convinced for months that I'd quit, and she kept reminding me how proud she was of me. Every morning before I left for the office, she'd whisper it in my ear. It killed me. And the deeper my guilt became, the more intense my thirst seemed to get."

The group shared uncomfortable glances and it angered him. They wanted him to share his damn story and here he was doing it to make *them* happy and they were acting like he was doing something wrong.

"Don't act like I'm an asshole. You all had stories just as bad. Wasn't that what you said, Georgia? Every story that someone tells, there's always one that's even worse?"

"Grant, maybe you should—"

"Right?"

She looked down at her pad, nodded once, then said, "Right."

"So here I am, telling you all what you've been dying to hear." He laughed a cold laugh without humor. "That's right. I had been *lying* to my fucking family. Lying to my wife, my daughter, and my son. Lying to every-damn-body. And you know what? It was hard work keeping that lie going. Hard as hell. So when I answered the phone, slurring my damn words together, and she could hear everyone partying in the background, she told me she was done with me. She couldn't just sit by like a supportive wife and watch me drink myself to death." He snapped his fingers. "Oh, right. I forgot to mention that the doctor told me if I didn't stop drinking I was going to be in a heap of shit because of how bad it was screwing me up or some bullshit like that…"

He noticed Kara twist in her seat. It made him realize he was losing his temper and he decided to ease up on his delivery. Grant felt like a comedian delivering jokes, *bad* ones. And to Grant, his story was the biggest joke of them all. It wasn't funny and that was what made it so unbelievably hilarious.

"But you know what? I also felt relieved when she found out. I didn't have to lie anymore because there was no way I could. I rushed out of the bar, didn't even pay my tab. I just ran right out." He jutted out his hand and whistled. "I decided to take the backroad home. It would cut off some driving time, and I could avoid the stoplights and driving through town. Too risky with the cops, you know. Plus I wanted to get there before Marion got home, and hopefully talk her out of leaving. And…I…"

He was having trouble again, but he shoved the grief away and kept going.

"I guess I either dozed off or passed out, don't know for sure which one it was. The next thing I heard was a loud crash. I didn't *feel* anything, only heard it. The crash, the shattering. It's kind of spacey after that. A lot of blank spots. I can remember hearing a man screaming…calling for help…and he kept calling for somebody named Josh. I didn't know what it meant at the time, but later I learned Josh was his son. Josh Hinshaw. The man screaming for him was Dennis Hinshaw."

He ran a hand through his hair. It was damp with sweat.

"Oh God, his screams…he kept begging for someone to help him. I remember a man stopping. Jerry. He helped me get my door open, used my phone to call 911. I told Jerry someone was at the bottom of the ridge, so he went down to check on them. I couldn't move—well that's not true. I could've, but I just didn't. I'm so ashamed of myself for that. Maybe if I would have gone down there when I first heard him calling, or if I would have at least called for help *myself,* maybe his son wouldn't have died, or his pregnant wife." Grant's throat felt like it was being squeezed. He tugged at the collar of his sweater, cursing himself for wearing something so thick and heavy. "He lost his family because of me."

Tears welled in his eyes. He looked at the group and found that the awkward witnesses were gone, replaced by a room of grim faces.

"I heard Dennis had a breakdown after that, spent some time in an institution. I only saw him at the trial a few times, and what I heard the reason for that was because he couldn't handle it. I mean, how could he? I *killed* his family! How could he sit in there and listen to me try to rationalize that? I wouldn't have been able to do it."

Grant paused, waiting for someone—*anyone*—to tell him what had happened wasn't his fault. Prayed that someone would tell him it was the booze that caused all of this. Nobody did. He hadn't really expected anyone to try and make him feel less responsible than what he really was.

"So what happened to me? Isn't that what you're all wondering? I'm sure some of you already know. See this lovely girl beside me, with the glasses?" He hooked a thumb in her direction. Heads turned to face

Kara, who uneasily smiled at them. "That's my beautiful and, much smarter than me, daughter. I put her, her brother and her mother through hell. First thing that happened right away was I lost my job. There was no 'take some time off to get better' bullshit when it came to me. Just *adios* there, fella, it's been a good run. Thanks for all the money you got us."

Heads slowly swiveled back to Grant.

"A few months later, I was sentenced to a year in jail." A few groans and disbelieving grunts resonated from the group. Like most others, they obviously didn't agree with the sentencing. There had been several articles in the newspaper about how he'd been handed a sweet deal by his friends in the legal system. And even his roomful of recovering peers was smart enough to know nobody with such odds against him could come out so lucky.

And they were right. Grant had been guided through the trial. The judge was a golfing buddy of his and even the district attorney was an old roommate from college. He'd known them all, and nobody was quick to make him suffer. Even his AA sponsor was an old friend, but at least she didn't sugarcoat his defects.

"I've recently started a small practice," Grant said. "Just to get back into practicing law again. It's nothing major, just something where I can tackle smaller cases at an easier pace. But I'm shit right now, nothing but total shit."

"No, Grant," disagreed Georgia. "You're *shitty*. Not shit. There's a huge difference."

"I don't see it."

"There is."

"It's all shit to me."

"Have you had anything to drink since the accident?" she asked.

"Not a drop."

"This is the truth? You've been dry for almost two years?"

"So dry I'm flaky. There isn't a day that goes by when I don't want to drink…"

"What stops you?"

"Christmas."

Georgia tilted her head, confused. Her brow furrowed to a crease above her nose. "I don't understand what you mean by that."

Grant took a deep breath, glanced at Kara and said, "My wife has agreed that we should take the kids to our cabin in the mountains, away from the house, for Christmas. Away from Leaf Spring, the town we live in...the town where the accident happened." He took another breath since he'd said all of that in one long gust. "We've been trying to reconcile ever since the accident. Haven't gotten very far with it, but God willing, we can work through it. I think. Christmas will either make or break it."

Georgia was shocked. "This is the first I've heard about this."

"I didn't want to say anything, just in case it didn't happen. It still might not. Marion might've changed her mind by the time I get home. I might chicken out. Bobby might threaten not to come with us. *Anything* could screw it up even before it happens. And I don't know where to even begin to try and make things right. But at least I have a few days to make up for all the hellish years I've put them through."

Georgia tapped the pad propped on her thigh with the ink pen. "It's going to take a lot more than a few days to prove anything to them. But it's definitely a good place to start."

Hearing her say it confirmed his fears. He was going to fail. He'd probably lose his temper, upset everyone and leave early on his own while they stayed behind to celebrate Christmas together without him.

Don't think like that. You'll do fine. Just try, honestly try.

"Well, Grant, I think you have made a tremendous amount of progress here today. You've really opened up to us. However, if you're in the cabin and feel like it's getting too hard for you, and you feel *tempted* to pick up the bottle..."

"I won't."

"Don't say that. Familiar faces make for familiar habits. You might find yourself wanting to drink even more being so far away from home with your family. And if that happens, please call me. It's the holidays, and that doesn't always mean happier times. With people like us, it means for a lot of hard work to stay straight."

"I promise to get in touch if I need to. Hopefully I won't have to."

"I believe you won't. You're a lot stronger than you give yourself credit for."

That was the first comment she'd said during his tenure at Second Chance that had actually made him feel slightly confident.

"Let's show Grant some love, what do you say?"

The group agreed, all of them standing. They took turns hugging him, each giving him brief words of encouragement.

CHAPTER TWO

"I can't believe you didn't tell me about your Christmas plans. I thought you were coming to the house and having dinner with Harry and me. I even bought a damn ham."

Georgia slapped the legal pad down on her small desk that was packed in the corner of her cramped office. She sat in the rolling chair. It cracked and popped, showing its age.

Grant shrugged. "I told you why. Besides, I'm sure Harry's tired of seeing my mug around your place for dinner. I know I would be."

"That's not true and you know it. You're my best friend, so naturally you're his too."

"I just didn't want to jinx anything or get your hopes up."

Georgia crossed a leg over her knee, leaned forward and slid off her shoe. Her foot was bare, and she flexed her toes as if they were sore. The toenail polish had faded and become chipped, showing the thin white of their natural color through the fissures.

"Well, it would've, but I still wish you'd told me. So Marion's really on board for this? I'm so happy to hear it."

"She seems very hesitant and I can't blame her for it. But she's willing, so that's a plus."

"Guess those sessions with the pastor are helping you guys, huh?"

Helping Marion, he thought, but Grant didn't find much comfort in them. Pastor Tom and his wife Carla meant well, but he didn't much faith in their biblical advice. To him, it seemed outdated and only Marion could understand the meaning in the verses. He'd told her he was reading the Bible on his own time, but that was lie. He'd read a couple chapters before giving up. So long as Marion was getting fulfilment and it meant getting beyond their broken marriage, then he was all for it.

Georgia, now completely barefoot, turned the chair around. She leaned over her desk, bracing her elbows on a calendar pad that took up most of the space. "I hope you're really sincere about not drinking anymore." She shook her head. "God, if your parents were still alive, it would've killed them."

Though Grant had often thought the same thing, it still stung hearing it said aloud. And coming from somebody he cared about made it worse. "You don't think I know that?" he said. "I'm the one living with it. Can't get the man's screams out of my head. They keep me up at night. And there's even moments during the day I'll hear them." Grant resisted a shiver, thinking about those agonizing cries for help. He couldn't ignore them now, because they haunted his life.

"With time, it'll heal," said Georgia. "You know that."

Grant didn't think they would ever go away, but he thought it best to respond, so he nodded.

"And if you need me, you know how to reach me. If it gets too rough for you at the cabin, Harry and I'll come pick you up. Weather permitting, of course."

"Well, if we get snowed in, none of us will have a choice but to spend Christmas together." He smiled. Georgia studied him with narrowed eyes. "It was a joke."

"Some reason, I doubt it. Seems like you just admitted your plan. And that could be very dangerous."

Grant sighed. He didn't need this right now. He turned and looked at the door. Kara was outside, waiting for him. "I better get going. Kara has to leave, and I want to walk her out."

"Before you leave, come back and finish talking to me."

Though he told her he would, he didn't plan on actually doing so.

Kara walked Grant to the back door, her arm hugged around his, her head on his shoulder. It felt good having her so close. Their bond was stronger than the excuse of one he had with Bobby, even after the Trey Riggs debacle. Maybe it was because she was the first born, if only by fourteen months. Or perhaps it was because she was his little girl. Grant didn't have the answer.

But he'd never been this comfortable with his son, even when he was little.

These days they rarely spoke to each other unless forced.

"I told you so," said Kara as they approached the metal door with a bar of meshed glass above the handle. Even though she hadn't spoken loudly, her voice bounced off the plaster walls around them.

"Yeah," he said. "You did."

"And you didn't believe me."

Grant pushed the latch on the door, throwing it open. Cold wind swarmed them. Their clothes flattened against their bodies as they moved through the frost-layered parking lot. It was nearing five in the evening and already the sun had sunk into the night pool, splashing the sky in a crimson sheet.

Kara's car was parked in the first space after the designated handicap plots. The back parking lot was rarely used, and even now it had been neglected by the other members. The front way was quicker, but Grant liked it back here because nobody driving by on Main Street would see him or his car parked out front. Although nearly everyone had to know he was in AA, he wasn't thrilled for them to spot him on his way in or out.

A pride thing, he knew.

Kara brandished her remote keychain and pressed the button. Not only did every door unlock, the engine revved to life. She'd told Grant she'd paid extra for the remote start feature so the car would be her desired temperature by the time she got in, whether it was winter or summer.

"What about when it's spring?" he'd asked.

She'd pushed another button on the remote and all the windows went down in synchronicity. "Just in case it gets too stuffy."

They'd both laughed at that one. That was a month after he'd been released from prison, eight months early. When he'd cosigned the loan with her, he figured he'd be taking over the payments a couple months after. And he still hadn't had to make one. She'd been maintaining a steady work schedule at Kohl's while juggling law school and so far, she'd been good at both.

He studied the car, the blue and white emblem on the trunk. It was the kind of car he'd like to have himself, but he was happy to still have his Mustang and Jeep. Paying off bills with the amount of money he made now was a merciless obstacle, and he'd had to dip into his savings account and inheritance left to him by his parents more than once. He wasn't scraping for pennies, but if he didn't get on his feet within the next year, he would find himself heading there.

Kara opened the door behind the passenger seat, tossed in her bag, and quickly shut it as if she was afraid the cold air might sneak inside.

"Thank you," he said.

Kara looked back at him, a smile curving the corners of her mouth. "What'd I do?"

"It's what you've *been* doing. You've really been there for me, through all of it."

"You're my dad. Of course I'll be there for you. No matter what."

Years back, he'd gotten into a drunken conversation while sitting at a bar with one of his colleagues. After a few beers, the man had turned glum and there seemed to be a cloud of despair in his eyes. Grant had tried to perk him up, but nothing he said seemed to work. Finally, the man admitted he'd been having an affair with a girl he'd met at the gym. His wife didn't know, but his daughter had somehow found out. As he was telling this to Grant, he'd suddenly broken down into a sobbing fit. But through the blubbering bursts of self-inflicted chastising, he'd said something that had stayed with Grant all this time.

If a little girl stops thinking her daddy is Superman, it's over. She'll never call him her hero ever again!

Those words still tormented Grant, although his daughter was not a little girl anymore. The fear she would give up on him had disturbed his dreams every night when he was in prison, and it hadn't left him, even standing next to her now.

"I'm going to make it right," he said.

"I know you will."

She was going to be a good lawyer, because he'd almost believed her. What gave her away was the subtle flick of her eyes. Right before she'd responded, she'd glanced down at her boots.

Taking a moment to whip up something to say.

Grant lowered his head. "I wish your brother felt the same way you did."

"You know Bobby." She shook her head, trying to keep the smile going. "Mom's been working on him. You know, trying to get him to open up."

"And I'm sure that's going wonderfully."

She laughed. "Yeah, right." She brushed a fallen strand of hair away from her glasses. "Plus we have Christmas. You two will have time to talk about things then."

"True." He sighed. Though he wasn't hungry, he said, "Want to join an old man for a bite to eat?"

She almost winced but managed to convert it to a slight grimace. "Oh...tonight?"

"Got plans?"

"Yeah...well...I've still got to finish packing for our trip..."

"We don't leave until Wednesday. You've got two days to pack your stuff. We're not *moving* out there."

"I know, I know. It's just that...I haven't even started."

"Let's head to the house and I'll help you. It'll be the best night I've had in a long time."

She made a sour face, as if the news she was about to share would sting. "I kind of have plans..."

"Oh, shit."

"What's wrong?"

"It's a date, isn't it?"

"Why would you say that?"

"Because it *sounds* like you have a date. Are you still seeing Chester Boseman's kid? I thought you two broke up."

Grant took a deep breath to calm down. The smell of exhaust drifted all around. It was strong with it being so cold out here. If Grant possibly had a rival, it was Chester Boseman. Alike in so many ways, but different in so many more. Boseman was a good guy, really, and had achieved his success without the scars. He'd done everything the right away, where Grant constantly seemed to mess up and make bad choices. In a bizarre world, Chester was the person Grant had strived to be in the early stages of his career. Grant was the type of guy that was Chester's constant reminder of how far you could fall.

And Kara had been seeing Chester's son, Derrek, for over a year now. They'd met in law school and, as Kara described it, sparks had ignited.

Kara shook her head. "We just took it easy for a while, Dad. School is our priority, but now that we can take it easy for a bit, we're..." She shrugged.

"The spark's firing again?"

Rolling her eyes and smiling slightly, Kara leaned forward, and gave him a gentle peck on the cheek. "Bye, Dad. I love you."

"I love you, too. I'll talk to you at the house later tonight."

Now she did grimace.

Grant's skin felt like it had shrunk tight on his bones. "You *are* coming home tonight, right?"

"I've got some stuff to do—it's gonna keep me tied up." She started moving around the front of the car. Glancing at her watch, her pace increased. "It'll be late when I get home!"

"Does your mother know?"

"She's the one who said it was okay!" She opened the driver's door. "Love you!" She blew him a kiss, then ducked into the car. The door banged shut.

She waved at him, a pale shape on the other side of tinted windows. The car clunked into gear, backing up with the tires whirring. He watched her speed away through the parking lot.

There was a quivery sensation in Grant's chest. It fluttered into his stomach, making his bowels feel loose. That depression that always seemed to visit him whenever he was alone, creeping inside at night to molest him in bed, tapped on his shoulder. He wasn't going to turn around and give it the benefit of making him feel sadder than he already did.

Nope. Not tonight, pal.

The depression seemed insistent tonight. As he began his hike to where his Mustang awaited him, it was like the depression was shouting at him: *Hey! Where do you think you're going? Come on, old friend! Let's get a drink for old time's sake!*

"Fuck off," he muttered.

He tucked his hands in his pockets. His fingers touched car keys. He wiggled them out. No fancy remote-start gizmos on his key ring, just the traditional one-button auto-lock feature. He glanced back at the rear of the church, knowing Georgia was probably in her office wondering when he was coming back. He saw her sitting behind her desk, pouring coffee in those foam cups for to them drink while they talked.

Sorry, Georgia. Just not in the mood tonight.

He'd text her later and let her know he was feeling up to chatting.

His car, a dusky purple, vehicle-shaped specter, sat under a cupola of shadow. Its headlights were like two round eyes that glowered dimly from the darkness. He called her Midnight Rain, but only in his mind. He knew it sounded ridiculous and people would only laugh at him if they knew it.

Midnight Rain sat alone at the edge of the parking lot, no other cars in sight. Even his car was lonely.

At least they had each other.

Grant climbed into his car and fired her up. He quickly began to fiddle with the heat settings, flipping the switch so the air would blast his cold feet. He didn't even realize another vehicle was parked at the curb beyond the parking lot. Because of the pine trees that ran alongside the road there were plenty of shades for concealment. This automobile had pulled up right after his and had waited for him to return.

Grant drove off, and the man sitting inside the unseen vehicle climbed out. He headed for the back entrance of the church.

CHAPTER THREE

September 7th

Dear Lindsey,

It's been over five months since the accident, but it feels like four years. Everyone likes to tell me that it'll take some time for things to not hurt as much. They're wrong. They don't understand. They do NOT get it. I don't mean they don't love you, Josh and Lilly as much as me. I'm not saying that all. I mean they don't know how it feels to me.

It feels like I died too, and I'm just this hollow, soulless body wandering around. It's so hard, Lindsey...and I miss you so much. The other morning, I thought I smelled coffee, and for a few minutes I forgot that you were gone. When I went into the kitchen and saw the coffee pot still sitting on the counter, untouched since the morning of the accident, I remembered it all over again. It was like I just found out that you all had been taken from me.

I've been going to a shrink. Can you believe it? Me, of all people. I don't want to, but the school is paying for it, so I guess I have to, at least for a little while. I sort of broke down at the school when I went in to get my things. They gave me an extended leave from April through June, and then I also had the summer to recover...whatever that means! I went to my classroom and saw Josh's drawings I'd hung up around my desk and just...lost it. I went a little ballistic, which isn't like me. The police had to escort me out. Had to escort ME out. I know you would've been so upset if you saw me.

Thankfully, Principal Horton understood and has allowed me to come back this year. But it was under the stipulation that I continue some kind of therapy. I go on Wednesdays, and now every Thursday morning he finds me in my classroom and asks how it went. I've had three sessions so far, and I don't know how I feel about the doctor. Sonja Dumont is her name, and I think she's probably a few years younger than us. She told me she's single with no kids, so how in the hell is she supposed to relate to what I have to say?

I'll go a few more times but if it doesn't seem like it's helping, I'm going to stop. Horton will just have to understand that too.

This was Dr. Dumont's idea, writing you. She said it might help me to not feel so lonely. She said I should do this for a while and sort of wean myself off of it. I thought, what the hell?

I don't understand why this happened. It makes no sense. Pastor Tom has been trying to contact me. He calls a couple times a week, but I don't answer the phone when I see it's him. I don't even answer the phone when anyone calls. I'm just not ready. Maybe one day I'll answer the phone when Pastor Tom calls and ask him why God took you away, why He took Josh away, and Lilly...a life that she never got to truly live.

I look at the gun in the closet every day and contemplate things. Dark things that shouldn't cross my mind. But the gun makes it easier to consider the influences of those dark things. The gun's still in the metal lockbox up on the top shelf. Remember when you told me to put it up there? Josh was three and he'd gotten into the nightstand drawer and had pulled the case out? I remember you were so mad. At the time, I thought you had overreacted because he was just a baby and there was no way he could figure out how to open the lockbox. Now when I think about it, I realize how stupid I was to say that. I remember thinking when I put it in the drawer that Josh would never actually look inside.

And I was wrong to think that, too.

I got the gun to protect you all.

A lot of fucking good it did...

Well, I guess this is enough for tonight. It's been a long time since I've written this much longhand, and my hand is cramping up. I love you. Please tell Josh and Lilly that I love them too.

Love always,
Dennis

CHAPTER FOUR

Marion left the church after five. She'd wanted to get home earlier so she could get dinner started and save them from being forced to eat late another night. But that wasn't going to happen. Again. Usually she was done at the church by three, but she'd worked over the last few evenings. With Christmas approaching and a big church service on Christmas Eve to prepare for, she'd worked extra hard to help organize it. She would be in the mountains on Christmas Eve, so she needed to be convinced she wasn't leaving anybody in a bind.

Pastor Tom had ensured her they would be fine. He'd been the one to encourage her to go out of town from the beginning. Tom, and his wife Carla, had also helped her through the last two years when so many had turned their backs, including her own family. Her parents hadn't spoken to her since Marion told them she wasn't going to leave Grant.

"Take half that fortune and start over," her mother had said. "You could probably get even more if you play your cards right."

It shocked her how easily her mother had turned malicious. Would she be so quick to destroy Dad if he did something wrong? She wanted to think it wouldn't happen, but the last conversation she'd had with her mother in almost a year suggested otherwise.

Her mother's voice: *Take his money. Hurt him. Ruin him.*

That wasn't what Marion wanted. Sure, it would have been easy to do. Grant had given her plenty of reasons to lash out, and a lot of evidence that would see any courtroom siding with her for whatever she wanted to get from him. The money, the house, the cars, the cabin and the beach house—all of it could be hers.

No thanks.

Marion wasn't vindictive, nor was she vengeful. She was just very sad, all the time.

And so was Grant. Through all his failings, he was very distraught and seemed to radiate grimness whenever he entered the room. If she didn't at least try to forgive him, he'd never forgive himself, and she couldn't bear to see where that led him. She hadn't forgotten the suicide watches he'd been placed under all those times during the first few months after his release from prison.

Marion steered her little VW onto Pine Ridge Lane. Winter looked to be in full effect here. The sky had turned into a purple screen with splashes of pink netting through. The tree limbs reached over the road from either side, touching high above the yellow line. She drove into the leafless chasm, the sky blotted out as if a dark blanket had dropped onto her. She cut the headlights on. Twin beams pushed against the shadows in front of her.

They'd searched so long for a house to buy. From frequent student loans and credit card debts, it had been nearly impossible to find a bank dumb enough to give them a loan after their wedding. Years of living as renters had gone by, and Grant eventually clawed his way up to a good salary. Finally, they'd saved enough for a decent down payment. And this time the banks weren't so tentative to give them a loan. Six months of house-hunting later, they found the one on Pine Ridge. It was all they'd ever dreamed of in a house. A decent-sized yard with plenty of trees to offer isolation from the neighbors, and woods behind it that led to a field on the other side. Though they were in a neighborhood, it never felt like it.

It had been a great area to raise Kara and Bobby. Perfect. And it had been perfect for a long time.

Until Grant's drinking ruined it...

Marion stopped the penitent feelings before they could pull her down into that familiar darkness. In that bleak separation, she usually began pointing fingers and blaming her husband for all their tribulations. That was a mood she needed to avoid. She was already tense over the trip and she didn't need the past to remind her how much was at stake here. If they couldn't get away and be a family for a few days, they'd never be able to make it work.

A lot of pressure on them all, she knew that, but it was the truth. She figured everyone else knew it too.

She slowed the car when she spotted their mailbox up ahead on the right. There was a slight dip where the driveway lowered to the road. Taking it slow, she steered the car onto the narrow path that carried up between trees. She heard a scraping sound underneath as she straightened the wheel and winced.

Every time.

She'd never managed to get on the driveway without bumping the undercarriage.

Marion drove up the incline. It leveled out in front of their large house. She loved the old Victorian design, the pillars on the front porch and the peaked window on the right. It was three stories, a walk-in attic being the top floor. Bobby used to utilize that space for playing music before he took all of his equipment with him when he moved out. He began Upton's School of Music this year and had found a cheap apartment in Granite Falls. Since she spotted his car parked off to the side of their swirled driveway, she made the logical assumption he was now home for the holidays. Relief flowed through her. She'd had doubts he would come home at all.

Reaching up to the sun visor, her fingers brushed the garage door opener that was clamped to the edge. She pushed the button. As she approached the garage, the door slowly rose to let her inside. Once the car was all the way in, she pushed the other button. The door clacked down the track, killing what little bit of light had managed to drift in.

Entering the house through the side door, she hung her keys on the wall-mounted key pegs. She closed the door behind her and stood there, listening. Silence. The only clue she wasn't alone in the house was Bobby's car outside.

Wonder what he's up to.

It was still hard not hearing the faint loudness of heavy metal coming through the ceiling whenever she got home. If Bobby was home alone, he used to crank the volume on his amp.

"Bobby?" she called. Her voice sounded very loud in the stillness of the house.

After a few seconds of waiting for a response, she decided she wasn't going to get one.

Marion walked through the short hallway and into the kitchen. She saw a loaf of bread on the counter that hadn't been tied back. The heel of the loaf lay part way out of the bag. Crumbs were sprinkled all over countertop. Ketchup and mustard bottles stood together, their caps flipped open.

"Way to clean up, kid," she muttered. She shook her head, setting her purse on the counter beside the mess. "Bobby?" She lifted the bread and spun it around, winding the plastic tail. After tying it, she stuffed it into the breadbox, then grabbed the condiment bottles and clicked them shut. Carrying them to the fridge, she looked behind her and called for him again.

A flitter of unease made its way through her. The house was big, but not *that* big. He should be able to hear her.

Unless he's hurt.

Marion's breath caught in her throat. She paused in front of the fridge, wondering where that thought had come from.

Why would he be hurt?

She saw him walking upstairs, sandwich in one hand and a can of soda in the other and tripping over his baggy pants. He liked to wear them baggy and long, so it could have easily happened.

Marion opened the fridge, putting the ketchup and mustard on the shelf in the door. She bumped it shut with her hip. Then she walked out of the kitchen and into the foyer area where the stairs led upstairs, her shoes clacking across the floor. She couldn't wait to get her shoes off and change out of this skirt. Though it was long, it still left her legs with a chill.

She walked alongside the stairs, passing the small closet under them.

Bobby's wrecked body wasn't at the bottom of them.

Frowning, she looked up. She listened. No sounds came from above. All she could hear was the drumming of her heartbeat, loud and fast.

What was her son doing?

"Bobby?"

Marion realized she was whispering. She took in a deep breath and felt cold tingling in her lungs. The whole house seemed a little cool. She should check the thermostat. It was supposed to get down in the teens tonight, but it already felt that way outside.

She gave one last quick glance up the stairs before heading to the right. She walked through the open set of double doors into the living room.

And saw her son sprawled on the couch.

Arms wide, a leg hanging off the side with his foot flat on the floor. An empty plate sprinkled with crumbs was on the coffee table. His eyes were closed, mouth slightly open.

Her heart gave a lurch.

"Oh no!"

She ran to the couch, but her steps quickly decelerated as she neared. Sitting on his chest was his iPhone. She saw the display screen had the cover of an album by some heavy metal band she'd never heard of. A wire twisted down from each ear and met where his finger tapped them to a beat Marion couldn't hear.

All her worry was shoved aside by anger. She marched the rest of the way to the couch, leaned over and grabbed the wire to his earbuds. She yanked down, plucking them from his ears.

Bobby's eyes popped open. He sat up with a startled gasp, looking around in confused panic. He turned his head to Marion, took a moment to focus, then his shock dropped into a scowl.

"Jesus, Mom! You scared the shi—crap out of me!"

"Good. Now we're even." She dropped the wire on his stomach. "I was calling for you and you didn't answer."

Shaking his head, Bobby grabbed the tiny device off his torso and swung his legs around. Leaning forward, he put the iPhone on the coffee table next to his empty plate. A can of Pepsi was beside the plate, and he grabbed it and drank.

"Can hardly breathe," he said between sips.

"Now you know how I feel." She folded her arms across her breasts. "I thought you were hurt or something."

"Really, Mom? Hurt?" He shook his head. "Trying to take a nap is more like it. It's a long drive home, you know."

Some of the anger drained from Marion, but plenty stuck around. "You left the doors unlocked."

"So? We always do."

"What would you have done if a psycho wandered in? Yell at them for not letting you take a nap?"

"Come on, Mom. I'm not ten anymore. Stop trying to give me a lecture about the importance of locking doors. Nothing happened. I'm fine. You're fine, though a little crabby. The house is fine. The psycho that wandered in is fine. He's using the toilet."

"Not funny." She shook her head. "You left a mess in the kitchen."

Bobby rolled his eyes, and for a moment, he was a younger version of Grant. Though Bobby's hair was hardened into a thick pad of spikes from a lot of gel, and his eyes were Marion's same sapphire hue, he looked nearly identical to Grant. She felt a flutter in her heart. Now she felt bad for being so snappy at him.

"I'll clean it up," he said, standing. He held the can in one hand and grabbed the plate with the other. "Thanks for the warm welcome home. It's good to see you too." He turned, walking the other way. There was another entrance on the other side of the living room that led into the dining room.

"I already cleaned it up."

Bobby paused, looked back at her. "Good thinking. Don't want a psycho to wander into a messy house."

Though he was upset with her, she couldn't help smiling at his comment. "Oh, hush."

"You look tired."

"I am."

"Planning on cooking dinner?"

"I thought about it." She shrugged. "Don't feel like it, though."

Bobby nodded. "I'll be back shortly."

"And where are you going? You just got home, didn't you?"

"A little while ago. I'll run out to Krispy Krust and grab a couple pizzas. What time is Kara supposed to be home?"

"Late, I think. She said was going out after your father's meeting."

"Ah, so when will the king be getting in?"

Marion hated the impudent nicknames Bobby seemed to whip up for his father. He hadn't called him *Dad* since the accident. "Your *father* should be home anytime now."

"Guess he's at a meeting."

"He was." She checked her watch and was surprised by how late it was getting. "He should be heading home now."

Bobby opened his mouth, about to say something snarky, most likely. But he stopped. He cleared his throat instead. "I'll be back in a bit."

"Need some money?"

"Nope. I got paid yesterday. I'm good."

Bobby had been working at Guitar Central since before he started school. While they were helping him move into his tiny apartment, they'd taken a break for lunch and driven into town to check out the area. Bobby spotted the music store and ran inside while Grant and Marion parked the car. When they entered the store, Bobby was shaking the manager's hand. He'd been hired on the spot without filling out an application.

Bobby was like that. Anyone who met him usually loved him right away. He'd inherited that trait from Grant as well. Marion wasn't the kind of person who could just talk to anybody about anything and strike up a friendship that would last a lifetime. She supposed Kara had gotten that from her, though nowhere nearly as severe. There was plenty of Grant flowing through her daughter's veins as well.

Marion blinked and saw Bobby was no longer in the living room with her. She hurried into the dining room, veered right and walked into the kitchen. She could see his plate in the sink, the Pepsi can on the counter next to it.

But Bobby was gone.

Marion suddenly felt very lonely. She hadn't seen Bobby since Thanksgiving, almost a month ago, and had ruined their reunion by yelling at him. Why had she done that?

I was worried about him.

She should've been pleased he was okay, not angry for scaring her. Marion sighed. She would apologize to him later. Maybe she could talk him into watching Jimmy Fallon with her tonight, or a rerun of *Law and Order*.

Marion returned to the stairs and climbed them. Her boots made hollow taps that turned soft and padded when she reached the carpeted floor of the upper hallway. The bedrooms were up here. She came to Bobby's first and peered inside. His bags were on his bed. His guitar was in a large metal case, leaning against the mattress like a slide. Seeing some of his stuff back in his room made her smile. His first Christmas back home. She wasn't pleased when she learned he would be going halfway across North Carolina to attend music school, but she wasn't exactly surprised, either. She knew most of it had to do with Grant and how their son wanted to get away from him.

And me?

Probably.

She could tell he was also angry with her for not throwing Grant out. But she hadn't been able to do it. Though they lived in this big empty house like two shadows that rarely crossed paths, she still loved her husband deeply. Hopefully she could start showing Grant just how much again.

She turned away from Bobby's room and headed down the hall, passing Kara's on the way to her bedroom.

Our bedroom.

Grant hadn't slept in here with her since coming home from prison. He used the guest room. She hadn't banned him from the bed, but she hadn't invited him back except for some lonely nights when she'd needed him with her. They'd made love those nights, and the mornings after, Grant had been ready to come back to the bedroom for good. But Marion still hadn't invited him. Those mornings when Grant was walking around with a goofy smile and whistling chirpy tunes, she was curled up in bed, depressed and sick with shame.

Grant hadn't brought it up since the last time they'd made love. It was in August, shortly after they'd left Bobby in Granite Falls. And it had been good. Everything had felt so right. When they were through, Grant had rolled over onto his side. On her back and panting, his seed trickling warmth down her inner thighs, Marion stared at the ceiling. She had felt his eyes on her and knew what he was about to say.

"Am I sleeping in here tonight?" he'd asked.

Tears had spilled from her eyes. No answer came from her mouth, but Grant had heard the cry from her heart. He'd slipped out of bed and, naked, left the bedroom.

Marion still felt awful. She shouldn't keep torturing him like this, but she wouldn't allow herself to become the faux-happy, naïve wife she used to be. Grant needed forgiveness, true forgiveness, and she wanted it to be legitimate. Not something she did just to make *him* feel better. And she thought maybe it was time the process began. But it wouldn't until she permitted it to. All she had to do was let it go. Stop holding her pain hostage and just release it.

Sitting on the edge of the bed, Marion pulled her skirt above her knees. She reached down, finding the zipper for her boot and ran it down her calf. Then she raised her foot, bracing it on the thigh of her other leg while she tugged off the boot. She let it drop to the floor, then removed her sock. Flexing her toes, her foot tingled and seemed to swell from the freedom of no longer being cramped. She quickly removed the other set and felt so much better.

Propping her arms behind her, she let her head fall back. Hair brushed the sides of her face and fell behind her. She felt exhausted. She was glad Bobby had offered to go get pizza, saving her from having to prepare a half-attempted dinner for the three of them. She wanted to take a shower. There was still packing to do.

Packing can wait. Shower comes now.

She stood up and crossed the room to her dresser, undressing along the way. In her bra and panties, she opened the drawers and found clean pairs. Bending over, she opened another drawer. Inside were her lounging clothes. She pulled out a T-shirt and pajama pants.

If Grant were to walk in right now, he'd get a shock.

She glanced over her shoulder, half expecting him to be standing in the doorway, a shoulder against the frame.

"Nice view," he'd say.

He wasn't there.

Marion couldn't help the disappointment she felt. In the old days, if Grant had been standing there, she would have turned around so he could see the front of her. But he wouldn't come into the room. He'd just watch, arms folded, eyebrows raised, as she slowly slid the straps of her bra down her arms. Watch as she reached behind her back and unhooked it from between her shoulder blades. Watch as she drew her panties down her long legs. Naked, she would walk to the bed, eyes locked on his, and sit down. As she crawled backward, Grant would enter, undressing on his way to the bed. He'd crawl on top of her, an arm on each side, matching her backward stride. Her legs would curl around his hips, hook behind his back.

And he would push into her, filling her, pushing against her walls to make room.

Marion shivered. The memory caused her to tingle all over. Four months. It had been four months since they'd been intimate, nearly as long since they'd had a full conversation other than planning this trip.

God, she missed him so much.

Holding her clothes to her chest, she walked out of the room. She was in the hallway when she heard the front door downstairs close with a muffled bump. It was too soon for Bobby to already be back, so that meant Grant was home. Though she was mildly tempted to wait for him at the top of the stairs in her bra and panties, she turned and hurried to the bathroom.

Inside, she shut the door. Her finger hovered above the lock. If she left it unlocked, would Grant come inside? Memories of him surprising her in the shower flowed through her. Head under the water, she would see the curtain slowly pull back. Grant would be standing there, naked and hard. She reached for him with a warm, damp hand. Stroking, she would guide him into the shower. Then she'd turn around, jut out her rump. With her arms bent against the wall, her breasts squishing on her skin, she'd tremble as his hands slid over her wet body. Since he was taller than her, he would have to crouch slightly to get his erection under her. When he stood, he would slide inside, lifting her against the wall. The smacking sounds his abdomen would make against her buttocks sounded like wet hands clapping.

What's wrong with me?

Her mind had been doing this to her all day, returning to the good times they'd had before everything was poisoned. Not just memories of sex; she had been visited by memories of vacations, conversations—moments that had caused her great joy. She shook her head, hoping to rattle them away.

Her finger twisted the lock.

Again, she was tempted to call off the trip. The temptation had come to her many times, and each time she talked herself out of it. But it was Carla's voice she heard in her head this time. It told her not be scared. This was what she'd wanted—a true shot at rebuilding from the devastation that had become their family. If she backed out of the trip, there would be no hope left. No more chances.

We have to try.

Decided once again, she turned on the shower. After adjusting it the hottest temperature she could stand, she stepped inside and pulled the curtain behind her.

The water pelted her scalp, the nape of her neck, down her back.

It felt wonderful. And she planned to relish the feeling for a very long time.

CHAPTER FIVE

Arms folded under his head, Grant stared at the ceiling. He couldn't sleep. Last time he'd checked the clock, he was shocked to find it was after one. Dinner was awkward and filled with a lot of silence. Bobby had come home with pizza, leaving two boxes in the kitchen for Grant and Marion. He took the third box up to his room with two cans of soda. Grant didn't see him again for the rest of the night.

Avoiding me.

Just like Marion had by hurrying into the shower when he'd come home. She hadn't seen him, but he'd seen *her* peeking over the railing upstairs to spot him. Then she hurried down the hall and into the bathroom, carefully closing the door so it wouldn't make a sound. It had taken her a bit longer to lock it, as if she had been contemplating her decision. The click of the lock twisting had resounded through the house like nails on a chalkboard.

At least she ate dinner with me.

She'd sat on the couch in her robe, her smooth legs curled under her. The robe draped her thighs, showing her bare skin from the knees down. Their smoothness showed she'd shaved them in the shower, and afterward rubbed them with lotion. Not only had he been able to smell the sweet scent, her legs seemed to glow in the soft light from the lamp. He'd stared at them from the corner of his eye while he'd sat in the recliner.

They'd watched the news together, barely speaking. But Marion had a look about her that reminded him of the good days, when she was in the mood to fool around and just wanted him to take the lead. He almost had tonight, more than once, but had refrained from doing so. He still worried she might reject him, and he didn't want to bring even more discomfort to the trip.

The news had been filled with the same crap as always—people killing each other, stealing from each other, hurting each other. But the weather forecast was why they'd decided to watch. The man on TV claimed if they got any snow at all, it wouldn't be very bad.

Grant wasn't sure about that. He'd heard on the radio that the storm had already left areas buried a foot deep in its wake with more coming.

Hopefully it piles down.

Georgia had called him out on his plan, and it annoyed him. Did Marion know he hoped they'd get stuck in the cabin? With nothing else to do, they would be forced to communicate. It might help them get over the bumpy spots that have caused them to avoid one another for so long.

Or it might blow up in my face, make things worse.

Grant sighed. And they'd be the ones *stuck,* not him. He would be in Heaven while they tried to claw their way out of the snowy grave they'd been buried alive in.

Closing his eyes, Grant wiggled his head into the pillow. He tried to settle his rocky thoughts. He pushed his fears far back into the black chasm of his mind, where he buried the majority of his doubts, hoping to stifle the urgings to drink they were causing.

Marion on the couch appeared in his mind. Her smooth shins, the section of thigh poking out from the flaps of her robe, glinting a soft bar of light from her skin. He felt his heartbeat increase as his penis hardened.

Don't think about that. Find something else to focus on.

He saw her sitting up, putting her feet on the floor. Slowly, she opened the robe at her chest. She was naked underneath. Her full breasts were dusky in the dim light, her nipples two dark dots that pointed at him. Finding the belt, she unknotted it, throwing the fabric aside. The robe flew open and fell around her. Putting her hands flat on the tops of her thighs, she rubbed them, working her fingers inward as her legs slowly spread.

"Come here," she said in a whispery voice that sounded slightly nervous, though her eyes looked inviting and open.

Grant sat up in bed, kicking the blankets away. He swung his legs around, putting his feet on the floor. Gripping the lip of the mattress, he leaned forward, took deep breaths. The fantasy had ended and began to fade into a memory from a few years ago. The kids had gone to stay with Marion's parents for the weekend, and it had somehow become a second honeymoon for Grant and Marion. They'd made love twelve times in three days. Both were sore and achy the following week, but neither could stop smiling.

Grant stood up, stretching his legs as he walked to the door. He thought some late-night pizza might be what he needed to keep him distracted. Besides, people were supposed to sleep better on a full stomach, right? Sounded reasonable to him.

He put his ear to the cold smoothness of the door and listened. Seemed quiet out there. Last thing he wanted was to run into anybody with a tent sticking out the front of his pajama pants. He tried pulling his T-shirt down, but it wasn't quite long enough to cover it.

Carefully, he opened the door. From the soft light of his bedside lamp, the hallway seemed smothered in dark. He couldn't see much, other than a glare that flashed each time he blinked. A heavy burst of quiet poured in. There was no sound, other than the pounding of his heart in his ears.

Pulling the door quietly shut behind him, he stood there a few moments. It took a little bit, but his eyes adjusted to the darkness. They used to have a nightlight in the hallway. He wasn't sure when they'd gotten rid of it, but it might be a good idea to bring back that custom.

He turned his head to the left. At the end of the hall was the closed door to his old bedroom. Marion was alone on the other side. Looking down, he saw a soft bar of light. It was so dim, it was hardly noticeable. He pictured her in bed, the pillows piled into a brace for her back, reading. She had her glasses on, her long lemon-colored hair pulled into a ponytail behind her head. He wondered if she had on a nightgown. She sometimes wore them, silky garments that clung to her and showed all her curves. For a long time, she slept naked, until the kids began surprising them in the mornings by bouncing on the bed and announcing it was time to wake up. When they grew out of it, Marion started shedding clothes at night again, but not as often.

Was she naked now?

She's probably asleep.

But the light was on. Probably her tiny touch lamp on her side of the bed. That meant his spot was vacant. Did she want him to fill it?

No. She's just reading. Can't sleep like me. Nervous about the trip. Probably dreading it.

He looked up and down the hallway, expecting to find faint light under Kara's and Bobby's doors as well. They were probably fretting over the trip also. He saw nothing but darkness. Though there was no light, he doubted they were sleeping soundly.

His head turned back to Marion's door.

Should he go knock? What if she wanted company?

I might just annoy her even more.

His feet started moving, carrying him to the bedroom door where Marion waited. Carrying him to the bedroom he once shared with his wife.

What am I doing? Turn back!

The floor popped softly under his footsteps, the carpet sinking as he neared the door.

She doesn't want to see me right now. I'm the last person she wants to talk to.

If I try to talk to her this late, I might just ruin everything. For a long time, he tried to talk to her too much about everything. Instead of giving her the space she needed, he smothered her with his alacrity to work it out. Finally, he'd stopped trying and thought letting her come around on her own would be best. The counseling sessions at the church had told him that was the best approach. Pastor Tom said she would talk when she was ready.

Months later, she still hadn't talked. And Grant was beginning to wonder if she ever would. They hadn't even had an argument or fight since the summer. Barely a word had been shared between them, unless they tiptoed around their problems with bullshit conversation.

Grant was tired of it. He wanted them to work this out. He couldn't show her how much if she wouldn't give him the chance.

"Grant?"

He jerked at Marion's soft voice. His heart dropped into his stomach. He looked around, realizing he was standing outside the door, a hand squeezing the frame. Slowly, he pulled his fingers back and let his arm drop.

"Is that you?" she asked. Her muffled voice came from the other side of the door.

"Yeah," he said in a husky voice. Clearing his throat, he added, "It's me."

There was a short pause. Then she asked, "Want to come in?"

Grant's throat suddenly felt very dry. His heart seemed to beat near his tonsils. "You're sure?"

Another pause. Then, "Yes." He thought he detected a slight quiver in her voice.

Grant watched the pale shape of his trembling hand lower to the knob. His fingers jittered as they closed around it. He opened the door, squinting as the dim light poured into the hall, a sweet aroma following it. The TV was off. Open suitcases were lined up on the floor at the foot of the bed. His eyes scanned the sheets, saw the familiar shape of his wife's legs under them and kept moving up. The light came from the lamp as he'd suspected, but a scented candle guttered on the nightstand.

Marion sat against the adjusted pillows, an open paperback on her chest, pages down. The sheets stopped at her silk-covered breasts. She was wearing a gown. Her hair wasn't pulled back but spread across the backdrop of the pillows like a woman on the cover of a romance novel.

Grant remained in the doorway, taking in the sight of his lovely wife and the wonderful fragrance the candle provided.

"Close the door," she said.

Grant nodded. He stepped inside, slowly pushing the door behind him. There was a quiet snick when it shut. He turned back to Marion. She lifted the book from her chest, folded down the upper corner of a page and closed it. She set it on the nightstand and leaned back.

"Can't sleep either?" he asked.

Marion took a deep breath that sounded a little shaky. She shook her head. "No."

"Can I sit?" he thrust his chin toward the bed.

A corner of Marion's mouth curled. "Sure." She scooted away from the edge of the mattress, patting the open space. "Sit."

"Okay."

The muscles of his legs felt limp and stringy as he walked to the bed. He turned and plopped down, shaking the mattress. Lifting his head, he looked around. The room hadn't changed since the last time he was in here. The last time they...

"Everyone else asleep?" she asked.

He couldn't see her now, so he twisted his hips, bringing up his left leg and laying it on the mattress. His knee brushed against the sheets, feeling the firmness of her body under them. "I guess so. What time did Kara finally make it back?"

"She didn't."

"What?" He felt a pinch of alarm. "Why not?"

Marion held up a hand as if to stop him. "I mean, she *hasn't*. Not yet. She texted me earlier and said she was going to be late."

"But we leave early..."

"She's already packed. So we don't have to worry about waiting on her."

Grant smiled. "She is?"

Marion nodded. "You know her."

"Yep. Always prepared, well ahead of everybody."

"That's her."

Grant's eyes drifted down from Marion's face, to the hollow of her throat. He saw the smooth flatness of skin before it swelled at her breasts. She had a couple freckles dotting the smooth patch, and more sprinkled across her back and legs. He loved them.

"Think it'll be a good idea to stop somewhere for breakfast?" he asked. "Or would I be playing with fire by prolonging the destination."

Marion frowned. "Nobody's going to back out."

Grant shrugged. "I'm not saying that. I'm just asking if you think it'll be a good idea to go straight there. If we can beat the traffic, we can get there in about two and a half hours."

"Sure. If we're in a rocket ship," she said. Grant smiled. "No way we'll get there that quick. Probably would be best to eat on the way. Empty bellies and cramped car rides make for irritable moods."

"Eat before we go?"

She shook her head. "It'll take too long to get on the road if we do. Then we'll definitely hit all that traffic on the way."

Grant nodded. "You're right about that."

He looked at Marion. A strand of hair had fallen across her face. Without thinking, he reached out, using his fingertips to brush it back. He realized what he was doing as he got it tucked behind her ear.

"Sorry," he muttered.

Marion ran her hand through her hair. "It's okay." The strand he'd tucked back fell onto her cheek again. She stuck her elbows into the mattress and squirmed a little higher on the pillows. The blankets dropped down to her stomach, exposing her chest. The gown was white, and from the light coming from the lamp, looked nearly translucent as it swathed her. He saw the dark shapes of her breasts, the even darker smudges of her nipples.

She didn't pull up the blankets to cover herself.

Must not realize how much I can see.

He looked down, feeling dirty for sneaking peeks at his wife.

"What's on your mind?" she asked. "I know you weren't just sneaking around the hallway because you couldn't sleep."

Grant snorted. "I wasn't *sneaking*…"

One of Marion's eyebrows lifted. "You weren't?"

Grant sighed. "Maybe a little sneaking. Was thinking about getting some pizza, but I saw the light was on and wondered if you were awake."

"And I am."

"Yeah…" He turned to her. "You are."

Their eyes locked. He felt her searching inside him, finding places deep within that she used to explore and had stopped visiting. Places that had cracked open and sprouted weeds from neglect. It felt good having her back in there, as if she was taking a tour inside his soul.

Her mouth was slightly parted, lips moist. The light sprinkled across them, made her bright eyes sparkle against the shadows around them.

"I'm sorry," he said.

"I know you are."

"I can't change what I did."

"I know."

"If I could…"

"Don't think about what you *could* have done. That's part of your problem."

He looked at her. "It is?"

"You're blaming yourself for not doing something differently, when you just admitted you can't change it. What you should work on is what is happening *now*. With us. With the kids. Stop trying to make us forget about what happened and help *me* save us from perishing because of where it's gotten us."

Tears dotted the corners of her eyes. One spilled out, trickling down her cheek. She used the back of a finger to wipe it.

"Marion…"

"Wait," she said, holding up tear-smudged finger. "I'm not finished." She took in a deep, unstable breath. "We can work through it if we try *hard* enough, but we can't change it. It's happened. It will have always happened. Nothing will make that not be a part of our life."

"You're right."

He knew all this. But hearing her say it somehow made it different.

"And *I'm* sorry," she said. More tears came, leaving wet crooked lines down her cheeks.

"You're sorry?" He shook his head. His chest felt tight and it was hard to breath. "For what? You haven't done anything wrong…"

"I have…" Now she used the back of her hand to dry to her face. "I have been punishing you. And maybe it's because I was angry that your friends helped you out so much…"

"I didn't ask them to do that…"

"But you knew they would. You *knew* they'd call in favors."

Grant lowered his head. He hadn't just known they would, he'd counted on it. And Marion had known him long enough to figure it out.

"I was wrong to do that," she said. "I shouldn't have held it against you for so long, but I did."

"You had every right…"

"Maybe. Maybe not." She cleared her throat, took in another deep breath and looked up at the ceiling. She stayed that way, as if collecting words from a swirling cloud above her. When she lowered her head, she was no longer crying. "I really do love you, Grant."

The strength drained from him. He slipped down from the mattress. His knees hit the carpeted floor, muffling his landing. He dropped forward and caught himself on his hands before falling on his face.

The blankets swished as they were thrown aside. The bed squeaked and groaned when Marion climbed out. Her bare legs came into view and dropped as she crouched.

The gown wasn't as long as he'd thought it was, reaching partway down her thighs and sagging between them. He felt the smooth skin of her leg brush his arm as she reached out to him. He thought she was going to help him up and he didn't think he could stand if she tried.

Instead, she hugged him. Her hand opened on his cheek and pulled his head toward her. He felt the softness of her hair as it covered his face, smelled the pleasant scents of her shampoo and natural aroma.

"I do," she said. "I do love you, and I'm sorry for everything I've put you through."

"*You're* sorry?" He noticed he was crying and had no idea when he'd started. "I'm the one who put you through…put you *all* through…"

"I know. You know. No more talking about it, okay? It's like we learned in counseling. We won't forget it, but not moving away from it will only make us weaker. We can't act as if it never happened, but we can't live our lives in a constant vault of misery because of it. We have to move on."

Grant lifted his head and turned. Her face was so close to his that he could feel the warmth of her breathing. He felt his head leaning toward her before realizing he was going to.

He kissed her. Nothing big. Just a soft kiss on the lips that lingered for a moment. Pulling away, he looked into her eyes. Marion stared at him, not speaking. Then she moved in and they kissed again.

This one didn't stop. They kissed for a long time before Marion began to lie back on the floor. Grant leaned back on his knees, pulling off his T-shirt.

Marion spread her legs in front of him, the gown falling back where it bunched around her hips. She wasn't wearing panties. Grant scooted back, lowering himself onto his elbows and putting his ears between her thighs. His erection pushed against the carpeted floor. He felt how she trembled, heard how her breaths came in jerky huffs. Then he pushed his face forward, tasting her juices.

Marion gasped. Her legs tightened around his head, crushing ears against her thighs. Her fingers reached into his hair, rubbing, fingernails tickling his scalp. Then her hand closed into a fist, gripped a handful, and pulled him up. She released his hair. As he wiped his mouth, she grabbed the elastic band of his pajama pants and shoved them down. His hardened penis dropped like a falling limb, bobbing as he crawled on top of her.

They began kissing again.

He slowly pushed into her, feeling her body tense as he went deep. He tasted her moans, swallowed them. Her wet warmth hugged him tightly as he went in, spreading to make room for him. It felt so familiar inside her, yet new and fresh like the first time. They'd had sex only a few times since the accident, but this was the first time they had *needed* to be this close. The others had been a way for them to get quick releases. This time was their rejoining, their way of becoming one flesh once again.

Grant's thrusting hit parts inside of Marion that caused her to grip him more tightly than ever before, to moan her love and admiration into his ear through her gasps. Her nails dug into his back. He pulled down the front of her gown, tearing it from the straps to expose her breasts. He squeezed them, flicked her nipples with his tongue, and sucked them.

Biting down on her bottom lip to stifle the noises, Marion huffed through her nose. Her moans sounded almost like whines. Grant could tell she wanted to scream but was holding it in to keep from waking anybody.

After Grant pumped and spurted inside her, they stayed on the floor, holding each other in a sweaty embrace. Marion fell asleep almost instantly.

Grant remained awake a bit longer. He couldn't shake the worry that this was only temporary, that Marion would return to being cold in the morning. He wanted to think that she wouldn't, because this time she hadn't thrown him out of the room afterward. This would be the first night they slept together in almost two years.

And Grant decided he wasn't going to let his uncertainties ruin it.

He closed his eyes.

Sleep came quickly.

CHAPTER SIX

November 23rd

Dear Lindsey,

Wow, my second legal pad already. I wonder if writing these letters is actually helping. They don't seem to be. Sonja swears that it will, but I'm not so sure.

School is out for the Thanksgiving holiday. I have opted to stay home this year. Your dad invited me out, but I told him I wasn't going to come. My family is meeting at Grandma's again this year. I said I might stop by, but I have no intentions of doing so. I'll probably skip Christmas dinner as well. Instead, I'll mail out cards with some money inside. The insurance checks have all come in, and I don't plan on using the money for anything, so I figured I would give some away for Christmas.

The rest can sit in the bank for all I care.

I feel like I have to tell you this, though I know you are looking down and saw it. Sonja invited me to her house for Thanksgiving dinner tomorrow. I told her no, but to be honest, I was tempted to go. She moved here from Alabama and has no family here. She claims to not have any friends as well. I can relate to that. You know how many friends I have. Barely one, and he hasn't talked to me since shortly after the funeral. I felt bad for her and told her that it sounded like fun.

But I can't do it. She said she understood, but I could tell she was very disappointed. I wanted to remind her that she's my psychiatrist, and it probably wasn't professionally appropriate that I come to her home and eat with her. I didn't say that, of course. If she had pressed the matter, I might have.

Now I feel bad for telling her I'm not coming. I should probably call her tomorrow and at least tell her "Happy Thanksgiving".

I tried to sort through Josh's room today and had to stop. It still smells like him in there. The toys, his bed, and his pillow. I climbed in the bed and took a nap. It felt good being so close to his smell, but it gave me bad dreams. I don't plan on going back in there for a while. I'm going to stick to sleeping on the couch. No more beds, not for a long time.

Grant Marlowe's trial starts at the first of the year. Can't wait to see him get what's coming to him.

I miss you. I love you. Give Josh and Lilly lovins from their daddy.

Dennis

CHAPTER SEVEN

From the backseat of the Jeep Cherokee, Kara studied her parents. Strange. Mom looked out her window at the blurry shapes of the distant hills. But that wasn't what Kara found to be so odd. Mom was smiling. *Really* smiling. Kara couldn't recall the last time she'd seen Mom in a *good* mood.

Dad glanced at Mom from the road, and also smiled, before returning his attention to the drive.

Kara frowned. Something had changed. She couldn't tell what it was, but *something* was noticeably different. Dad was smiling more, and Mom seemed to have lost some of the melancholy in her eyes.

Somehow, they both looked younger.

Their behavior reminded her of friends who'd started secretly seeing each other. *No way.* Kara tried not to grin. She'd known coworkers that screwed around off hours, and somehow the rest of the staff could figure it out without either of them talking about it. Something just hovered around them, an ambiance that was easy to sense. And her parents were radiating it.

They're acting like they got laid last night and are trying to hide it.

She'd tried talking to Bobby about it at the restaurant after breakfast. Mom had gone to the bathroom and Dad went to pay the bill.

"You're crazy," he'd said. "Mom wouldn't..."

"I'm telling you. Something happened last night."

"Well, I didn't hear any beds rocking, and I was up half the night."

Kara hadn't told him their father didn't sleep in his room last night. She was already awake when Mom's bedroom door opened. She'd heard whispering in the hall, then Dad's door opening and closing. A few minutes later, Dad snuck down the hall and took a shower. While he was indisposed, Kara had snuck into his room and saw his bed was still neatly made. The bed cover wasn't wrinkled.

Could mean anything.

But she doubted it.

Judging Bobby's reaction to the little she'd shared with him, she thought it best to drop it altogether. For now. Unlike Kara, he didn't want their parents to mend things. He'd never quite connected with Dad like she had, so his relationship was already strained. After Dad's accident, what little bit of cordiality they'd managed to hold on to was completely obliterated. She didn't know if they could ever come to any kind of rational terms again. She also didn't know if either man knew how to try.

In the back of the Jeep, Kara turned and looked at her brother. Bobby, head resting back on the seat, had his earbuds in. His mouth was slightly parted. *Sleeping.* He'd said he was up late last night. Hopefully he wasn't fooling around in some video chat that he shouldn't be. One day during the summer she'd come home and found him watching a young woman pleasure herself live in a streaming video feed. She was calling Bobby's name as she reached climax. Thankfully, all he'd been doing was *watching.* She never brought it up, and she supposed he might not even know she'd seen as much as she did.

"About to cross the bridge," Dad said from the front.

"Yay," said Kara, twisting so she could look out her window. She reached back, slapping Bobby on the arm. "Wake up."

Bobby snorted, smacked his lips. His eyes fluttered open. "Huh?"

"We're about to pass the bridge, Sleeping Beauty."

"Blah..." He closed his eyes. "It's just a damn bridge."

Kara felt her features drop into a frown. She imagined it was the same look her father would give Bobby when he was frustrated. Rolling her eyes, she faced the window again. Brown fuzzy fields led to a canvas of hilly slopes capped with white. Beyond that were the pale shapes of jagged peaks that looked like a smeared painting. If they were about to cross the bridge, that meant they were getting close to the cabin. Thirty more minutes to go.

Just as she would when she was younger, Kara smiled as they crossed over Lake Mitchell. The water was bright green and looked like glass far below them. A rock protruded from the emerald flow like a giant brown fingertip, frothy where the water splashed against its sleek surface. The lake curved through a narrow cove between an awning of thick trees.

Such beautiful scenery never failed to take her breath away.

When she was fifteen, she'd taken a picture of the scenery. Dad sent the photo in and had it turned into a jigsaw puzzle that Kara put together. When she was finished, she'd painted the puzzle with glue. And it still hung in a frame on her bedroom wall.

The wheels made a *thunk* when they left the bridge and returned to the blacktop.

Minutes later, Dad took the exit and drove them off the highway, cars zipping by behind them. They reached the end of the turnoff and stopped when they reached the sign.

Bear Creek. Population 504

You'll come to visit, but you'll stay to live.

Kara smiled. It had been three years since she'd seen the wooden sign with the pine green background. There was a golden crest of a bear crossing underneath the lettering. The last time she was here was Fourth of July, nine months before the accident. Dad was in the middle of another alcohol detox and had been very moody the entire vacation. He'd burnt the hamburgers and they'd had to eat hot dogs by hand, dipping them into the condiments since he'd forgotten the buns. She prayed this time would fare much better.

"Getting close," said Dad.

He wasn't directing the statement to Kara. It had been meant for Mom.

Mom turned to him, smiling. "Yes, we are."

Between the tight gap of the front seats, Kara saw movement. Fingers locked together.

They're holding hands?

Tears filled her eyes, making the golden lettering on the sign look daubed.

So she was right. Something had happened that made the last couple years suddenly seem like a bad dream. For the first time since the accident, Kara felt something filling her with warmth inside.

Hope.

She'd forgotten what it felt like. When Dad started attending AA classes, she had *wanted* him to do well. Though she wasn't a regular attender, she'd visited the church throughout the week just to borrow the worship center for some prayer time. She'd begged God to heal her father. But she'd never truly believed He would. But now she had real *hope* that everything might work out.

And all it took was seeing her parents hold hands like they used to.

Strange...

What would she do if she saw them hug? How much would change then? Maybe Bobby would finally believe things could be better. She hated that he was asleep and had missed the small token of affection that had exterminated Kara's reservations.

"You okay back there?" asked Dad.

"Um..." Kara used a knuckle to wipe her eyes. "Yeah, I'm fine. The elevation...it's getting to me. Stopping up my ears."

"Take deep swallows," said Mom, like she always would whenever Kara complained about it.

Nodding, Kara wiped her eyes. She could see better now. Dad was turned in his seat, looking back at her. He smiled, showing he knew what was really wrong. Kara understood him without words being spoken. The soft look he gave her told her all she needed to know.

"We've still got higher to go yet," he said. "Guess we better buckle down and get our bearings under control, huh?"

Kara snorted a laugh. "Yeah, I'll get right on that."

Dad gave Bobby a glance. For a brief moment, disappointment took away his smile. When he looked at Kara again, the smile returned. "Hang tight. We'll be at the cabin soon."

Kara nodded again. She looked at her mother and saw she was watching her in the rearview mirror. Her eyebrows rose above her sunglasses. One flicked down before reappearing again. Smiling, Kara winked back. Now she felt as if she was in on the big secret. And doofus Bobby was clueless to it all. She wanted to punch her brother in the side.

They forged ahead on the isolated road. Naked trees towering above them, lightly coated in a sprinkling of frost, shaded the road. The only green came from the pines and evergreens, but the color was so vibrant, it suggested winter had never come. All she needed for a reminder was to check the digital thermostat in the instrument panel.

Forty-four degrees.

It looked nearly dusk as they traveled deeper into the woods and higher up the mountain. The sun was hidden under a blanket of gunmetal gray clouds that looked low enough to drop.

Dad dodged a felled branch in the road that had broken into pieces when it landed. Farther up, they passed by a doe that stood on the verge of the road, lifting its head to watch them drive by.

Bobby didn't see that, either. Can't complain that he misses everything since he sleeps through it all.

Kara saw the giant boulder that was shaped like a snake's head stretching out from the ridge as if to swallow cars. She remembered the times they used to park behind it, and she would race Bobby to the top. He never won. She would like to do that again, but it was too cold to even think about trying.

Maybe we'll come back in the summer.

She hoped so.

Kara couldn't stop smiling as she looked out her window. Whenever they passed an overlook, she stared at the haze-shrouded summits that looked as if they'd been painted by a very talented artist. So many familiar sites that she'd forgotten about but seeing them again made it feel as if she'd never been away. She couldn't wait to see the cabin, her old bedroom. Hopefully they could roast marshmallows in the fireplace like they used to.

"I wonder what shape the cabin's going to be in," said Kara. It had meant to be a thought, but her mouth pulled it from her brain and made it audible.

"I'm sure it's fine," said Dad.

"Have you been there recently?" she asked.

His head shook. "No. But that's what we pay a caretaker for."

Mom laughed. "I bet he's loved us being gone so long. It's probably become his vacation spot."

"Who, Edgar?" asked Dad. Mom really laughed at that, though Kara didn't know why. "Please. He probably hasn't set foot in the cabin since we left until I told him we were coming out."

Still laughing, Mom said, "Probably spent the whole week cleaning his ass off!"

Now, Dad exploded with laughter.

"Mom!" said Kara. "I can't believe you said that."

"Oh, honey, I'm just teasing."

"Still," said Dad. "It's probably true."

Kara remembered Edgar very well. A nice man, but he had an odd look to him. A very tiny head that seemed to have been plucked from a child and put on the body of an old man. When she was about to meet Edgar for the first time, Dad had turned to her and Bobby with a serious look on his face.

"I'm only telling you this because you need to be cautioned, okay? Edgar looks a little—strange. His head…" Dad's lips tightened into a line. "It's just really small, okay? That's the only way I know how to describe it."

"Why are you telling us this?" Bobby had asked.

"Because I don't want you snickering when you see it. Maybe my warning will kill the shock of it."

Kara hadn't expected it to be as bad as Dad had made it out to be. And she was right. It was much worse, which made Dad's forewarnings pointless. Kara and Bobby had to quickly walk away. Once they were confident they were out of earshot, they laughed until they cried.

Edgar's head was like a walnut placed on top of bodybuilder. He also had very tiny teeth, so his lips were always pressed together and wrinkled like wet laundry, which bulged out his cheeks like he was holding a deep breath.

Thinking about him now, Kara felt bad for him. She remembered him being married and wondered what his wife looked like.

Nice, Kara. Why don't you try to picture his hideously deformed kids while you're at it?

They drove through the main strip of Bear Creek. Old-fashioned shops accommodating businesses were on either side of the road, the buildings designed like something from a western. Everything had a front porch, a porch swing and rocking chairs. Most were closed for the season; the only ones still open were for the essentials meant for the locals: a grocery store and a service station. A doctor's office. The Sheriff's Department.

Smoke curled from chimneys. Christmas wreaths hung from the eaves, and the pillars and porch posts were wrapped in colorful garland. She saw cardboard Santas and snowmen, a plastic display of the nativity scene from the Bible.

"Do you want to stop and stock up now?" Dad asked, glancing at Mom.

She seemed to think about it for a moment. "Nah. Let's get to the cabin and unpack. We can make a list and take a quick trip back out here after we've figured out what we need."

Nodding, Dad drove past Ridgewell Grocery. "That's going to be a very long list."

Mom smiled. "A couple pages."

And then they'd left the town behind, the Jeep entering another tree-smothered chasm. A wall of toothed rock sprouting moss was to Kara's right. On top were even more large trees. She could smell the sweet fragrances of pine and burning wood coming in through the vents. She smiled.

They passed several driveways that went uphill, curling through the trees. Mailboxes sat at the end, some crooked, others dented, but mostly fine. Kara didn't see any other mailboxes for a stretch of time until theirs came into view. The flag with the bronzed M fluttered in the breeze below it like a tongue.

The car slowed down, triggering a pang of flutters in her stomach. *We're really here.*

She elbowed her brother in the arm. Nose wrinkling, his eyes remained shut. He stuck out his lips as if about to pout.

"Wake up," said Kara. "We're here."

Bobby slowly opened his eyes. He glanced at Kara, then turned to gaze out his window. Seeing they were heading up with trees nearly touching them on the other side, he sat up. "Wow. How long was I asleep?"

"Almost the whole way," she said.

"Hmmm…"

Bobby arched his back, lifting his bent arms. He reached out, stretching. His hands pushed against Kara's face, fingers brushing her nose. She knew he was doing this on purpose, so she jabbed him in the ribs. Not hard, but it was enough for him to know he'd better knock it off.

"My bad," he said, grinning.

"Sure," she said.

But Kara couldn't help grinning back.

The driveway seemed to rise for a long time before it somewhat leveled out. To the right side of the Jeep were dense woods, but to the left was a steep drop off that sloped back down to the main road. Trees reached up from the edge, branches spreading along to make a twiggy barrier. If the Jeep was to drift in that direction, no way would the branches be strong enough to stop them from plunging.

This part of the drive had always rattled Kara the most. They'd passed plenty of areas just like this on the way in but knowing there was no kind of barrier keeping them from falling to their deaths made her a shaky wreck. Adding that with her already distraught emotions, she was starting to sweat.

The woods seemed to spread apart, making room for the driveway that widened into a graveled lot beside the two-story cabin. A small pickup truck was already parked there, waiting. The cabin's wooden exterior was capped by a green tin roof. A sheltered wraparound porch looked out onto a big yard that surrounded the vacation house and the trees that enclosed their property from the rest of the mountain. Though much older than she remembered, the shed toward the back looked mostly the same. Its flat structure was shaped like a toolbox with a pair of doors in the front. The large structure blocked her view of the large oak tree where the treehouse used to be until a storm knocked it down. Dad strung up a tire swing from the fattest branch a couple months later. She used to have such a fun time, sitting in the tire while either Bobby or Dad pushed her. Soon as they'd unloaded their luggage, she was going to sit in it again.

If I still fit.

The truck's driver side door opened as Dad pulled up beside it.

Edgar dropped out. He wore a bedraggled pair of coveralls under a heavy red-and-black-checkered flannel coat. A hunter's cap with fluffy ear-warmers pulled low on his head made his head appear even smaller than usual. Maybe it was the addition of his heavy wardrobe that made it look so much tinier. He looked nearly the same as Kara remembered him, only older with more wrinkles and obvious gray hairs in the brushing of beard on his cheeks.

"It's the voodoo guy from *Beetlejuice*," whispered Bobby.

"Shut up," said Kara, fighting back her laughter. She shouldered open her door and climbed out. The air was a brutal slap of cold on her face. Reaching into the pocket of her coat, she removed her beanie and put on. Then she zipped up her coat and buried her hands inside its pockets.

Edgar waited at the front of the Jeep for Dad.

"Edgar," Dad said, holding out his hand. "Good to see you."

"Much obliged," he said, taking Dad's hand in his own glove-covered one. He turned to Mom. "Mrs. Marlowe, always a pleasure."

"Likewise," she said, keeping her hands in her own coat.

Edgar's tiny eyes landed on Kara, gazing slowly down her body. She could feel his stare trying to see what she looked like under her clothes. Then they glanced at Bobby briefly before returning to her.

She wished she wouldn't have worn her yoga pants. They clung to her like a dark layer of skin, showing the jut of her rump and the shapes of her thighs and the crescent of her pubic mound. If only the coat was a little longer…

"You kids sure have grown up since I saw you last."

"Some more than others," said Bobby. "As you can tell."

Edgar's tiny eyes went round as heat spread through Kara's cheeks. Bobby must have noticed Edgar's lingering gaze as well. Though she shouldn't feel proud for what Bobby said, she did.

Dad gave Bobby a look that showed he got what Bobby was doing and wasn't pleased about it. He turned back to Edgar, whose face had turned red. "How's the cabin?"

"Huh?" Edgar blinked. "Oh, it's fine. Cleaned her up really nice for you. Some of the tile in the kitchen was cracking. Used some filler and paint to patch it up. Can't even tell now."

"How much do I owe you for that?"

"I'll get you an invoice after the holidays, no rush."

"I appreciate that, Edgar."

"I changed the filter in the central air and heating system, swept the chimney, and made sure all the plumbing was working as it should. The hot water heater is fine, too. We're going to get snow, so I made sure you have plenty of gas for the generator. All the cans are full. Everything's in order."

"Sounds great, Edgar. Thank you."

"Yes," agreed Mom. "Thank you so much."

"Only thing I didn't get to was chopping enough firewood. Had to take down that old tree on the side. Big limb broke off and damn-near crashed against the house. She was old. Rotted too much that she didn't sprout any leaves this year. Been sawing it down to logs all week. You got a little bit to hold you over tonight, but it won't last. I can cut you up some more wood for the fireplace off that if you want me to."

The tire swing tree?

Knowing the tree was gone made Kara's throat tighten. She wondered if Edgar had at least saved the tire or thrown it away.

Dad shook his head. "Not necessary, Edgar. You've done plenty. Head on home and spend the holidays with your family."

"Yes sir, you got it. I left the spare key under the mat."

"Thanks."

Edgar started to turn away, but stopped. He looked back at Dad, frowning through his sagging lips. "There's something else…but I don't know if I should say something in front of the kids or if we should speak in private."

"They're practically adults, Edgar, it's okay."

"If you're sure." He removed his hat, twisting it in his hands. His cotton-white hair was mussed and flat. "Had a prowler out here the other day. Came back last night."

Cold dripped down Kara's spine. Here? She'd never seen anybody out here other than Edgar.

"A prowler?" said Dad. "Are you sure?"

"Oh, I'm sure. I saw him those two times, could have been here more. Didn't get a good look at his face. He was wearing a hat, had it pulled down real low to block his face."

"Did he try to break in?"

"Not that I saw, but he was looking through the windows last night. I was here late, working on the tile, and I felt like I was being watched. You know that feeling?" Dad nodded. "Well, it came over me all of a sudden, and when I looked at the window, I saw him standing there. Couldn't see much on account of it being dark, but I saw his hat and coat. The same hat and coat I saw the other day on a guy wandering around the backyard."

"Did you tell the police?" Dad asked.

Edgar made a face that seemed to ask Grant Marlowe if he thought Edgar was an idiot. "Of course I told them. Sheriff came out last night and we walked around but didn't find anybody. He was long gone. The first time I called, they said if he came back to call them again. So's what I did."

"Good job, Edgar," said Mom.

A miniature-teethed smile parted Edgar's wrinkled face.

"Other than those two times, you haven't seen him?" Dad asked.

"No. That's it."

Dad nodded. "Thanks for letting us know. We'll keep an eye out."

"Good. I didn't want to say something on account of scaring the wife and kids."

"It's fine. Thank you, again."

"You're welcome. I hope y'all have a merry Christmas."

Kara didn't hear what Dad said back. She was too busy hoping the same.

CHAPTER EIGHT

August 14th

Dear Lindsey,

I'm back home. I've missed this couch. Feels good to be in it. The house looks fine. Your mother kept it up and fed the cats while I was at the institution. But it will be her last time here. She boxed up all of Josh's things and was still working on yours when your dad brought me home.

I got very upset, lost my temper. When your parents left, your mom was crying, and I thought your dad was going to punch me. I threatened him with a baseball bat and put a hole in the wall. Told him the next one would be his head. He said he was going to call the institution and have them come pick me up. I don't think he really will, though. He seemed pretty scared when he left. I'm sorry I did it, but I had to make them understand how upset I was.

The doctors said I was suffering from anger issues because of my 'inability to cope with the change.' They gave me a lot of drugs and, after a while, they started to help. I was seen as fit to leave, so I got to come home. *Seeing the boxes with your names written in black marker on them brought it all back.*

I've decided to stop taking the meds.

I start my sessions with Sonja again tomorrow. She came to see me a few times while I was away. She was the only one. None of my family bothered. None of yours bothered. Nobody from the church bothered. They all seem to be slowly phasing me out of their lives, just like they have already done with all of you. It angers me…

I'm tired. Turning in early. Spent the entire day unpacking the boxes. Almost have it back to the way it was before.

I love you all. Please forgive me for the way I spoke to your parents. I figure never seeing them again might be best for all of us.

Love always,
Dennis

September 5th

Dear Lindsey,

They let Grant Marlowe out early. I'm speechless. He's out. Not even a year behind bars, and they let him out? How could this happen? Not even a year???

It's hard to see…my head is pounding.

He's out!

October 4th

Dear Lindsey,

I drove past Grant's house today. It wasn't hard finding out where he lives. Just looked it up online. Plus, his house is like a landmark. So big. Believe it or not, it's the house we used to admire when we would take drives in that wealthy neighborhood. Our dream house. All this time, Grant's lived there. Had I known, I would have killed the bastard and prevented everything from happening…if only I could go back in time.

November 15th

Dear Lindsey,

Today wasn't so bad. Lunch at the park with Sonja was actually kind of fun. It helped…I don't know…distract me from Grant Marlowe for a little bit. Sonja doesn't know I've been following him around, only you do. It's our secret. I knew he was going to be at the park today with his wife, so when Sonja asked where I wanted to go for lunch, I told her the park.

It was elevating, seeing him so miserable. He looks so much older and I could tell he was trying really hard to make his wife smile. She didn't. She looked miserable. I try to imagine what it must be like being married to a murderer and knowing he got away with it. I bet it's hard. But I guess their bond can't be broken, even though it looks like she's suffering. If she would just let that bond die, Grant might actually get some kind of punishment from this. Or if he lost his family, maybe he would finally wipe that artificial grin off his smug face.

They didn't stay at the park long. But Sonja and I stayed for a couple hours. It was fun.

December 24th

Dear Lindsey,

Christmas number two without you. Our last Christmas together was when we gave Josh that Corvette Power Wheel. Remember how much fun it was watching him drive it around the yard? It was so cold outside, but he wouldn't stop driving it. His cheeks had turned pink and his nose looked like a radish. We couldn't get him off the thing until the battery died. Today I wondered what sort of toy or video game Josh might want if he was here. Probably something expensive.

I found the videos I recorded of him and watched them. It was so good hearing his laugh again. I'd almost forgotten what it sounded like. The way I remember it is completely different than what the footage reminded of how it truly sounded. Yours was too. You've always had a wonderful smile, but that Christmas it seemed to be even more powerful than normal. I'm planning on transferring all the videos to the computer and burning them to DVD, for posterity.

Doesn't seem to get any easier like everybody promised. Actually, it feels like it only keeps getting harder.

I have such horrible nightmares, where I'm out of control and I find myself in a room with Grant Marlowe. I kill him, slowly, torturing him until I can't control it and finally ram the knife into his throat. It feels so good watching him gurgle blood as he chokes on the blade. I wake up screaming and the thing that helps me get back to sleep is remembering the dream. Weird how it scares me awake, but also soothes me back to sleep. I don't understand it.

I thought watching our home movies might help. They didn't. I'll kill Grant in my sleep again tonight, I'm sure. One thing I've noticed is my screams aren't as loud as before.

Last night I woke up laughing. Help me!

I miss you all so much it hurts. I feel like I'm in pain all the time. It's hard to move. Tomorrow is going to be awful.

Merry Christmas. I love you all.

Love always,
Dennis

March 14th

Dear Lindsey,

I lost my teaching position today. Was told it was a budget decision, but I know it's not. They can't stand seeing me anymore. I guess who I am now is a constant reminder of who I used to be. I can never go back to who I was before, and I'm not happy with the man left behind. I've changed. I know I have. And nobody wants to be near this new Dennis. Sonja says people care about me, but I disagree. She says she cares about me, but I told her she only does for two hours a week, and she cares about others for the same amount of time on different days. That seemed to really hurt her. She offered to cook dinner for me again. I told her I'd think about it, and I will. Telling her no all the time seems to really make her sad.

June 11th

Dear Lindsey,

Grant's in AA. Can you believe it? All this time I thought he was going to church to pray, but he's taking AA classes there. Marion Marlowe has started working there as an office manager. She used to work for Pinyan's Trucking Company as their office manager, and I doubt she left for the church because of financial gain. There's no way they can match what she was probably making at Pinyan's.

What do they think they're doing? Who are they trying to fool? Does Grant think that attending AA classes means anything? Before long, he won't even remember the accident. He won't remember you or Josh or Lilly. I've been cursed here to always remember. And I'll be DAMNED if he's going to sweep this under the rug like the Grant Marlowe he's famous for being.

April 1st

Grant and Marion went on some kind of date tonight. I followed them to Bender's Bar and Grill. Grant did his usual performance—lots of smiles, overly loud laughter, like he was trying to go out of his way to show he was having a good time. Even Marion seemed to smile more than usual. I could tell she was enjoying herself, even if only a little. But it's more than Grant deserves. His daughter is out of school for spring break. Saw her hanging around that Boseman boy a lot the last few days. Wonder how Grant feels about his daughter palling around with the son of his attorney.

Grant and Marion didn't stay at the restaurant very long. Just long enough to eat. No dessert. And no drinks. But I could tell how much Grant wanted one. Whenever he wasn't looking at his wife, Grant was looking at the bottles being carried around, dabbing his mouth with a napkin.

May 13th

Followed Grant into the grocery store. Actually passed him on the canned soup aisle. He didn't seem to recognize me. I even walked and stood beside him while he selected packages of Ramen noodles—chicken and oriental. Our eyes met and he gave me a single nod before returning to his shopping cart. Nothing. Not even a glimmer of recognition. Has he already forgotten who I am? Sure, I don't look exactly the same, but neither does he. And I know who HE is. I'll never forget HIM.

He will not forget me. Grant needs to remember.

July 25th

Grant will remember. He has to know what this feels like. If only he knew the hell I'm trapped in.

I'm so lonely...

August 23rd

Had sex tonight... Can't believe I did it. What was I thinking? I wasn't, that's where I went wrong. Sonja and me. I guess I should have known it was leading to that. But I never expected for a moment I would've given in.

I liked it. A lot. She was amazing. Felt wonderful. She's so beautiful...so great...makes me feel good. Almost happy.

I can't be happy. Not with what's happened. It's wrong to forget. Wrong to move on. So WRONG!

I bet she's upset with me. I ran out afterward. Left her in the bed, naked. She's calling me now.

I'm not going to answer.

August 28th

I'm not the only one having sex lately, it seems. Grant and Marion did tonight. I was under the bed. Snuck in when they left to help Bobby move out. They came home and Marion asked Grant to lay with her for a while. I knew what would happen. Sure they also knew. Sounded pretty loveless, but both of them seemed to enjoy it.

Shortly after, Marion made Grant leave. I was able to sneak out later. Marion, popping a couple of sleeping pills, zonked out pretty quickly, so I got out without being seen. While I was under the bed, feeling the mattress brush against me as it rocked, I thought about Sonja. Was reminded why I can never let myself become weak again. It's not fair to Lindsey. Not fair to Josh or Lilly. I have wronged them so much by my relationship with Sonja. I'm supposed to go to our session tomorrow. I won't be there. Those will have to end now as well.

Now I'm focused. And I think I might know what I have to do. I don't WANT to, but it might be the only way to make Grant understand. Won't be long before Marion caves and is back with Grant, pretending we don't exist.

If that happens…I might have to remind them all.

CHAPTER NINE

The shed door swung open, throwing smoky light inside. The shapes of Grant and Bobby's shadows were dark against the dirt floor. Grant was a little surprised to see his son was now slightly taller than him. He thought Bobby would have stopped growing by now, but he seemed to have shot up another inch since Thanksgiving.

Bad memories of their Thanksgiving dinner tried to force their way into his mind. He shut the door to them, hoping to keep them locked out.

Grant entered the shed, leaving Bobby standing in the doorway. His son was not thrilled to be out here, and it wasn't just because it was so cold.

Doesn't enjoy the idea of cutting down a Christmas tree.

Maybe if Grant weren't here, Bobby would actually smile.

It had been Marion who'd pointed out they didn't have a tree. They were in town getting supplies for the next few days and she'd seen a tree displayed inside the store. So they'd driven around, hoping to find a lot selling them. When their hunt turned up nothing, they stopped back by the store and asked if there were any nearby.

"Nope," the old man behind the counter had said. "You can drive out to Moreland's Tree Farm in Franklin. They'll probably have some."

Grant knew where Moreland's was. It was a long drive from their cabin. The last Christmas they'd spent out here, they'd made the drive and gotten one. Bobby was fourteen then, and it had been a pretty good time. Grant knew another long drive on top of the one they'd already had would be pushing it with the mood his son was in.

Then Grant came up with the idea of chopping one down. Marion and Kara had loved the idea, but Bobby had only made a farting sound with his lips. Grant had figured since he'd have to get some firewood ready, he could use the ax and chainsaw for a Christmas tree as well.

Hopefully the chainsaw still worked.

Edgar probably gave it a tune-up, if he used it to cut down the tree in back.

Though Grant hadn't showed it, he was upset about the tree. He owned the cabin, not Edgar. So it should have been Grant's decision whether the tree stayed or went. He wished Edgar would've gotten his permission before cutting it down. The tire swing used to be in the tree, and Kara loved it.

Now the tire leaned against the wall. The rope was still wrapped around it, leading to a frayed tip that showed where Edgar had made the cut.

Grant looked away. Seeing the tire was upsetting him more than he wanted. His eyes landed on the chainsaw. Edgar had set it on the workbench that had been built against the back wall by Grant's own hands. Light coming through the window on the other side highlighted the faded paint on the blade in a dusty glow. Though it showed use, the chain looked rather new.

"Want to grab the chainsaw while I look for the ax?" asked Grant, nodding at the workbench.

"Whatever." Sighing, Bobby entered the shed. He stepped past Grant and made his way between the lawnmowers and boxes in the center.

The shed had plenty of space inside, with a pair of front doors that locked from the outside and in. Another single door was on the side, but Grant couldn't remember if they'd ever actually used it.

Bobby grabbed the chainsaw by the front hand guard. Dragging it across the table, he let his arm drop. The chainsaw made clacking sounds as it swung by Bobby's leg.

"Careful," said Grant. "It can still cut you."

Bobby made a sound that was supposed to be a shocked gasp. But Grant knew it was his son's way of telling him *No shit*.

Grant turned right, walking toward the yard tools. He passed the rakes, some shovels and a sledgehammer. He had no idea why there were so many tools in here. He'd never used the majority of them and probably never would. Some still looked smooth and sported the barcode sticker on blades that slightly shined in the dim light from lack of use.

The ax was propped in the corner, the aging double-headed blade on the dirt floor. He'd had the ax for a long time. It was the first tool he'd gotten after they purchased the cabin. Grant gripped the handle and turned, feeling the pokes of old wood against his hand. He'd have to wear his gloves for sure or he might get splinters when chopping.

Walking back to the doorway, he dragged the ax behind him.

"Ready?" he asked.

Bobby looked down at the chainsaw. "Let's not and say we did."

"Come on, Bobby."

"Why can't we just ride out to Moreland's?"

"Because there's no adventure in it."

"It's a warm car ride. We're going to turn into frozen meat pies out there." He pointed out the window to the side of him. Frost painted the panes. "It's cold. We'll look like Jack Nicholson at the end of *The Shining* before the day's over with."

"Nice image," said Grant, shaking his head. He started for the door. "Come on. Your mother wants a tree. So does Kara. And I do, too. I'm sure you wouldn't mind having one either."

Bobby sighed. "Do we even have any Christmas decorations?"

"In the attic."

"Suppose you'll make me climb up there and get them."

"There's an idea."

He smiled at his son. Bobby rolled his eyes, killing Grant's humor. This was going to be a catastrophe. The demise was already starting. After a huge breakthrough with Marion, Bobby's attitude was going to ruin it. If he was giving Grant this much of a hard time for wanting to cut down a Christmas tree, he hated to think what Bobby was going to do later.

"Forget it," said Grant. "Go inside. I'll do it myself."

Bobby made a face that was a mixture of confusion, anger, and sadness. He shook his head, and the expression became complete frustration. "Yeah, right. And upset Mom?" He started making his way back through the clutter. "You may be okay with doing that, but not me."

Already with the quick jabs. Can't wait to see what he's working himself up to saying.

Grant exhaled a heavy breath through his nostrils that hissed like air leaking from a tire. It made thin cloudy trails in the air. Bobby walked outside, leaving him alone in the shed. Grant gave another look around as he started for the open door and spotted Bobby's old mountain bike hanging on the rack with the others. It looked too small for his son now.

And that depressed him even more.

Kara put the last plate in the dish drainer. Water made little tapping sounds in the tray underneath as it dripped from the soaked dishes. Hopefully she'd washed enough. Looking at the full drainer and the spread-out dampening towel on the counter with pots and pans drying on top, she figured she did.

Though covered in dust, everything had been where it was supposed to be. When she found the drinking glasses had old spiderwebs clinging across the tops, she'd begun pulling them down and carrying them to the sink.

Thankfully Mom thought to get dish soap while we were in town.

Mom was good at that, details. Dad seemed to only be concerned with getting to the cabin. She figured it was because he wanted to get it over with, knowing that once they were there, nobody would be apt to leave anytime soon.

Except for Bobby. She still needed to have a talk with him.

Maybe tonight, after Mom and Dad have gone to bed.

Kara flapped her hands, throwing the access water off fingers. Then she grabbed another towel and dried her hands. With tomorrow being Christmas Eve, tonight might be the only chance she'd have to be alone with him so she could tell him about what she saw in the Jeep.

Holding hands.

She couldn't remember the last time her parents held hands. Maybe after Dad quit drinking the first time.

Something crashed at the back of the cabin.

Her mother yelled.

Dropping the towel, Kara dashed out of the kitchen. She stood between the stairs and the front door, looking around.

"Mom!"

Thoughts pranced through her mind about prowlers. She envisioned her mother being attacked by a man in a hat.

"Up here!" called Mom.

Her voice came from upstairs. Kara stood on the bottom step, looking up. "Are you okay?"

"Yeah…I'm fine." She sounded depressed. "I don't know if the decorations are, though."

Kara ran up the stairs. Reaching the upper floor, she saw the attic door was down and the foldout ladder was extended. A box lay on its short side on the carpet, dented and crumpled. The packaging tape had ripped up the middle and spilled gaudy ornaments all over the floor. Most had shattered, including a little porcelain stocking Kara had painted in art class when she was in eighth grade.

"How bad is it?" Mom asked.

Kara looked up. Mom's head peeked over the edge of the square-shaped hole in the ceiling. Blond hair hung around her face.

"Totaled," said Kara.

Mom's eyes closed. "Shit."

"Mom. If you're going to work at a church, you can't keep cussing."

"I think I'm allowed a couple here and there," Mom said, opening her eyes.

"I'm not sure that's how it works."

"You're probably right." She took a deep breath. "Did *anything* survive?"

Sinking to a crouch, Kara dug through the flashy-colored debris.

"Don't cut yourself," said Mom.

"I'll be fine."

Kara felt a sharp sting on her fingertip, but ignored it so her Mom wouldn't say anything else.

Way to prove Mom right.

Hopefully it wouldn't start bleeding.

Kara grabbed the jagged chunk of her ornament and held it up. "This didn't make it."

"Aw, Kara, I'm sorry. I loved that ornament."

Though Kara thought *So did I,* she only nodded.

"Coming down," said Mom.

Kara stepped back. Mom's head vanished from the opening and her rump appeared, wiggling backward. A foot reached out, softly kicking air until finding one of the risers. The other followed. Once both feet were together on a rung, Mom swung around to face the ladder. Then she started climbing down.

"Careful," said Kara. "We don't need you to look like this box down here."

"You don't have to tell me twice."

Mom made it without error. She turned around, brushing off her hands. She pursed her lips and blew softly, her face flustered. Sweat was sprinkled across her forehead. Looking down at the mess, she frowned. "Way to go, Marion."

Kara nodded. "Ready to survey the damage?"

"I guess."

Together, they got on the floor. Kara sat cross-legged and Marion, with her legs folded under her, braced herself on the backs of her legs.

They began to sort through the decorations, making piles. The bashed pile was growing much quicker than the salvageable one.

Mom sighed. "This is awful. Some of this stuff we've had since you and Bobby were little."

"Good thing Bobby wasn't here to see it or he'd make a big dramatic scene about it."

"Kara!" Mom laughed.

"It's true. You know how he is, so overdramatic sometimes. If any of his stuff's broken, we'll just hide it. He probably won't even notice."

Mom smiled, though it was without cause. "I hope he's not being a turd to your father right now."

Kara tossed a silver cap with sharp pieces of broken bulb sticking out the bottom onto the bad pile. "You know he probably is."

"I don't know why Grant didn't want us to go with, to be peacekeepers."

"I think Dad wanted the time alone with him."

"Oh, he's getting that, all right." Marion shook her head. "I just hope he doesn't regret it. Your father's so sensitive right now. Bobby says the wrong thing..." She shook her head again.

Mom actually seemed concerned about Dad, which was nice. But it also worried Kara. "Mom..."

Mom looked at her. Saw the expression Kara was giving her. Her eyebrows angled down. "What is it?"

Kara wanted to say a lot. But sitting in front of the shattered remains of their holiday decorations was not the place for it. "Forget it."

"What's on your mind?"

"It's Dad..."

Mom briefly closed her eyes, took a deep breath. "I know, honey. This isn't an easy trip for any of us..."

"No. It's not that. I'm glad we came out here."

"You are?"

Kara tried to smile, but her lips felt strange. "Yeah. Dad's doing much better now. He's tried really hard to...you know—change."

"I know he has."

"Are you going to give him an honest chance?" Mom's eyes seemed to weaken. Her posture slightly drooped. "And I mean an *honest* chance? I saw you holding hands on the way up here." Mom's mouth opened to speak, but Kara didn't give her the opportunity. "Because, honestly, if we spend Christmas together, and you're taking all this time to hunt out the decorations while Dad cuts down a tree, and we open presents and eat a big dinner and you *don't* give Dad a chance..." Kara paused. She huffed out a breath that rattled her cheeks. "I don't think I'll be able to handle that and I just might start acting toward you like Bobby does to Dad."

"Kara..."

"I'm serious, Mom. My opinion? You've punished him enough. It's time to either let him go or to work through it."

Mom sat up straight, pulling back her shoulders. She pulled her hair away from her face. "I'll talk to you like an adult, since you are one."

"I hoped that you would."

"Your father spent so many years lying to people that it became who he was. Is he that person now? No, I don't think he is. Do I think he's working really hard to be someone different? Yes. Do I want things to go back to normal? Yes. Will they?" Mom held out her hand, palm up. She shrugged. "I don't know. I don't think they can, no matter how hard we try. So, what I'm going to do is just keep working to adjust to how things are now. They're not perfect, by any means, but I'm not doing a whole lot of good by moping around."

"Have you forgiven him? Dad?" Kara saw the switching of expressions on her mother's face and knew that she hadn't. "Will you be able to? You know things will never be okay unless you can."

"I have forgiven him for a lot..." Mom's jaw shook, lips made soft fluttering sounds as she breathed in. "But not everything."

"Do you still love him?"

Mom tried to smile, but it somehow made her look even sadder. "Would we be here if I didn't?"

"Does he know that?"

"Probably not. He probably thinks I won't ask for a divorce because I found Christ..."

"Is that it, though?"

Mom rolled her shoulder in a weak shrug. "It might be what originally kept me from doing it. But it's not all of it. Not anymore."

"What changed?"

"Nothing. I just stopped trying to punish him."

Kara nodded. That was enough for now. Mom had told her plenty, but it wasn't Kara who she should be saying it to. Maybe she'd already told this to Dad, but she doubted it.

Sighing, Kara looked at the busted box that had vomited broken ornaments all over the floor. Being here felt more like visiting the house of a dead relative than a family vacation. She supposed most of their outings would feel like this until things got better. But if they ever would, Kara couldn't say.

However, she guessed they were on some kind of right path to trying.

This week won't be a good time to tell them about Derrek.

She looked down at her finger, remembering how it had looked with the engagement ring on it last night. She smiled.

"Come on, kiddo," said Mom. "Let's finish up here and get some hot chocolate going. The boys will need it when they get back."

Though they talked nearly the whole time, neither of them mentioned the previous conversation.

CHAPTER TEN

Bobby stepped out from behind the tree, zipping up his pants. The trail was empty. The ax leaned against a tree with the chainsaw on the ground in front of it. Dad hadn't come back yet. He must still be behind his own tree, pissing into the cold.

Maybe it froze.

He pictured his father stuck to a thin golden line of solid piss that connected him to the ground and snickered. Now that would be a sight. He'd have to take a picture of it with his phone.

Bobby stood on the trail a bit longer. Raising his hands to his mouth, he gripped them together and huffed hot air into the small pocket his palms made. It warmed his skin for a too brief moment before turning cold again.

What's taking him so long?

He'd left a good ten seconds before Bobby decided to go on and empty his bladder as well. Frowning, Bobby lowered his arms, putting his hands into his heavy coat pockets. "What's the hold up?" he asked. His breath hung in the air.

"Bobby?"

Something wasn't right. Dad's voice sounded serious. "Yeah?"

"Come here a second."

Bobby started walking but paused before leaving the trail. "Got everything tucked away?"

Dad huffed. "Yes. Just get over here."

Bobby couldn't help but smile as he stepped off the trail onto the brittle leaves that carpeted the forest floor. His steps sounded like walking on a plateau of potato chips as he moved between trees. Walking down a short slope, he saw his father farther up. His back was turned to him, both arms hanging by his sides. The hood of his coat covered his head, but Bobby could see his breaths in a curling trail from the side.

Why's he just standing there like that?

"What's up?" asked Bobby, raising his voice to be heard over the crunching of his footsteps.

Dad turned, then stepped back. He held out his left hand as if showcasing some kind of prize. "This."

At first, Bobby couldn't see it. Dad's bulk was still blocking his view. When he stood next to his father, he saw it clearly.

Scorched sticks had been assembled into a crooked pyramid inside a ring of stones. Frost painted the sticks' blackened skin. The ground a few feet away was trampled flat in a wide spread, probably by a tent.

Seeing the rigged campsite caused Bobby's skin to tighten. "What the hell?"

"My thoughts exactly," said Dad.

"Do you think Edgar...?" Before he could finish, Bobby realized how stupid that would be. Why would Edgar have himself a little campout on their land?

"I doubt it," said Dad.

"How far out are we from the cabin?"

Dad breathed heavily through his nose as he thought it over. "Not real far."

Bobby turned and looked into the trees, as if he might be able to see the cabin from where he stood. He couldn't. The woods were dense, filling his vision with tall pines and leafless trees. Maybe they weren't *real far* away from the cabin, but it had still been a pretty good hike.

He looked back at the charred timber. His stomach felt weird. "Think this belongs to Edgar's prowler?"

"I'd say it's a good possibility."

Nodding, Bobby walked around the side of the old campfire. He pointed at the compressed brown grass and broken leaves. "A tent?"

Dad nodded. "Good guess." He pointed down to the right. "And he left tracks."

Bobby squinted his eyes. Off slightly to Dad's right foot were some depressions in the dirt. He couldn't tell if they had been made by feet or not, but he assumed so. Bobby turned away from the tracks and his eyes landed on a small stack of cut wood. "Here's more for the campfire."

"I see it."

"Why would he leave everything out like this?"

"I guess he planned on coming back."

Bobby's stomach felt like it was going to flip over. A tingling current traveled down his colon. "You really think so?"

Dad held out his hands, as if saying he wasn't sure of anything right now.

Bobby frowned. "But he took his tent?"

"Maybe seeing Edgar made him think twice. Plus, it's way too damn cold to camp."

As if to prove Dad's point, an icy gust blew across Bobby's face. His cheeks felt frozen, but still burned slightly. Removing the beanie from his head, he brushed his fingers through his hair. Though it was freezing outside, his hair was damp with sweat and the cold air stung his scalp. He pulled the beanie back onto his head and felt better.

Dad waved Bobby over. "Come on. Let's get moving."

Nodding, Bobby started walking, not taking his eyes off the campfire. Seeing somebody who didn't belong had used this area to keep warm left Bobby feeling squirmy inside. He pulled his eyes away from the burnt pile, but could still *feel* it back there, as if it was watching him walk away.

"Are we heading back?" he asked Dad.

"Not until we get a tree."

Bobby stopped. "Are you serious?"

Dad was almost to the trail when he stopped. He looked back at Bobby. "Of course I am. Why?"

"Why?" Bobby stared at him. "Oh—I don't know, maybe because we found evidence of the guy Edgar was talking about? Somebody's trespassed on our property? Shouldn't we report it?"

"It's been reported. Sheriff came out here himself."

"So?"

Dad closed his eyes like somebody trying to keep his calm while trying to understand a foreign language. Sighing, he opened them and stared at Bobby. "Fine. I'll call when we get back if it'll make you feel better."

"Sure. No rush." Bobby threw his arms in the air. "No reason to worry."

"There's not. Obviously, he's gone."

"For now."

"For good."

"How do you know? You have a crystal ball that tells you these things?"

"No. I just know people. He knows Edgar saw him, probably knows the police have been here. He won't be back." Grant turned away from Bobby and started walking. "He's long gone by now."

Pushing some drooping limbs out of his way, Dad vanished when they swung back together. Bobby couldn't believe Grant Marlowe's stubbornness. But he wasn't surprised by it. His father had been blessed with a notable career because of such hardheadedness. That was Grant Marlowe for you. Once he was convinced of something, nothing would deter him from it.

"Asshole," muttered Bobby.

He joined his dad on the trail. Dad, holding the chainsaw by the hand guard, turned when he heard Bobby. "Grab the ax, will you?"

Bobby saw it leaning against the tree. He grabbed the handle, tilted it up and let it slide down through his fingers. He caught it under the head, stopping the ax's drop. Carrying it with him, he followed his father up the trail.

They walked in silence for several minutes.

Dad killed the quietness by saying, "Do me a favor."

"Let me guess—don't tell Mom or Kara about what we saw."

"Bingo."

"Should've known."

"What's that?"

Bobby sighed. "Nothing."

The trail curved to the right. A cluster of pine trees was off the trail, gathered in a circle of bright green. Two looked small enough to cut down but the rest were way too big.

"How about that one?" asked Grant, pointing at the fuller of the two smaller ones. "Think we can carry that back with us?"

"Does it matter what I think? If you say we can, then by surely, we can."

Grant lowered his arm. "Got something you want to get off your chest?"

"Like what?"

"It's just the two of us out here. You can say what's on your mind without worrying about your mother or sister stopping you. I'm sure there's something you want to talk about."

Bobby knew what Dad was doing. He wanted Bobby to lose his temper and release his pent-up anger. In Grant's eyes, it would get it out in the open and Bobby could start to relax. Not going to work. Bobby smiled. "Really? You want me to let it out, huh?"

Dad nodded. "I think it would help. What you say might hurt, but I'm sure I need to hear it. No matter how bad…"

"I'm flunking out of school."

Dad stopped talking. His head slowly turned away, gazing over Bobby's shoulder as if looking at something in the woods. Bobby felt his lips arching into a smile. The way it shaped on his face, Bobby figured it must look nearly proud of his academic situation.

Taking a deep breath, Dad let the chainsaw drop to the ground. "Not what I was expecting to hear…"

"Didn't think it was."

"And you're serious, aren't you?"

Bobby tilted his head, smirking.

"Of course you're serious," said Dad. "Why would you joke about that?"

"I wouldn't."

"No...you wouldn't." Dad rubbed his temples with both forefingers. "How...?" He paused as his face scrunched up with pure frustration. "Tell me how the hell a musician as talented as you flunks music school?"

Bobby held out his hands. "It's easier than I ever would have thought."

"What is? Flunking?"

Bobby nodded. "Just don't try. That's usually the quickest way." He started walking toward the tree, suddenly feeling chipper. "This tree?" He grabbed one of the branches. The needles were thick and coated in a thin skin of ice. "Good eye. I like it."

"Bobby...this is serious."

"I know. If we get one that's too big, we'll have to cut the branches and then sap will leak onto the floor..."

"Stop!" Dad's voice ricocheted off the trees around them in an irate reverb. His eyes were narrowed, eyebrows pointed down. His mouth hung slightly open, lips quivering, shoulders rising and dropping with his quick breaths.

Bobby hadn't seen him this mad since he caught him smoking weed in the backyard. And he felt some kind of selfish pride knowing he'd caused it.

"Is this a joke to you?" asked Dad.

"Am I laughing?"

"I believe you are on the inside. Actually, I can almost hear your arrogant cackle from here."

"Nice. Sounds a bit like yours, doesn't it?"

"That's what this is about? Really? You're going to ruin your future just to get back at me?"

"Nope. You already ruined my future, Pops. I'm just following the path you laid out for me."

"Oh, get over yourself, Bobby. You think you're the only one that's been affected the last couple years?"

"No. I'm the only one who's not pretending to be okay with it."

Dad's mouth hung open. He licked his lips. "So you're going to flunk out of school because you have issues with me?"

"My band's sent out demos. We have interest from two labels. One even wants to come out to watch us play live. We're on the verge of making it. That's where my focus needs to be. Not at some school of music that you can brag about to your friends."

"Bobby, I don't have any friends to brag to. And you're going to finish school. That's not a request. That's an order."

"An order? In case you've forgotten, I'm not a kid anymore. I'm nineteen. That pretty much entitles me to be able to do what the hell I want. Even if it makes the almighty Grant Marlowe angry."

"Almighty? Why don't you tell me what this is really about?" Dad folded his arms across his chest. From the heaviness of his coat, it looked as if he was fluffing out his chest.

Bobby stared at his father. The ax felt heavy in his hands. A brief image flashed through his head of him swinging the double-bladed weapon at Grant Marlowe's head. It shocked him how satisfying of a vision it was.

He tossed the ax at his feet. "I'm done," said Bobby.

"Done?"

"This stupid holiday was your and Mom's idea. You guys can have it. I don't want any part of it. I'm leaving."

"Bobby…you can't…" Grant rubbed his mouth. It was the familiar gesture he used to do whenever he wanted a drink. "You rode with us…"

"I already have a way out of here, a contingency plan. I'll text my girlfriend and she'll come pick me up."

"Girlfriend?"

"Yeah. See what you'd learn about me if you just asked?"

Bobby turned around and started walking.

"Bobby!" His Dad's voice sounded weaker than usual, a little shaky. "Bobby…please…"

"Up yours! I'm done with you, too." Bobby hurried back to the trail. He paused to look back at his father.

On his knees, with his back to him, his shoulders shook. His head was down.

Seeing he'd caused his father to cry didn't bring him the pleasure he thought it would. He felt pretty lousy.

Went too far.

He wondered if he should apologize. Hearing the sniffles of Dad's soft sobbing made his heart feel heavy. Bobby took a step forward. He stopped.

Forget it. Let him cry.

He deserved it.

Bobby turned away, started walking. When he was up the trail a little ways, he pulled out his cell phone and scrolled through the list to Sheena. He sent her a text that said he wanted to be picked up.

CHAPTER ELEVEN

November 26th

What a cabin! Wow. Big enough to house a family of six, and the Marlowes use it maybe once or twice a year. None since Grant killed my family, but they will be soon.

Had to break into the church and look over Marion's session notes. She's ready to move on, but doesn't know how to tell Grant this without thinking she's over the accident.

Accident...sure.

The pastor's notes states that he believes Marion fears "forgiving" Grant for her own anxieties that stem from the car wreck and Grant's condition leading to it. She's apparently afraid if she forgives him, he will revert back to the old Grant, thinking he got away with everything.

She's wrong. Grant already believes he has.

I'll remind him that he hasn't.

Looking over the layout of the property in Bear Creek, I have a pretty good idea of how to move forward. I'll need to see it in person.

Time to plan the trip.

December 2nd

Have everything prepared for the trip. I'm leaving tomorrow morning. Just for a day drive. Scope things out.

December 4th

An old man was fixing the place up. Watched him cut down an old tree that had a tire swing hanging from one of the branches. I wonder how many good memories were created with that tree. Would have loved to have something like that in our yard, but we just didn't have the space. A tire swing. I remember swinging on the one at Grandpa's lake house and having such a good time. Josh would've loved it too. He used to love swinging at the park. When he was a little older, he would've been able to do the tire swing.

Looks like the Marlowes are planning on spending some time at the cabin after all. Marion must've agreed, or the old man wouldn't be there getting the place ready. Today's Thursday. Marion has another session this afternoon…

December 5th

Home from the church. Marion is supporting Grant's idea of taking the family to the cabin for Christmas. She believes it will be a huge leap to making their family a unit once again.

Marion is such a damn fool. No wonder she hasn't left her husband. Just when I was beginning to think she couldn't be tricked by Grant Marlowe's flashy speeches and charming good looks, she proves me wrong. Should've known she would've fallen for it. She's the oldest of all his sheep, the longest punchline of the Grant Marlowe joke.

Her faith is leading her to these decisions?

I have to disagree.

December 15th

The old man saw me today. Had to get out of there pretty fast. Left my stuff behind. Hopefully he doesn't find it. I'll go back in a few days and gather it up. Hopefully the police won't be waiting on me.

December 21st

Spotted by the old man again! How does he keep seeing me? My own fault. Shouldn't've looked through the window. Had to know for sure Grant wasn't there. Don't know what I would've done if he had been.

Probably would've changed my plans.

I wish he would've been there.

CHAPTER TWELEVE

"Maybe we should rethink all of this," said Mom. "If Bobby's already making such a big deal…"

"We're *not* going to rethink anything," said Grant. He must've regretted the tone of his voice because he took a deep breath and tried to smile. Instead, his lips just sort of twitched. "Sorry. I didn't mean to snap."

"I understand you're upset."

"Upset?" Grant snorted. "I stopped being upset twenty minutes ago. Now I'm *furious.*"

In the kitchen, Kara sat at the table. Her arms were on top, fingers slowly stroking the ring of her coffee mug. She slipped her finger through the hole and gripped the mug. Lifting it to her mouth, she blew the steam away. She sipped some of the hot liquid and grimaced. Though it should taste warm and sweet, it seemed bitter and nasty.

"Losing your temper isn't going to solve anything," said Mom.

Damn it, Bobby.

"Who's losing their temper? He was the one…left me back there…"

Kara shook her head.

Had to start your shit, didn't you?

And who was this girlfriend Dad talked about? Bobby had kept her a secret from all of them, apparently. Kara twisted in her seat. She looked to the glass bay doors. The blinds were open and she could see Bobby through them. He sat in a chair, a foot hooked on his knee. Elbow planted on his thigh, he held the phone up. His thumb moved in a blur over the bright screen. The collars of his coat were upturned, blocking most of his face. But she could tell he was smiling at what he was tapping into the phone.

Obviously the message was for the mystery girl.

"You should have heard him out there," said Dad. "I get it, okay? I *fucked* up. The last ten years of my goddamn life have been a series of ultimate fuck-ups…"

"Grant! Don't shout and don't you dare talk like that!"

Now Mom was shouting.

"Forgive me, Marion. I forgot how you're suddenly sensitive to cuss words!"

Kara squirmed in the chair. She hadn't heard her parents fight like this in a long time. Sure, they'd hardly spoken to each other in over a year, but when they would, it was at least civil.

"You said you wouldn't make fun of my faith anymore, Grant."

"I'm not making fun of it. I'm really not. You just have to understand how out of line it is to point out how I'm speaking when I'm pissed off, and not acknowledging *why* I'm so fucking pissed off!"

"I know why you are! But that gives you no right to talk to me like that!"

Something loudly clattered, followed by a crash. To Kara, it sounded like somebody had either dropped or thrown their mug of hot chocolate.

"Sorry…" said Dad, his voice low and overly soft.

Kara didn't know what he was apologizing for, but the sputtering sobs from her mother showed her it was coming too late.

And they were doing so much better today.

Holding hands, smiling. They'd even joked together.

All ruined. She turned and looked at Bobby. Thumb flapping back and forth. Smiling.

Rotten asshole.

Kara stood up so fast her rump bumped the chair, causing it to fall backward. It landed on the tile with a rigid smack. She left it where it landed as she headed for the bay doors. She hardly noticed Dad's calling for her because of the rushing sounds in her ears.

She gripped the doorknob with a palsied hand and jerked it toward her. Cold air washed over her heated body, but she hardly cared.

Gasping, Bobby dropped his phone, but managed to catch it before it hit the deck's wood floor. Kara marched over to him, raising her hand.

"Jesus, Kara! You scared the shit out of—"

Her fist swung down. Kara saw it going right for his eye and quickly averted its direction. It cuffed the top of his head with a muffled *whack* that sent a bubbling jolt up to her elbow.

"Ow!" yelled Bobby.

"Damn!" Kara yelled back. She pulled her fist to her stomach, holding it with her other hand. She tried to open her fingers, but they felt locked in place and tingled as if hot rice filled them from her knuckles to fingernails.

Holding the top of his head, Bobby looked up at her. His face was twisted in pain and confusion. "What the *hell* was that for?"

Kara shook her hand. It seemed to only make the pain worse, so she put it close to her stomach again. "For being such an *asshole.*"

"Me?"

"Yes! Mom and Dad are in there arguing because of you."

"Whatever. I didn't do anything wrong."

"You went out of your way to be a complete ass, didn't you?"

"I only said what was on my mind."

"And you couldn't have kept it toned down some?"

"Who told you what I said?"

"Nobody. But it's you, so I can imagine it."

Bobby took his hand away from his head, checking his fingertips as if expecting to find blood on them. Seeing that there wasn't any, he let his hand drop into his lap. "I think a lump's forming…"

"Oh, please, I didn't hit you that hard."

"You *punched* me."

"You're lucky I changed my mind when I did."

"Yeah, lucky me."

"Stop being a baby."

He reached up, rubbed the top of his head again. His fluffy hair fell back into place when he was done as if he hadn't touched it at all. She didn't like the color of his hair now. He'd added some kind of highlights to it, obviously to try and mimic some popular rock star's style. Kara didn't know who that would be since she didn't listen to a lot of modern music. She loved the classics.

"Did you really tell your girlfriend to come pick you up?"

"Mom told you?"

"No. I heard her telling Dad. After you came back, I went and found Dad. He was trying to lug back the tree, chainsaw and ax all by himself."

"Well, he didn't, did he? You were there to help. Always the favorite, always eager to please."

"Oh, up yours. Don't try to twist this around on me."

"I'm not. And yes, I texted Sheena. She's on her way. Probably be here tonight."

"Sheena?" Bobby nodded. Kara held out the hand that didn't hurt, fanning the air to coax him into saying more. "And?"

"And what?"

"Who is she?"

"My girlfriend."

"For how long?"

"None of your business."

"Does she live in a bell tower somewhere?" Bobby's nose wrinkled. Apparently he didn't get the reference. "Nobody knows her, so she's either make-believe or really ugly."

"Whatever. She's damn hot. I didn't tell anybody about her because I knew you'd all want to meet her."

"And why's that so bad?"

"Kara? Are you even aware of our family matters?"

"Text her back and tell her to stay home."

"Too late. She's already on her way."

"Then tell her to plan on staying."

Bobby shook his head. "Hell no."

"How long has she been *on her way*? Was this before or after your pleasant chat with Dad?"

"I told her to be ready to leave at any moment."

"Wow. Got her trained well, huh?"

"Piss off, Kara."

"What's gotten into you?"

"Nothing."

"You've changed."

Bobby rolled his eyes. "Sure. That's expected. What gets me is that you haven't changed at all."

"What's that supposed to mean?"

"Can't keep pretending everything's the same when nothing is."

"It's better than being a nonstop prick like you. You don't think I hate how screwed up we are?"

"*We're* fine. It's him." Bobby raised his chin toward the cabin. "*He's* screwed up. Now he's screwing all of us up with him."

"That's not fair...you shouldn't say that about Dad. He needs us right now."

Bobby shook his head. "Not me. I'm done with this family."

Her brother turned blurry as hot tears filled her eyes. She didn't want him to know she was crying, but knew there was no way of hiding it. She pulled the sleeve of her sweater over her hand and used it to dry her eyes.

"Stop crying," said Bobby. "What's done is done." He leaned forward in the chair, peering around her hip. "You hear that? I'm *finished* with this shitty family and all the pretend affection it has for each other. I can't just grin and bear it. Sorry, Mom. I'm not as good of an actress as you are. And Dad, to me you died in that crash with that little boy."

Kara turned around and saw her parents standing in the doorway. She had no idea how long they'd been standing there. She suddenly felt as if they'd caught her stealing money from their wallets.

Her eyes turned to Dad. She thought she could actually see what little bit of potential he'd managed to keep firmly clutched in his heart flap away. His shoulders slouched, mouth dropped open. His eyes, usually vibrant even through his despondency, dimmed so much they hardly seemed to be there at all.

Though Mom's face was streaked with tears, she looked numb.

"Merry Christmas, everyone," said Bobby as he stood up. Without another word, he walked to the doorway. "Excuse me."

Mom turned and walked away, opening up a space for Bobby to pass through.

Dad leaned against the doorway. Kara realized if it wasn't there to support him, he would've dropped to the floor.

"Oh, Dad…" She started walking to him, holding out her arms. The one she'd hit Bobby with still throbbed.

Dad held up his hand. "Don't, Kara. It's okay. You don't have to pretend anymore."

"Dad…I never pretended…"

Dad offered a crooked smile. His lower lip trembled. "No more performances, okay? I think Bobby said what was on everyone's mind. There's no point. Right? It's over."

"Dad, don't say that." Kara's voice had turned to a whine by the end of her sentence.

"Good night. We'll leave in the morning."

"Tomorrow's Christmas Eve."

"Go spend it with the Bozeman kid."

Kara's eyes shot toward her finger. Though there was no band on it, she could feel it like there like a ghost ring. And she figured that somehow Dad could see it.

"Good night," he said.

Walking like somebody who'd been a coma for months, Dad made his way back into the kitchen.

The strength left Kara's legs and she had to grab on to the back of the closest rocking chair. She pulled it back and dropped into it.

Leaning forward, she put her elbows on her knees and buried her face into her palms.

And sobbed.

CHAPTER THIRTEEN

The GPS told Sheena where to turn. She slowed her tiny Honda to a crawl and made the turn without dipping the tires into the deep ditch. She hated the mountains, hated driving through them even more. Plus she could hardly see a thing. It was late in the evening and heavy purple clouds seemed to have swallowed up the daylight. They were thick and hovered above the mountains like a mauve-colored cowl. The weather app on her phone said it was snowing in the nearby areas, but so far she'd only seen a few flurries drift down and melt into clear dots when they hit her windshield.

Before pushing her foot down on the gas, she sent a quick text to Bobby.

Be ready. Getting close.

He responded nearly right away.

Hurry.

"I am," she said. And smiled.

Sheena bounced in her seat from the excitement she felt. Kind of like a hero, like she was a knight and Bobby was the princess trapped in some tower. She understood the genders were all wrong, but she did feel as if she was coming to rescue him.

He would love her forever for this.

And she was just fine with that.

Sheena had no idea when she fell for Bobby completely, but she'd never forget when she realized that she had. They were at the movies. Before going into their theater, she'd asked Bobby to hold the popcorn while she ran to the bathroom. When she'd come out, she saw him standing outside the theater's entrance, an arm hugging the big bucket of popcorn and the extra-large drink in the other. Seeing him standing there had changed everything. The realization that she wanted to spend the rest of her life with him had hit her all at once.

And this insight came *before* he'd told her about the possible record deals. She was sure there would be people out there who thought she was only with him because of his potential future. If it was up to her, she'd rather he not sign any contract that would keep him away from her for months at a time. She didn't want to be a band groupie, but if Bobby's band took that step, she would support him. Just like she knew he'd support her if she was selected to sit in a chair in an orchestra somewhere. He'd follow her and she'd follow him.

That was what made them so right for each other. Their commitment to each other. The comfort in knowing that somebody had your back no matter what.

And she had his back right now. If he ever had any doubts about her intentions before, her driving all this way to pick him up should remove them.

The GPS's monotone voice announcing her turn was up ahead made her gasp. With the radio off and windows up, the faux female voice was like a shout in the quiet car.

Her headlights pushed two bright tunnels through the wan light in front of her. A mailbox seemed to shine in the powerful glow.

I'm here.

Her heart began to beat faster. Reaching for the turn signal, she saw how much her hand was shaking. God, she was jittery. She took turns wiping her sweaty hands on her thighs. Then she slowed the car to turn onto the driveway.

The trees seemed to shield her from what little bit of light remained. Darkness smothered the inside of the car as it started to climb the mountain.

She kept her speed low. She looked out the windows and through the windshield. No sign of Bobby. She'd expected to find him walking down to meet her, though they'd never decided how they were going to do this part. Not wanting to drive right up to the front door, she wished Bobby would have thought to meet her halfway.

Maybe he still would.

If not, she hoped his family wouldn't cause a scene. She pictured Bobby walking out to the car with his parents chasing after him. One of them tries to pull him back inside while the other comes to her window, demanding to know why she is here to take their boy away from them.

Please don't let it come to that.

Sheena had no idea how she'd react to such a situation. Hopefully she wouldn't soon find out.

Dusty fog swirled in front of her, throwing the glare of her headlights back at her. She switched off the high beams, but all that seemed to accomplish was making her slow travel feel even more treacherous. She could only see a small space of the gravel driveway in front of her before it was hidden by the curling pillars of gray.

Sheena eased her foot off the gas pedal even more, bringing her speed to a nudge. When she tried to see out her window, dense blackness blocked her view. She figured if she was heading up, all that was beyond the dark outside was down.

She swallowed hard to get the lump forming in her throat to go away.

Another curve and she tapped the gas to go around it. The car straightened out.

Headlights pushed back at her through the fog, filling her windshield in a blinding glow.

Sheena stomped the brakes. The car jerked to a halt. Since she was traveling such a sluggish rate, the tires didn't slide, but she was still thrust forward. The safety harness jerked her back. Her hair flew into her face, obstructing the harsh brightness.

Huffing, hair was sucked into her mouth and blown back out from her breaths. Her hands, tightly gripping the steering wheel, trembled when she made them let go. She parted her hair and pushed it back on her head.

And gasped.

Somebody stood between the headlights in front of her, a man's dark shape between two bright orbs.

Bobby?

Nope. The size and posture was all wrong. This guy was planted with his shoulders high and his head low. His arms hung by his sides like stiff appendages, showing small crevices of light coming behind him. Plus she couldn't see any hair. Bobby's hair was fluffy on the sides and stuck up on top.

Unless he's wearing a hat or something...

As if to show her he was, the man's head turned slightly, showing an arc above the darkened face.

Baseball cap?

Bobby never wore them. He liked fedoras and beanies.

Who is this?

Maybe her fears of being trapped in a family dispute were coming true. This very well could Bobby's dad, cutting her off at the pass, going to tell her to leave.

I'm not. He can't make me either.

Technically, he could. All it would take was a phone call to the police and they'd make her leave.

But he can't keep Bobby here if he doesn't want to be here.

Sheena continued to stare at the black figure that cut a shape in the light, hoping she wouldn't have to remind this lurking presence of that fact.

The shape stepped forward. A cry tickled Sheena's throat. Her heart sledged, pounding her chest.

What the hell's wrong with me?

She couldn't stop shaking. Looking down, she saw her hand hovered above the gear stick. About to throw it in reverse. She hadn't even realized she was going to until now.

Her mind told her hand to return to the steering wheel. It stayed poised above the knob, fingers curling down to grab it as if opposing her demand.

The person was closer now, cutting to the left to approach her window. The light caught him as he turned, revealing partials of his clothes and face. He wore a heavy dark coat, a ball cap as she'd suspected, and had a cheek shady with stubble.

Turning her head to look out her window, she squealed when a hand appeared. Knuckle extended, it rapped on the glass as if he was a cop wanting to see her license.

Get out of here, Sheena...something's not right.

Her body seemed to buzz with warning. Ignoring her apprehensive feelings, her finger pushed down on the button in the door panel. The window whirred down. Cold air drifted in with the smell of car exhaust and pine.

"Y...yes?" Her voice sounded higher than normal, a little frazzled.

"What are you doing here?"

The voice was deep and blank. Nothing distinguishable about it, other than it was devoid all emotion.

Like a gruff robot.

One thing she recognized about it right away was this person did not want her here.

"Um..." She almost told him she'd come to pick up Bobby, but decided it wasn't a good idea to just divulge information to some random guy on an isolated, fog-shrouded driveway.

"Who's asking?" she said.

The person leaned down. She caught a whiff of him that reminded her of how her father smelled after a long day of working outside. His face was veiled in the shadow the hat's bill provided. But she saw his eyes, and realized they weren't pleased by her question.

"Are you going to see the Marlowes?" he asked.

"Why are you asking?"

"I need to know who you are..." He looked behind him, as if expecting someone might try to sneak up on him. His head turned back toward her. "Why are you *here?*"

"To pick up Bobby," she said. She'd had enough of this and decided to divulge the information and hoped he would choke on it. "Are you the doorman of the forests or something? Want to move your car out of my way so I can get by?"

"Pick up Bobby? He's leaving?"

"Yes. With me. Are you his dad?" Even as the question left her mouth, she knew he wasn't. Seemed too young.

"Bobby can't leave," he muttered, more to himself than her.

A cracking sound came from under his fingers. Sheena noticed how they were turning white, and realized his grip was making the padding on her door pop. Maybe being snarky with this guy wasn't the best approach.

"You're not supposed to be here," he told her. "It's just supposed to be the four of them. *You're* not part of this."

Sheena felt herself shrivel inside. "Part of...what?"

"You have to get out of the car...I'm sorry."

The phone beeping from the passenger seat made Sheena jump. She knew without looking who'd just sent her a text.

Bobby.

Wondering where she was, most likely.

The man leaned closer, looking past her. Was he trying to see who was on the phone?

"Listen," she said. "I think you better step back and let me by."

The man exhaled a slow breath that smelled like coffee and beef jerky. "I'm afraid I can't do that."

Sheena glanced at the phone from the corner of her eyes. The screen, a block of light in the dark, dimmed as the alert faded. If she could text Bobby to tell him that some stranger was blocking her way in, he would do something about it.

Why aren't you out here, Bobby?

"Leave me alone," she said.

"Get out of the car."

"I told you…" She looked at the harsh light, trying to see how wide the driveway was.

He must've known what she was doing for he said, "You can't get by. The driveway is too narrow. You'll drive off the side."

She slapped the steering wheel. "What do you want?"

"Get out of the car…"

Sheena reached for the gearshift, ready to throw the car into reverse and back down the driveway. Her hand didn't stop there and shot for the phone. Cell service had been terrible for calls, but texting had been working fine.

And she needed to try now!

With one hand slapping at her phone, the other pushed the button on the door panel. The window started to rise.

"Don't!" The man yelled.

The climbing window forced his hand away. He lunged toward the door, flinging his arms forward, but they bounced off the glass when it thumped into place.

Sheena groaned with relief, but screamed when his fists pounded the glass. Her hands jerked, and the phone slipped through her fingers. It hit the console, tumbling down into the floorboard on the passenger side. The screen flashed bright, shining on the carpet of the floor mat.

No!

She leaned up, reaching into the shadows below the passenger seat.

The seatbelt snapped rigid, yanking her back. "Damn it!" Sheena fumbled around the latch, trying to find the button. It was as if she'd never operated a seatbelt before. Her fingers slipped over the button, unable to push it in. For some reason her hands just couldn't make it work.

The man outside the car slapped and punched the window. She heard the glass squeak. Somewhere it must have cracked.

Deciding to stop trying for the phone, she leaned back and grabbed the gearshift. She was about to wrench it down to reverse, but stopped.

The man was gone.

Outside the window was solid blackness except for the thin swirls of either fog or car exhaust. She looked out the windshield. The headlights from the other vehicle still poured its bright light onto her car, but she saw no movements.

It was as if the night had swallowed him.

Sheena hoped that was what had happened. That the night had suddenly opened its maw and the man had fallen in. But she knew nothing like that could ever come to be and she needed to get out of here.

She hated to leave Bobby, but she had to. When she was back on the road, she'd text him. Tell him what happened. He'd fix it. He fixed everything.

Her foot pushed down the brake. Her hand closed around the gearshift's knob. She started to pull down.

The window exploded.

Sharp tips of glass left tiny lines of fire as it glanced across her skin. A long dark bar flew into the car, in front of her eyes. She saw the bowed fulcrum, the pair of teeth pointing at the ceiling on either side of a small hollow.

A crowbar?

It turned around, the teeth pointing to the back of the car. She tried to dodge the tool as it was yanked back. Failed. It hooked her arm and jerked her toward the door. Pain flashed through her. This time the seatbelt worked in her favor when it locked. It kept her from being pulled through window, though the sharp tips raked across her shoulder, down her arm. The bits ripped her coat open, tore her shirt sleeve and dug rents into her flesh that quickly filled with blood.

The crowbar went back out the window.

Sheena knew she had limited time before it came back. She tried to lift her hurt arm, but it wouldn't and just hung limply beside her.

Come on, arm! Move! Damn it, move!

It didn't move. Her right arm was now useless.

Sheena turned slightly, using her left hand to grab for the gearshift. It was too far away, so she twisted her body in an awkward way to make it work. Her fingers brushed the top.

An arm, covered by the thick sleeve of a coat, reached in and grabbed the door handle. It pulled it up and the door was jerked open.

"No! Stay back!"

The man snatched her hair and jerked. Sheena yelped. Her hand, still holding the gearshift, was pulled loose but the lever remained in place. Swatting and slapping with her good hand, she screamed at him to let her go. He pushed the crowbar against her chest with one arm, pinning her against the seat. The bar pressed into her chest, making it hurt and hard to breathe.

The man had no trouble unfastening the seatbelt. Grabbing her by the coat, he yanked her out of the seat and threw her down. Her breasts pounded the ground. Before she could try to get up, the man grabbed her hair again and tugged. She was dragged across the dirt road, her coat making scratching sounds as it skidded along. Her breasts and stomach lit up with a flurry of stings as the ground ripped her shirt open, tugged at her bra. A breast became exposed, the cup jerked down. Her nipple scratched the ground and caused her to scream. When she was clear of the car, he let go.

Sheena, holding her tattered shirt together with her wounded arm, tried to crawl away. Her hand slipped out from under her. She rolled, landing on her back. Her right arm fell beside her, still not cooperating. Her shirt hung around her like a useless rag. Pushing with her elbow, she tried to sit up. The man stood over her, a foot on either side of her. Looking up, her eyes scanned the long bar of the crowbar as it was raised above his head with both hands. He held it with both hands at the top, like a sacrificial tool to be used in an ancient ritual. She'd never seen one so long. The headlights glinted off its dark metal.

"Please..." she said, crying. "Please don't hurt me..."

"I'm sorry," he said. "You weren't supposed to be here."

The crowbar came down. She felt the blunt pressure on her chest as it punched in, bone cracking as the bar crushed her ribcage. She felt it plunge through. There was a juicy crunch as it burst through her back.

Sheena wanted to scream. Couldn't. Her throat only emanated high-pitched groans as her trembling hand felt around the bar protruding from her chest. Blood soaked her exposed breast, flowing down into the cup of her bra. Trying to sit up was impossible. The crowbar had her pinned to the ground, like a stake hammered into a tent. Giving up, she let her arm drop, her head fell back.

The last thing she heard before darkness consumed her was her phone beeping to alert her of another text.

From Bobby...

CHAPTER FOURTEEN

Grant held the blade of the ax above the wood. He tapped the top a couple times, picking his spot. Then he raised the ax high. He slammed it down, splitting the wood into halves. They collapsed onto the stump that had once been a large tree. Smiling, he was proud of himself for still being able to split wood after all these years. It'd been a long time since he'd done it and hadn't missed a beat.

He looked at the chopped logs lying around and nodded.

Should be enough.

He slammed the ax down again, the blade imbedded into the stump. He left it there, sticking out like a large wooden lever. Grabbing the logs, he turned and chucked them into the wheelbarrow. They rattled when they bounced inside of the tub. He stood up straight, brushed the sawdust and wood flakes off his gloves and grabbed the handlebars. Lifting the wheelbarrow, he started rolling it toward the back of the cabin.

From this angle, he saw nearly every window was bright with light. The bathroom, his and Marion's bedroom, the living room, study and den. Each one brightly illuminated.

Though it was lit up all over, he doubted anybody was downstairs. The others, most likely, had retreated to their bedrooms to avoid him.

He was surprised Bobby was still here. The way he'd talked, his *girlfriend* would have been here by now to pick him up. He didn't know what had delayed her, but he didn't feel bad that she was late. But he also didn't really relish the idea of an angry Bobby chomping at the bit to unleash more hateful slander at him.

Slander? Not really. True facts.

The wheelbarrow bounced over ruts in the ground, the tire squeaking like a bad shopping cart. The night was quiet and very dark and cold. Clouds blocked the moon.

Probably have snow all over the ground in the morning.

He didn't feel the excitement about it now that he had earlier. Bobby had killed it. Because of his leaving, he'd ruined their trip. Grant wasn't really angry at his son for wanting to leave. There was more heartache than anything. He'd hoped for a Christmas miracle that would see his family working through their qualms; instead he got a reminder of how pathetic his reality had become.

My fault. Should've known better.

And he'd lost his temper with Marion again. Stupid. He'd made progress with her and now it was all shot to hell.

He reached the side door and set the wheelbarrow down on its pegs. Standing upright, the muscles in his back ached from the work and cold. He had no idea why he'd felt the need to chop the wood. It was late. Besides, his original plans of them spending the evening roasting marshmallows in the fireplace wouldn't happen.

Most likely, everybody would stay in their rooms for the rest of the night. Grant hadn't spoken to Marion since Bobby's outburst, but he figured he'd be sleeping on the couch tonight. Last night would be chalked off as another one of Marion's moments of weakness and she would be back in her meetings with Pastor Tom and his wife Carla asking for advice on how to proceed from here as soon as they got back into town.

Grant looked at the cabin, scanning it up and down. Probably need to sell it, or give it to Kara as a present when she finished school. She'd appreciate it. Out of everyone, she loved it here the most. She used to talk about wanting to move out here when she was an adult.

She's an adult now.

Grant nodded, decided. Kara could have the cabin. It was paid for. Let her enjoy it.

He opened the screen door, and braced it open on his hip. Then he opened the other door and gave it shove so it would open wide. It swayed back a tad, but stopped. With the door open, he bent down and found the chip on the screen spring. Pushing it as far to the coil as he could, he let it go and the screen door shook when it caught. Now he could go in and out without needing anybody to hold the door for him.

Why am I bothering?

Because he'd paid for the damn marshmallows. And he'd eat the whole damn bag by himself to make sure they weren't wasted.

It took two trips, but he got all the wood inside and stacked on the hearth. Selecting three off the top of the pile, he tossed them into the opening, arranging them in the way he was taught by his father. Then he reached into his pocket, removed the wadded newspaper and unfolded it on the floor in front of him. He'd picked up small pieces outside to use for kindling. He put it all in, plus the newspaper, then struck a long match across the stone paneling. Lowering the flame to the corner of the newspaper, it ignited pretty quickly. The flame spread through the kindling, fiery tongues reaching out from between the logs. Satisfied that the fire would continue to grow, he sat back on the rug and watched the flames lick.

The room filled with the sound of pops and crackles, spreading heat across him as the light slowly began to grow with the fire's size. He took off his coat and he tossed it across the room where it landed on the couch. The gloves came off next and landed on top of his coat. He held his hands in front of the fire, rubbing them as if washing them with heat. The fire covered the logs. A writhing orange glow covered the walls.

The marshmallows.

Grant looked up and saw the corner of the bag sticking over the mantel's edge. Standing, he grabbed the bag. He was reaching for a skewer from the assortment on the mantel when his eyes landed on a framed photo. The picture had always been here. He'd put it in the frame himself and placed it there in the center so it would be the first thing you saw when you got near the fireplace. It was one of his favorites. He'd seen it countless times, just passing by, glancing at it. But something tonight made the image seem brand new.

It was a shot of the family, at Lake Mitchell State Park, about to embark on a picturesque boat tour. Kara had been sixteen, Bobby about to turn fifteen. The four of them had on bright orange lifejackets. Grant's face was chubbier, dotted with pink cheeks and swollen eyes—showing the symptoms of a man who enjoyed his alcohol. At least in this picture his flushed cheeks could be blamed on too much sun.

How'd nobody know?

They knew. Even Grant. But they'd all chosen to ignore it because they knew he couldn't be convinced he had a problem.

Took me smashing into a car. Killing people. Destroying a family.

Grant shook his head, still focused on the picture. The flickering glow of the fire reflected in the glass's dusty surface. He remembered it being a good day. They'd camped at the state park overnight and came back to the cabin the next morning and stayed another week.

Maybe it was the memory that caused the tears in his eyes. He doubted it, though. What he assumed had caused the warm streams now trickling down his face was the proof they'd once been a happy family. His hand shook as he reached for the frame. It had been so long since he'd seen his family genuinely happy, he'd almost started to believe they never had been. Now he had verification that showed it hadn't been a dream.

"That's a good picture."

Though Marion's voice was very soft, Grant still jerked and nearly dropped the picture. He looked over his shoulder. Marion stood in the doorway, leaning against it, her hands fidgeting with the belt of her robe. It was the thick white one that she usually put on after her baths.

The damp hair showed she'd recently bathed. Even with no make-up, she was a lovely sight, awash in the fireplace's dim shimmer.

"One of my favorites," she added. Her eyes were puffy. She'd been crying.

Grant nodded. "Mine, too."

"So, Bobby's still here..." She stopped, letting the statement hang in the air.

Grant nodded again. "Yeah. I guess his ride's running behind."

"Maybe he changed his mind, told her not to come."

Grant shrugged a shoulder. "Maybe." He doubted it. Bobby was probably pacing a gulley into the carpet in his bedroom, wondering what was taking her so long.

Setting the frame back on the mantel, Grant turned around. The bag of marshmallows hung from the fingertips of his hand. Marion, noticing the pudgy sweets, frowned. "That just looks so depressing."

"What does?"

"A man about to roast a bag of marshmallows by himself."

Grant choked a laugh. "Well...yeah. It *feels* as depressing as it looks. Want to join me?"

She grimaced. "None for me tonight. Don't know if it's a good idea on my stomach right now."

"Upset?"

"No. But I'm sure splitting a bag that big will be a bad idea for both of us."

Grant nodded. "True." He turned back to the mantel, dropping the bag on top. He faced Marion again. "Want to sit and watch the fire?"

Marion smiled. She looked so tired, stressed. But the smile seemed to peel off a lot of it. "Yeah." She came into the living room and stood in front of Grant. There wasn't much space between them when she put her hands on his shoulders. "Were you planning on sleeping down here tonight?"

"Well..." Grant looked her in the eyes. "I don't know what I was planning."

"When I was upstairs, I started packing..."

Grant nodded. He'd figured this was coming.

Marion continued. "But I stopped. I don't want to let Bobby's objections stop us right now. We need to keep fighting forward."

"But Marion, without the kids' blessings, we can't just..."

"We can, and if we work hard enough, we will. Kara is pulling for us. Right now it's too hard for Bobby. In time, I think he will come around. We just have to give him the space he needs."

"I'm afraid if we give him too much space, we'll lose him forever. He's already dropping out of school..."

"I'm sure a lot of that was just his idea of ruffling your feathers. I don't think he has any intentions of doing so. Not unless he becomes some big famous rock star."

Grant groaned.

"Come here," said Marion.

She pulled Grant close, hugging him. Grant folded his arms behind her back, holding her tightly. The back of the robe was warm under his hands. She turned her head sideways and placed her face against his chest. She said, "If we do this right, we'll get through it. I think my biggest fear was that you were only working on changing your behavior, but I can see how much you're trying to change your character. And that proves so much to me." She looked up at him, her bright eyes rippling orange from the fire.

Grant loved this woman so much. He knew when he met her on spring break in Myrtle Beach that he wanted to spend the rest of his life with her. She was a beach bunny, born and raised in the ocean, but by the time spring break was over, she was working on transferring to North Carolina to finish up her Bachelor's in accounting and finance. They'd been together since the following summer.

And if Grant played his cards right, they would be together forever.

He lowered his head. She came up to meet him.

They kissed.

When Grant started to pull away, Marion pressed herself closer to him. She wriggled against him, moaning into his mouth. He slipped his hands into the robe, felt smooth warm flesh and realized she was naked underneath.

Together, they made their way to the couch, stepping in a synchronized rhythm. Grant plopped down first. Marion climbed on top of him, putting a knee on either side of him.

"Wait…" he said. Marion, reaching for his belt, paused. "The kids."

Marion looked up at the ceiling. She looked back at him, a sly expression on her face. "I don't want to stop…"

Grant would hate for Kara or Bobby to walk in on them, but he also doubted that either planned to leave their rooms unless Bobby's ride happened to show up.

We should be able to hear them if they try to come downstairs.

Then what? Tell the kids to give them a minute to finish up?

He looked at Marion. The robe was opened a tad, slipping back on her shoulders. The slopes of her breasts uncovered. Freckles dotted up the middle, as if drawn on with magic marker.

Grant decided it was a risk he wanted to take. He unraveled the cloth belt.

Grinning, Marion tugged at his belt.

He'd left the van beside the Jeep, leaving the engine running as he walked toward the cabin. He had the girl's cell phone in his hand. After reading over the messages, he ascertained that she was coming to pick up Bobby. They were going to stay in a hotel tonight and go to her parents in the morning.

Luckily, he'd gotten here early. Bobby might've left. The plan would've been ruined.

He sent a quick message to Bobby, saying the roads had gotten bad and she didn't know if she'd make it out there tonight. He waited for Bobby's response, which quickly came.

This sucks! I want to get out of here!

He responded: *Sorry! I miss you!*

Bobby told her he missed her too and to keep him updated.

Reading over the old messages showed the girl truly cared about him. He assumed Bobby's feelings were very similar. He hated the girl had to die, but she was in the wrong place at the wrong time, trying to drive a wedge through the plan. What surprised him was how easy it had been to kill someone who hadn't been part of the plan. He felt hardly any remorse.

The plan is good.

He'd been here a few times before, so he was familiar with the surroundings. The blueprints had shown him the interior layout, so he knew what the inside looked like without having ever set foot through the doors.

Walking up the stone path, his shoes made soft crunching sounds on the wind-strewn debris. Another heavy gust wafted over him, freezing his pants, making his testicles feel as if they were soaked in cold water. It would snow soon. He'd been listening to the forecasts on the radio all night and the storm was making its way here. Once it finally dropped down, they would all be trapped here together.

He stopped at the front, looking up at the house. It was dark all around, but a lot of lights were on. He couldn't go in yet. But he could still take a quick look around, just to survey the area one last time before he got started.

Walking alongside the house, he looked around, up and down. Nothing had really changed. He passed a wheelbarrow parked beside the side door on his way to the back. He paused, gazing at the sawed-up tree. He saw the ax stabbed into the stump, the handle a pale line in the darkness. The safety light atop the power pole glinted off the blade's tarnished surface, looking like a winking demonic eye. His eyes moved to the right, to the shed. It was hidden under a dome of shadow. He kept walking.

Coming out on the other side of the house, he was near the living room window. Soft flickering light spilled onto the ground. He quietly stepped up to the window, keeping his back to the house. Once he was right beside it, he slowly turned. He looked inside.

At first, he only saw the fireplace going. It struck him as odd that nobody was close to keep an eye on it. Then he looked to the left. His eyes landed on the couch. He saw Marion's back, the muscles flexing and tightening as her hips worked back and forth. A pair of knees protruded from between her legs, pants gathered around the shins.

Hands roamed her skin, squeezing her buttocks, gripping them tightly and spreading them. Her skin seemed to glow in the firelight under a sodden luster. She threw back her head, damp hair flapping, arching her back as if to gaze at the window upside down. Her large breasts pointed at the ceiling.

Now he could see Grant. Leaning back against the couch, head pushed into the cushions, his eyes were closed and mouth hung open. His face was wet with sweat, hair clinging to his forehead in thick curls.

He stared at them as his blood turned hot, flowing under his skin like rage-filled lava. His heart kicked his chest, as if wanting to punt a hole through his ribcage. He almost headed straight for the door, about to kick it in and put things into motion. Rubbing his eyes, his fingers nearly gouged them out from how hard they pushed. He pulled them down his face, stretching the skin and leaving burning trails behind.

He held his breath, counting to ten several times. Finally, he felt calmer and exhaled, rustling his cheeks.

Let them have this moment. It would be their last.

He turned away from the window, not wanting to see any more. He wasn't a voyeur, or a pervert. He got no thrill from watching them perform. But it did seem to leave him with an empty sensation inside.

And what made it worse, he saw Sonja in his mind, naked underneath him as he pushed into her. Her fingers digging into his back, leaving red marks on his skin that lasted for days.

Guilt turned his thoughts to Lindsey. And Josh. And the unborn Lilly.

The plan came back into focus, filling him with a soothing comfort.

He returned to the van and climbed inside. Quietly, he pulled the door shut. He'd disabled the cab light, so there were no worries of anybody seeing it.

The heat blowing from the vents made him uncomfortable, so he shut it off and rolled down a window. Sweet aromas from the woods seeped inside, slightly tainted by the oily smell of the van's engine.

His leg bounced. Fingers drummed the steering wheel as his stomach cramped with restlessness.

Soon.

He took a deep breath.

This will all be over soon.

CHAPTER FIFTEEN

Kara peeked into the living room. The fire had dwindled to a soft flame that lazily flapped on top of the black wooden chunks. Her parents were on the couch, embraced in their sleep, a blanket coiled around them like a cocoon.

She smiled.

At least they're doing okay.

After what happened earlier, she thought they would have reverted back to a nonspeaking relationship. Didn't look like that would happen this time.

Tempted to put the fire out completely, she decided to let it burn itself down. It was almost there now anyway. Plus, she didn't want to wake them up. They needed the rest and they looked content with being in each other's arms.

Kara went back upstairs. She sneaked over to Bobby's door, putting her ear to it. No noise came from the other side. She looked down and saw a dim bar of light at the bottom of the door. He was probably in there moping since his girlfriend hadn't shown up. It was after eleven, and Kara figured she wasn't coming. She quietly walked away, shutting off the hallway light.

Returning to her bedroom, she grabbed a suitcase and heaved it onto the bed. She unzipped the lid and threw it back. Her clothes were inside. She dug around and found pajamas, panties and socks. She put them on the bed, then grabbed her small carry bag. She threw the strap over her shoulder, grabbed her clothes and headed to the bathroom.

She locked the bathroom door and cut on the fan. Other than making a lot of racket, she didn't know what good the fan was for. It never seemed to actually filter out the steam. Whenever she got out of the shower, the bathroom was always filled with a balmy mist. But she'd gotten so used to having these fans running while she was in the bathroom it'd be odd showering without the steady hum.

Kara put her clothes on the rim of the sink, setting the bag in the bowl. She stepped over to the toilet, raised the lid and turned around. She pushed down her pants and panties, then sat down. The ring was cold against her buttocks, making her flinch. It didn't take long for it to warm up so she could relax and do her business. When she finished, she pulled her feet out of her pants and picked them up. Her panties were stretched across the inner seam. She chucked them at the door.

In nothing but her sweater and socks, she stepped over to the tub. Pushing back the stiff curtain with her shoulder, she reached in and cranked the shower dial as close to the H that she thought she could stand. Then she returned to the sink with the hiss of water behind her. She quickly unloaded her toothpaste and toothbrush, her hair ties and brush, spreading them across the sink. Done with that, she turned the bag around and opened the pocket in the front.

Looking inside, she smiled.

The ring case was in there. She took it out, opened it. The diamond wasn't very big but it shimmered vibrantly under the light as if to make up for its size. Kara didn't care how small it was. She was happy with what it represented. One day she would be Kara Bozeman. And that sounded just fine to her.

She pulled the ring from the case and slipped it on her finger. Perfect fit. She felt better, having it on. Holding her hand out, she wiggled her fingers. It looked good. She'd planned to tell everybody on

Christmas, but if Bobby was leaving she didn't know if it would be the right time.

Derrek might get mad if I don't tell.

She'd promised him she would.

Cross that bridge when I get to it. Need to play it by ear.

Steam curled through the bathroom, making the mirror foggy. She pulled her sweater off her head. She saw herself in the mirror, in her bra, pushing her breasts up. She held up her hand, turning it so she could see the ring in the glass. The light hit the diamond, making it gleam like a small flashlight in the valley between her breasts.

"Looking good, Mrs. Bozeman."

She winked, then reached behind her and unclasped her bra. It slipped down her shoulders. She pulled it off and dropped it on her pants. Then she pulled off her socks and headed for the shower.

The water was way too hot at first and she had to stand away from the spray as she tried to adjust the dial. Finally, it cooled enough for her stand. She walked into the gust, lowering her head to let the hot water tap her scalp.

She didn't plan on moving for a while.

The sound of knocking shocked Grant awake. He stared at the pale ceiling. The scent of wood smoke was heavy around him, mixing with the sour odor of sweat. That odor was coming from him and Marion. She was on top of him, her legs spread over his waist, his penis still inside and slightly limp. He remembered how they'd made love, but he had no recollection of how they'd wound up tangled together like this.

Another knock, heavier than the first.

"Marion," he whispered.

"Hmm...?" Marion didn't move. Didn't open her eyes.

"Marion? Wake up."

"I am awake."

Still, she didn't move. Grant smiled.

That one must have really taken it all out of her.

"Somebody's at the door," he said.

Marion's head lifted up. Her hair hung in her face like a veil of yellow. She shook her head, making the hair fall away. "What?" Now her eyes were cracked open.

The knocking repeated, longer, heavier. Marion jerked on top of him, squeezing him inside. Grant sucked in a breath.

Marion twisted, turning her head as if she could see behind her. "I guess Bobby's ride is here."

Grant sighed. "Yeah…"

Squirming, Marion sat up. The blanket fell away from her, exposing her nude torso to Grant. She had ruddy markings around her breasts and neck from his kissing and sucking and groping. Twisting her hips, she felt around the bunched blankets. She found her robe and pushed her arms through the sleeves.

"You better hurry up and get dressed," she said. "Bobby'll probably be down in a minute."

Grant nodded. Marion pulled the robe around her front, covering her breasts, then stood up. His penis pulled out of her. It felt much colder in the open, without her soft warm walls. He quickly found his clothes and started dressing.

Throwing on his shirt, he walked to the doorway. He looked back at Marion. She tugged the belt tight around her waist. She nodded, telling him she was ready.

"Be right back," he said.

"Be nice to her," she said. "She's only here because Bobby told her to come."

"I know."

Grant walked away. On his way through the foyer, he decided the best approach to this situation would be to not say anything at all. He'd open the door, let her in, and go tell Bobby she was here. Nothing more. If Bobby wanted to say anything, he would let him. But no matter what, Grant would remain silent. No point in saying anything that might worsen the condition that was already awkward for everyone.

He was almost at the door when the knocking resounded again. Being this close, he felt the vibrations on his skin from the strong hammering. The girl had some serious strength to pound on the door like that. Maybe she was knocking loud like this, hoping Bobby would be the one to hear her.

Everybody should be able to hear that.

Grant reached for the knob. He paused with his fingers just grazing the cold, slick metal. Something deep within him threw up some red flags. Why would the girl just come to the door and knock? Wouldn't she have called Bobby to tell him she was here? She would want to avoid any kind of contact with anyone, Bobby probably would too. His son would want to spare her from any uncomfortable confrontations. Why would she announce her arrival like this?

Grant wished they had a peephole, or some windows in this door. There was neither. Just a wall and a solid door that gave zero indication to who was on the other side.

He felt his instincts trying to pull him away from the door. He shook his head, to knock them free.

Don't be ridiculous. There's nothing to worry about.

But if Bobby had already left…

Grant could picture it—him sleeping with Marion on the couch while Bobby snuck outside and got into the car with his girlfriend. Somewhere along the way, they wrecked. Too busy celebrating their reunion and fresh sense of freedom, they didn't see the curve in the road.

And this is the police officer coming to tell Grant his son was dead.

Grant suddenly felt cold. He trembled. His hand shook as it gripped the knob. The other flicked the light switch to turn on the porch light.

He pulled the door open. Cold air rushed in. It was snowing, not very heavy, but thick dots of white floated down in a steady pattern.

A cop wasn't outside.

A girl wasn't outside.

It was a man. His head was down, the bill of his cap blocking Grant's view of his face.

Couldn't see his face on account of his hat. Edgar's voice.

Grant stiffened. This had to be the guy who'd been peeping in their windows while Edgar worked. "Can…can I help you?" asked Grant.

The man's head lifted. The bill of the hat moved up, pulling back the shadows to reveal a face. A deep scar ran down from his temple, over his cheek, and ended on the jawline. He smiled a wicked smile that seemed to say: *I got you.*

Grant knew he recognized this man, but his mind seemed to be locked and wasn't allowing him to access his memory. It was seeing the man here, at his family's cabin, which had caused the hiccup in his brain. How'd he know about this place? Why was he here? How'd he find them?

How'd he find me?

"Grant?" Marion. "Who is it?"

Marion's voice seemed to tear him loose from the numbing shackles. Recognition dropped onto him hard enough to make Grant fall against the door's edge. He had to grip onto the knob to keep from falling.

Dennis Hinshaw.

The man nodded, knowing that Grant realized what was about to happen.

"Oh my God..." said Grant in a harsh whisper.

Dennis's arm went high. Grant glimpsed the crowbar in his hand when it swung down.

Marion heard a wet punching sound that reminded her of a mallet hitting beef. There was a sharp groan, followed by the commotion of something heavy hitting the floor.

"Grant?!"

Marion ran. The bottom of the robe fluttered behind her like tails on a kite. She didn't care that she wasn't wearing anything underneath. All that mattered was getting to Grant. Something had happened. He was in trouble.

He needed her.

She almost slipped when her feet came off the carpet and onto the hardwood floor of the hallway before the foyer. Cold air blew against her. She could see the front door. It was open, swaying as the heavy breeze shook it. Snow was blowing in. In her jarring vision, she looked down.

A scream scratched the back of her throat.

Grant was on his back in the foyer, feet sticking through the doorway, arms splayed wide above his head as if he'd tried to perform a backward dive into an empty pool. Snow had sprinkled across his pants and shirt, leaving patches of white flakes around his body. A trail of dark fluid led from the gash on his forehead, down his face, and spread into a blob on the floor beside his head.

"Grant!"

She dropped to the floor, her knees skidding across the hardwood. Ignoring the searing pains on her skin, she leaned over Grant. Her hands stayed above his chest, as if afraid to touch him.

"What happened? Grant? Are you okay? Please answer me!"

His eyes were dark slits, clear moisture leaking through the tight spaces. He was also bleeding a little from his nose. She could hear the rattling sounds of him breathing through the globs of blood.

He's alive! Thank you, God!

Now she touched him, knowing she wouldn't feel a chilling empty shell. He felt warm, almost hot.

"Grant, wake up! Please! What hap…?"

Footsteps behind her made her look back.

He came from the darkness, as if birthed from the shadows. A long metal bar was extended from his hand like a sword.

Marion didn't have a chance to scream before he was on her.

CHAPTER SIXTEEN

Kara twisted the dial all the way down. The spray shut off, turning to a drip that sprinkled from the nozzle and smacked the tub. She pulled back the curtain and stepped out. Her feet came down on the bathmat, the fuzzy hairs tickling slightly. She pulled a towel from the rack and shook it loose. Hugging it to her soaked skin, she began to dry herself.

She'd stayed in the shower a lot longer than she'd intended. The water had begun to cool before she could finally force herself to turn it off. It just felt so good being in there that she hadn't wanted it to end. Her mind had wandered, thinking about the future, a little afraid but more excited.

She stopped drying long enough to look at the ring on her finger.

Two years from now, I'll be married.

She couldn't believe it. Once she graduated college, she'd have the summer to relax, then she would marry Derrek in the fall. He already had a job lined up for him, so she could take her time that following year, finding a firm to work for. She didn't want to work for any that had given her dad his start. She wanted to earn whatever she got, without Dad's influence, whether it was a good one or bad one.

She wrapped the towel around her body, tucking a corner between her breasts to hold it up. Taking down another towel from the rack, she bent over and used it to scrub her hair. When she stood up straight, she was a little dizzy. She stepped over to the sink, wiping the mirror with the towel. When it was clear enough to see herself through the mist on the glass, she tossed the towel onto her dirty clothes.

First, she brushed her hair. Second, she brushed her teeth. Pulling the towel free from her breasts, she added it to the pile on the floor. She was chilly, standing naked in the room. Now the steam that hovered seemed to be trapping her inside a cool box. She quickly dressed, but it wasn't until she pulled on her socks that she felt warmer.

Lastly, she removed the ring, unable to find anything to prolong it any longer. She held it up, pinched between her fingers, and smiled.

I love you, Derrek.

Then she put it back in the case and put the case in her shoulder bag.

Opening the door, a mass of steam expelled into the hallway. She stepped through the swirling cloud, dirty clothes held close to her stomach, bag dangling from her shoulder. She dropped the clothes in the hamper inside the closet in the hallway.

Then started for her bedroom.

She glanced at Bobby's door, noticing it was partway open.

Frowning, she halted. Wasn't it closed earlier? She thought so. She remembered putting her ear to it and listening.

The light was still on, spilling a sheaf of luminosity onto the carpet. Did he leave? She wondered if his girlfriend had shown up while she was in the shower. If so, he could have come to the bathroom door and yelled that he was leaving.

Jerk.

Kara slowly walked to Bobby's room. As she neared the door, she noticed the knob was smudged with some kind of dark grease. Grimacing, she reached out, lightly fingering the tacky smear. It felt cold and sticky on her fingertip. She held up her finger, squinting to try and figure out what it was.

Too dark.

She held her finger in the light spilling from Bobby's room and saw it was red. It looked like…

Oh my God!

Kara pushed Bobby's door. It swung wide. She froze in the doorway. What she was seeing didn't quite register, and instead seemed to slow her mind down.

A man was in Bobby's room, leaning over the bed. Bobby's head was turned to her. He looked asleep, except for the welt on his forehead that was dripping blood onto the pillow, turning the pillowcase dark and sodden. Her eyes moved away from Bobby, landing on the man.

His head swiveled in her direction. She saw a scar. His face was speckled with blood. His eyes were wide and wild, his mouth plastered with a nasty grin.

Oh God…that's…

He stood up straight.

What'd he do to Bobby?

Lowered the elongated crowbar by his leg. Blood streamed down the arched tip, dripping off, making crimson dots on the carpet.

Other than trembling where she stood, Kara couldn't move. Her feet felt rooted to the floor, as if she'd simply sprouted from the carpet to watch this scary man lurch toward her, grinning maliciously.

The bag fell from her shoulder, landing with a rattling bump by her foot. The soft noise was like a clapping hand in the eerie silence.

Kara blinked. "Stu…stay back…" Her voice was barely audible. Whispery and shaky, she hardly heard it at all.

If he heard her, he gave no indication. He kept coming. Each step closer, he raised the crowbar a little higher. Now the blood current reversed, trickling down the bar and oozing over his fingers gripping the flat end.

Why wasn't anybody coming to help her? How'd he get in? Where were her parents?

Where's Dad?

He promised he'd never let anything happen to her. She remembered the day. She was nine years old and Melissa Rudy had been making fun of her pigtails all day long at school. She'd come home and cried in her father's arms while telling him about it. He'd explain how Melissa was only jealous because she had short little boy hair and couldn't put hers in pigtails. They'd talked about how sometimes people can be mean for no reason other than to feel better about themselves. He'd promised while he was around, nobody would ever hurt her.

But this man would hurt her. He'd hurt Bobby. And she was next.

Help me, Dad!

The man reeled back the blunt weapon as if it were a baseball bat, splashing blood across the door. Some dots flicked against Kara's face, making her flinch. Her arms began to move, her knees bent.

She screamed, "Dad!"

The man swung.

Her knees kept bending until they hit the carpet. The crowbar cut through the air where her head had been, cracking the door frame and imbedding into it.

Kara, hands folded around her head, looked up. She saw the middle of the crowbar was deep into the wood, wiggling, making the wood groan as the man tugged with his bloodstained hands. He looked down at her, yelled, and turned his focus back to the lodged crowbar. His efforts looked to be working.

Get up, Kara! Run, damn it!

Kara spun around, squatting like a frog. She flung herself away from the doorway. Her shoulder hit the carpet, face slammed down and dragged across. Burning sensations ripped through her cheek and nose. She didn't stop rolling until she was a few feet away from the doorway. Getting back to her knees, she whipped her head back toward Bobby's room.

The man jerked the crowbar free with a splintery crunch.

He lurched.

Screaming, Kara crawled backward. Her hand dropped down, hitting the wooden step and slipping across the smooth surface. Its fall seemed to jerk the rest of her to the stairs. Rolling onto her stomach, she put both hands flat in front of her and stopped her plunge. She gripped the railing and pulled herself to her feet. Her socks tried to snatch her feet out from under her, but she gripped the railing and didn't fall.

She looked back, seeing that she was a quarter of the way down the stairs. The man started climbing down, a hand on the railing, the other holding the crowbar over his shoulder like an umbrella.

Kara screamed again, and put her back to him. She expected to feel the brutal whack of the crowbar between her shoulder blades, but she felt nothing as she started to run down. Because of her slippery socks, she couldn't go the speed she wanted. But she was still ahead of him, and that was what really mattered.

Her feet slapped down on the floor and shot out in two directions. She dropped forward, throwing her hands in front of her to catch herself. It looked as if she was doing a split, or warm-up exercises before a big run.

The heavy thuds of his footfalls came from behind her, growing rapidly closer.

Kara pushed herself back upright. She wanted to check and see where he was, but didn't waste the time. He was close enough that she could hear him breathing, and that was much too close.

She ran.

Hung a right at the intersecting hallways.

Her eyes landed on her father. He was supine in front of the door, arms spread wide, blood pooling around his head. Mom was draped across his chest as if she'd simply fallen asleep while resting her head on his shoulder.

Seeing them unleashed another wild shriek that tore at her throat.

Then the man suddenly appeared in front of the door, coming from the right. He'd gone through the kitchen to intercept her. He was already dashing up the hall, heading straight for her!

"No!" Kara slid to a stop, spun on her heels and ran back the way she'd come.

The living room was straight ahead, but it exited to the dining area which would only lead her right back to here.

Gotta get help! Call the police!

Good luck on that. Her cell phone was in her room.

A landline was in the kitchen—an old touchtone phone mounted on the wall. But was it working? It had been the last time they were here, but that was a few years ago. She decided to chance it.

So, when she reached the transecting hallways, she swung her body left and dashed for the kitchen. She saw the phone right away, a red shiny hump on the wall.

Please work! Please!

Her speed was too fast for her stop, and she plowed into the wall beside the phone. Her shoulder pounded it hard. A pegboard with notes and old coupons above the phone was rattled free. It bounced off her head on its way to the floor. Ignoring the pain the wooden corner had raked down her skin, she snatched the phone from its base.

And cried with glee when she heard the dial tone buzzing in her hear.

The buttons were on the receiver, so she turned it around to see the keypad. She punched 9, then 1, and was about to hit the final 1 when she felt a heavy wind that ruffled her hair, heard a high-pitched whistle just moments before the base exploded beside her. Pieces of plastic nicked her skin. When the debris cleared, she saw the crowbar was against the wall. Behind it were the shattered remains of the base. The comforting drone of the dial tone vanished.

Kara traced the long metal stem of the crowbar to the man. He stood off to the side, gripping the other end with both hands. Pulling the crowbar from the phone, he stepped toward her.

Shaking her head, Kara took an involuntary step back. "No..."

"I'm sorry, Kara."

The phone cord pulled taut and jerked the receiver from her hand. It hit the floor and slid to the wall, dangling from the destroyed base above it.

Kara, holding up her hands, patted the air. "Stay back! Please!"

The man made a sad face like somebody watching an invalid trying to walk. He shook his head, raised the crowbar.

Gasping, Kara's feet tangled, jerking her down. Her rump pounded the floor, jarred her, made her teeth clack together. Pain jolted her spine. She fell back, catching herself on her elbows. She didn't stop, kept dragging herself, her elbows squeaking on the tile.

The man stalked her, matching her pace. Each small scoot she made, he easily stepped to catch up. He seemed to pity her. As if he knew what she was doing was a waste of her time. And Kara was starting to agree. She was so tired. Her body hurt. Hurt elbows felt like they were being rubbed raw as she pulled, and pulled.

Finally, she gave up, letting her back fall flat on the floor. Her elbows stayed pointed into the tile, her hands up and hanging like limp ornaments. She stared up at the ceiling, the lights above turning into a bright smear as tears filled her eyes.

"Please..." she said again. "Don't do this..."

He stood above her, his face a blurry darkness. "I'm sorry, Kara. You're a part of this. You all are."

Kara rubbed her eyes clear and wished she hadn't.

The crowbar was soaring at her.

She felt it hit, then nothing at all.

CHAPTER SEVENTEEN

December 22nd

Dear Lindsey,

I know it's been a long time since I've written you. You probably know why. I knew if I told you what I was doing, you'd talk me out of it. I'm leaving in a few minutes. If things go how they're supposed to, I won't be back.

I'll be with you again soon. I'm coming to see you and the babies.

You're coming with me. And when this is over, we'll be together forever.

Grant Marlowe will understand why I'm doing this. He'll have to. He won't have a choice.

Soon, Lindsey. Soon.

Love always,
Dennis

Sonja Dumont finished reading Dennis's final letter again. She couldn't keep count of how many times she'd read it. She flipped the pages of the legal pad back to the front, reread the angry scrawls on the first page, and set it on top of the stack she'd brought with her. It confused her how he'd alternated between letters to Lindsey and the mad ramblings that seemed to be his inner voice being put to paper.

Didn't make any sense to her.

"Ms. Dumont?"

Sonja looked up. A young woman in a deputy's uniform stood partway out from behind a door across the hall. She was a thick woman who filled her uniform, but Sonja guessed there wasn't a trace of fat on her. The deputy smiled. "Sheriff Massey will be with you in a few minutes. It's getting bad out there and accident reports keep piling up."

Sonja attempted a smile of her own. It felt odd on her face and she supposed it looked it as well. "Thank you. I'll be here."

The deputy nodded, then stepped back into the room. The door snicked shut.

Sonja took a deep breath and held it, hoping to settle the swarming feeling in her stomach. Holding her breath seemed to make it worse, so she exhaled. It was a loud flapping sound in the quiet hallway, bouncing off the thin walls.

It was like waiting in the hospital for bad news. They take you into that quiet area, away from the crowds so they can tell you somebody died. That way, nobody will be around to hear you lose control.

Sonja shuddered. She hoped nobody had died. Hopefully she'd gotten here in time.

At least I managed to beat the snow.

Sure, she'd gotten here before it started coming down. But now it was dropping in endless coatings outside. Last time she'd peeked out the window, the parking lot was a cream-colored plateau under the glow of the sodium lights. The cars looked as if they'd sprouted fluffy white hair. Spikes of ice hung from underneath the doors and wheel wells, sharp and winking light.

The sun would be up soon, but the temperature wasn't supposed to climb above freezing. And forecasts predicted more snow later in the day.

She wished she would have gone to Dennis's yesterday—well, the day before, now that it was nearly dawn. She'd gotten tied up in the office, trying to file as much paperwork before the holiday break as she could. But Dennis had been on her mind constantly. He always was. She loved him, and wanted nothing more than to help him.

Sonja was afraid, especially after reading his writings, that she'd only caused him harm. She looked at the stack of legal pads, had to be at least thirty that she'd brought with her. But inside his house, she'd found a few hundred, easily.

Some of those she'd flipped through. There were other haphazard scribblings of incomplete thoughts, drawings that didn't make any sense and some that had such clarity they'd filled her with chills. She wondered what was in the others. If she would've looked through them all, she'd still be there.

"Sonja Dumont?"

Sonja looked toward the deep voice and saw a man in his late forties or early fifties approaching her. He had a kind, slightly chubby face, with a net of thin dark hair that he'd brushed to the side. He wore a tan-colored uniform under a green coat with a furry collar and puffy sleeves.

"Yes?"

"Sheriff Massey." He held out his hand. Her tiny hand was consumed by his when she shook it. It felt warm. "I understand you want to talk to me."

"I do." She grabbed the legal pads, groaning when she hefted them onto her lap. "People are in danger. I don't even know where to begin, I…"

Sheriff Massey held up his hand. "Whoa, slow down. Let's go into my office. Tell me everything in there."

Sonja started to say more, but stopped herself. She nodded. "Fine."

Wasting too much time. Doesn't he get what's probably happening at this very moment?

If he'd seen the cemetery, he wouldn't be so relaxed. He'd feel sick inside, like her.

"Help you with those?" he asked.

She looked down at the legal pads. "No. I've got them."

"All right. Follow me."

He turned, heading to the door the female deputy had poked her head out of earlier. Opening it, he put his back against it and ushered her inside.

Sonja stepped through, hugging the writing pads to her chest. Her purse dangled from her shoulder, and smacked her hip as she walked. On this side of the door, the station was a frenzy of ringing phones and voices. She saw the female deputy sitting behind her desk, a phone to her ear, and a pen in her hand that was trying to keep up as she jotted something down.

"It's hectic this morning," he said. "You'd think nobody was expecting the snow." Pointing down a small hallway, he added, "We're heading that way. My office is the first door you come to."

Nodding, Sonja hurried through the melee. She kept her head down, eyes focused on her shoes. On her way to the hallway, deputies crossed her path. One nearly bumped into her, but stopped to let her by. She smiled nervously, apologizing for being in his way.

He said nothing in return and hurried by once she had passed.

They reached the sheriff's office. Though the door was open, the light was off inside. She stood aside, letting him enter first. He flipped on the light, then held his hand out to the chairs in front of his desk.

"Have a seat."

"Thank you." She dropped down in the first chair.

"Want some coffee? I can go grab us some."

Coffee sounded wonderful. It might eliminate the deep chill that had burrowed into her bones. But that would only delay things further. She needed to talk to him before he was pulled away from her. Her alone time with the sheriff was very limited. "Maybe later," she said.

He nodded. "Okay." He pulled back the large rolling chair behind his desk. It was leather, with a heavily padded back. It made popping sounds when he sat down. "Now, tell me. How can I help you?"

Sonja set the writing pads on the desk. "Like I said, I don't really know where to begin. I feel like no matter how I explain myself, I'll take too long and that could make things too late."

Sheriff Massey's eyes narrowed. "Too late? This sounds serious. First, let's start with who you are and what you do."

"Well, you know my name. Sonja Dumont. I'm…" She thought about telling him all the degrees she had and the different titles and associations she'd earned in her short career. Instead, she opted just to say, "…a psychiatrist."

Massey nodded. "Okay. So what brings you to Bear Creek? I imagine it has something to do with those legal pads."

"Right. This is only a sample of what I found. There's so much I shouldn't say because it violates patient and doctor confidentiality, but the proper people can pull my charts and I'm afraid you wouldn't believe me if I didn't at least share some of it."

"You're rambling, Ms. Dumont. Just get right down to it."

"You're right. I am. I do that." She took a deep breath. "I think Grant Marlowe and his family are in danger. I'm afraid that a patient of mine, Dennis Hinshaw, has come out here to kill them."

Massey stared at her for several moments that felt endless. "What brings you to that assumption, Ms. Dumont?" He tapped the legal pads. "These?"

"That's part of it. There're other things I could get into, but it would only waste time. I told Dennis it might be a good idea to write letters to his deceased loved ones—I'm sure you heard about the accident Grant Marlowe was in almost two years ago."

Massey nodded. "Who hasn't? He used to be a regular vacationer here, so it was the talk of the town."

"Right. Well, Dennis was the other person involved."

"He lost his kid, right?"

"Yes. And his pregnant wife."

"Jesus. And this is your patient, correct?"

"Yes. My idea with the letters was to give him a way for him to write down his feelings, addressed to her, and that it would help comfort him through the early stages of recovery and remorse. I couldn't imagine what my simple suggestion opened up. There were legal pads stacked all over his home, Sheriff Massey. You know of newspaper hoarders?"

"Sure. My grandmother had old newspapers arranged like skyscrapers all through her house. My brother and I used to pretend we were giant monsters trying to smash the paper buildings."

Sonja didn't acknowledge his story. "Picture that, but with handwritten letters inside writing pads. In that pad on top he wrote about going out to Grant Marlowe's cabin and snooping around, being spotted by a caretaker, and in his last entry, he wrote a letter to his deceased wife saying that he was going to put an end to this and he'd be with her soon."

"Sounds like a suicide to me. Have you sent anybody to check on him?"

"I was at his house before I drove out here. That's where I saw his...writing collection. He wasn't there."

"And where'd you acquire these?" He picked up the pad from top, started flipping through the pages. The paper rustled softly as he looked through.

"His home."

Massey looked up. "How'd you get in?"

"Carefully."

Something that was almost like a smirk showed on his tired face. "Okay. I won't ask."

"But I also found blueprints of a cabin off Shady Pine Road, pictures of the cabin." Sonja's voice went thick as she recalled the wall. "He had pictures of the Marlowes, taped to the wall, with their schedules, like he'd been following them around for months."

"Pictures *he'd* taken?"

Sonja nodded. "Yes. There was a large map with little stickers that I guess showed all the places they'd been, or the places they liked to go. He must have been stalking them for a long time."

"And you had no idea?"

"No. None. I actually thought he was doing better for a while. But he stopped coming to our sessions, stopped accepting my phone calls. With the holidays coming up, I decided to pay him a visit since he wouldn't answer the phone anymore. And this was what I found."

"I know Grant Marlowe fairly well. They do own a cabin on Shady Pine Road. And Edgar Whitley *did* file a report about a prowler a couple days ago. But getting out there is going to be almost impossible

149

with the roads a mess from the snow. Besides, we don't even know if they're actually there right now."

"But Sheriff…"

He held up his hand. "Let me track down the phone number and I'll give them call."

Sonja closed her mouth, breathed slowly through her nose. "Fine."

Massey pushed a button on the base of his phone. "Gale?"

The speaker buzzed back. "Yeah, Sheriff?"

"Can you get me the phone number for Grant Marlowe's cabin? It's out on Shady Pine."

"I know the place," replied Gale's crackly voice. "Give me a minute?"

"You got it. Thank you."

"No problem."

Massey turned to Sonja. "We'll just confirm he took his family out there."

"The graves had been dug up."

Massey flinched as if she'd shouted. "What? What graves?"

"Dennis's wife and children. He talked about going to see them in the letter, so I hoped to catch him at the cemetery. It was after dark by the time I got there, so I had to climb over the fence. That wasn't easy, Sheriff. I nearly impaled myself on the spikes on top of the fence."

"Whoa, so you've admitted already to breaking into a residence and now a cemetery?"

"And I went to the graves. He'd dug them up. It looked like he'd thrown some of the dirt back into them, but…" She shook her head. "I think he took the bodies."

"What town is this?"

"Leaf Spring."

"And you didn't report it?"

"I did. I phoned in an anonymous tip on my way out here. I decided they could handle things on that end and I'd come out here. I was going to drive right out to the cabin, but the weather started getting bad. I figured coming here would be the next best thing."

"Jesus H. Christ."

Massey pushed the button on his phone to summon Gale. This time he told her to get him the number for Leaf Spring's police department.

When he looked at Sonja again, Sheriff Massey seemed paler and somehow older than when she'd first met him. "Anything else?"

"Yeah. I think we might already be too late."

CHAPTER EIGHTEEN

Grant was in some kind of lake, cold water wrapped him up to his shoulders. The sun hadn't broken through the early morning clouds yet, leaving everything gray. A heavy mist hung over the water. It impaired his vision, making it impossible to see beyond the churning gray barrier. He had no memory of how he'd gotten there. He treaded water easily enough, kicking his legs underneath him. The exertion didn't make him tired, though his legs felt heavy because of his waterlogged pants.

"Dad!"

"Bobby?"

Grant spun around. Moments ago, he was alone, but now he saw his son, struggling to remain above the surface. His head bopped up and down, going under, but he fought to come back up.

He spit out water, yelled, "Dad!" Bobby reached out, fingers extended.

Grant started swimming. His clothes felt heavy on his body, trying to pull him under the water like a soggy anchor.

"Dad!"

Grant stopped. He looked over his shoulder, which was strange, since he was no longer swimming. Though he felt no surface under him, he remained above the water.

Kara was a few yards away, struggling just as hard as Bobby. Her long hair was drenched and stuck to her face in wet streaks. "Help me, Dad!"

Grant started toward her.

"Dad! What are you doing? Don't leave me!"

Grant looked back. Bobby was sinking fast, his chin going under. A few more moments and he would be submerged entirely. "Please!" His cries became groaning burbles as his mouth became submersed.

"Bobby, no!"

Grant went back for Bobby, but Kara's cries stopped him. He looked back, saw her go under. "No!" He sprung through the water, leaping forward as if diving. He was almost to the rippling surface where she'd been when he heard another cry.

"Grant!"

Marion!

Upside down, Marion's head hovered above the water. Her hair had fallen, dipping into the murky depths. She wore her bathrobe, but it remained in place around her body and didn't hang open. Her ankles were clutched by a pair of hands. At first, Grant couldn't see who the hands belonged to because of the wall of mist.

The mist thinned, parting, as if knowing he needed to see the person dangling his beautiful wife above the water like a worm over a nest of baby birds.

Dennis Hinshaw—dressed in dark clothing and a ball cap. He grinned madly, like a scientist that had just restored life to a cadaver. "Can't save them all, can you Granty ol' boy?"

"Leave her alone!"

"What about your lovely daughter? I'm sure she's wrestling for air about now."

Grant looked for Kara. He could no longer tell where she'd gone underneath. The lake was a solid mass that didn't undulate. All he heard now were the slurping sounds of water.

"Ka...Kara?"

She was gone.

"And your poor son?" Dennis smirked. "Always turning your back on him, aren't you? Can never give him your full attention, no matter how much he needs it. Am I right? He's a hard one to figure out, you know? So unique with his attitude and behavior, but so much like you with his pigheaded personality. You just don't have the patience to try to identify with him. And this time, your neglect let him sink!"

Bobby was nowhere around. A spiraling tentacle of mist was all Grant saw.

Grant turned around. Water slapped against his chest, splashing his neck. He looked at Dennis, holding Marion's ankles in one hand without any effort.

"And now the question is," said Dennis. "Can you save your poor wife? Or will you fail her too?"

Dennis began to laugh as he slowly lowered Marion. She winced when the top of her head touched the water.

"Grant!" she cried.

"Marion!" Grant tried to swim. He couldn't move. The water felt as if it was tightening around him, turning gummy as it held him in place. "No!"

Marion's head dunked, her screams turning to bubbles when her mouth vanished.

Dennis continued to laugh, continued to sink her.

Her shoulders went in next, then her chest.

Grant struggled against the watery constraints, feeling them give slightly. He shoved forward and tore free.

Arms reaching, hands open, he dived for his wife.

Dennis released her ankles. Marion dropped. Her feet vanished in the splash, throwing water against Grant's face.

"No! Marion!"

Grant flinched and jerked, unable to move his arms. Down by his sides, elbows bent and forearms out, he couldn't lift either of them. Something tight held his wrists down on something flat and hard. Blinking water out of his eyes, Grant raised his head. He glimpsed the living room before pain pounded through his skull, making his vision go blurry. His stomach twisted and seemed to work like a slingshot, firing its contents up his throat in an acidic torrent. He quickly turned away and vomited onto the floor. It splattered across the hardwood, thinning in the middle and throwing thick glops out to the side. Warm spatters nicked his ankles.

"Finally! Grant Marlowe's awake! Thought I might've hit you too hard. Took three splashes before you finally came to."

The echoing voice alternated pitches through the fierce ringing in his ears. Though the tone shifted from high to low and quiet and loud, Grant recognized it as belonging to Dennis Hinshaw.

With each gasp of breath, the back of Grant's throat burned from the tart bile coating it. He spit some out, but more quickly foamed up to replace it. He was careful when he turned his head this time, moving slower. It still felt as if his brain was being compressed between two bricks. His stomach heaved, threatening to toss out more, but he managed to hold it down.

He looked ahead of him, saw where he was and realized the lake had been a bad dream. But now that his eyes were open, he realized he had only swapped a make-believe nightmare for a genuine one.

His family was in front of him, hands and feet tied to the arms and legs of the chairs from the dining room. And Grant was at the head of this gruesome Marlowe pyramid. Marion was seated directly across with Bobby to his left and Kara to his right.

They were either unconscious or…

Dead.

How their heads hung limply, chins nearly resting on their chests, Grant feared they might be.

No. They're not. They're NOT!

Grant's accelerating heartbeat pumped agony inside his skull. Looking around, he didn't spot Dennis right away.

Then he suddenly saw him. He stood before him, arms hanging by his sides. A tin bucket hung from a thin metal handle in his left hand.

"You…" said Grant. He spit again.

"Did you think it was all a nightmare?"

Before Grant could answer, Dennis dropped the bucket. It hit the floor with a tinny clatter. At first, the bucket confused Grant. But his soaked clothes and the water sluicing down his face made him realize Dennis had used tossed water on him to jar Grant awake.

Dennis spun around, moved toward Bobby. He stepped beside him, leaning over his shoulder. Bobby had a welt that had swollen to the size of a golf ball around a gash above his eyebrow.

Dennis dug his thumb into the scabby fold. "Wake up, Junior! Wake up!"

Bobby awoke, screaming.

Grant flung himself forward, but didn't go anywhere. The snug rope burned as it tugged against his wrists. "You son of a bitch!"

Dennis jerked his thumb out of the wound, blood coating it to the knuckle. He held his arms out. "Looks like he's awake too!"

Bobby's eyes patrolled the room in a wild search. They paused on his mother, his sister. Then they shot toward Grant. Seeing he was awake, Bobby's eyes narrowed. He winced, as if doing so caused him agony. "Duh-Dad?"

"Yes, Bobby! I'm here."

"What...what is this?" He tried to move his arms. "What...? What's going on?"

"Don't worry," said Grant. "Everything's going to be all right."

Bobby didn't look at him. His eyes were on his wrists as he tried to work them free. Grant could see the coarse rope leaving dark bracelets on his skin.

Marion began to rouse, head slowly rising. Her hair hung in tangles around her face. The left side of her face was a half sheet of bruises. Seeing the purple coating with patterns of red and yellow spread throughout, Grant felt a combination of sadness and anger. "God...Marion...what'd he do to you?"

Marion's eyes looked swollen and weak; their usual brightness was a dim spark. "Grant...?" She looked down at her hands, flexed her fingers a couple times before returning her puzzled gaze back to Grant. "I...what...?" Her nose wrinkled, mouth cracked to bare teeth.

"Well," began Dennis. "While Marion regains her senses, let's wake up the little princess."

Grant looked at Kara. Her head was canted to the side, eyes closed. Crooked lines of dried blood spread across her forehead, making her thin eyebrows clumpy.

Dennis stepped behind Bobby, who still fought with his ropes, and headed for Kara.

Grant pulled his arms up. The rope held. He stopped trying to free himself and leaned his head forward. "Stay away from her, you bastard!"

Dennis paused behind Kara. He looked at Grant, brow narrowing as his eyes shot hate across the room. "What did you call me?"

"You heard me. Stay away from her or I'll *kill* you."

Dennis bolted forward. He crossed in front of the family, going straight for Grant in a rushing blur. Grabbing Grant by the front of his shirt, Dennis pulled him forward. The chair legs tooted across the floor. He reared back his fist to strike.

Grant closed his eyes, ready for the hit.

A scream blasted through the small room.

Grant cracked open his eyes. Dennis's fist was so close to his face it was flesh-colored distortion. He pulled his head back, looking past Dennis to see Kara's mouth opened wide as the scream petered to a whispery wail. She took a deep breath in and started to cry.

"I'm awake," she said through her sobs. "Please…leave him alone…I'm awake now…"

"Oh, sweetie," said Grant. His throat felt tight. "Oh sweetie…sweetie…"

Kara took in another breath and screamed until her voice ran out. Then she bawled, shoulders shaking, head jerking as tears flowed down her face. Thick globules fell from her jawline.

Dennis turned, putting his face close to Grant. He stared at him, saying nothing. His eyes were so wide open that it looked as if he didn't have the socket capacity to hold them in.

"What do you want?" asked Grant. Dennis didn't answer. "What do you want with *us*?"

"Give it a rest, Grant. *You* make me..." Dennis's hands formed around Grant's throat. "*Sick!*"

The hands squeezed.

Grant couldn't breathe. Dennis's hands gripped him with such force that his vision was already darkening. The ringing in his ears intensified, nearly overpowering the cries of his wife and children. Trying to breathe made it worse, made his brain feel as if were inflating and might crack his skull open. His lungs felt like they were twisting, shriveling like a leaky balloon.

Dennis's eyes, still wide and evil, were somehow narrowed and angled toward his nose. He bit down on his bottom lip, as if concentrating on something important. A wedge of tongue prodded from the corner of his mouth.

Grant felt himself starting to fade. His skin burned...

Then the pressure suddenly went away. Dennis stepped back, holding up his arms as if he was about to hug somebody, hands by his head. He gaped at Grant, worried.

Grant gagged and coughed. Air pushed into his lungs, stinging as if being poked with tiny needles.

"I almost went too far..." whispered Dennis. He spoke as if he was the only one in the room. "Not yet. Not yet. Just stay calm...calm..."

He turned away from Grant, and walked across the room. Keeping his back to them, he faced the wall.

"Are you okay?" asked Marion.

Grant took in a breath that sounded like a bicycle tire losing air. His throat felt too small to allot the proper volume of air he needed. He couldn't answer his wife. His mouth moved, but all he managed to do was wheeze.

His son and daughter gawped at him. The fear in their eyes had reverted them back to children waking from a nightmare and begging him to let them sleep with him. They pleaded for protection from another kind of monster. This time Grant couldn't shine a flashlight under the bed or inside the closet to show them there was no monster. He wanted to say something that would ensure them, encourage. Just one word would do.

But his voice was temporarily disabled, making it impossible for him to lie to his children. And it proved he was as helpless as the rest of them.

"Please, let our children go!" shouted Marion. She turned her head, trying to see behind her. "Keep us, but let *them* go!"

Dennis spun around. "Quiet!"

Marion cringed. She sucked in her bottom lip, lowered her head and cried.

Dennis held out his hand, wagging his finger. "I need a minute…to think." Dennis walked out of the room, shaking his finger.

It was a bit before Grant tried to speak. He leaned as close to his family as the ropes would allow. "Is everybody okay?" he asked in a strained and croaky voice.

"I'm scared," said Kara. She sniffled, lips quivering and breaking Grant's heart.

"I know," he said. "Me too, sweetie."

"My head's pounding," said Marion. "But I'm okay."

Grant nodded, turned to Bobby. "Are you all right?"

Bobby snorted. "Oh, sure…just peachy…what the hell *is* this? Is he…the guy, you know?"

Grant nodded. "Yeah."

"From the accident?" Bobby asked, confirming.

"Yes, Bobby. It's him."

"He has to be the one Edgar saw, right?"

Grant closed his eyes. They didn't need to talk about this now. "Later, Bobby."

"And we saw *his* campfire in the woods? *He* camped out there, right? We should've left when we saw that. We shouldn't be here! We could've been long gone before he showed up!"

"We don't know that, Bobby…" Grant paused to calm down. The last thing they needed right now was an argument between himself and his stubborn son. Before he could speak again, he was interrupted.

"What campfire?" asked Marion.

Grant looked at his wife. "Let's not talk about it."

Bobby turned so he could see his mother. "Dad and I saw a campsite in the woods. He told me not to tell you." Bobby leaned his head further to look at Kara. "Or you, either."

Marion looked at Grant, mouth opening in shock. "Grant? Is this true?"

Grant didn't have to answer her. She could read his eyes and know that it was. She slowly shook her head.

"You knew I'd want to leave, didn't you?"

"Yes, Marion, but—"

"And you kept it from me?" she asked.

"Marion, now's not the time…"

The chirping of a phone made all of them jump.

Dennis entered the room, a stack of cell phones in one hand and holding the screen of another close to his face. "Well, Kara, Derrek has been blowing up your phone all night. I guess since you haven't texted him back, he decided to start calling. Guess he wants to know if you told your parents yet."

Grant realized he had no clue what time it was, but if Derrek was calling Kara it must be late enough in the morning he figured she'd be awake. A quick glance at the window showed him nothing since the blinds were down. Dennis must've done that.

Kara chewed her teeth a bit before she finally asked, "How'd you know about that?"

"Please, Kara. I know a lot more than you think." He pointed the phone at Grant. It had stopped ringing. "Probably isn't easy telling *him* you're engaged to his enemy's son, huh?" Dennis extended his neck, swaying his head back and forth as if trying to find something on Kara. "Don't see the ring. Got it hidden somewhere? You can't wear it if Grant doesn't know you're engaged, right?"

Grant felt like he was hit in the chest with a baseball bat. His sore head seemed to ache even more. Kara was engaged to Derrek? When had this happened? How long? Why didn't she tell him?

Kara looked at Grant, then Marion, her eyes wetting as she whispered something that Grant couldn't hear.

160

"You mean you haven't even told your mother?" asked Dennis. "I thought for sure she would've been the first to know."

Dennis's boots clacked along the floor on his way to the fireplace. Grant watched Dennis sink to a crouch in front of it. The flames were curling high. He hadn't noticed a fire was even going before now. Dennis must have lighted it while they were still knocked out.

Hunkering in front of the fire, Dennis looked back. Wriggling lines of orange and black slithered across the scar of his face. He removed his hat and tossed it onto the flames. There was a *swoosh* as the flames began chomping. The hair underneath was thick and damp, flattened in the front and nearly hanging in his eyes. "Kara? I asked you a question."

"I…" Kara didn't look up. "I don't know…"

Frowning, Dennis shook his head. "Just like ol' Papa, aren't you? Keeping secrets. Guess that's a common thing in the Marlowe house." The phone fired up again. Dennis squinted at the screen, holding it slightly away as if he couldn't quite read it. "Derrek. Again. I don't know about you, but this is going to get on my nerves really fast." He chucked Kara's phone into the fire.

Kara gasped. "Why'd you do that?"

Dennis winked. "We don't want anybody bothering us, now do we?" He tossed all but one phone in. It was covered in a pink case with purple star on the back. Looking at the phone, Dennis took a deep breath and sighed. "Sorry, Bobby. Sheena won't be able to make it."

Bobby slowly lifted his head. "What'd you…?" His eyes widened when he saw Dennis holding the phone. "No…please tell me you didn't."

"Sorry, Bobby. She wasn't supposed to be here."

Bobby's jaw shook, his lips quivering as he sniffled. "Not her…"

Grant felt terrible for his son. Though he didn't know the girl, Bobby's reaction showed how much he cared. Did Dennis *kill* her?

When Dennis tossed the phone into the fire, Grant assumed that he had.

Brushing off his hands, Dennis stood up.

Grant looked away from Dennis, eyes focused on his daughter. She gnawed at her lip, as if trying to stop its trembling. She sucked in a quivery breath.

"Please, sir," she said, "please stop…"

Tilting his head to the side, Dennis looked at Kara with sympathy. "Stop? I *can't* stop." He sighed. "We've got a long day ahead of us." He looked at Bobby when he said, "Already had too many setbacks." Then he turned to Grant. "Storm knocked the power out, but I've got the generator going, so we should be good for a while." He took a deep breath, letting it out slowly. "Guess we better get started."

CHAPTER NINETEEN

Sonja held the paper cup to her mouth. She felt the coffee's steam on her lips. She sipped. The bitter taste made her shiver, but it was better than nothing. Taking another nip, she held her breath as it went down, to mask the tartness.

It needed more sugar. A lot more.

Sheriff Massey had excused himself after bringing her the coffee. So much was going on in his town with power outages and accidents that he hadn't been able to talk to her much.

Sonja stood up, walked behind Massey's desk to the window and bent down a slat to peek out the blinds. Daylight had pushed the darkness back into the mountains, turning them into pointed dark shapes in the distance. The white streaks of snow on the mountains and the milky caps that covered their tops reminded Sonja of peppermint and ice cream. She could almost smell Christmas at her parents' house. What she saw through the window was beautiful and it made her realize this was why Massey chose this office to be his. How he got any work done with such a view, she had no idea.

Taking a tiny swig of coffee, Sonja felt herself begin to sweat. She didn't know if it was the waiting, the horrible coffee, or both that was causing cold drips to slide down her sides. Her stomach was also starting to hurt, but she assumed that was mostly hunger, since she hadn't eaten since lunch yesterday.

Sonja let the blinds snap shut, then turned around. Her eyes landed on the writing pads. She pulled one to her, flipped through the pages, and glimpsed some of Dennis's frantic scribbling. It was like reading something written by a lunatic stranger. These words were nothing at all like the Dennis Hinshaw she'd come to know...come to love.

She did love him. A lot. Never before had she had any kind of feelings other than congenial for her patients, but Dennis was different. The moment she'd met him, she knew he was unlike anybody she'd ever known. He was loyal, wholesome, and had a loving heart. She didn't think people like him existed anymore, unless they were in the pages of those cheesy romance novels she liked to read by Laura Kelly.

The accident had broken him, physically and mentally. But she also thought she could help put him back together.

Like Humpty Dumpty.

Smiling, Sonja remembered when she'd referenced the old children's rhyme to Dennis.

He'd looked at her, confused. "So...I'm like a giant broken egg?"

In Sheriff Massey's office, Sonja laughed. So sweet. How could the words on these pads have come from him? Almost like a mental argument put to paper. She'd never seen anything like it.

And why had he stopped writing to Lindsey? Until the final letter, he hadn't written to her in months. It made no sense to her, and she could usually figure these things out. It was her job. She'd had enough training that Dennis's behavior should be easy to diagnose. Lack of theories aside, she was certain of one thing:

I caused this. He wouldn't have started writing this stuff if I wouldn't have recommended it.

It wasn't fair to shoulder the blame, but she could think of no other reason.

Was he writing his thoughts in hopes of talking himself out of it?

She didn't think so. It was almost like there were two Dennises—Dr. Jekyll and Mr. Hyde.

164

Massey pushed his door open and stepped inside. He had some papers in his hand. His nose wrinkled when he saw her standing behind his desk.

She smiled. "Sorry. Had to move around."

"Yeah. The coffee'll do that to you." He held up his other hand. Small white cups were on his palm. "Creamer?"

"Thank you." Sonja took the cups, peeling off the tab of one without reading the label. She poured it into her coffee, then took a sip. Hazelnut. "Better."

"I know it can be a little strong to somebody not accustomed to it." He entered, leaving his door open. "Got some information for you."

"Yeah?" She walked around the other side of his desk as he came around to his chair. She dropped back down into her seat as Massey returned to his groaning chair.

"Well..." He put the papers on his desk, folding his hands over them. "The cemetery checks out. The graves were disturbed. Concrete was used as a barrier over the coffins and somebody chiseled through."

Oh, God...

"And..." Sonja swallowed the dry lump in her throat that tasted like Hazelnut. "The bodies?"

Massey took a deep breath, pressed his lips together. He shook his head as he exhaled. "Gone."

Closing her eyes, Sonja sank in the chair. "Damn."

"I haven't been able to reach anybody at Marlowe's cabin. I don't think the phones are down in that area, but there are massive power outages all over. If they have a cordless phone, they have no way of knowing we're calling. So, I called Edgar Whitley, the caretaker, and asked him if he'd seen the Marlowes."

"Has he?"

Massey nodded. "They're out there."

"Oh my God..."

"But we don't know for sure if Dennis Hinshaw made it out there before the snow hit, or if he even went out there. Since it's my jurisdiction, it's my call."

"Your call? For what?"

"On how to proceed on this end." He took another deep breath. "As you've seen, my manpower is very limited, especially under these weather conditions. The roads are treacherous right now and with snow and heavy fog making the skies unsafe, we have to rule out helicopter coverage for the time being."

"Where does that leave us, then?" She put the coffee on the corner of his desk. The smell was starting to nauseate her. "I know with all my heart that he was going there. He's probably there now."

Massey nodded. "Our other option is this: I have a Frontier with all-weather tires on it. I like to go off-roading when I'm not here. I'm going to drive out there myself."

"But the roads?"

"Will be hell to travel on, but I should be able to make it. It's just going to take me some time."

"I'll go with you." She stood up.

The sheriff looked up at her. "Thought you might."

"Maybe we can stop him before he goes too far."

"Ms. Dumont, if what you're telling me is true, and so far, the evidence is supporting your claims, he's already gone this far, and I'm afraid he has no intentions of stopping."

Edgar stood on his back porch, inside the cube of screens, gazing at the white undulating hills that led to the mountains beyond. The wind blew through, shaking his coat and fluttering his pants. The evergreens were striped in white, and the bare trees glistened under an icy shell. A fuzzy mist drifted all over, curling between the trees and above the ground like hazy vines. It was the wind causing it, stirring the snow like sand. But it looked eerie as he watched it breathe and pulsate, as if alive.

His house was in heavy isolation, away from the main roads and the tourists and the seasonal occupants that made up Bear Creek. He liked it out here, which was why he'd built their little two-bedroom home in the heart of the woods. Sure, it was smaller than Wanda liked sometimes, but it was all they really needed since the kids had moved off to start families of their own. Selling the old farmhouse and banking most of the money was a good plan, and Wanda agreed. But if she had her way, they would sell this house too and move closer to the children and grandchildren. Edgar was just fine where they were, and he supposed the kids were happy with the arrangement as well. He wouldn't be able to live somewhere that couldn't provide him such wilderness for cover and roaming and hunting.

He drank from his aluminum thermos. The scotch-tainted coffee was what he needed to get him alert. What he was thinking about doing was crazy, but after the sheriff's phone call, he hadn't been able to think of anything else.

"Edgar?" Wanda shuffled outside, letting the storm door bang behind her. Her replacement knee had been acting up because of the cold. She walked like somebody with a wooden leg, practically dragging it behind her. "What in Heaven's name are you doing standing out here?"

"Thinking." He sipped from the thermos. The brew left a warm path down his throat that spread through him.

"You can think inside where it's warm. Too damn cold out here."

"Naw, it's fine."

She stepped up beside him, grabbing the lapels of her coat and pulling it tight in front of her chest. He saw how far it bowed out because of her large breasts. Even at her age, they still sat high and firm on her chest. He supposed it was what caused her such bad back pains. Her hair was short, cut almost like his and matched in color. Since her eyesight had dwindled to nearly blindness over the years, she wore glasses that looked like goggles on her tiny face. He liked them, but she hated how huge her eyes looked behind the lenses.

Wanda huffed, her breath turning into a thin veil around her mouth. "The kids called. They're all holding up at a hotel in Linville. Guess they decided to meet there and then drive out here, but now they can't. They're going to try and make it tomorrow, depending on the roads. Merry Christmas to us, I guess."

"Figured as much. Told them they should have gotten here last night."

"I know you did, but you know how hardheaded they can be."

Edgar nodded, drank, and ground his teeth against the burn. It wasn't just those reasons, he knew. The kids didn't want to hang around any longer than they had to. Eating dinner, swapping gifts, and having some hot chocolate around the fireplace was the most they could handle. Usually after a couple hours, they left for the long drive back to their homes. Maybe they'd see each other again in the spring, maybe not. It depressed Edgar. Somewhere during their childhoods, he'd screwed up as a father. Now he was too old-fashioned for them, too boring, and not very fun to be around for extended periods of time. He knew this, he'd accepted it, but Wanda was clueless. And he hated seeing how much it broke her heart witnessing her grown babies' and grandbabies' visits become shorter and shorter.

There were times where he considered moving closer to the kids for her sake, but he knew it would only be worse for her. Right now, the kids had excuses for why they couldn't stay long. If they were closer together, Wanda would have to face the truth, and he didn't want her going through that.

"Who called earlier?" she asked, raising her clasped hands to her mouth. She puffed hot air between her thumbs, rubbed her palms together.

"The sheriff."

She dropped her hands, concern on her face. "What'd he want? Something happen?"

"Well...don't rightfully know. He called asking about the Marlowes."

Wrinkling her nose, a corner of her lip arched. "Why?"

"I don't know." He sighed, turned to face her. She looked really cold. Her cheeks had tiny red blossoms that were growing. He still found her to be beautiful. The same short, yet stout, body. The smooth face that showed no hint of age, but was evident of how tired she really was. A hard worker, a good wife who loved him unconditionally, though he'd done things in the past that didn't deserve her forgiveness. Trying to be good husband, he'd vowed long ago to never put her through those things again.

168

And he hadn't.

Which was why he knew he couldn't keep anything from her even now.

"I think something's wrong," he said. "The sheriff didn't say anything about it, but I just got one of my feelings about it."

"In your gut?" He nodded. "Never been wrong before."

Edgar sighed. "Nope."

Those buzzing sensations he'd feel in his stomach always proved to be accurate. Never once had they steered him in the wrong direction, and he supposed they weren't now. Something was going on, and he wasn't so sure even the sheriff knew what it was. Why else would he call looking for confirmation that the Marlowes had showed up at the cabin?

Why wouldn't they have?

That was what Massey really wanted to know. And he assumed the sheriff's unease also stemmed from the prowler, though he wasn't sure why.

And Wanda must've read his mind. "Did it have to do with the guy you saw?"

Edgar shrugged. "I don't know. Maybe. I'm thinking it did, though he didn't say one way or another."

Now Wanda frowned. "What are *you* thinking? I'm guessing you wouldn't be standing out here, freezing your biscuits off, if something wasn't on your mind."

"You're right about that." He tipped up the thermos, draining the rest of the coffee and scotch brew down his gullet. He slapped the thermos down on the table he sometimes played solitaire on, belching softly to himself. "I'm going to head out there."

"Edgar, have you lost your mind?"

"Probably."

"You can't drive in that mess out there! The roads ain't clear! More snow's coming later on. You're bound to get yourself killed."

Edgar's back tightened as if being gripped by cold claws. He understood Wanda was trying to prove her point, but it was her third opinion that threatened to make him tremble. Steeling himself, he resisted the palsied sensations that tried to work through him.

For some reason he couldn't understand, he thought she might be right.

"Why would you *want* to go?" she asked.

Edgar groaned. He didn't have the answers she needed to hear, nor did he truly have a reason. Just that same damn feeling that had kept him safe throughout his life, but sometimes led him into the biggest bouts of trouble any man should ever experience.

He didn't know which he'd face this time, but he *did* know he'd find out soon enough.

"I have to," he answered.

They stared at each other for several moments. Wanda stayed firm for a bit, then her defense began to slowly dissipate. It started with her shoulders slacking, next came her back slouching, then the hardness left her face, returning it to the sweet, amicable appearance he'd fallen in love with almost fifty years ago.

He stepped past her and headed inside. From the coldness outside, the heat felt wonderful. It wafted across his frozen face, thawing the mask of ice. He stepped into the living room. Since the power had gone out sometime last night, he'd cranked the generator until this morning. They'd gotten the fireplace going and after breakfast had shut it off. He could hear the steady rumble of it running again, so he assumed Wanda had fired it up.

Crouching in front of the fireplace, he added some fresh logs, stoked the fire and stood up. His rifle rack hung above the mantel. Grabbing the 30.30 Winchester, a lever action rifle he'd gotten from his father on his sixteenth birthday, he slipped his fingers through the lever and jacked a round into the chamber. He reached higher, patted around the shelf above the rack and pulled down a box of shells. Those he slid into his pocket.

He turned around. Wanda stood in front of him, arms crossed over her chest. "What do you think you're doing with that gun? Thought you said it jams up all the time."

"I oiled it." He attempted a smile. "Just making sure I'm prepared."

170

"For what?"

He stuck out his lips, huffed through his nose. "Wish I knew."

"Think you might just be going off half-cocked? Running off of stubbornness or paranoia?"

"I really hope so."

"Let me pack you up a few things…if you really think you should go."

"I think I should."

But he didn't know why. He imagined he'd know before the day was over whether he'd done something good or made the biggest mistake of his life.

CHAPTER TWENTY

Dennis dropped a book bag on the floor. Crouching, he unzipped it and began rummaging around inside.

Kara looked around. She saw everybody else silently watching him. The only noises came from Dennis's shuffling and the very faint rumble of the generator under the house. Nobody tried to get free, nobody even moved. They only stared. There was no point in doing anything else. It was Dennis's show now, and they were his prisoners.

We're not getting out of this.

Nobody knew he was here. The snow had made it impossible for them to get away. And even if the roads were clear, nobody would come to check on them. The only person who could've was Bobby's girlfriend and she was dead. Dennis killed her.

Kara never got to meet her.

Dennis stood up, holding a clear case in his hand. Kara could see a shiny disc through the plastic. "I want to show you something." He marched to the TV, squatted in front of it, and pushed the button on the DVD player. The lights came on, the tray rattled open.

"What are you doing?" asked Dad.

"I just want you to see this."

Dennis cut the TV on. A message on the screen said: *Service Temporarily Unavailable.*

Satellite's out. Power's out.

Kara wondered if the phone lines were down, but realized it didn't really matter since Dennis had smashed the phone.

Dennis switched the input over to one of the Video channels, then put the DVD in the player. He nudged the tray forward, triggering the closing mechanism. Sitting back on the floor, he pulled his legs up, hugging his knees.

A few seconds later a video appeared on the screen. A little boy, running around a grassy backyard, had a water pistol. Shooting everything he saw with spurts of water, he made booming sounds with his mouth. A cape fluttered behind him, torn up the middle of the giant S logoed across it. The camerawork was jerky as it tried to keep up with the quick youngster.

"That's Josh," said Dennis. "My little boy. He'd just turned four here…" He took in a slow breath that sounded shaky. "I transferred our home movies to DVD, you know, for posterity."

The little boy was adorable, with shaggy hair that hung close to his eyes. He had bright eyes, full of happiness and a bell-like laughter that cackled and squeaked. Seeing the innocent boy made Kara's heart feel heavy and sluggish. She could tell he was a very happy kid.

Dennis suddenly appeared on the screen, growling like a monster. He held his arms out, then pounded his chest with his fists. "King Papa attack!" Brandishing a squirt gun of his own, the Dennis on TV began chasing a wildly laughing Josh. Though he looked much younger without the puffy bags under his eyes, fuller hair and a lack of stress wrinkles, she recognized him easily enough.

Dennis laughed from the floor. His eyes had turned watery. Wiping one with his thumb, he said, "He loves that…running around the yard like that, shooting me with water." Smiling, Dennis looked at them. "I'd be pretty soaked by the time we were done."

He spoke to them as if they weren't bound to the chairs, like old friends he wanted to share his memories with.

And in a way, they were. They were connected by a cruel fate.

Watching the footage, Kara felt worse each passing moment. What was on the screen was this man's whole world. And Dad destroyed it.

The video suddenly cut to another scene. Josh was sans the cape, but he still had the water pistol and was running alongside a field with tall dandelions, blasting the petals with strings of water. A gorgeous woman stood to the left corner in a pair of brown shorts that made her toned dark legs look very bare and a tank top that showed the muscle in her shoulders and arms. Long dark hair hung far down her back, shimmering in the wan daylight on the video.

Dennis spoke on the screen, but it sounded quieter, so he must've been the one filming at this point.

"Want to play with my squirt gun?" he asked.

The woman looked at him from over her shoulder, smiling coyly. Her face seemed to light up from the simple act of arching her lips. "Is that recording?"

"Yeah."

She playfully rolled her eyes, still smiling. "Is the gun loaded?"

"You know it is." He laughed.

The woman laughed. "Don't we already have video of that?"

Dennis's cheeks reddened as he watched the video. "Forgot about that part," he muttered. "That's my wife, Lindsey. God, she's beautiful. I have no idea how I got so lucky. Look at me. I'm not exactly something to brag about."

In normal circumstances, Kara would've disagreed. Other than the scar and heavy bags under his eyes, he was a very good-looking guy. But it was hard for her to see him in any other way than a walking nightmare.

"Dennis, please…" Mom shook her head, trying to get her hair out of her face. Bruises streaked her cheek like a purple map. "Please."

The sentimental calmness drained from Dennis's face when he looked at Mom. Hate filled his eyes, making them dark. He didn't speak. Didn't have to. Those horrible eyes told all he wanted to say.

Dad swiveled his neck. "Marion?" Mom turned to Dad. He shook his head. "Don't…just let him get through it."

Mom nibbled at her lip, nodded. Then she looked at the TV again.

"She was six months pregnant, Grant. You know that, right?"

Closing his eyes, Dad sniffed. She saw pale lines of moisture on his cheeks that might have been tears. "Yes, Dennis. I know that."

Dennis shut off the movie, stood up. Turning to the family, he took a couple steps toward them. "Lilly lived for about four hours after Lindsey died. I'm sure you heard about that too. It was in the paper, a featured story that made the cover. Had this horrible picture of my little girl all hooked up to these machines by wires and tubes." Wincing, he shook his head. "But for some reason they neglected to focus on that in the trial. Didn't flash that picture around to gain the pity of the jury or judge. Of course, I didn't have the money at the time to afford the kind of lawyer you did. What'd he do, Grant? Persuade the right people to omit that part?"

Dad stared at the floor, reminding Kara of a child being lectured by his parent. Guilt seemed to cover him like a dark glow. How much string-pulling had he done during the trial? She was there for most of it, and remembered how lousy she felt for her father. He'd looked so pitiful behind that table, head always down, grief-stricken and vulnerable. Seeing him being put through the ringer like that, knowing the life he'd worked so hard for was over, had made her feel so sorry for him and her family. Sure, she felt awful for Dennis, but she wasn't as affected because she wasn't *directly* related to it. In an essence, she was, but there was still a thin barrier of safety.

And now it wasn't there. She was facing it just like the rest of them.

Dennis stood next to Dad now, a hand on the back of the chair gripping it so tightly the wood made soft popping sounds. "Our anniversary was coming up that weekend. We were going to go to the beach, spend the weekend together. Josh was going to stay at the in-laws and give us a few days to ourselves before Lilly came. We were excited. Time alone didn't come often, so we were eager to accept their offer to watch him."

Standing over Dad, Dennis glared at him, his eyes round angry orbs. Dad turned, meeting his eyes. Neither looked away.

"I want you to come outside with me for a second," said Dennis.

"I'll go with you under one condition," Dad said in a calm voice.

175

Dennis made an impressed face, poking out his mouth. "Bartering?"

"Yes. It's me you want to punish, not them. Just take me away and leave them here. You'll get what you want. They're not a part of this, Dennis, you know that. It's me you want to hurt...it's *me*."

"Is that right?"

Dad nodded. "You know it is."

"Well, you're forgetting one thing." Dennis stepped over to the book bag, picked it up and started walking to the group.

Kara realized he was heading for her and started to squeal.

Dad stiffened, his back straightened. "Dennis? What are you doing?"

"You forget about this, Grant," said Dennis. He moved past Kara. She could no longer see him. Turning her head this way and that, she couldn't find him but felt his presence behind her. Dad's eyes were aimed above her head, growing wider.

She heard Dennis shout from behind her, "I'm the one who's calling the shots around here!" Then her hair was jerked, pulling back her head. Something cold pressed against her throat. It felt sharp as it dimpled her skin, though it wasn't pushing quite hard enough to cut her. Not yet.

"Dennis!" cried Dad. "Please, no! Stop!"

Bobby and Mom screamed.

"Get away from her, you asshole!"

"No, please! Not her!"

All the cries and pleas blended together into a suppliant harmony. Kara could no longer distinguish the voices. All she heard was her own frantic thoughts that seemed to stampede through her. The cold steel against her throat pushed tighter, beginning to burn.

"She's bleeding!" cried Dad. "Stop it!"

"Then come outside with me. Help me get something out of the van! Stop trying to make deals with me!"

Mouth agape, Dad nodded. His eyes spewed tears. "All right, Dennis, okay! Whatever you say—you're in charge."

"Thank you," said Dennis.

The cold sharpness moved away from Kara's throat, leaving a warm line across it. She felt thin trickles of heat moving down her skin. It reminded her of shaving her legs and accidentally nicking herself with the razorblade.

Dennis stepped in front of her, twisting the knife around in his hand as he walked slowly to Dad. He turned the knife so the blade pointed at her father. When he thrust the blade forward, Dad flinched. For a moment, she thought she saw the knife punch into his stomach and quickly looked away. Sawing sounds called her attention back to Dennis. His back blocked most of her view, his arm moving back and forth.

Ropes dropped.

Dad's arm did too, freed from the binding.

"Don't try anything," he told Dad.

Thank God...

It was the ropes being cut, not her father's flesh.

"I can't feel my arm..." Dad muttered.

"Good. It'll keep you from trying to be a hero." Dennis moved down to Dad's feet. He cut only one of them loose. "All right, listen to me. I'm going to free your other hand, but your foot's going to stay tied. In case you try to run, you won't get very far."

Seeing the disappointment on her father's face, Kara recognized right away that he'd been planning something and Dennis had just prevented it from happening.

"And if you still try something stupid," said Dennis. "I'll kill them all. Do you understand me?"

Dad nodded. "I won't try anything."

"Good."

Grabbing Dad by the arm, Dennis made him stand. Dad swayed a few times, but Dennis held him up. Kara imagined it was like waking up in the middle of the night, when your muscles didn't want to work how they should and you stumbled your way to the bathroom.

Dennis turned around, aiming the knife at the rest of them. "That goes for you guys too. If you try anything, I'll kill *him*. Got it?"

Nobody spoke. Kara nodded.

Desolation

She believed everything he said.

CHAPTER TWENTY-ONE

Grant wished Dennis had let him put on his coat, or at least shoes. What clothes he had on did very little to warm him, and his feet felt numb yet throbbed with stinging pain as he stumbled through the snow. The chair, dragging behind him, left lines in the slushy white. Its added weight made his trek difficult and clumsy. If Dennis didn't have such a firm grip on his arm, he'd probably fall on his face.

But seeing how the knife was aimed at his sternum, he knew falling would only bring him down on the blade.

"What are your plans, Dennis?" Grant hated how much his voice shook, sputtering little clouds in the air. Mostly it was the cold, but his fear also helped. His lips felt dry and cracked as he tried to talk.

"It'll all make sense in a minute."

Grant wanted to ask more. He was afraid to. So he stayed quiet as they took the stone path down to the yard. He saw his Jeep and felt a surge inside.

So close.

There was a spare key under the front bumper in a storage case. If he could somehow get it, sneak it in with him. Later, if he had a chance, just a short opportunity to get away from Dennis, he could get his family free. Together, they could run out of the cabin, pile in the Jeep and flee. He saw an old white work van parked beside the Jeep that must belong to Dennis. No way could that block on wheels make it down their driveway in the snow. That meant Dennis wouldn't be able to come after them.

If I can get the key...

They wouldn't have to waste time trying to find his set of keys later. Dennis had probably done something with them anyway.

He was just a few feet away from the Jeep, close enough that he could see the frosted headlights. The snow piled around the wheels. This close, he felt jittery inside, antsy, as if an invisible current flowed from his vehicle into his body. It made him fidgety. Hopefully, Dennis wouldn't notice.

They stepped onto the snow-covered gravel. Their feet made powdery crunching sounds as they walked. They moved past the front.

Then Grant looked down at the tires. The piled snow wasn't all that made the wheels look low. The tires had been slashed, hanging around the rims in a fat black ribbon. The second wind of bravery Grant had been building was washed away. Seeing Dennis had already crippled their way out of here suffocated any morsel of hope he had left.

More tears began saturating Grant's cold-dry eyes.

He heard Dennis make a whispery snigger from beside him. "Stings, doesn't it?" he asked. "And if you were thinking about the spare key, I already grabbed it."

Now Grant cried. Not a full-on bawling, but he no longer tried to hide his anguish. Dennis had thought this through more than Grant would've ever guessed. And why wouldn't he have? He'd had two years to plan this out. Every detail. He probably had a counteraction for *anything* Grant might attempt, even the things Grant hadn't thought of yet.

It was hopeless.

They walked around the front of the van, moving beside it. In the corner of Grant's eye, he thought he saw the dark smear of a person sitting behind the thin sheet of ice covering the passenger window. Though he was tempted to look closer, he kept walking, giving it none of his focus. The chair was sliding across the snow pretty easily now. And if he paused to give the window a glance, he might somehow throw off the intricate coordination he had going now.

Grant slowed as they neared the van's side door.

"No," said Dennis. "Around back. Keep going."

Grant did. He walked on legs that felt tight and achy. The snow squished between his toes, though he couldn't feel it. He had no idea if it was the lack of sunlight making them look purple or if they actually were.

They stepped around the back, to the rear doors. Grant slipped as he tried to turn around. Again, Dennis's tight hold didn't let him go down. The strength in his arm was impressive.

"Open it," said Dennis. "It's unlocked."

Tentative, Grant raised his hands. They floated in front of the twin latches, as if touching one might somehow hurt. His worry was probably close to accurate.

Pain burst in his ribs from Dennis's elbow slamming into him. "Do it, Grant! Do you think I enjoy shouting like this? Think I enjoy *doing* this?"

Dennis elbowed him again, knocking Grant against the van. Grant caught one of the latches. His arms jerked, making his shoulder pop. Holding himself up by one hand, he looked over his shoulder. His feet had shot out behind him, toes cutting little gulches through the snow. Had he fallen, he probably would have cracked his head open on the corroded bumper.

"Damn it, Grant," said Dennis.

Grant felt hands grip him under his arms and jerk up. Grant shot back to his feet. They kicked the snow, trampling it flat as they found purchase. He leaned against the door, panting. Sweat dribbled down his forehead.

"We're wasting time," said Dennis. "I'm afraid one of your gutsy offspring might try something stupid."

Grant agreed. Head resting against the tinted glass of the small window, he pictured Bobby inside working hard to squirm his way out of the bondage. If he didn't hurry up and get back inside, Bobby might get them all killed.

"Okay," said Grant. He pushed himself off the door and was disheartened by how sore and fatigued he already was. "Okay."

Grant pulled the latches, pointing them toward each other. The right side clicked open, the left stayed shut. Carefully, he pulled it open, not knowing what to expect.

Nothing happened.

He gazed into a dark, stuffy cab. Pale light came through the windshield, dimmed by the frost and ice. Though it barely showed any luminosity, he could make out the contours of the middle row, the front seats.

And the dark shapes of heads...

Before Grant could ask about what he was seeing, Dennis said, "Grab it."

Grant turned to Dennis. From the gloomy dark inside the van, the cloudy light hurt his eyes. "Grab...what?"

Dennis pointed into the shadows. "That."

Looking inside the van, Grant followed Dennis's finger aimed at the floor of the trunk area. Hardly noticeable was an obscure lump against the blacker shades around it.

"What is it?" Grant asked.

Dennis reached around the shut door, fumbling along its edge. Something clicked, then he pulled the door open wide. Light spread inside, pushing the dark back a couple feet.

And unveiled a body bag.

Zipped tight, the silver line of the zipper's teeth glowed like a lopsided metal grin. The body-shaped lump showed something was inside.

Cold tumbled through him. His scalp went prickly, feeling as it were sprouting little legs.

"Ever seen one of those before?" asked Dennis.

"It's...no...a body bag?"

"Pick it up," said Dennis. "We're taking it inside."

Grant looked at Dennis, reaching for his arm. His fingers snagged Dennis's sleeve. "You can't be serious."

"Don't make me repeat myself. Just do it."

Grant peered down at the black vinyl form. It looked like a giant leech in the darkened trunk area. He was convinced if he reached in, something would gobble his hands. But he also knew if he didn't do what Dennis said, the madman would make him regret it.

So Grant extended his arms. His hands slid across the smooth texture, making soft popping sounds like a tarp. He felt something hard through the canvas that didn't sink when he pushed down. Not allowing his hands to linger on the solid piece, he reached underneath and began to drag it toward him.

Something inside shifted. He dropped the bag.

"Shit!" He snatched back his hands, holding them to his chest. "Something moved!"

"It was bound to happen."

"What's in there? What are you trying to pull?" He grabbed Dennis's coat, jerking him close. "What is this, Dennis?"

Dennis shoved him away. "Don't ever touch me!" Grabbing Grant's shoulder, he turned him around and forced him closer to the body bag. "Pick it up!"

Instead of arguing, Grant only nodded. After taking a few deep breaths, he tried again. This time he pulled it halfway out, then squatted, letting it hang on his shoulder. Standing, he pushed his shoulder into the middle and hoisted the heavy bag up with him. It was awkward getting it situated, and he nearly dropped it a couple times, but he was eventually able to stand with the bag balanced across his shoulder like a hefty box. Whatever was inside was stiff, remaining mostly level as he tried to turn around.

Now the chair was causing problems.

"Could you untie me from the chair?"

"Yeah, right." Dennis started walking, tugging on Grant's sleeve like a dog harness. "Let's go."

CHAPTER TWENTY-TWO

Bobby studied the rope on his wrists. It looked as if Dennis had simply wrapped it around them several times, tying a knot under the arms of the chair. It kept his forearms taut against the wood. The ropes weren't coiled around his actual wrists.

He was in a hurry. Wanted us all tied before somebody woke up.

Looking down at his feet, he saw the ropes there had been looped around his ankles several times, then snarled to the chair. Bobby figured he'd done those last, after getting the hands secured.

Is he going to retie them a little more thoroughly?

He hoped not. Because he felt his right arm beginning to move a bit as he tried wiggling it from side to side.

If only Sheena would've gotten here sooner...

Sheena.

Dead. Her cell phone was burning in the fire, a blob of coagulated plastic and wiring. If he would have texted her earlier, she'd have picked him up before Dennis even got here.

And everybody else?

Bobby wouldn't allow himself to think about that. Actually, he shoved those thoughts away, ashamed of himself for even contemplating such possibilities.

"What are you doing?" asked Kara.

"Trying to get loose," he said, a little more vicious than he'd meant. There was no time for apologies, though.

"Well, stop it," she said.

"Shut up."

"Bobby," said Mom. "You heard what he said. He'll *kill* your father."

"I heard him," said Bobby, still jiggling his arm.

"And don't you care?" she asked.

Bobby paused. He was surprised by how little the chance his father might be slain affected him. Surely he still loved him, didn't he?

Moments ago he'd wished Sheena had taken him out of here before Dennis broke in.

Now Bobby's lack of movement was triggered by his thoughts, not Mom's warnings. He'd spent so much of the past two years telling himself he needed to hate Grant Marlowe. Had he actually started to?

Of course Bobby was furious for the accident, betrayed by Dad's constant lying about his drinking. But back then, he still loved his father. And it had angered him nearly as much as what Dad had done. Bobby figured nothing would ever change those feelings. But Bobby had *wanted* to hate him, so he'd kept up the charade until Mom, Kara, and especially Dad was convinced the act was legit.

During the course, did his feelings eventually did change without his realizing it?

Bobby had put on the performance for so long, it had absorbed him. The character had influenced the performer. Infected his heart. He looked up at his mother, his eyes flicking back and forth from her to his sister. He realized that it had not only perverted his stance on Grant Marlowe, but it had distorted his love for the rest of his family.

My God...

He would have kept trying to get loose. Might have actually succeeded. The pressure in the ropes seemed to be slacking. Eventually the rope might've become so loose he could just slip his arm out. And what would he have done then? *No clue.* Probably not much, other than instigate the brutal deaths of his loved ones.

And just like Sheena, he'd have nobody to blame but himself.

His eyes began to itch, filling with moisture. His chest felt tight and painful.

"Bobby, what's wrong?" asked Kara.

"I'm…" He couldn't even say it. He shook his head. Apologizing was admitting that he had screwed up. And Bobby wasn't one to say sorry. His actions these nearly two years were just as deceiving as Grant Marlowe's had been. Bobby had also been living a lie. And even now he couldn't confess his imperfections.

Guess he was more like his dad than he'd wanted.

The side door opened, banging against the wall and making them all jump. Thumping noises resounded from the side hall, followed by a horrible grating sound of wood draggling across wood.

In synchronicity, they gaped at the doorway.

Several long moments later, Dad appeared. A long black object that looked like a flattened tent was braced on his shoulder. Half pointed forward, the other half behind. The chair bounced and dragged behind him. Dennis entered right after, the tip of the knife directed at Dad's back.

Dad turned toward the bound group. From this angle, there was no mistaking what he was carrying.

A body bag. And it wasn't empty.

"Oh…shit." Bobby muttered.

Though the girls seemed just as disturbed as Bobby, they kept quiet. Not even a gasp. Bobby noticed he'd gone tense and had to remind himself to breathe.

Dennis stepped around Dad. "Put it on the floor, where everybody can see." He pointed with the knife and Dad obeyed, carefully placing it at the head of the assembled chairs. Dad stood, breathless, his hands rubbing his lower back.

Dennis stepped next to him. "What are you waiting for? Open it."

"I don't want to, Dennis," said Dad, winded. "I don't want to see what's in there. Don't want my family seeing what's in there."

Dennis's lips squirmed around his teeth. "I had to see the body bags opened in the morgue. It's your turn to know what that feels like! Open the goddamn bag!"

Bobby surprised himself when he shouted, "Don't do it, Dad!"

"Shut up, Bobby!" Kara fired back.

Bobby looked at her, surprised.

"*Both* of you shut up!" barked Dennis.

And both of them did. Bobby held his tongue in place to keep it from causing more problems.

"Calm down, Dennis," said Dad in a composed voice. "I'll open it."

"Of course you will," said Dennis. "There was never an option not to."

Dad sank to a crouch beside the body bag, the rope pulling the chair toward him. It bumped against his foot and stopped sliding. Bobby saw how dark the skin of his toes and his ankle had become. He wondered if it was frostbite.

Dad's hand shook as he pinched the zipper and slowly ran it down. The strained concentration on his face showed that he wondered what was inside, but was afraid of finding out. Looking up at Dennis, Dad's eyes begged to let him stop.

As if reading his mind, Dennis answered, "Keep going."

Shoulders slumping, Dad's neck suddenly turned weak, letting his head drop with a heavy exhale. Dad grabbed the edges of the undone flaps and flung them wide. Seeing what was inside, he jumped back, screaming.

Mom's shrieks tore through the room, drowning Dad's machine-gun yells and drilling into Bobby's ears. Kara bawled. She shook her head, as if doing so might make what she was seeing not real.

Bobby only stared at the corpse, his eyes fixated on the bruises across its insipid face. Where a throat had once been was now a deeply carved gully, ridged points of bone could be seen through the dried sinewy curtains of the esophagus.

Though the damage was severe, Bobby still recognized Georgia.

Through his jittery vision, Bobby saw Dennis drop down to one knee beside Dad. On all fours, Dad heaved as if vomiting air.

"Feel that?" Dennis had to shout over the ruckus of all the shouts and cries. "That cramp in your chest? Almost like your heart's twisting and folding in on itself? You can't breathe, can you?"

Dad stared at the corpse with fat eyes, pushing his brow into his hairline. Mouth wide open, he screamed and screamed.

"Feels like your heart's locked up like an old engine. And you're wondering if it's going to start beating again or if you're just going to drop dead right here. And you hope that God will just let you drop because what's still to come will be even worse than this—"

Bobby didn't even realize his Dad had spun around until his fist pounded the side of Dennis's face. The force of the blow threw Dennis back, throwing his legs high. His back smacked the floor, followed by his feet. The knife flew and Bobby lost sight of it when it hit the floor and skated across the hardwood.

The tumult of pain-filled cries was silenced as if someone had pushed the power button on their grief.

Dad shot to his feet, arms held out, hands clenched into fists. The chair was no longer tied to his foot.

And the family cheered him, shouted his praise. For the first time in what felt like an eternity, Bobby was proud of his father.

He ran to Bobby first, probably because he was the closet to him. But he still smiled at his father like a puppy being selected from a box full of others. Kneeling before him, Dad started working at the knot. The same one Bobby's squirming had started to loosen. Leaning sideways, Dad angled his head under the arm for a better view.

More of the rope's tension went away.

And Kara's screams called Dad's attention, triggering Mom to start as well. Dad pulled his head out from under the chair's arm, turned around and jerked rigid.

Kara had noticed first. If only Bobby wouldn't have focused all his awareness on his father, he might have noticed Dennis coming first.

Instead, Dad was whacked to the floor. Before he could attempt getting up, he was kicked hard in the stomach. Dad rocked forward and back, coughing, face red as he clutched his midsection. Dad was going to be down for a while, so Bobby started wriggling his hand again. This time it was much easier, but still gave him trouble. He wasn't free yet, but much closer.

"That's it!" screamed Dennis, killing everybody's cries. He kicked Dad's stomach again.

"Stop it!" Bobby cried.

If Dennis heard him, he didn't show it. "Now I'm going to make you watch something else. I wasn't going to, but you brought this on yourself."

He stomped over to Dad's chair, picked it up and dragged it to the TV. He positioned it facing the screen. Then he returned to where Dad lay on the floor, moaning. Dennis made him stand up, jerking him to the chair. Dad dropped into the seat, still holding his stomach as Dennis got more ropes from his magical duffel bag of torture and tied him back up.

Bobby noted how this time Dennis tied Dad's hands in a stricter way; starting with his wrists, he strapped them to the chair's arms. Arms bound, he could no longer hold his hurting gut. He winced with each breath, which prompted a coughing spell. Bobby knew his father was in tremendous pain and it both angered and distressed him.

Dennis went back to his duffel bag and crouched. His hands rummaged around inside. When they came back out, they held another DVD case, a small white box and what looked like some a roll of packaging tape. Then he walked back to Dad and got on his knees beside him.

He dropped the DVD case onto the floor, keeping the box and tape. "I hate to do this, Grant. I *really* do. This isn't who I am at all. This…" He waved his empty hand around. "…is *not* me."

Dad took in a breath that sounded like he was trying to breathe through a tight straw. "Then…stop it…"

"I promise you I will. But not until we're done. And we're not to that point yet. Soon. Very soon." He looked at Dad with sympathetic eyes. "You've got to learn. And people like you never do unless you're forced to. So I'm going to *force* you."

Dennis set the tape on his thigh. He pulled the tab out of the box and turned it upside down. Nothing fell out. Shaking the box, metal items dropped into Dennis's palm. The light glinted off them, making the tiny things look like chrome fireflies.

It wasn't until Dennis had peeled off a strand of tape and began lining one of the items against the adhesive strip that Bobby realized it was a razorblade. Holding it to Dad's face with both hands, he lined it directly under his right eye. The sharp end was just below the white of his eye.

"If you try to close your eyes, you'll be sliced."

Dad cried out. Thin trickles of blood ran down from his eye like murky tears.

Dennis smiled. "Whoops. Even if you *blink,* you're going to feel a nick."

Dad looked as if he was gasping in frightened surprise as he tried to keep his eyes open. "Dennis! This is crazy! I can't…" Dad screamed again, making the red tears turn even darker.

Ignoring Dad, Dennis grabbed the DVD case and carried it over to the TV. He opened the DVD player, removed the home video disc and swapped it with the one from the case. With the previous disc inside the case, he snapped it shut.

Aunt Georgia, bound to a chair in a similar fashion as the rest of them, appeared on the screen. Hysterically crying, her eye makeup had left black squiggly trails down her cheeks. Though she was gagged, she still screamed with all she had.

Bobby pulled his stare away from the screen. His eyes landed on Aunt Georgia's mangled corpse and he quickly looked away. This time he saw his mother, his sister, bound and crying. Everywhere he looked was carnage, even if he closed his eyes, he would still see it.

Dad sucked in a breath that sounded thick with grief and groaned. "Oh God, Dennis…no. Don't make us watch this!"

Ignoring Dad, Dennis walked away from the TV. He passed the chairs and bent over. When he stood up straight, he had the knife again. Bobby wanted that knife. If he could just get the ropes loose, he'd put an end to all of this.

But there was no way he could even begin to try. Not right now.

Dennis moved back to the chairs, stepping between Mom and Kara. Both of them softly begged Dennis to stop all of this, but he was deaf to them. "Every time you look away from the screen," Dennis said, "I'll stab a member of your family. I'll start with your wife and work my way around. It won't be enough to kill them, but they'll still have been hurt because of you." Dennis turned to Bobby, gazing at him with eyes boiling with hate. "Understand?"

Bobby grinded his teeth. Through a clenched mouth he said, "I'm going to kill you."

Dennis leaned over, putting his face closer to Bobby. His eyes didn't flicker, didn't even blink. This only angered Bobby even more.

"Bobby, please stop," said Kara. She whined in a way that reminded him of when he used to dig his fingers into her armpit to try and tickle her. "You're not helping anything. Just shut up."

Her words also riled him up. Bobby sniffed hard and long, feeling a thick globule of mucus being siphoned from his nose into his throat. He hocked it back up and spat. The green gobbet smacked Dennis's cheek, splattering against his skin like a busted paintball. Phlegmy bits clung to the hairs of his freshly growing beard.

Dennis didn't even flinch.

Bobby felt the anger that tricked him into thinking he was strong retreat, leaving him trembling in the chair. He tried to keep his mouth still, but it made soft clicking sounds as his teeth tapped together.

Shit. What did I just do?

Slowly, Dennis raised the knife to Bobby's face, a silver blur close to his eyes. Bobby trembled, his breaths coming fast and short. "No. Don't." Around him, his family also begged. The knife moved down out of sight, leaving a thin line of fire on his cheek. Bobby wanted to remain as emotionless as Dennis and not show any pain, but he closed his eyes and cried out. He leaned his head to the side, rubbing his dampening cheek on his shoulder.

He could hear Kara and Mom screaming at Dennis some more.

Dad must've looked away from the TV, because Dennis shouted, "Don't do it, Grant, or I'll stab your wife!"

It took a short bit, but eventually the crying and screams dwindled to soft sniffles and jerky breathing.

The stinging in his cheek only worsened as his sweat mixed with the blood. He felt another scream tickling his throat, but the hollow sounds of Aunt Georgia's sobs beckoned him to lift his head. He didn't know why he looked at the TV. She was dead, and the condition of the body showed she had died brutally. He didn't want to see what had caused it.

But he didn't look away.

Aunt Georgia stared off camera, her curly hair wet and hanging around her face in tangles. The gag pulled her mouth, forcing it open and shoving her cheeks back into ridges that showed her teeth. Her eyes widened as Dennis stepped into the shot.

On screen, Dennis said, "It's not *entirely* your fault that you didn't do the right thing. Your brother and his legal team were the ones that dragged you into this. But the fact of the matter is you're a part of it. I hate the place you've all put me in. But I will do what has to be done."

Georgia screamed behind her gag, shaking her head rapidly, flinging her hair all over as Dennis approached her. He held a clear plastic drape in his hands, spreading it wide as he neared her. He moved past her, getting behind her as Aunt Georgia pleaded and prayed muffled and pointless words.

Bobby looked at his father. Dad closed his eyes, holding them shut as he growled in pain. They shot open. His eyes were red and filmy, spilling crimson runnels down his face. He whimpered through his huffing breaths.

And watched.

Bobby could tell Dad was forcing them to stay open, though he didn't want to watch his old friend die. She was more than that to their family. She was one of their own and it got her killed.

On TV, Dennis threw the bag over Georgia's head and pulled it back. The tight sheet mashed her nose, pulled her eyes into tight slits. Her breaths turned raspy, sounding as if she was blowing up a balloon. A tiny bulge of plastic turned foggy over her mouth as she sucked it in and huffed it out.

Watching, Bobby felt as if he couldn't breathe. His lungs felt tight.

Aunt Georgia's tongue pushed and prodded, licking moist trails across the plastic.

Bobby looked away again. Kara was staring at him. She was slightly blurry with his tears, but he could see the woe on her face. Her lips were pressed tightly together, her eyes partway shut and wet. She breathed through her nose in hissing spurts.

The sounds of Aunt Georgia's fight faded in the background. A few moments passed and Bobby heard the rustling of plastic.

When he turned to check the TV, he saw the Dennis on the screen punch a knife into his aunt's throat and start to twist.

Hot bubbles rushed up his throat. He quickly looked away, swallowing to keep his stomach acids down. It made his stomach cramp as he fought against the urge to vomit.

Wet tearing sounds came from the TV's speakers, reverberating and juicy in stereo sound quality.

Dad's shouts made him look back.

Blood was seeping from the dark jagged hollow in Aunt Georgia's throat.

Growling, Dad swung his feet and kicked out. His bare soles kicked the screen, spinning the TV sideways. It tipped over the edge and crashed to the floor in a burst of sparks and sizzles.

Dennis jumped, looking more surprised by Dad's outburst than angry. Running over to Dad, he held his arms out. The knife was pointed away. "What the hell are you doing?"

"You son of a bitch!" Blood sprayed from Dad's lips. "Why her? This is between *us*! She had nothing to do with it!"

Dennis pinched the end of the tape and yanked the razorblade away from Dad's eye. He flung it aside. The metal hit the floor with a soft clatter.

Leaning closer to Dad, Dennis said, "Your sister was just as guilty as you, the cops, our lawyers, the judge—all your contacts that got you off so easy. It was her testimony that helped sway the jury. She spoke so highly of how hard you'd tried to stop drinking and how the success of the case and the peer pressure at the bar led to your relapse. That was bullshit and all of us in this room know it. You'd never *stopped* drinking, just kept on guzzling and guzzling and lying to your family about it. If that was me, and I murdered three innocent people, I would have been put away for life! But you? You were out in a less than a year! Monitored on probation for only six months? And here you are, a free man, already got your license back and driving. There's no gizmo in your car for you to breathe in before it starts. You can just come and go as you please."

Dad shook his head, not listening. "Let my family go right now. Do what you want to with me, but let them go."

Dennis threw back his head and laughed. "As if it was that easy."

"It is…they're *not* guilty. I am."

"They're as much a part of this as we are. The two of us pulled them into it. You pulled in mine, and now I've pulled in yours. We're all in this together to the very end."

Bobby understood what that meant.

It was too late. Their fates were already condemned.

CHAPTER TWENTY-THREE

Edgar downshifted and the truck's engine steadied. The drive had been harder than he'd anticipated with how much snow blanketed the road. He might have had a somewhat easier hurdle if he'd taken the main road, but that would have added a lot more time to his journey.

And he wasn't sure if he had time to spare.

The closer he got to the Marlowes, the more his stomach felt like insects were buzzing around inside. The cold grip in his chest seemed to squeeze tighter.

He drank some hot chocolate Wanda had made for his trip. It did nothing to warm him. The vents blew hot air against him, and he still shivered.

Nerves.

He was more worked up than he had been when he was about to lose his virginity. So nervous that night with Wanda, he hadn't been able to keep his erection for longer than five seconds at a time. He eventually got the job done, and the second time was much easier, but he'd been a wreck that first time. He didn't want a second chance with this, though. He figured one time would be enough.

Better not be wasting my time.

Now that was a dumb thought. Would it somehow make this difficult journey more worth his efforts if something *was* wrong? What if he got there and the Marlowes were just sitting around the table for a meal, looking at him as if he'd stepped off a spaceship? Would he consider this a waste of time?

Of course not. But it was that damn nagging in his gut that had set him out, risking his life on this damn bumpy, uneven road, packed with snow that the tires kept slipping in and jerking his truck this way and that.

If his gut was wrong this time, he doubted he'd ever trust it again.

But deep down—*not too deep*—he hoped it was wrong. Maybe he was just going senile, or had gotten so old he was no longer able to recognize stubborn paranoia when it flared up.

And maybe I'm right.

Another shiver. Edgar held the wheel in one hand and chugged more hot chocolate. It burned his throat going down, but seemed to cool as it moved through him.

He checked the time on his dashboard clock. He'd been traveling for over half an hour. At this rate, he might reach the Marlowes sometime after lunch. Hopefully the weather would hold out so he could get back home if nothing was amiss. Going downhill on a snowy road with his half-bald tires, and the likelihood of even more snow coming later, he doubted he'd reach his house without winding up in the ditch.

If only that was all he had to worry about, Edgar would surely feel better.

The seat was comfortable, and it held Sonja like a giant soft hand. The padded cushion under her and the warmth in the cab made her feel cozy. She thought she might be able to take a nap like Massey had suggested. But her thoughts wouldn't allow any kind of sleep to come. Plus, her eyes were glued to the road ahead of her.

Or what she supposed was the road.

Snow obstructed everything, hiding any traces of blacktop or yellow lines. For all she knew, they were driving through a field.

There were tire ruts in the snow, little ridges of treads pressed deep. Somebody had come this way before them.

She wasn't surprised a short ways later when they spotted a truck similar to Massey's on the verge of the road, abandoned. No more tracks were beyond where the vehicle had been left behind.

The truck slowed. Massey leaned forward to look past Sonja. She looked out her window as well. Nobody appeared to be inside the other truck. If they were, they were lying down.

Massey honked the horn, holding it down for a few seconds. When he took his hand away, Sonja's ears were slightly ringing.

Nobody sat up. Nothing stirred in the other truck.

"Well, guess he gave up," said Massey as they trudged by.

"Or he's smarter than us."

Massey huffed a short laugh. "That's probably it."

"I really appreciate your doing this," she said. She looked at Massey. He faced the road, both hands firmly pried to the steering wheel. "Thank you."

"Don't thank me. I feel like an incompetent ass."

Sonja choked on her laugh. "Why do you say that?"

"Well, a sheriff in a real town would have sent out a team to the cabin. But all you get is a dimwitted sheriff and his four-wheel drive." He shrugged. "That's the best I got."

"So this isn't a real town?"

Massey laughed. "We have people living here. Guess that makes it a town."

"Must be something, or they wouldn't have you at all. Right? My cousin lives in a tiny town in Georgia and their police force are volunteers."

"We have tourists that like to act up during the peak months. That's why I'm here."

"Well, if you weren't here at all, I wouldn't have a ride to the Marlowes. So it all works out."

"I suppose you're right."

Sonja recognized the true meaning behind Massey's words, and she could probably accurately define where they thrived from. Somebody in his life had made comments that stung, probably about his job, which had left a complex that probably would never go away. She felt bad for him.

There I go again. Relating. That's what screwed up Dennis. My connecting with him on an emotional level.

Her poor Dennis. All she'd wanted was to help him. Like everybody else, she'd heard about the accident. Who hadn't? If you lived in Leaf Spring, you knew about it. And you knew Grant Marlowe. She'd met Grant at some fundraisers in the past. He was always the life of the party, a drink in his hand and a funny story to tell. Everybody loved him. And everybody went out of their way to help him when it got too real.

And that was what seemed to really bother Dennis—those cliques Grant was associated with. How his family's fates were swept under the rug of Grant Marlowe's reputation. Still, Marlowe didn't walk away from this unscathed, and that was what she'd tried so hard to make Dennis understand. Just like Dennis, Grant had also lost his job. Word going around was that his family life was a total ruin, and now he was no longer invited to those parties he used take over without anybody realizing it. Politicians no longer asked for his endorsements. He was hardly the same guy he used to be, and everybody saw it.

Everybody except for Dennis.

What he'd failed to understand was he was a lot like Grant Marlowe. They shared the same outcome, albeit their variances.

She'd heard stories of people in similar situations as Dennis completely forgiving the responsible person. But Dennis couldn't even consider it. Maybe he could've eventually gotten to the point of no longer blaming him had Grant's punishments been easier to recognize.

I told him all about it. He knew. But in Dennis's eyes, Grant hadn't truly been punished, because he didn't truly understand how much misery he'd caused.

Dennis's thought patterns made a little more sense to her.

Massey said something, but Sonja didn't quite hear it all.

"I'm sorry." Sonja shook her head. Thoughts of Dennis faded like smoke. "What'd you say?"

Massey glanced at her and gave her a pleasant smile that showed he understood. "I asked what kind of guy am I dealing with?"

"Dennis?" Massey nodded. "Not the kind of guy you'd expect."

"That doesn't really tell me anything," Massey said.

"Whatever expectations you're building up, they're probably wrong. He's so sweet and very harmless."

"Not that harmless, obviously. Or you wouldn't be here."

"I know. That's why I can't understand."

"Let me ask you something. And it's personal, so I don't expect you to answer it."

"Okay."

"Did things between you two go further than they should have?"

Sonja sighed. What was the point of keeping it from him? "They did."

Massey nodded. "Thought so." There was no judgmental tone in his voice. "So, you're blind to this."

"Blind? Not hardly."

"Yes you are. And I'm not trying to throw blame. But do you think you might have stopped seeing how messed up he actually was because of other feelings getting in the way?"

"I don't... You can't just..." Sonja shook her head. She made sounds at the back of her throat as she tried to get words to surface. Either they weren't there, or they were too scared to come out.

"I've seen women in abusive relationships make up excuses for why their spouses beat them within inches of their lives," said Massey. "I've seen that a lot. Women in hospital beds with broken arms, legs and even necks, still talk about the guy who put them there like they were God's gift to the world."

"I am not trying to pull wool over your eyes..."

"Didn't say you were. But I'm saying you've come this far, why don't you stop sugarcoating your feelings and *really* tell me what kind of guy he is. That way I know how to address the situation, and hopefully without anybody getting hurt."

Sonja saw Dennis sitting across from her at her the Japanese restaurant, struggling as he tried to hide how much he hated sushi. He ate it, though, and fought the shivers the taste caused him. She saw him on one of their many walks through the park, stopping to feed the ducks. Squatted at the lake shore, the ducks surrounding him, quacking and begging for pinches of bread. She saw the photographs of him with his son, the complete happiness on his face as he held the little boy in his arms. The photos of him with Lindsey had caused subtle twinges of envy at first, but it grew to full-blown jealousy because she couldn't win his complete affection like Lindsey had. She'd wanted it, oh how she'd wanted it, but even then knew he'd never give it to her.

She saw him crying in her office, unable to walk because his strength had left him when he talked about how much he missed his family.

She saw his desperation, the desolation of his spirit as he succumbed to the pain that blackened his heart.

Now she could clearly see the rage inside him that he tried to hold back like a wall of tissue paper in front of a tsunami. She saw the torrents seeping through, turning the paper dark and thin. She saw the soggy paper rip down the middle as the surging waters poured in, covering everything. The tissue paper dissolved in the currents, giving no indication it had ever been there.

"Oh my God..."

Sonja put her finger to her mouth. She could feel her lips trembling against her knuckle. Heat moved up her neck and through her nose. Her eyes turned misty, itching with tears.

Massey was right. She'd made herself blind.

"You all right?" asked Massey.

The truck bounced, rocking Sonja in her seat. The motion made her knuckle shove against her teeth, so she let her hand fall into her lap. It made a soft smack against her jeans. "No, I'm not okay." She took a deep breath. "I guess the Dennis Hinshaw we're going to see is somebody I don't know at all. The illusion I fell in love with died with his family."

Massey didn't respond, so Sonja looked at him. He gave her a quick glance from the corner of his eye. "Then I think we should be prepared for anything," he said.

Nodding, Sonja used a fingertip to wipe her eyes.

CHAPTER TWENTY-FOUR

Dennis had placed the TV back on the stand. Now that it was set up once again, he pushed the power button. Nothing happened. Frowning, Dennis put his hands on his hips. "It's shot."

After Dennis had mercifully resealed Aunt Georgia's body bag and moved it into the other room, he'd dragged Dad back to the family. Kara watched him. Her father hadn't moved since Dennis returned his chair to where it had been. He stared ahead of him, eyes glazed over, as if he was on some kind of medication that had made him loopy.

Kara looked away from him and watched Dennis. He headed to the fireplace, stabbed the knife into the mantel and crouched down.

"Thought it was getting a little nippy in here," he said.

"Dennis?" she said.

Stooping in front of the weakening fire, Dennis tossed a log in. "What?"

"May I please go to the bathroom?"

Bobby groaned. His legs bounced. Obviously, he needed a potty break as well.

Kara's bladder felt near rupturing. It made her lower back and stomach ache.

"Why?" Dennis asked.

"I have to use it."

"Me too," said Bobby.

"Please?" added Kara.

"Sorry, but no." Dennis added what was left of the wood to the fire. Then he used the poker to stir up the flames. He put the poker away, but didn't move. "We're running out of wood. We need to get this show going."

Bobby groaned, then dropped his head. The slice on his face had stopped bleeding. The blood that had spread on his cheek looked tacky. The wound on his head, though it didn't secrete anything fresh, still appeared wet.

Knowing that her only option to pee was doing it in her pants, Kara started to cry. "What do you want with us, Dennis? Really? What do you want?" She hated how pathetic she'd sounded, so whiny.

Dennis didn't answer. His eyes never left the fire.

His silence only egged her on. "Do you want us to die? Do you want us to live? What do you *want*?"

From where she sat, Kara could only see Dennis from the side. He stared at the fire as it began to rise. "I met Lindsey in college. I fell for her hard. It was nothing like I'd ever felt in all my life."

Bobby's legs wouldn't stop bouncing. He looked at Dennis's backside. "I'm sorry about your family, man. I really am. But you have to know doing this isn't going to bring them back."

Dennis acted as if Bobby hadn't spoken. "Her family didn't really like me at first. I'm not sure they ever truly grew to accept me, either. But they acted like they did, after I got my teaching degree. English. Went to college to learn how to write fiction, came out with a teaching degree." He chuckled without humor. "Her parents have a lot of money, and I think even though I had a good job, they could never be content that their daughter married somebody who didn't make as much as them. Did they not think I wanted my children to be able to brag on career day that their father was a writer? I made all the sacrifices a good father should make, and didn't mind doing them. But her parents never seemed satisfied with me. I wanted a great life for us, but what I didn't realize at the time was how great it already was."

Dad blinked a few times, as if waking up. "Dennis..."

Kara could actually see Dad's voice physically altering Dennis. It added strain to his muscles, made his shoulders pull back.

Dad must not have been able to recognize it the way she did. He kept talking. "I know the holidays make the pain worse. It reminds you how different things have become. But Dennis, please listen to me when I say this: I am *very* sorry for what I did. Please believe me. I've lived with it, and the guilt kills me more and more every day. If I could go back in time...if I could take it back, I would."

Dennis stood up, turned around. His wrathful disposition came back as if a switch had been flipped. "You've lived with it every day? Imagine how I've felt. Just think about this a minute. I can never hold Josh on my chest while he takes a nap. He loved falling asleep while listening to my heartbeat. I can't curl up next to my wife or reach over her and place my hand on her stomach to feel our daughter kick. I can't feel her breathing on the back of my neck anymore when we're in bed."

"Neither can I!" Dad took in a deep breath. "Do you think I've been able to do that with *my* family?"

"For a very brief amount of time, I thought you were finally judged. More than once, I was told your time was coming. Well, if *your time* meant putting you all back together so you can eat a ham, open presents and be jolly, then I'm stepping in and changing things."

"We don't have any presents," said Dad. "We don't have a tree..."

"I saw it outside, leaned against the house. The presents are in the back of your Jeep. Saw those too."

"They don't want to be here, Dennis. It was my idea. I made them come here. I trapped them here. Bobby was going to leave. This wasn't going to work out and I was stupid to make them humor me into thinking it would."

"They came because they wanted to," said Dennis. "They knew, same as you, if you got through this Christmas fine, then the new year would be filled with new beginnings. New beginnings that I won't get to have. And neither will you."

Dennis pressed his face close Dad, squishing his nose against Dad's cheek. He jabbed his finger against Dad's chest. "The last memory I have of my wife is a closed casket. The body inside was too chewed up to permit an open lid."

"May I say something?"

Mom's voice.

"We've all been affected by this. All of us were hurt by th—the accident." Mom pursed her lips, exhaling a heavy breath as if trying to keep her composure. "I know you were hurt most of all. But we understand what you're going through. We've all lost somebody close to us, we know how you feel."

"You don't know at all," said Dennis. To Dad, he said, "I watched my wife bleed to death in front of me."

Dad's sobs turned to bawls. Kara hated seeing her father cry. It somehow made him seem less human, weaker, like somebody she didn't know. There was only one other time she'd seen him weep like this, and he didn't know she'd been watching. Last year she'd gotten up in the middle of the night, needing to pee as she needed to now. She'd heard weird noises and tiptoed downstairs to find her father sitting on the couch, crying over an opened photo album. She couldn't see the pictures inside, but it had broken her heart.

"Oh God, Dennis," wept Dad. "I'm so sorry! So sorry! I was dr—"

"Drunk," said Dennis, flat. "You were drunk. Yeah, I know."

With tears trickling down his cheeks, Dennis stood up and walked away.

"Where's he going?" asked Bobby in a harsh whisper.

"I don't know," said Mom, not taking her eyes away from Dad. "Whatever he's doing, I'm sure it's part of his plan."

Dennis grabbed the duffel bag and brought it closer. He dropped it on the floor. The items inside rattled and clinked. In his hand was a bottle of whiskey; the dark fluid looked like cola as it sloshed inside the glass. As he twisted off the cap, he walked over to Dad. The cap landed on the floor and rolled under Bobby's chair. Gripping Dad by the back of his hair, he jerked his head back so his face was pointed at the ceiling. Dad's mouth yawned open, groaning in pain.

"I bet you were wasted," said Dennis, raising the bottle. "On a cloud while my family died all around me. Luckily for you the booze saved you from feeling anything but fantastic. But that's how it's supposed to be, right? I mean, that's what alcohol's for—to escape. So how about it, Grant? Let's escape!"

Dennis upturned the bottle, splashing Dad's face with the murky liquid. The whiskey washed away the coagulated blood, soaked his eyes, sluiced down his face and into his wide-open mouth. Wincing, Dad coughed and spat, trying his best not to swallow any. Kara knew there was no way he could avoid all of it.

"How's that, Grant? Have you forgotten all about what's happening? Did the booze make you forget about watching your sister die, about seeing her in a body bag? Are you at peace? Are you in your happy place?"

While Mom and Bobby screamed at Dennis, Kara only watched her father's face being washed in whiskey. The slit on his eye must feel like it was being bathed in acid, but a part of him must be swimming with joy from the insalubrious reunion. His struggles lessened, the squirming reduced, but his mouth remained wide. His throat worked as the booze went down without choking.

He's drinking it!

And loving it.

Dennis must've noticed the same thing, for he threw the bottle across the room where it exploded against the wall. The impact left a large dark spot that drooled down the paint.

"It's not going to be that easy, Grant. I hope you know that."

Dad gasped as if he'd just come up from under water. Whiskey dribbled down his chin. Eyes closed, he ran his tongue across his lips.

"You're not going to numb yourself to this," Dennis said. Then he turned away and stormed out of the room again.

After a short while, Dad's coughing killed the quiet. He took a few deep breaths before opening his eyes. The right one was slightly pinched, probably the slash preventing him from opening it all the way.

"I'm sorry...I'm so sorry..." Dad sniffed, the corner of his mouth arching. "I got you all into this...I'm so sorry, guys."

"Grant," said Mom. "Don't."

"I'm sorry to all of you, to Dennis, to Lindsey, Josh...I deserve this. I do. Not you. If we would've left...like Bobby said, then we wouldn't have been here."

Bobby frowned. "I shouldn't have said that..."

"But you were right. You were right." Dad was so winded. "Marion, I should've listened to you about the weather, we should've stayed home. But I wanted us to get snowed in, you know. I thought if we were stuck here together, it might force us all to bond again. I'm such an idiot."

Mom jerked forward as if attempting a lunge, making her chair bump on the floor. "Grant, damn it. You need to snap out of *whatever* it is you're letting yourself become. You sound worse than you did a year ago. We all need to be strong. We need *you* to be strong. We're in this together. Doesn't matter how it happened, we're here. All of us. We're a family. And we have to pull together, we have to..."

Mom stopped talking, her eyes rising.

Kara followed the path of her stare, gasping when she saw Dennis entering the room. He held Mom's canner pot in one hand, the other hand behind his back. Everybody stopped talking, stopped moving. They watched him as he walked over to Mom, placing the pot on the floor beside her chair.

"What are you doing?" asked Dad. He still sounded out of breath, and Kara noticed he was shaking because his body craved another drink.

Slowly, Dennis pulled his arm out from behind his back. Something in his hand glimmered. When he turned it to the side, taking the light's glare away, Kara saw the object was a meat cleaver. She recognized it from when Mom had used it to cut a whole chicken. Kara had joked about how she must've stolen it from Jason Voorhees because it was so big.

And now Dennis had it...

Kara felt an icy prickling work up her spine.

"Mrs. Marlowe?" said Dennis.

Kara looked at Mom and saw her eyes widening at the sight of the cleaver.

"No," said Mom, shaking her head. "Dennis. I know what you're thinking…"

He shushed her.

Kara had no idea what he wanted to do. Somehow, Mom did.

"What are you planning?" she heard Dad say. "Whatever it is, please don't do it."

"Stay away from my Mom, you fucker!" Bobby.

Ignoring the pleas and angry demands from the men, Dennis began untying Mom with his free hand. He held the cleaver up by his face in a chopping position as he worked. He freed both her hands, letting the ropes hang to the floor. "Do your feet. And don't even think about running. You won't have a family to try and save if you do."

Mom held her right arm in her left hand, using her thumb to rub it. "I won't run. I promise I won't." She leaned over as if about to put on her shoes and began on the first foot.

"Thank you," said Dennis, calm. "This is hard enough for me."

She finished with the first foot, moved the left. "I know it is, Dennis."

When she was finished with the left, Dennis took her arm and helped her up. Mom's legs folded under her, but Dennis quickly pulled her back up. "Easy," he said. "Let the blood start flowing."

Swaying, Mom looked at Dennis. "You don't have to do this," she said.

"I wish I felt that way," he said.

Kara still couldn't figure it out. What was he going to do?

"Dennis," said Dad.

Mom held her finger up to Dad, silencing him. "Stay out of it, Grant. Nothing can change this."

Dad's mouth moved around sounds that weren't words. Kara could tell he wanted to say plenty, but knew that he wouldn't because Mom told him not to.

"Ready?" Dennis asked.

Mom nodded, sucking on her bottom lip. It was a habit of hers that she always did when in deep thought or prayer. Probably a hefty dose of both caused it now.

By the arm, Dennis guided her to the TV. Then he situated her beside it, so she faced the side of the TV stand.

"Get on your knees," he said without any kind of emotion.

Mom nodded, wincing all the way down.

"Give me your arm," he said.

What he planned to do clicked in Kara's head. "No!" she cried.

"Kara," said Mom.

"Leave her alone," said Kara.

"Stop it!" shouted Mom. "Just stop..." At first Kara thought Mom was yelling at Dennis, but when Mom looked her way, she realized she'd been talking to her. "Stop."

Crying now, Kara nodded.

Mom sucked in a sob, bit down, and obliged to Dennis's order. Dennis, holding her arm by the wrist, guided her arm to the stand. He put her hand flat down.

Tears blighted Kara's vision, so she blinked to clear her eyes. More quickly replaced them.

"Are you sure this is what you want?" asked Mom. "Will this really make it better?"

"It's what must be done. Doesn't mean it's what I want."

"Stop it, Dennis!" Dad shouted. "Don't!"

"What's that saying, Grant? An eye for an eye? Blood for blood?"

Kara tried to spring forward, forgetting the ropes. The chair didn't even scoot a fraction. She could only sit here, trapped and helpless, watching Mom as she stared down at her flat hand, the fingers spread as if making a plaster cast.

"Don't do it!" begged Dad.

Dennis looked down at Mom. "I'm very sorry. I hope you believe me."

"I do." Mom looked up. Her hair fell back, showing her bruised face was no longer contorted with trepidation. She was at peace. "And I forgive you."

Dennis looked as if the strength left his legs. He stumbled forward, arm going slack. The top of the cleaver hit the stand, acting as a brace to hold him up. He looked up at the ceiling. On the verge of tears, he took deep breaths through his nose, releasing them out of his mouth as he groaned.

The groans became growls, as if to work him up.

He raised the meat cleaver.

Dad screamed. Bobby screamed. Kara couldn't make a sound.

Mom lowered her head, closed her eyes.

Dennis slammed the meat cleaver down, chopping off Mom's arm just below the elbow.

Blood showered from the stump, gushing across the TV stand and spilling over the sides.

The room filled with screams, but none louder than Mom's as she stood up. She held her arm under the gory nubbin as blood pumped down, covering her dismembered arm in a sleeve of thick red.

Dennis didn't try stopping Mom when she wobbled away from him. He stood with his head down as if ashamed, remorse evident on his face.

Dad screamed pointless threats at Dennis as Mom staggered toward him, holding her arm as it ejaculated blood. Dad was doused, crimson shooting into his wide-open mouth. Wincing, he turned his head away, shaking it as if someone was trying to make him eat something awful.

Mom turned a circle, hitting Bobby and Kara. As the hot spray silenced Bobby's cries, it jerked Kara's from her throat.

Then Mom's shoulder bumped the wall and knocked her sideways. Her stump dragged across, bone scraping paint away and drenching the wall as her feet tried to walk through the puddles.

As if her legs were yanked out from under her, Mom collapsed on the floor. She landed on her side, her arm pinned under her and pointing out. Other than the squirting blood, she was motionless.

Kara looked away, her eyes landing on the TV stand. The cleaver was imbedded into the wood, and just beyond was a severed arm atop a gloppy blob of blood.

Mom's arm...

Kara passed out.

CHAPTER TWENTY-FIVE

Edgar gripped the steering wheel with both hands as the truck struggled up the driveway. The snow shifted under the tires, pulling the truck this way and that. His knuckles hurt from the fierce hold on the steering wheel. Tightness ran up his arms and into his locked elbows.

"Just a bit further," said Edgar, encouraging his old truck. "Almost there, baby."

Sweat slid down his brow, clinging to his eyebrows. He felt more dripping down his sides, tickling as it went down. He wanted to pluck his shirt away from his skin, but didn't dare take a hand off the steering wheel. Felt as if any jerk might throw him over the edge. He pictured the truck flipping down the ridge, crashing against a tree farther down the side and bursting into flames. It made his stomach pinch and he held his breath.

The tall trees blotted out the sky, throwing down a muffle of shadow. But the ice sheathing the branches somehow twinkled like crystals. A beautiful sight, like an image on a calendar that showed you stunning vistas that could kill you.

A car appeared on the driveway.

Gasping, Edgar pulled his foot away from the gas pedal. He almost stamped the brakes, but stopped himself in time. As the truck slowed down, he stared at the car. It was a small model, but the name was covered in snow, so he didn't know for sure which company had built it. The back window was buried under soft white that piled down onto the trunk. The tires could hardly be seen.

Edgar put the truck in neutral and set the emergency brake. Leaving the truck idling, he shouldered the door and hopped out. His feet sank in the snow, covering him midway up his shin. He looked down the driveway, seeing the grooves in the snow his tires had made. Though they were pretty deep, he still couldn't see the driveway in the trenches. He turned back to the car and that feeling in his gut returned even stronger. It felt as if his insides were being gripped by a frozen hand.

Walking toward the car, Edgar kept checking around him. The woods seemed empty. And silent. He could hear nothing but the chugging of his truck and the soft howls of wind in the distance as it cut through the trees.

"Hello?" he called. His voice sounded flat, dying in the cold air.

He didn't recognize this vehicle. The license plate showed North Carolina, so it wasn't an out of state registration. But it didn't belong to anybody he knew. Was it the prowler's? On his way up to the cabin and the snow just became too much.

Edgar doubted it.

I would've seen the tracks it made in the snow.

No footprints either. No sign that anybody had been out here other than him.

Then he noticed the window was open. Snow clung to the frame. As he closed in on the car, he saw the seatback was sprinkled with white that looked like powdered sugar. A morsel of sharp glass stuck up from the gap where the window should be like a single clear tooth. Beyond the window, dark filled the car.

Edgar stopped walking. The window had been broken. He looked around once more, and again didn't see anybody. Nothing moved. The shadows seemed steeled, like dark curtains between the trees.

He brought his gaze back to the window, took a few more steps closer. Putting a hand on each side of the open space, he lowered his head and peered inside. Glass was all over the floor and on top of the dashboard. It looked almost like ice, but he could see the faint tint of green, so he knew it had come from the window.

Somebody had busted it from the outside, thrown the glass inward.

Damn.

Whoever had been inside was gone. Probably pulled out.

Edgar lifted his head out of the car, then trotted back to his truck. He got in and pulled the door shut. From the coldness outside, the inside of the car felt warm and wonderful. He pointed all the vents to him and sighed.

The windshield began to fog, so he switched the heat over to defrost. As the foggy obstruction cleared, he saw the car again, sitting in the middle of the driveway. Going to the left would surely end with him falling off the side. But there might be enough room to the right. It looked tight, but his truck was narrow, so he could probably pull it off.

He shifted the gear into first, popped the emergency brake, and curled his fingers around the steering wheel. He felt cool dampness soaking into his gloves. Easing his foot onto the gas, he turned the wheel, slowly. Already, the tires felt as if they were starting to spin out. He took his foot off the pedal, angled the wheel to the right, then reapplied the gas. The truck sluggishly moved, bounced a few times before the back wheels started scooting.

Again, he took his foot off the gas. Now he was at a slant behind the car, the front end pointing toward the trees. It should be easier from here on, though he needed to be careful so not to bump any of the trees. Wouldn't take much to get him stuck at this point.

A few minutes later, he had finally maneuvered the truck beside the car. He was about to apply the gas and turn the wheel to the left when he took his foot off the clutch too much, stalling the truck. He did this three more times before he finally got the truck heading in front of the car.

A grinding noise came from his door. He felt the nudges as his truck scraped across the corner of the car, rocking him. Chewing on his tongue, he squinted his eyes and let out a soft groan as he tried to correct himself. It looked as if he was going to come out too close to the other side.

A tree in front of him seemed to grow, filling the windshield as he tried to get the truck straight. He bumped the tree. Glass shattered at the front. The engine stalled again.

There went my headlight.

He was stuck between the car and the tree. Turning around in the seat, he looked out the back window. The car's front wasn't in sight. All he could see was the snow-heavy top.

Edgar faced forward again. The tree blocked his vision of anything else.

He could attempt another back and forth try. It would take some time, but he could probably get the truck right without any other accidents. But time was something he was convinced he didn't have. So he cranked the truck, shifted it to reverse and backed up.

The rear end made crunching sounds as it dug into the car behind him. He felt the truck shifting and held the wheel with all he had to keep it steady. The tree shrank in front of him as the truck pulled away. There was a rubbed spot on the bark where his headlight had smacked it. When it felt he was far enough back, he put the gear back into first and kept his grip firm on the wheel as he started forward.

This time, the front end entered between the trees and he was back on the track. He didn't straighten the wheel until the back of his truck quit scraping the front of the car. When the horrible scratching of metal stopped, he turned the wheel the opposite way. Then he was heading back up. He could faintly smell the sweet odor of antifreeze coming through the vents. Hopefully he hadn't damaged anything under the hood, but it sure smelled like it.

In a few more minutes, he'd be at the Marlowes.

CHAPTER TWENTY-SIX

*T*ink!

Bobby jerked.

Tink!

He looked at the pot, where the hollow drips of his mother's blood were tapping the bottom.

Tink!

Seeing her in this condition was awful, but he couldn't cry. He'd heard people say they were out of tears and he truly believed he just might be. The empty feelings were there, the tightness in his throat and chest and burning itch in the eyes. But there was no salty wetness to accompany them. Maybe he was becoming dehydrated. Maybe he'd pass out and be spared of watching his mother bleed to death. His lower back felt tight and sore, his ass feeling as if it had been slowly rammed into his spine.

Dad gazed woefully at Mom. His skin was white like the belly of a fish. His eyes were darkened circles, swollen from crying and pink where they should be white. He looked dead.

Like Aunt Georgia. Like Mom will be.

Bobby shook his head, trying to jar those thoughts away.

Kara was crying, little sniffles that made her breaths sound jerky. He actually felt bad for his sister. There were times where he referred to her as *Grant's Princess* because she was the obvious favorite. She hated when he called her that. Though she'd never said so, he figured she understood why he did. He'd never been able to win Dad's graces, so he'd stopped trying and began to work as hard as he could to be the exact opposite. He regretted it now, regretted so much more.

And now they were all here together, nothing keeping them apart, but none of them trying to bring an end to it. They still weren't working together as a team to figure out a way to stop it.

It's up to me.

He looked down at his arm. It was so loose already. If he could work at it a little longer, he could get free. What he'd do from there, he had no idea. Saving Mom was his top priority. If she didn't get help soon…

Don't think about that. Focus on getting her out of here.

He needed some kind of a distraction. If he could get Dennis to go away…

That's not going to happen.

Bobby looked over his shoulder. Dennis still sat on the couch. Leaning forward, his elbows were propped on his thighs and his face mashed into his hands. He wasn't going anywhere. He was waiting for Mom to die, to prove his point to Dad.

"Hey."

All heads turned to Mom. She was looking around, her head dipping as she tried to focus on the family.

"Marion?" said Dad in an almost whisper.

Bobby stared at his mother, surprised she was able to communicate at all. She looked so haggard, so white, her skin a faded brown hue like old bananas. Her gaunt eyes had sunken back. The blood was very red on her robe and leg. He kept his eyes diverted from the stump that was tied down, pointing at the pot.

But she was smiling as she looked at them all. "I'm all right. Tired…but I'm all right."

"It's okay," said Dad. "You shouldn't try to talk. You need your rest."

"No," said Mom. "I can't rest." She looked around the room, face wrinkling with confusion. "Where's the tree?"

"The tree?" said Dad.

"Didn't you and Bobby go get a tree?"

Dad almost broke down, but he fought to contain the shudders of his sobs. Kara could not. She turned away from Mom, leaning her mouth onto her shoulder, and cried.

"Yes," said Dad. "We got the tree. We'll decorate it later."

Mom smiled at that. "Good. I'm so glad you and Bobby are getting along. That's what I've wanted...for the two of you to...forgiveness. It's what this family needs."

Bobby felt his chest pinch, making it hard to breathe. "I do, Mom."

Mom's head swung toward him, sinking lower.

"I forgive him," Bobby said.

"Thank you, Bobby." She looked relieved, as if he'd just delivered her wonderful news. "That's go great. I've been so worried about you two. A father and son shouldn't have so much hate...for each other. You should be there. Love each other. The son should carry on with what the father taught him, so he can teach his own son..."

Then she lowered her head and didn't lift it again. At first, Bobby thought she had died. He stared harder and could just barely see her head rising with each slow breath.

His heart ached, feeling as if a hand of spikes was squeezing it. He looked at Dad. His face was a clear, burnished sheen from tears. He caught Bobby's eyes. Neither of them spoke a word, but somehow Bobby knew everything Dad was thinking. And he knew Dad understood his own thoughts.

The sound of the crackling wood filled the room, blending with their quiet sobs.

Then another noise filtered in. It was a hum, a steady acceleration as it grew in volume. Though it sounded muffled, it was close.

Dad's snuffles stopped. His eyes widened. He looked around, first at Bobby. He nodded once, then turned to Kara. She must've heard the sound too. She had also paused her crying, lifted her head. Her nose wrinkled as she listened.

Someone's coming.

A buzz of adrenaline tore through Bobby. It pushed all his remorse aside and made him alert, energized. He tugged at the rope, feeling how loose and limp it was.

Something clattered behind them, making them jump.

Dennis stomped toward Dad. "Who knows you're here?" he asked.

Dad looked puzzled. He shook his head. "Well...I don't know. A lot of people."

"Who are you expecting to come here?"

Sheena?

Bobby knew it couldn't be. He saw her phone burn. And Dennis had said, well, not exactly said, she was gone.

She has to be.

But what if he was wrong?

Don't even think like that. You know it's not her.

Grief wanted to rob him of his freshly developed energy. He couldn't allow that to happen. Later, once he'd gotten his family out of this, he would hole himself up for weeks to mourn. But now he couldn't be bothered with it.

Sorry, Sheena. Forgive me.

He continued working with the rope, slower now that Dennis was so close.

"We're not expecting anyone," said Dad.

Dennis looked frantic, eyes wide with worry and confusion as he ran his hand through his sweat-damp hair. He gripped a handful and held it for a moment. Then he rushed over to his duffel bag of horror and dropped down to his knees. He tore into the bag and pulled out some duct tape. He quickly tore off pieces and moved from person to person, slapping a strip across their mouths. It made it harder for Bobby to breathe since his nose was so stopped up.

Mom was startled awake by Dennis applying the tape. Her weak eyes stared dumbly at him as he smoothed the tape out across her lips. He was much easier with her than anybody else.

Finished, he chucked the tape behind him as he ran to the window. Leaning against the wall, he eased the blinds back. He wouldn't be able to see the driveway from here. Realizing this, Dennis looked as if he was about to snarl. Probably frustration combined with the wondering of who might be here.

Bobby didn't care who it was, so long as they were here to help. He looked at his wrist and started twisting and tugging. When Bobby checked on the window, Dennis was gone. The blinds shook slowly, then went still. He looked around, but couldn't locate Dennis anywhere.

He's gone to see who's here.

And he'd kill whoever it was, Bobby was certain.

He went back to work on the knot with total intensity, knowing if he didn't get his arm free this time, he probably wouldn't have another chance to try.

CHAPTER TWENTY-SEVEN

Edgar parked beside the Jeep. He stayed in the seat, looking past Grant's vehicle at the van on the other side. Like the car, he didn't recognize it, either. Looked like a maintenance van, or something that belonged to a plumber.

The prowler?

That squirming feeling of dread pounded his insides like a triggered alarm. He looked beside him. His rifle leaned against the passenger seat, the stock end on the floorboard. Gripping the barrel with one hand, he opened the door and climbed out. He dragged the gun across the seats, looking around. More frozen quietness, in the distance soft howls of wind that would never reach him. No other sounds could be heard until the crunches his footsteps made when he started walking. Afraid the slightest thump might sound like a grenade blast in the stillness, he left his door open.

He slipped three fingers through the finger lever and his forefinger in front of the trigger. A round was already in the pipe. His thumb hovered over the hammer block a moment before he moved it back. The safety would stay on for now. As jumpy as he already was, he didn't want to risk accidentally shooting one of the Marlowes by mistake. For all he knew, the van might belong to a family member who'd come up for Christmas.

Don't think so.

But he wasn't going to take the chance.

He moved between some evergreens in front of the cabin, his shoulder bumping the sagging branches. Snow sprinkled down, landing inside the collar of his coat and stinging his neck with cold. He flinched, hissing as he made his way through.

"Shit," he muttered.

On the other side of the tree wall, he reached behind his back. He plucked his collar and began to shake his coat. More cold bits dotted down his back and made him shiver. Giving up, he lowered his arms and stood up straight. He held the rifle, barrel pointing out.

Standing at the launch of the stone pathway, the cabin was ahead of him. It looked quiet. And spooky. Sinister. The windows were dark, reflecting the scenery outside. Blinds were drawn or curtains had been shut. He felt as if he was looking at a picture of a haunted house, not something that was real and he could touch.

He didn't want to touch it. Didn't want to go near it.

I have to.

Edgar swallowed. Something was wrong here. The house oozed maliciousness into the air, turning it into something Edgar could feel and smell. Smacking his lips, he tasted the foreboding flavor on his tongue and realized it reeked of gasoline. He focused his ears. He detected the very faint chugging sound of the emergency generator from under the house.

Power's out.

Edgar frowned.

Nothing was right.

Alert, he started forward. His footsteps chomped through the snow until he reached the sidewalk, then they became soft scraping sounds on the stone as he headed for the porch. The snow here was hardened and he could see footprints and a pair of narrow tracks that looked as if something had been dragged. He studied them as he walked—two different pairs, two different sizes. Both adult from the looks of them.

Other than that, they gave him no useful hints as to what had happened here.

Might be nothing.

And it could be something. Something bad.

Quietly, Edgar climbed the old wooden steps to the front porch. The wood popped from the cold as he kept his steps soft, rolling from his heel to the front of his foot.

He reached the front door.

Edgar moved the rifle away from the door and leaned his shoulder against it. He put his ear to the wood, flinching from the shock of cold that zapped into his head. This time he didn't touch the door, bringing his ear as close as he could.

He heard nothing. No groans in the floor of people walking around, no talking or TV. With the generator pumping power into the cabin, he would expect to hear some kind of proof there were people inside.

He sniffed.

Wood smoke.

The fireplace was going. So somebody was inside.

Edgar stepped back and raised his fist to the door. He hesitated. What would Grant's reaction be if he opened the door and saw Edgar out here with a gun? He might shoot Edgar, especially if it turned out that car his truck scraped up belonged to a relative.

His gut seemed to tremble, telling him none of those things would happen.

Edgar's fist pounded the door. The noise echoed around him like cannons. He waited a moment and knocked again. He still heard no sounds from inside that would indicate anybody was home.

"Grant? It's Edgar. You there?"

Nothing.

Dread moved through him, stiffening his muscles. Nothing was right about this. Looking down at the knob, he was tempted to try turning it. If it was unlocked, he'd just poke his head in and call out for Grant. Surely somebody would hear that.

They should've heard the knocking.

His hand was a little sore from how hard he'd banged it against the wood. Maybe they'd missed his shouts, but surely they would've heard the loud pounding.

Edgar tried the knob without giving it another thought. It was locked.

Damn. Damn.

"Damn," he muttered. He took a deep breath, and let it gust out, puffing his cheeks. "Grant!"

Thump!

Edgar jumped. Spinning around, he pointed the rifle toward the yard.

Nobody was there.

Where'd that come from?

Sounded like wood banging wood, a door being slammed or something.

Frowning, Edgar walked to the end of the porch. His midsection bumped the railing. Staring out, he saw the woods on the far side of the yard, the dark streaked in white like cotton. He saw the field leading to it. He turned his head to the left, scanning the side yard.

The shed.

The door was wide open, rocking slightly. He could hear it gently knocking against the wall.

Was that open the whole time?

Edgar tried to recall if it had been open when he got here, but he couldn't think. He hadn't been paying attention.

Something rattled inside the shed. He heard it hit the floor with a tinny bump and make a metallic *whir* as it rolled into view in the doorway. Looked like a can of some kind.

Edgar stumbled back, bringing the gun up. His thumb shoved the safety to the off position. He turned around and hurried across the porch, down the steps and into the yard. He kicked through the snow, throwing up bursts of white. He held the gun tightly, keeping his finger away from the trigger so he wouldn't accidentally fire it.

Arriving at the shed, he slowed down and sidled to where the door was flush against the wall. He tried to see inside the dark shed from this position.

"Who's in there?" he asked.

Silence answered him. The wind blew harder now. He felt the cold seeping through his pants like ice water. He slowly scooted forward, keeping his back against the door. The can was on the dirt, almost touching the snow. He recognized it—an old coffee can that Grant kept fishing weights in. He saw the metal pyramids sprinkled across the floor.

Edgar took another deep breath and stepped to the doorway while bringing the rifle up in one swift motion. He stared into the darkness, giving his eyes time to adjust but looking for any movements. He took a couple steps closer and was surprised to find the shed appeared to be empty of human life. He walked all the way in. Nothing was inside other than the usual items.

"What the hell's going on?" he muttered.

Edgar turned around. His eyes glimpsed cracks of light in the wall. He stared at the dark mass as his eyes concentrated. They began to make out a whitish rectangular shape against the intense shadow around it. It was the side door. It hadn't been shut back all the way.

Somebody had *definitely* been here.

But they're not now.

Frustration mixed with his discomfort. He lowered the gun. Shaking his head, he began to think his gut was just full of shit. It hadn't been that old feeling motivating him to come here, it was gas. A good fart might make him think entirely different.

Drive all the way out here to find an opened shed? Big deal. He was going to be in a lot of trouble with insurance companies for the damage he'd done to his truck and that strange car. Plus the hell he was going to catch from Wanda when he finally got back home. He'd never hear the end of this one and it would be deserved.

Sighing, Edgar started for the door. He planned to go back to the house and knock some more. If nobody answered, maybe he'd go inside one way or another. That way he'd at least know for sure that he was an idiot to risk his life driving over here.

As he was about to step through the doorway, he heard a rushing sound of something cutting through the air. He saw a dark streak swing low at his body. His chest felt the impact like a mule kick, burning hot but quickly turning cold as something shoved its way inside and knocked him back. His arm flew high, finger squeezing the trigger. The rifle bucked and jumped out of his hand. Dust sprinkled down on him as he heard his rifle hit the ground. He nearly tripped over it as he stumbled in reverse.

His mind tried to piece together thoughts, to understand what had just happened. Why did it feel like he had an additional weight on his chest now that seemed to drain his energy in a rapid fashion? It felt like a cold block pushing his ribcage apart.

Looking down at himself, he saw his answer.

The double-edged ax was imbedded in the center of his chest. It looked as if it had veered in at him sideways, like somebody swinging at a baseball. He saw the other blade sticking out, pointing at the doorway to the dark man-shape between the frames, as if to show him who'd just killed him. The blade was turning slick and dusky with blood. *His* blood. It dispensed from the wound in murky waves.

It took great effort to bring his arms up and grab the wooden handle. He didn't have near enough strength to pull the ax out. In his darkening vision, he spotted his rifle on the ground. He started for it, but his legs folded and jerked him down. His knees pounded the dirt. Trying to stand was useless since he could no longer feel his legs. It felt as if his heart used all his efforts to keep beating. He couldn't even bring his hands in front of him to break his fall when he pitched over.

With what little bit of strength he had left, he rolled to his back. His head turned toward the door. The man who'd been standing there was gone now, so he could see outside.

It had started snowing again. Thick white fluffs fluttered down from a darkening sky.

CHAPTER TWENTY-EIGHT

Bobby stopped twirling his wrist when he heard the gunshot. He looked up at Dad and Kara, who watched him with wide eyes. The tape over their mouths had wrinkled, but showed no signs of peeling off. Dad nodded, urging him to keep working at the rope.

Bobby glanced behind him, looking at the hallway. Dennis had rushed that way when they heard the vehicle. Somebody had shown up.

Edgar.

All of them had heard his shouting. The gunshot proved he was here. Maybe he'd shot Dennis. Any moment now they might hear Edgar calling out, telling them the horror was over.

Don't get your hopes up.

No problem there. Bobby doubted any of that was true. But the gunshot had happened, so something was going on out there.

Bobby lifted his arm and shouted into the duct tape over his mouth at how far up he could go. The rope was nearly completely untied from the chair's arm. He looked at Dad again and saw the excitement on his face too. Now Dad nodded frantically, shouting something behind the tape that sounded like *Go!*

And Bobby did. From the combined efforts of his own twisting and Dad's loosening the knot earlier, he almost had his right arm free.

Almost. Just a little more.

The rope slid up the chair's arm, constricting as Bobby pulled, twisted and tugged. It looked as if he might be now working the opposite way, tightening it instead of slackening it.

No!

It was like a damn bread tie, you're turning it one way to open the bag and all of a sudden it starts going taut around the plastic again.

So Bobby worked the other way and it began to relax again.

Dad and Kara grunted and shouted in the background, but Bobby paid them no attention. He focused on the rope, moving his wrist, following the tied pattern.

His hand flew away from the chair's arm so quickly, he accidently socked himself in the chin. With his hand so numb, it felt like somebody else had struck him. Holding his arm out, he stared at it in disbelief. It was free. He checked the chair arm to be sure and all he saw there was the loose rope draping it.

I did it! was what Bobby had tried to say, but the tape stifled it. Reaching up to his mouth, he tried to work his fingers around the tape, but they tingled too much to grip the thin edge. Later. He'd worry about the tape later. He had other things that were more important.

Bobby immediately got to work on his left hand. The rope was thicker and easier to grip with his throbbing hand. It felt as if tiny pebbles were under his skin, making his fingers feel fat and dull.

But he still got the knot untied rather quickly.

Kara whimpered and squealed as Dad grunted like a caveman. Though it was impossible to know what they were saying, he could take a guess it was all positive. They rooted for him as he bent over and began working on his feet.

He wanted to see if Mom was watching him, if maybe seeing his progress had somehow relit the spark inside of her. If she saw how close he was to being free, it might energize her once more.

But he didn't risk it. The last glance he got of her had nearly caused him to give up. She had been so pale she was almost blue. And the bucket no longer made any kind of sounds as it collected her blood because her blood had stopped dripping.

No, he wouldn't look. He'd keep going…

His left foot came free. Raising his leg, it felt as if he had bricks strapped to his ankles. His muscles strained and screamed. His bladder pinched and shot his lower back and abdomen with hot pain. Though it hurt to move, it also felt wonderful as his muscles awakened.

One more foot to go. He started working on it.

Then he paused. He tilted his ear up, listening.

Very faintly he could hear the sounds of hasty footsteps in the snow. He couldn't tell exactly where they were, but they were close enough that his ears registered them. He looked at his father and sister, saw their heads had turned toward the window. Nobody could see outside because of the blinds, so they had no idea where Dennis was.

Oh God…

Bobby picked up the pace. His right arm was almost completely useful, but his left struggled to keep up. He pulled a piece of rope out of the knot, shrinking the nub in size. Somehow, the knot became even tighter. It was too small for him to dig his fingernails into.

Damn it! Come on! Don't do this! I'm so close! Please, God, PLEASE!

It was no good. He didn't have the time to fret with the knot. He needed something thin to slip between the ropes to work the other piece out.

Forget it!

Bobby stood up and his back straightened in a series of pops that made him feel more flexible. Swinging his arms, he worked the muscles around his shoulders. It hurt doing so, but he did a few more quick reps until his muscles started to burn. Then he knocked the chair over, raised his free foot, and brought it down on the leg of the chair. It broke with a sound like a felled tree.

Bobby nearly tripped over the chair as he stumbled sideways, but he got his feet under him and managed to stay up. He checked the rope and saw it hung slack around his ankle. Leaning over, he held the rope and pulled his foot out.

Now he was completely free. Though he heard Dad and Kara cheering behind him, he couldn't celebrate this victory. He turned to his family and gasped behind the tape when he saw his mother. Her head hung forward, hair swathing her face. Her skin was almost the color of pool water.

Bobby went to her on legs that felt weak and wobbly. He dropped down in front of her, trying to speak, but remembered the tape. This time he was able to grip it and tear it from his lips. It burned so much, he wondered if his lips had come off with the tape.

"Muh—Mom?"

Carefully, he started to remove the tape. Her skin stretched, adhering to the sticky side and dropping back down when it tore loose. The backside of the tape was soaked with slobber. His fingertips were wet when he tossed it away.

Though she didn't acknowledge him, he could smell her breaths. Somehow, he could detect the weakness in them, the slow death.

"Mom?"

Dad's groans called his attention. Jerking his head to the left, Dad was signaling for him to come over there.

Bobby moaned as he got up. His body felt the same as on the mornings after a night of partying, still slightly drunk as the hangover tried to take control. He reached Dad and Kara, standing between them. With each hand, he gripped a strip of tape and yanked. Kara gasped and cried out while Dad sucked it in and snarled from the sting. The tape left pale rectangles across their faces.

"Sorry," said Bobby. Shaking his hands, the tape dropped off his fingers and flittered to the floor. He started working at the rope on Dad's hand.

"No," said Dad. "Bobby, don't waste your time."

"It'll only take me a second," he said.

"You're being stupid, Bobby." Kara.

Bobby looked at her, shocked by what she'd said. "You're stupid if you think I'm going leave you here. We can't sit around and wait for him to kill us. Mom needs to get to a hospital. Now."

"Listen to me, son…"

Ignoring his father, Bobby pulled a piece of rope through the knot.

"Bobby," said Dad, raising his voice some.

Now Bobby looked up. "What?"

230

"Just go."

Bobby couldn't believe what he'd heard. "What do you mean…?"

"It's going to take too long to untie us. Get out of here. Leave us here."

"I can't just leave you—"

"Go, now!" said Kara through gritted teeth, supporting their father.

Those tears Bobby thought he'd run out of returned in heavy blotches, turning his vision into smudges. He took his hands away from the rope and rubbed his eyes.

"I love you, son," said Dad. "Go."

Bobby couldn't remember how long it had been since Dad had told him that. It was wonderful to hear, but also seemed to sap the fight out of him and make the tears thicker.

"Dad," Bobby said in a thick and shaky voice. "He'll kill all of you when he sees I'm gone."

"If you don't hurry," Kara said, "he'll kill us all before you even have a chance."

"No," said Bobby. He shook his head. "I'm not leaving you all here to die."

He started working on Dad's knot again, but it was hard because his hands trembled.

"Baby?"

Bobby paused at his mother's frail voice. It was an indistinct ghostly whisper. He looked over his shoulder. Her position hadn't changed and he began to wonder if he'd truly heard her at all.

"Run," her voice shifted in pitch.

"What are you looking at?" asked Kara. "Bobby?"

"Mom?" he said. "This doesn't feel right, leaving you all…"

"Go…"

It was odd hearing her talk but clearly seeing that her body wasn't moving. Not even a twitch. But he obeyed her just the same and stood up.

"You can do it, son," said Dad. "I believe in you. I *love* you."

"I love you, Bobby," said Kara.

He turned to see them. Both heads were pitched back, gazing up at him with wet eyes and worried faces. "I love you, too."

After one last glance at his mother, he started running. He paused briefly at the hallway and looked down. The door was open, but the screen door was shut. He could see snow falling in thick blots outside.

Dennis had gone that way and would come back in from the same direction. Bobby could just grab a fireplace poker, stand off to the side and bash his head when he entered.

He smiled at the idea. It was perfect.

The smile died on his face when Dennis appeared at the door, holding a rifle. He pulled the screen door open and started inside.

Shit!

Bobby hurried away from the hallway and ran on his tiptoes into the kitchen. His legs throbbed with soreness, but he ignored it. He saw the porch through the glass doors and remembered the argument he'd had with Kara. Those cruel remarks he'd said to his parents reverberated through his mind.

I'll make it up to them. I swear.

His coat hung on the rack. There were a line of shoes on the mat. He saw Kara's, Mom's and his own. He hurried to the door, grabbing his coat as he slipped his feet into his shoes. Then he quietly opened the door.

"Things are getting out of hand a lot quicker than I thought." Dennis's voice. "We should start wrapping this up." A pause. "Where is he?"

Dennis's angry shout filled Bobby with coldness. He tensed up and dropped his coat on the porch.

"Run, Bobby!"

Dad's voice was the kick in his ass that he needed. He picked up his coat and ran. He leaped from the porch, his feet hitting the snow and sliding. He quickly twisted to the side to keep from tumbling over.

He started for the cars, shoving his arms into the sleeves of his coat as he ran. Snow smacked his arms and turned clear as it dissolved on his heated skin.

Please let them be all right. Please don't let Dennis hurt them!

"Bobby!"

Dennis's voice sounded deep and possessed with evil as it resonated from not far behind him.

There was a kicking boom behind him. Something whistled past his ear and smashed into the tree to his left. Bark exploded, throwing shards that cut his neck and cheek. Screaming, Bobby ducked, hugged his head. He turned a sharp right and ran in place while his feet fought to find purchase on the snow. A rachety click came from very close, too close. Bobby's shoes caught and he ran.

Bobby headed into the thicket of evergreens as another blast zipped by.

He's shooting at me!

The slice Dennis's knife had made on his cheek awoke in a stinging line as he continued to scream. He burst through to the other side of the thicket, throwing the branches out of his way. Snow hit his face, aggravating his wounds like salt. He saw Dad's Jeep and right away noticed the tires. Though he felt defeat working at him, he fought against it.

He briefly paused, looked each way. A vehicle was on either side of the Jeep. A van and a truck.

Edgar's truck...

He realized Edgar was most likely dead.

"No," he whispered.

Bobby looked behind him. He could see the green bristles shaking, snow falling off and sprinkling down. Dennis was coming.

Poor Edgar.

Bobby screamed again. This time it was directed at Dennis and filled with hate. He turned around and started running.

CHAPTER TWENTY-NINE

Sonja thought the highway had been a rough ride, but now that they were on the back roads she realized how wrong she was. There had been no salt dumped here to keep them somewhat clear and the snow had piled down into a mattress of dangerous beauty.

But it didn't feel like they were driving on a mattress. No, it felt like a waterbed from how much the truck rocked and slid. She'd never been one to get carsick, but she could feel that putrid coffee from the station trying to work its way out of her churning stomach.

"A little bumpy," said Massey. "I know."

"My God..."

She gripped the handle above the window. Friends in high school called it the *Oh-shit-bar*, and now she understood why.

"Sorry we have to go this way," he said. "The power company will have that part of the highway blocked for a long time. We'd be waiting all day."

A colossal tree had collapsed to the road, bringing down power lines with it. The power company and a service crew had gathered on the narrow two-lane highway to fix it.

"Might be safer if we had," she said. "It's still going to take us a long damn time to get out there from here."

"Not too long," he said. "We'll be there before you know it."

"Maybe if I pass out from stress, it'll feel like that."

Massey chuckled. "Maybe you should. Unless you want to drive."

"No!"

Now he laughed. Knowing he was having such a good time ribbing her pissed her off. But she didn't say anything about it. It was his defense system, she knew. She supposed he turned to humor in situations of crisis to make them seem not so threatening. How did he act around victims? Tease their tears by accusing them of being a rainy face?

Sonja couldn't do that. She'd never been able to handle anything bad other than an accurate way. Her mood was always influenced by the situation and usually it passed to frustrated anger.

Maybe that's my defense system. Being a bitch.

And she was being one now.

Sonja's sigh turned into a sour-tasting burp that she muffled by closing her mouth. Slowly she exhaled out the corner of her mouth, away from Massey.

God that smells terrible.

Her stomach gurgled and for a moment she thought she was going to spew.

Not now. Please not now.

The gripping nausea eventually passed, leaving her stomach feeling sore and hollow. She knew the issues weren't completely caused by the trip, but the reason behind it.

Dennis.

What have you done?

She didn't want to know. Hopefully it was nothing. She wanted so much for the snow to have kept him away, but deep down she knew the bad weather had done nothing but keep him there.

Subtly, she leaned toward Massey and checked the instrument panel. She saw the gauges. The speedometer stayed at twenty like a stiff red line. It could have been colored on there with a magic marker. Quietly sighing, Sonja leaned back in her seat, holding her hand over her stomach. It was taking forever to get to the cabin. She understood that any other means of transportation was limited. Especially since they had no idea for sure something was amiss. She was grateful Massey had taken the initiative upon himself to drive them there. She just wished they would go a little faster.

The CB radio crackling made her jump. She let out a soft squeal and felt embarrassed. Raising her hand to her eyes, she dug her fingers in and rubbed. They were painful to the touch, so exhausted they ached.

"Sheriff? You riding around out there somewhere?" The voice was female and very Southern. Cute in a backwoods kind of way.

Massey didn't respond. There was no noise to indicate he'd even reached over and grabbed the mouthpiece.

Another cackle, followed by a shriek of static. "I know your vacation's started, but Deputy Holden is trying to get ahold of you. Said he tried your cell, but it must be shut off or you don't have a signal. It's not urgent, but he had some questions…"

Vacation?

Odd. Hadn't he said earlier that he was going to be working all day?

Slowly, Sonja lifted her face from her fingers. She peered over at Massey from over her hand.

Another fizz of static. "Did you get that woman with the car in the ditch taken care of?"

Sonja studied Massey. The color drained from his face. His mouth was a frowning tight line. He gave her a sympathetic glance, then reached for the mouthpiece. He brought it to his mouth.

"Hey, Shirley. I'm still out in this mess. Making my way home."

"There you are, Papa Bear." She laughed. "Everything handled?"

"Getting there," he said. "Tell Holden I'll call him later if it's not urgent."

Shirley laughed again. "It's not. I'll let him know. Have a good Christmas, if I don't talk to you before then."

"You too."

"Enjoy your week off. I envy you."

Massey laughed. Though it probably fooled Shirley, Sonja knew it was forced.

"I will," he said. "Merry Christmas."

He put the mouthpiece back on the clip.

"Merry Chris—" Shirley started to say but it was cut short when Massey turned off the radio.

Massey sat back in the seat. He sighed. His eyes looked grim. Sonja waited for his explanation. He stayed quiet. What was this girl-in-a-ditch business? Vacation? Why would he lie to her? Why would he lie to Shirley? Everything suddenly seemed out of place. As if she was in somebody else's life and was trying to make sense of it.

She felt her eyes being pulled toward the radio. He'd shut it off.

So he wouldn't be bothered?

Don't think so.

So she couldn't grab it and scream for help into the microphone?

Oh God…

Everything made sense so suddenly she felt dizzy. No wonder he'd brought her into his office. No wonder she'd gotten weird looks from people as she'd walked back there. They were wondering why she was being escorted by the sheriff to his office. He'd asked for people to check on things, but they couldn't have known for what reasons. He'd kept her hidden from them, for the most part. And if anybody asked, she was a woman he was kindly helping get her car out of the ditch.

Why? What's he trying to pull?

Massey could have read her mind. "I could try to convince you that whatever you're thinking is wrong."

Sonja wished he would try. Anything other than what she assumed was the truth would be wonderful.

"But what's the point?" he asked. "Later, you'd just put pieces together. Might ask too many questions to the wrong people and bring a heaping of shit down on my neck."

"I'm the woman who's stuck in a ditch?" Sonja asked in a trembling voice.

Wincing, Massey shrugged. "I didn't want it to happen this way." He shook his head. "Damn Shirley's loud mouth. I guess I should've cut the radio off before we left, but I didn't want you to suspect anything."

"Suspect—what the hell are you talking about?"

"Reelection's coming up, and it's expensive funding for a campaign." He shrugged. "I just took a little to look the other way. Promised not *pay attention* to what was happening at the Marlowes, until it was over. It was enough to fund the campaign and a little extra. I did it because I work *so* damn hard and don't have the paycheck to show for it." He looked at Sonja. "You understand, right?"

"Who did this? Dennis? He *paid* you?"

"Said he'd be finished by tonight. I figured I would take the long way out there, driving around with you to stall time. I don't think he counted on your showing up. I was surely surprised myself, so I improvised, thinking by the time we got there, he'd be long gone. And if he wasn't, I'd just put a bullet in him and call it over."

Sonja's dizziness turned to a floating sensation. She could hardly feel the seat underneath her. Her stomach no longer cramped and now felt as if it was swelling with cold. She couldn't fathom what Massey was saying. Dennis had thought enough ahead to ensure the police were handled. And not just any bum cop, the *sheriff.* How could he have known Massey would take the bribe?

He researched it. Just like he'd researched everything else.

She remembered the wall of tacked maps and photos. There was a map of Bear Creek, a small speck on it that had been circled half a dozen times in heavy black marker. Surely that was the cabin. He'd known he might raise suspicion snooping around, so he'd made sure he had somebody to divert it.

Until I messed it up.

"That guy," said Massey, shaking his head. "He really thought of everything. I mean, he had his plan so thought out, covered it *all*." He gave Sonja a glance. "But I don't think he considered for a minute that *you'd* head out here. At least not today."

Sonja stared at him, unable to speak.

Massey shook his head once again. She saw his leg move and felt the truck begin to slow down. She faced forward, looking through the windshield. Snow spattered against the glass in powdery bursts, only to be knocked away by the wipers. They were on a narrow road that curved ahead and vanished around a protruding section of rocky crest. The stone formation reminded her of a giant snake's head poking out from the mountain. The truck's front end moved to the right, onto a flat of white path that led behind the rock. The snow-heavy road vanished from her view, replaced by white caps of rock and gaunt icy trees.

He's stopping.

Massey downshifted, then wiggled the stick back and forth for neutral. The engine's rumble dropped and steadied. Her heart began to pound, punching her ribcage with pain. Looking around, she saw no markers to indicate where they might be. All of this was unfamiliar to her.

"What are you doing?" she heard herself say. She couldn't believe how pitiful she'd sounded. Sonja had worked all her life to not lapse into that kind of pathetic blubbering. How quickly things had changed. When she felt tears saturating her eyes, she really despised herself.

Don't do this! You can't let him…

Kill her. He was going to kill her.

Oh, God. Please no. I don't want to die.

Sonja took a deep breath and swallowed down the panic. It dropped to her gut inside a painful bubble.

Massey looked pained, as if he was about to deliver awful news. Sonja figured the face was an accurate depiction to what he had to say. "That damn Shirley," he said again. "I really don't want to do this."

"Do what?"

Her arm slowly moved to the door, fingers brushed the paneling.

He huffed through his nose, shoulders lifting and drooping. "We both know what."

"No!" shrieked Sonja. Her hand gripped the handle and jerked it back. She slammed her shoulder against the door, expecting it fling open. It didn't. The door remained shut. She let out another "No!" and yanked the handle repeatedly.

The door didn't budge.

"Enough of that!" Massey's deep voice boomed in the confined space.

Sonja froze. Her fingers remained curled around the narrow handle. It was in the open position, but the door was still closed. She looked over her shoulder. Massey had brandished his handgun and was pointing it at her. The barrel looked very large and had a dark hole the size of a pecan at the tip.

She felt herself shrink inside. "Please..."

Stop begging!

"I'm sorry, Ms. Dumont. There's no other way."

Her body trembled and it took a lot of effort to make it stop. "I don't want to die..."

"I don't want *anyone* to die, but I'm out of options. Shirley..." He shook his head again. "She might have to be let go after the holidays. She's the kind of person who always has to have her nose in everybody's business."

He's really going to kill me. I'm about to die.

Sonja couldn't believe it. All her hard work would be for naught. The struggles she'd had during her teenage years, finding herself once she went to college and graduating as a new person—all of it wasted.

A slideshow of her childhood ran through her mind in rapid fire.

"I'm going to need you to hand over your cell phone," he said.

"My...? What?" She couldn't recall what such a device was or if she even had one.

"Just give me your whole damn bag."

Sonja looked down at her feet. Her purse was on the floorboard between them. As if in a trance, she reached down and grabbed the handle. Lifting the bag, she was tempted to swing it at the dopey sheriff. But she knew it would be a wasted effort. She didn't have the space to make a sufficient swing. She'd probably even miss entirely.

Reluctantly, Sonja handed the bag over.

Holding her purse in one hand, Massey gave the gun a few quick jerks to usher her along. "Go."

"Where?"

"Get out."

"The door..." She pulled on the handle again. Nothing happened. "It's broken."

Massey frowned. "It's not broken, it's locked."

"What?"

"The door's locked. You locked it yourself when you got in."

Locked?

Sonja twisted her head. The lock tab was down. In her car, the doors automatically unlocked when somebody pulled the handle. Being an older model, this truck didn't have that feature. She saw her hand reaching for the tab, fingers pinching the top. She pulled up. There was a click and when she tried the handle this time, the door popped open. The wind whistled as it squeezed cold air through the small gap.

She looked back at Massey. He was still frowning.

"Let's get this over with," he said.

CHAPTER THIRTY

Bobby, keeping low, ran around to the passenger side of the van. His original idea had been to wait for Dennis to come through the trees and ambush him from behind. But he had no weapon and he also couldn't be sure which section of evergreen he'd emerge from. With there being a row of them in the front, Dennis had many places to cross through. So Bobby scratched that idea.

The next idea was to run and hide. That was nixed because his footprints would lead Dennis straight to him.

Now the plan had altered into one of desperation. He was going to find a weapon and fight the crazed man.

A quick check inside Edgar's truck came up with nothing. Though he knew his dad wouldn't have anything in the Jeep, he'd done a rushed search inside. Other than an ice scraper for the windshield, he turned up nothing.

Now he was approaching the sliding door to the van. Dennis was close enough to hear his footsteps squelching through the snow. He'd be here in mere moments.

This is a waste of time! Just run!

Though his instincts screamed to haul ass away from here, his mind forced him to stay. Besides, if he managed to leave Dennis behind, he'd only return to the house and kill his family. Bobby needed to kill him. It was the only way he knew for sure to bring this madness to an end.

He put his hand on the sliding door and pulled the handle. Surprised it was unlocked, he threw it wide.

A body tilted out. The seatbelt snagged it, catching it from falling out. Long dark hair flapped around a withered face. The dehydrated skin was the color of driftwood and crinkled around the mouth to show teeth between the gnarly lips. The eyes were thin lines that looked as if they'd been scribbled onto flat sections. Pruned lumpy hands were crossed over the breasts, flat on each one. It wore a nice dress that had faded and turned splotchy with stains.

Bobby jumped back, screaming as the body seemed to shift in the seat to look at him. He knew it was really just the wind making it twitch, but at the moment that didn't matter. He was looking at a dead body, a rotted corpse that has been dead for a very long time.

In his frantic vision, his eyes scanned the cargo area of the van. Two dark shapes behind the body caught his eye. He saw the booster seat, another safety harness draped across it. The form behind the strap was motionless, stiff like a doll as if posed by human hands. A baby carrier beside it faced the back of the van. He glimpsed a bunched blanket, pink and fluffy. The light that spilled inside showed him just enough for him to gather the skin on the small bodies matched the woman hanging partway out of the van.

She stared at him through the tight empty slits that used to be her eyes.

Bobby screamed. Shaking his head, he staggered back. The snow shifted under his feet, almost yanking them out from under him. He hardly noticed. Nothing could divert his mind from the sight before him.

It's his family! Jesus Christ! Shit! His dead family!

Bobby's mind tried to wrap around this gruesome reveal and instead crumbled like a poorly constructed foundation. He noticed Dennis appear at the back of the van, glance inside and turn to face him. Dennis readjusted the woman in her seat, pulling on the harness to tighten it. Then he threw the door shut. It rolled across the track and boomed when it closed, once again hiding it from Bobby.

But Bobby knew the image would never leave. He'd be haunted by this forever.

Dennis turned, raising the rifle. He put the stock against his shoulder as Bobby only stood there, trying to catch his breath. His throat made sharp squealing sounds with each inhale.

"I'm sorry, Bobby," said Dennis. "But it's over."

Bobby realized he was about to be shot. Death was imminent. It still couldn't move him. The horrible discovery had caused his legs to become useless.

Dennis stared down the barrel, jacking the lever. Bobby flinched at the clacking noise, but remained where he was.

"Please forgive me," muttered Dennis to either Bobby or God.

Then he pulled the trigger.

Click!

Bobby stumbled back, yelling as if a cannon had been fired. He looked down at himself, still shouting, patting his chest. He found no wounds, no bullet holes. Looking at Dennis, he saw him pulling the lever down and snapping it back. He quickly pulled the trigger.

Click!

Bobby nearly squealed. The gun was either out of bullets or it had jammed.

"Shit!" Dennis threw the rifle down. He reached behind his back and came back with the large knife. The same one that had left the soon-to-be scar on Bobby's cheek. "Come here!" Hands held out, knife up, he charged Bobby.

And it snapped Bobby out of the stupor that had been gripping him. He shook his head, turned, and started running. He quickly realized he was heading for the woods when he knew he should be going to the driveway, making his way down to the road.

It didn't matter. Bobby was just grateful to be moving again.

He ran into the woods and was enveloped by shadows that seemed to choke the light and absorb the sound. His foot falls sounded hollow and far away. Branches whipped him. Though his coat was heavy, he still felt their stinging lines across his body. Snow smacked his face. He leaped over tree stumps, jutting roots. His foot came down in a hole, vanishing in the snow momentarily before he snatched it back out. Thankfully he didn't crack his ankle.

He saw a tall tree ahead with a thick trunk and ran around to the other side. Putting his back flat against it, he stood there, trying to catch his breath. Everything around him was spinning. He could feel his body trying to shut down. He'd gone all day without food, water, sleep. He ached all over, his head throbbed. And he still needed to pee.

After a few more quick breaths, Bobby leaned up and peered around the tree. All this time he'd been going downhill and hadn't realized it. He closed his mouth and breathed in through his nose, trying to get control of himself once again. He breathed out through his mouth. Again and again, he did this until his heartbeat was steady. Though it still drummed, it no longer seemed about to burst.

Get moving!

Bobby nodded to his thoughts.

And ran.

Now that he knew he was going downhill, the trek seemed harder. Slower. He slipped and bashed his ass against the earth two times before the ground began to level out. His foot came down on a loose patch of soil and snow and he was jerked down once again. This fall was the worst yet, jarring his spine and clacking his teeth together.

He began to cry as if he was a child and had just fallen off his bike. He looked up. The trees above him seemed to reach over, connecting into a network of thin branches. It kept a lot of the snow out, but left just enough to make the ground slick and insuperable.

As much as he wanted to stay here and wallow in his pain and misery, he couldn't. He had to get back up, had to keep moving. Not just for his safety, but his family's.

He saw his mother, tied to the chair, head canted far to the side.

She needs me.

Groaning, Bobby put his hands on the frozen ground and shoved. He shuffled to his feet, swaying as he looked around. Now his hands throbbed not just from pain but from the cold snow clinging to them. He wiped his hands on his pants, then started moving again.

The second wind that had powered him to dash frantically down the hill was gone. Now he ambled along the trees. Bit by bit, the spaces between them grew, spreading and thinning out. He left them behind and stepped onto a small path that ended before a large field. It looked barren, as if it had been many years since anybody had set foot in it. Brown weeds protruded from the tarn of white like stiff hairs.

Bobby walked along the path, pausing at an old, rusting barbwire fence that ran in two lines vertical to the field. The wire sagged at the post, nearly touching the ground. Carefully, he stepped across the wire, making sure he didn't catch his leg on a barb as he entered the field.

Just as Bobby cleared the fence he was hit from behind.

Bobby crashed into the snow. His chin dug into the ground as he was crushed underneath something heavy. He heard ragged breathing and felt a hand trying to grab him.

Flat on the ground, Bobby managed to swing an elbow back. He felt it hit softer flesh, heard somebody grunt. The burden fell away from his back. Getting on all fours, Bobby turned and glimpsed Dennis sitting in the snow behind him. His legs were spread straight out as he patted around the ground. When his hand rose, it held the knife. The blade twinkled in the gray light. Glops of snow stuck to it.

Bobby turned away. He started to stand. Dennis's legs snapped together around Bobby's ankles and twisted, throwing Bobby back. His rump pounded the ground, pushing into his spine again. His back tingled with a prickling current that spread in the shape of a leaf.

He tried to sit up. Dennis's legs closed around his waist. He punched them, clobbered Dennis's thighs, but through his tingling arms, he could have been patting them. His coat was tugged back, pulling Bobby with it. As if Dennis was trying to show Bobby how to swing a golf club, he reached down Bobby's front. The hand coming down clutched the knife, the tip heading from Bobby's stomach.

"No!" Bobby yelled.

He brought his arm up to block the knife's plunge.

And missed.

The knife punched into his stomach, sinking to the hilt. Bobby felt the blade moving around inside him, slicing things as Dennis twisted his wrist. Bobby arched in pain, pushing his back against Dennis. His arms flapped, swung behind him. They made soft smacks when they struck Dennis.

There was a wet tearing sound and Bobby felt his stomach being split. The strength in his arms flowed out. They dropped at his sides. The snow was cold, but felt a tad soothing on his skin.

"I'm sorry, Bobby." Dennis whispered into his ear. "I truly am sorry."

The knife continued to climb. The pain lessened as if a numbing blanket was pulled over Bobby's body. Things around him began to darken.

Bobby's head felt heavy and swiveled on his neck. He glimpsed his stomach, his intestines curling out like balloons being inflated.

Though it sounded very far away, Bobby could hear Dennis crying. Warm tears dripped down the nape of his neck. Like a dream, nothing seemed logical. But he understood everything and knew without having to ask that he was dying.

I'm really dying.

And he felt no fear, no pain. Just exhaustion.

When Bobby looked up, he spotted somebody across the field—a woman with gorgeous flowing yellow hair that stabbed lustrous blades through the darkness all around him. She waved, then turned her hand and began motioning for him to come to her.

Bobby felt himself going, though he knew he wasn't walking.

When he got closer, he saw the woman was his mother.

She was no longer tied to the chair and had both her arms again. They felt cozy and soothing as they hugged around him. His body filled with warmth in her caring embrace.

CHAPTER THIRTY-ONE

Nearing another thicket of trees, Sonja slowed down. The barrel of Massey's hand cannon jabbed her in the back. "Ow," she said.

"Quit stopping."

"I'm not."

Though Massey didn't argue with her, she knew he was right. She had been stopping, coming up with any reason possible to prolong this.

Her *death*.

Again, the thought of her demise made her legs go weak. They trembled as she started walking again.

"Please don't do this," said Sonja.

"Ms. Dumont, do you really expect me to think you'll just drive back to your home and forget about everything if I let you go?"

Sonja said nothing. There was no way she could do that and Massey knew it. It was pointless to lie. He wouldn't believe it.

"That's what I thought," he said.

"But they'll trace the bullet back to your gun."

"No they won't."

"How can you say that?"

"Because I'll be heading up the investigation. This isn't the movies, honey. We're a small town. We don't have fancy-dressed detectives in the department. Sure, they can be *brought* in, I suppose—if you were somebody important. But you're not. Plus, after the business at the Marlowes is finished, I'll just make sure you get swept under the rug with everybody else. No problems."

Sonja sucked in a quivery breath. Cold air went into her lungs and made her chest feel tight, as if she'd just left the gym. Her muscles ached all over and the pain seemed to worsen the more she walked.

Trees shaded the ground, but she could see fine from the glare of the snow. To her right were some small oval-shaped prints that she thought probably belonged to a deer. The woods were filled with the crunches of their footsteps and the quiet ticking of branches being strained by the snow's added burden. A white mass dropped down and splattered on the ground ahead of her. It was a small mound on the flat smooth surface of the ground, powdery like chalk.

"This should do it," he said.

"Don't. You can handle this in a different way." Her voice rose. Tears flooded her eyes.

"Hush it. No, I can't." He sighed behind her. "Get down on your knees."

"Oh God…"

He's really going to do it. He's not just going to kill me, he's executing me!

"Please, Massey—Sheriff. Don't *do* this!"

"Get down!"

Massey's order ricocheted off the icy trees around her. There was no echo, just an amplifying effect that made the voice loud *inside* her head.

"Okay, okay…"

Nodding, Sonja got down on one knee. Cold soaked through her pants, shocking her joint. She winced and brought the other knee down. It wasn't so bad this time, but still sent Arctic prods through her legs. She leaned forward, placing her hands on the ground to brace herself. They sunk into the softness, bringing her closer to the forest floor. The snow felt cold and wet on her palms.

"Sit up straight," he said.

Sonja squeaked low in her throat as she leaned back. He was going to shoot her from behind. Couldn't even look her in the eye when he did it. She was kind of glad it would happen this way. She wouldn't have to see the huge barrel in her face, wouldn't know when it was coming.

But the not knowing also made it worse. What did he plan to do with her body afterward? Just leave it out here?

Probably.

He'd come back and get it later, or "discover" it after the Marlowes' investigation had begun.

Sonja's hands throbbed as if she'd let them soak in a bucket of ice water. Looking down, she saw her skin had turned pink. At least she wouldn't have to worry about frostbite.

Something like a lame attempt of a smile tugged the corner of her mouth, which brought more tears. She tilted her head, using a frozen finger to wipe her tears. It felt like an ice cube was pressed to her eye. Done with that, she let her hands drop onto her legs.

And saw the tiny mound of snow that had fallen earlier.

She knew it was just a minute ago, but it felt like an hour had passed since then.

For some reason, she kept looking at the snow. It seemed to be telling her something that she couldn't understand. Just like trying to communicate with her cousin's daughter. Being two years old, she couldn't say a whole lot, but she could get her point across without words.

I'll never see her again...

The hammer cocked on the gun, a loud grating click in the stillness that made Sonja jump. Her breaths intensified, her heart sledged. The air made high-pitched wheezing sounds as she sucked it in.

Now the snowy knoll seemed to be screaming, grabbing her by the shoulders and shaking her. She just wasn't listening, wasn't understanding. It was so simple if she'd stop dwelling on her imminent death and *grasp* what was right in front of her.

Grasp!

Sonja understood. Her eyes widened. The rapid breaths snagged in her throat.

"I want to say a prayer," said Massey. "Do you mind?"

Sonja slowly shook her head, gazing at the hump of snow with round eyes. The cold weather dried them out, made her want to blink. She didn't. She worried if she took her eyes off the snow, it would somehow vanish.

"Heavenly Father, please be with Sonja in this moment."

Oh, I think He is. He has to be!

Who else would have showed her this plan that was quickly forming in her mind without any design of her own?

"She is innocent in this situation, Father. You know this. I am not. I pray for your forgiveness for what I'm about to do. It's not right—I know this. But I don't know what else to do. I let the enemy trick me into his plan, not yours. Please guide me out of this and please guide Sonja to the other side. Forgive her for all her sins, and send your son to embrace her at the gates of Heaven. I pray you let her in."

Sonja's hand slid across the slow, making its way to the white hump.

"Again, Father, I ask for your forgiveness."

"Amen..." muttered Sonja.

"I pray in your son's name. Amen."

She heard Massey huff out a breath of air as if he was nervous. Her hand closed around the hill of snow. It formed into a perfect ball in her clenched fist.

Then she dropped sideways, spinning on her knees. She heard Massey cry out in surprise. Sonja brought her arm around, extended, her fingers opening around the snow. The compacted ball flew from her hand.

And smacked Massey's face.

It burst into a cloud of white that covered his eyes and nose. He let out an "Ah!" as he stumbled back a couple steps. "Damn it!" With his empty hand, he dug at the snow in his eyes. "Son of a bitch!"

With his eyes temporarily blinded, she crawled to his legs, throwing snow all around her. She got back on her knees, hooked her fingers in his pockets and jerked down. His pants shot down his legs, stopping just below his knees.

"What the hell?" screamed Massey. "You bitch!"

His legs were nearly as white as the snow, peppered in black hairs. She saw freckles and moles spread across his pasty skin.

Sonja quickly scrambled back, putting distance between her and Massey. With his eyes closed and pants down, he raised the gun and swept it from side to side as if trying to decide where to shoot first.

Sonja froze. She closed her mouth and controlled her breaths through her nose. If she made any noise, he'd fire countless rounds in that direction.

Giving up, Massey lowered the gun. With his other hand, he reached down for his pants. His fingers pawed at his legs, trying to find the top. "Shit!" He reached up to his eyes, rubbed, and made another grab for his pants. "Shit-shit-shit!"

Sonja snickered.

And cringed when Massey jerked his arm in her direction.

No!

She quickly padded out another snowball and threw it. This one pegged him in the crotch in a rupture of white. Massey's mouth shot open into an O shape. Flakes of snow sprinkled down his thighs.

The gun fired.

It sounded like an explosion as the retort bounced off the trees around her. Sparks showered from the barrel. The ground in front of her knees blew apart, throwing snow and sharp bits against her face.

The buck of the blast threw Massey's arm high. He shouted another expletive at Sonja as he stumbled in reverse. His feet shot out from under him and went in the air. He came down hard on his back, let out a groan, and went silent.

Sonja quickly wiped her face, then clumsily got to her feet. She walked slow and stilted over to Massey. Her sense of alert was up and she waited for anything to happen. As she neared Massey's supine form, she began to make out soft choking sounds.

She frowned.

Her eyes scanned up his body. Starting with the knobs of pale knees, they moved up his plain white briefs that were now soaked in yellow.

Pissed his pants...

She should find that funny, but she didn't.

Her eyes moved to his chest. She saw his uniform shirt between his open coat. The front was dark with fresh stains. Her eyes moved slightly higher.

A jagged tip jutted through his throat. It stuck out from under his chin, slick with crimson.

A branch?

Looked like it. When he fell, he must have landed on it.

My God...

It had gone all the way through. And he was slowly choking on it as he studied her with unblinking round eyes. He looked almost confused, as if he wasn't sure what had happened.

Sonja didn't feel glorious in her victory as she watched him suffer. She felt awful. As if she'd been the one to drive him out here to die.

He was going to kill me.

Still, she shouldn't have...she could've...

Could've what?

No alternative plans came to mind. And it wasn't like she'd thrown him onto the branch. He'd just fallen in the wrong spot.

Yeah, that's going to help me sleep at night.

It was sad to think so, but she figured it would ease some of the guilt. It was his fault, not hers.

His arm suddenly appeared, the gun aimed at her. For a brief moment, Sonja felt terrified. It quickly passed. She snatched the gun out of his hand, and stared down at him, contemplating putting a bullet in him so his misery would end.

Sonja aimed the gun at his head.

His breaths sounded like whistles as they sped up, obviously thinking she was going to shoot him.

She couldn't make herself do it.

"Sorry, Massey," she said.

Then she started back for the truck as snow continued to fall down from the sky.

CHAPTER THIRTY-TWO

Kara jerked awake and at first she thought it had been an awful nightmare. But as she became more alert, she realized how wrong she was. She was still bound to the chair, her bladder full, and the muscles in her neck felt stiff and tight. Turning her head was unbearable, causing her to grit her teeth and huff through them.

Mom looked the same. Her body in the same leaning position in the chair. The remnant of her arm was still tied, angled down. Blood no longer sluiced from the wound, not even a drip. Her skin was the color of bruised fruit.

Kara felt herself sink inside, as if a cork was pulled and drained what remained of her essence into a black hole. Tears wetted her dry, crackly eyes, washing away the sleepy crumbs.

Mom was dead.

Aunt Georgia was dead.

And…

Kara gulped, fighting back another body-racking sob fit.

Bobby was dead.

Dad and Kara had been waiting on Bobby to come back, both knowing in their heart that he would return with help. This horrendous ordeal was going to be put to an end. Mom would be swept away to a hospital where she could be treated. It would be rocky at first, Kara knew, but eventually she'd overcome her injuries. The arm couldn't be saved, but it was a small price to pay if it meant her mother being alive to see her get married.

To keep her eyes off Mom, and Dad's thoughts away from his heroic son and his bleeding-to-death wife, Kara had started talking. Just casual comments at first, anything to distract them both, but it eventually led to more personal topics when silence returned.

"Dad?"

He'd already started looking at Mom again, his face crumpling. When Kara spoke this time, it went away, and he somewhat looked like himself. He turned to her and smiled. "Yeah?"

She hadn't wanted to ask this question at all, even if their situation were different. But if there was a chance they never made it out of here alive, she *had* to know. "Were you and Mom going to get back together?"

"Oh, honey, don't..."

"I mean, *really* get back together? Not the roommates business you've been doing, barely acknowledging each other in the house. Were you going to be a husband and wife again?"

"Honestly?"

She nodded. "I have to know, just in case we don't..."

"Bobby will be back soon."

"The gunshots we heard could mean—"

"It's been too long since we heard them last. Bobby couldn't have been shot. He's fine."

"Please, Dad." Dad stopped trying to avoid the subject with reassurance of her brother's safety. He stared at her, his eyes glowing dimly from the dwindling fire in the fireplace. A strong odor of wood smoke filled the room. "Just in case."

Dad nodded. He opened his mouth. She heard him take a breath in before answering.

Then the side door banged open, making them jump. They heard the screen smack the house, heard the tittering howls of the wind coming up the hall. Footsteps pounded the floor on the way to the living room.

Kara held her breath, knowing it was Bobby. He hadn't brought help, but had somehow managed to subdue Dennis, maybe even kill him. She felt no regret for hoping for the latter.

But it wasn't Bobby who'd entered the room. It was Dennis.

His clothes were dark and wet. Snow had sprinkled all over him, attached to his hair. His eyebrows were light with frost and his skin had turned pale. He was winded, shoulders bobbing as he stared from Dad to Kara.

Dad's mouth trembled. "Dennis..." Dennis looked at Dad. "Did Bobby...?"

The rest of the question faded in the air, but Kara heard it in her mind.

Did Bobby make it?

Dennis slowly shook his head, telling them that he had not. He was dead. The blood covering Dennis was her brother's.

Kara could vaguely remember shrieking as Dad screamed Bobby's name. She'd passed out shortly after, for the second time today.

She had no clue how long she'd been out. No idea what time it was. It seemed darker inside, though the fire still crackled and popped, the flames higher than they had been earlier. She saw chair legs had been stacked inside, the fire's hot tongues licking black across them.

She looked at Dad. The only indicator that he was awake was his eyes. Open and dull, they stared ahead at the empty space where Bobby's chair had been. Its remains were what now burned in the fire.

"I've been fighting with myself for a long time, Grant."

Dennis's robotic voice carried across the room. Kara turned toward the couch. Nobody sat on it. The recliner, which usually was beside the couch, had been turned away from her, the front facing the fire. She figured Dennis was in it. How long had he been talking? Probably hadn't stopped since he'd come back.

"I almost killed myself so many times. Put the gun in my mouth. The oil left a sour flavor that I could taste for days, no matter how much I brushed my teeth or rinsed with mouthwash. When it would finally go away, the urges would come back. So in the gun went again, and I just sat there. It never felt right, you know? No matter how badly I wanted to die, I couldn't do it. I wanted to, though. To die? Just couldn't make myself do it. I pawned the gun, thinking that with it out of the house, the temptations would go away, but they didn't. Last Christmas was the first one without Lindsey and Josh, and it was hard. This one is worse. Didn't seem to get any better after last year's passed. I just keep feeling worse and worse and worse. It hurts me physically to get out of the bed in the mornings. And when I do sleep, I'm plagued with horrible nightmares."

Kara knew Dad had nightmares. Sometimes at night, she'd hear his screams. She expected Dad to tell Dennis how he could relate.

Dad didn't move, didn't blink. He only stared.

"People say time heals all wounds." He paused. "Such a damn lie. You never heal, because there's nothing out there that *can* heal you. Who can? God? No, if He's real, He surely doesn't heal you. In fact, He doesn't even acknowledge you're still here, wondering why He took those you love away." Another pause. "I thought about that one for a long time and began to wonder. If God's real and...*does* have a plan like people say, and He took them away, He did it so I would come and take yours."

Kara should have been appalled by Dennis's words, but she wasn't. Somehow, beneath the lunacy of his speech, there was reason. And it made sense.

Sins of the father.

Pastor Tom had preached about that a few weeks ago. She'd gone to church with Mom and the message had been about somebody planting seeds far in the past that are just now starting to grow. And Dennis was the seed her father had planted. It sprouted a wicked, poisonous crop that killed them all.

Dad looked as if he hadn't heard anything Dennis had said. But Kara knew he was hearing every bit. He'd been there that Sunday, had heard the same message she had. She didn't doubt he was playing it back in his mind right now just like her.

"It's time you bury your son, Grant. *Just as I had to bury mine.*" Dennis enunciated the last few words, letting each one linger.

The recliner creaked and tipped forward. Dennis appeared on the other side of it, letting it rock back. Knife in hand, he stepped around the recliner and moved behind Dad. He placed a hand on Dad's shoulder, squeezed. Dad didn't seem to notice.

"Come on, Grant. It's time we finish this. We're almost to the end."

He quickly untied Dad from his imprisonment. Slowly, he helped Dad stand. It looked hard for Dad and he dropped back in the seat a couple times before he was able to stay up on his own. His stiff joints came alive with a grunt.

"You're right, Dennis." Dad sounded a little out of breath, and very tired. "Let's finish it. Too many people have been hurt."

"Don't try anything funny," said Dennis. "You know what the outcome will be. I'm sure you've figured out how this story ends."

Dad looked Dennis in the eyes. "Whatever it takes, I will make damn sure it ends."

Dennis shook his head as if he felt sorry for Dad's stupidity. "Just remember this: I don't have anything to live for. But you do." He glanced at Kara, then Mom.

"What are you going to do with my dad?" Kara asked.

"We're bringing this into the final act," said Dennis. "Your father and I have agreed it's gone on long enough." Dennis used the knife to motion Dad forward, pointing in the direction Bobby had taken when he'd gotten loose.

Dad shambled forward like a zombie. As he walked by, he glanced at her. She saw something in his eyes that hadn't been there until now. Though it was very small, she could still decipher it through the guilt and pain.

Determination.

Dad had said he'd make sure this ends. And she could tell that there were at least minimal workings of a plan brewing inside his head.

CHAPTER THIRTY-THREE

Dennis walked next to Grant, nudging him with the knife. The point felt sharp as it jabbed him through his coat. Dennis had told him to put it on. He'd said they had a long walk ahead of them and Grant would freeze to death without it.

The snow made the hike through the yard difficult. Grant was more tired than he'd ever been and wasn't sure how much he had left inside. He saw footprints all through the snow, leading in different directions. The fresh falling snow was filling them in, but their presence was still prominent. He followed their paths to the shed. The door was open, something lying inside. Daylight glimmered off what looked like the blade of his ax jutting at an angle from a dark lump low to the ground. Strange. Grant had left it lodged in the tree stump the other night.

No, last night.

Didn't seem like it was only that short amount of time. Felt like a week had passed.

Another painful poke of the knife and Grant's lower back erupted in a fury of stings. Though he winced, Grant bit down to keep from crying out.

"Keep going," said Dennis.

Grant hadn't noticed he'd slowed down. He put more speed in his stride, making his gait stretch. Dennis directed him to the van with even more quick pokes. Grant saw Edgar's truck parked next to his Jeep on the way. He wasn't shocked to find it there, since he'd heard Edgar calling for him earlier. What had possessed him to come over in this weather? Had something happened? Grant had no clue, and he couldn't allow himself to dwell on it. He needed to keep his mind clear and open. This would most likely be his last chance to stop Dennis. He needed to be ready when the moment came.

He glanced at the truck one last time and grief tried to squeeze him.

Poor guy.

Something had brought Edgar out here and it had probably gotten him killed. He wondered what Dennis had done with the body.

Did he leave it with…?

Grant stopped the thought before it completed. Bobby was okay. He had to be.

But the blood…so much blood.

Tears welled in his eyes and he held his breath to stop the sobs from coming. He would not allow himself to be convinced Bobby was…dead. No. It wasn't acceptable, and he wouldn't even consider it. Dennis wouldn't go *that* far.

Georgia's dead. Did you forget about her?

More a moment, Grant *had* forgotten. But now he remembered.

And Marion? You know she's already gone.

Grant nearly screamed at his mind to shut up. But Dennis stepping ahead gave Grant the distraction he needed. He watched the man move like a cautious cat, ready for a shoe to be thrown as it tried to sift through some garbage. He stepped up to the side door, gave a quick look around and pulled it open.

Grant's skin pulled tight at what he saw. If it shrank any more, it might rip open.

What is this?

Grant knew exactly what it was, but his mind seemed to question every aspect of it. The rotted flesh, the stringy hair, its stiff form posed like some kind of morbid Halloween decoration, was easy to determine. But the setting was all wrong.

Dennis reached into the van as if the corpse wasn't there, searching through the inside.

Grant shook his head, as if telling the scene before him no. Maybe if he repeated it over and over, this vision would go away. Couldn't be real. His mind was playing tricks.

But when he saw the kid carrier occupied by a little body and the decomposed small body on the other side of the van, Grant knew nothing could make this not be real.

My God, Dennis.

Grant fell against the side of the van, grabbing the top to keep from collapsing. He rested his head against the metal. It felt cold and slick on his heated skin.

Dennis had completely lost his mind. He wasn't even human anymore.

And it's my fault. I made him this way.

"God," muttered Grant.

His forehead slid across the metal as he turned. Dennis was still leaning inside the van, his back to Grant. Right now would be a good time to strike him from behind. He might even be able to grab the door and pull it shut on his head. Good plan, if only Grant had the ambition to do so. Right now, blinking felt impossible. Seeing those bodies—*corpses*—had wiped out what vitality he had left.

Those bodies in the van are my victims.

He'd killed them.

Dennis leaned back, holding a flashlight. He held it out to Grant. It was one of those with the large bulb in the front and a plastic handle. Before the idea of bashing Dennis's face with it could present itself, Dennis had already stepped away from the van. He dragged a shovel out as he moved back. The metal head made scraping sounds inside the van, then dropped out, hitting the ground with a padded thump.

He held the shovel by the wooden bar next to him, the knife pointed out. "We've got some walking to do."

"Where?"

"Just start walking that way." He pointed to his right, the blade directed at the dark woods. "I'll tell you which way to go."

Grant saw the footprints in the snow and right away recognized Bobby's. A cold hand squeezed his heart. "I think I can find it," he muttered.

"Yeah," said Dennis. "Just follow the trail he left. It's what I did."

Unwilling, Grant started walking. He supposed the flashlight would be needed eventually, but right now he had no use for it. There was light to see by, though it would be gone once under the canopy of the trees. He wasn't sure what time it was, but it had to be late afternoon.

He walked, following Bobby's prints as snow fell into the sneaker-shaped hollows. They led him into the woods. He lost them briefly, but spotted another trail leading around a pair of evergreens to his left.

Kara couldn't stand the silence any longer. It was so quiet in here that it felt like a presence on her shoulders. Other than a few splintered spits, the waning fire made no noise. Faintly in the background, she could hear the kitchen's wall clock ticking. She listened for breaths other than her own and heard none.

Mom wasn't breathing.

And Kara knew it had been some time since she had been.

Now that it was quiet in here, all she could do was focus on the silence from her mother. She hadn't moved, not even a twitch. Her head hung sideways, hair flaccid over her shoulder. It had lost its yellow glow and now looked off-white and fake, like a wig.

"Mom?" Though she only whispered, it sounded like a shout in the silent room.

There was no answer, nor would there be. The realization of her mother's death punched her. The wind huffed out of her chest. Kara looked away from her mother's back, down at her arms. The rope was so tight it had pressed lines into her skin. She could see ruddy smears spreading around the indentations in her flesh. She tried moving her arms, twisting them as Bobby had to no avail. How he was able to do it, she didn't know. Her ropes were way too tight.

All she wanted was to go to her mother, hold her. But she couldn't move. Couldn't hug her mother, kiss her good-bye.

Good-bye.

Kara cried. As her body convulsed, it triggered the swollen pressure in her bladder and reminded her of how badly she had to pee. She'd been holding it for almost a full day. There were moments where she just kind of forgot about it. She wished she could forget now, but the pain was building to a breaking point.

She squeezed her thighs together, knees touching. Her bound ankles made it difficult to remain in this position for very long. To her body she could have been on the toilet. Her bladder fought to release, and she fought to keep it in. Now she shook all over, sweat breaking out on her forehead and under her arms.

Please don't!

Too late. Her bladder didn't obey her any longer and suddenly opened up. She felt hot fluid gushing out of her, soaking through her pants. The seat of her pants became drenched in the ammonia-scented wetness. It filled the chair, splashed her legs and spilled over the side. She heard it tapping the floor like rain. It kept coming, making her shiver from how great it felt to relax and the softening pressure.

And now she really cried. Mixed with her agonizing grief was the humiliation of soiling herself, but with it came the heavy relief of not having to go anymore. Somehow that seemed just as bad, if not worse, than everything else she'd endured today.

Once again, she prayed for an end that she wondered would ever come.

It took her a minute, but Sonja found the switch for the headlights. It was a knob on the instrument panel that needed to be pulled out. Light appeared in front of her, throwing a wide bright puddle onto the darkening road. The trees on either side shaded her path, making it look as if it was in the early stages of night. It wasn't, but she couldn't believe how long it had taken to make any distance.

Should've gotten on the road quicker.

Easier said than done. After she'd gotten back to the truck, she'd planned to use the CB to radio in for help. Massey had chucked her purse into the trees on the other side of the road. She'd heard it bouncing off limbs on its way down the mountain. Her cell phone was inside. Nearly her whole world was inside. And it was gone. Her only option left was the radio inside Massey's truck.

Snatching the mouthpiece from the compact radio, she thumbed the button on the side. "Um…hello?"

Silence.

"Is anybody there?" She released the button. Nothing still. Trying again, she said, "Please! Hello! Anybody there?"

Massey shut off the radio.

Yes. She remembered now. Leaning over, she gazed at the small box mounted under the control panel. She saw a couple knobs, a few buttons, but the painted labels had rubbed off with age, rendering it impossible to read what worked what.

So she tried them all. After a couple failed attempts, shrieking static burst from the speaker. Sonja jumped, emitting a tiny squeak and nearly dropped the mouthpiece. Managing to hold on to it, she squeezed the button again.

"Hello? Is anybody there?" A ghostly siren sound called back to her, fading to a rumbling drone before going quiet. "Come in, anybody. My name is Sonja Dumont, and I need help."

The CB peeped and whistled. No human voices talked back. Sonja thought about trying more knobs and buttons, but changed her mind. That was probably where she'd messed up to begin with. Probably changed the channel or something, and she had no clue how to fix that.

Hell with it.

Sonja let the mouthpiece drop.

With the radio out of commission, her only other option was to forge ahead. She'd come this far and the Marlowes was much closer than the police station. It didn't matter that she'd never driven such a large vehicle before, or that she was inexperienced with four-wheel drive. The steering wheel felt large and awkward in her hands, as if she was trying to hug a wagon wheel. Driving had been an obstacle and hell on her nerves. Rarely had she even driven on roads in weather considered inclement. But her choices were nonexistent and only one thing seemed to make sense: she needed to continue to the cabin.

She had Dennis's notes with her and after scanning through some of them again, she thought she might be able to find the Marlowes' cabin on her own.

Just don't screw it up like you did the radio.

The truck was much bigger than a radio, but she felt a tad less intimidated by it.

Not much less…

But she'd needed to go back to Massey's body and get the keys first, since they weren't in the ignition. That had been a chore she wasn't prepared for. She was worn out from the two hikes she'd already made in the woods and a third and fourth seemed to drain what bit of energy she had left. The snow had already begun to conceal Massey under white flakes by the time she reached him. His blood had turned tacky and was starting to freeze. Thankfully his pants were around his knees and she didn't have to touch any of the crimson frost as she hunted for the keys. They were in the first pocket she tried, and she was also grateful for that.

Then she headed back to the truck. It constantly felt as if she was being watched and she stopped to check behind her many times. At one point she thought Massey's body was gone, but as she looked harder, she realized the snow had just covered it that much more. A few more feet and the trees blocked him from her sight, making her feel even better.

In the truck, Sonja took her foot off the gas and put it on the clutch, stepping it to the floor. The truck decelerated as she reached another sharp curve. She saw a metal guardrail running alongside the road, bent and warped in several places from vehicles smashing into it. A small track of ground was on the other side before a narrow gap. On the other side were trees that she couldn't see the bottoms of. How far down was that drop-off? She didn't want to know.

If only she could drive faster and know she wouldn't take herself right off the mountain.

At least I'm moving. Hopefully I'm not too late.

Something inside told her she already was.

The road straightened out and Sonja gently reapplied her foot to the gas. It would take her a little while, but she was going to get to the cabin.

CHAPTER THIRTY-FOUR

Grant walked slightly ahead of Dennis, sweeping the flashlight here and there. Sometimes he lost Bobby's prints and would have to stop long enough to find them again. Each time, Dennis would give him a painful nudge with the knife and tell him to keep moving.

They'd been walking down hill for a while now. The woods had grown darker with each passing minute. All Grant could hear were the soft trickling sounds of snow and the padded scrape of the shovel dragging behind Dennis.

Many times Grant's mind tried to think about Bobby and each time he managed to stop it. He wouldn't allow himself to believe his son was dead, but somewhere inside he felt an empty space that hadn't been there before. Something was absent. And it told him all he needed to know.

He's okay. Probably hurt, like Marion, but he's okay.

Marion was not hurt. She was...

Stop!

He shook his head hard, jarring those thoughts free. The scraping of the shovel being dragged filtered back into his ears. They were farther down the incline now. He wasn't sure how long he'd been lost in his thoughts this time.

"Dennis?" The man behind him didn't respond, but Grant knew he'd heard his name called. "We're alone out here. And you said it was time we ended this, so end it now. Just you and me. *Kill* me. Let the kids get their mother to the hospital, leave them out of it now. Finish it. Kill me."

"I wish it was that simple."

"It is," said Grant. "I'm the one to blame. *I* did it. Not them."

"I've always blamed you, Grant. Always." Dennis spoke calmly, slowly, as if Grant would have a hard time understanding the words. "It was hard for me to not kill you while you slept. Sometimes I stood over your bed for hours at a time, a knife pressed to your throat, willing myself to slit it open."

He's been in my bedroom? In the house?

Of course he had, Grant realized. He knew everything. Even knew they were coming here for Christmas.

Christmas.

It was Christmas Eve. Grant had hoped they would be settling down for a nice meal about this time. He'd planned on letting the kids open a gift early, just like they used to do. Not one of the bigger ones, just something small that they'd asked for. It always seemed to get them even more excited for the big day.

Tears dotted the corners of his eyes. He sniffed. Then he wiped his nose with the back of a cold hand. He could barely feel the connection when he touched his face.

I killed them. All of them.

Grant held his breath, straining as he shoved those punitive thoughts aside.

Through gritted teeth, Grant said, "Why my family, Dennis? Huh? Why? For what happened to yours? They didn't do anything wrong."

"Neither did mine. And just like your actions took mine away from me, mine will take yours away from you. I couldn't just kill you. It'd be letting you off too easily. You've already gotten through enough in stride. Not this time. Truth is, I don't plan on killing you at all."

They reached the bottom of the hill. Grant, out of breath and completely exhausted, paused by a large tree and waited on Dennis.

Grant put the flashlight on Dennis's chest. He saw the dark bar of the shovel pointing up. Dennis talked as he approached. "Just like me, you'll have to live without them for the rest of your life."

Grant shook his head. "It won't change anything. Your family will still be dead. Their bodies—that's all they are, just bodies. They're not alive." Grant saw the putrefied corpses of Dennis's family, propped in the van as if taking a morbid road trip. "They're *dead*."

Dennis stared at him. "Walk."

"Dennis…"

"Walk!"

Grant sighed, nodded. "Okay."

Putting his back to Dennis, Grant shined the light on the ground. Bobby's prints tracked through the snow forward. It looked as if the woods actually ended not very far ahead. He couldn't believe how far Bobby had gone. He felt proud of his son for being able to keep going when Grant felt as if his legs would stop working at any moment.

They shambled along, Grant leading the way. Dennis stayed close, the shovel sliding across the snow, making whistling sounds as it bounced over the ruts and roots. Reaching the verge of the woods, Grant stopped. In the waning light, he saw a field before him. It was deep and wide, ending on another barrage of trees. The black jagged shapes of mountains could be seen beyond the woods. The landscape looked as if it was under a filter of purple from the plum-colored clouds above.

If Bobby had crossed the field and made it to the other side, there was a good chance he'd left Dennis behind.

The blood. Dennis is covered in it.

He wished his head would shut up. Anytime hope tried to manifest, his thoughts quickly exterminated it.

The blood could be Edgar's.

Grant tried to recall if Dennis had been soaked when he'd come inside and found Bobby had escaped. He hadn't noticed, but he also hadn't been looking. It was hard to miss such a heavy amount of blood, and he figured he would've seen it.

But maybe not.

Before Dennis could poke him again, Grant swiveled the flashlight. The beam threw down on the ground, finding Bobby's tracks. He followed them out of the woods and onto a flat stretch of land. His feet sunk down to his ankles as he walked behind the trail Bobby had left. He only vaguely noticed Dennis wasn't as close as he was before.

He saw posts spread alongside the field. One was tilted to the side, making the barbwire fencing sag. A line of barb was on the ground, vanishing under the snow.

Then he saw the protuberance on the far side of the felled fence. It was fairly large in size.

Grant's breath was crushed in his throat. He stopped walking. His chest began to feel as if something was slowly stepping on it.

"My God," Grant choked. "What have you done?"

He felt the blunt tip of the shovel handle prod his back, shoving him forward. "Go."

Grant's legs carried him, though it felt like they were touching the ground. Everything around him began to swim, turning spacey and warped. As he moved closer, the lump became highlighted under the flashlight's beam. The light traced Bobby's head, his usual spiked hair that had gone flat and hard. It looked almost white from the ice, adding years to a handsome face that was nearly a replica of Grant's except for the slash on his cheek and knot on his head. His eyes and mouth were open, frozen in shock. The light showed his outstretched arms, fingers curled and pointing at the darkening sky. Snow fell into his palm like fluffy white coins.

The light shook as it scanned his midriff. A large open wound stretched from the bottom of his stomach up to his chest, leaving a wide gulley that spewed dark innards. The blood had turned crispy around the serrated edges, making it look sculpted from wax. All of Bobby somehow seemed artificial, as if molded by a ghoulish artist.

The smear of light on Bobby's torso jerked and shook so much now it looked as if it was coming from the front of a train. Then it suddenly went away as the flashlight fell from Grant's hand. He only knew this because he no longer felt the weight of it and heard the muffled bump of its landing.

Grant juddered as an electric current of sorrow flowed through him. He heard the shuddering stutters of his voice as he tried to speak, felt the clucks of his words lodged in his throat. He stole a glance of Dennis, who stood off to the side. Though his face was veiled in shadow, he saw enough to read the expression. There was no malice, no vengeful gleam, only a mourning frown that pulled his face downward.

Then Grant dropped to his knees, his legs no longer able to support him. He started to fall forward, but slapped his hands into the snow to catch himself. He gazed down at his murdered son, watching his tears make ripples in the thickening blood. Collapsing onto Bobby's hardened form, Grant pressed his face to his son's cold cheek and began screaming his anguish. The breaths of his shouts stirred the snow.

"You can't describe what you're feeling right now, can you?"

Though Grant still cried and shouted, he'd heard Dennis's question. The voice asking it had sounded sad, on the brink of tears. And Dennis was correct. There was no description; just an overwhelming sensation of loss that Grant hoped would take him with it.

"That empty feeling in your heart came on so quickly it almost stopped, didn't it? But it won't stop. It'll keep beating. Even though you don't want it to, it'll always beat." Dennis's voice was rising with each word. "It'll *beat* and *beat* and *beat!*"

"*Oh-God-my-son!*" Grant gripped Bobby's extended arm. It was like clutching a pole shoved inside a thick coat.

"I know the feeling, Grant!"

"No, you don't! You can't possibly know!"

"I found my son's body..."

"You *tortured* him! My son was older! He was a part of my life longer! You son of a bitch! You butchered him!"

Dennis seemed momentarily swayed by Grant's harsh comments. He stuttered over his words, trying to say something back.

Grant pushed himself to his knees. "This is nowhere *near* the same! I didn't torture your family! I didn't kill your friend…I didn't do any of the things you've done!"

"Shut up!"

"You're a murderer! A cold-blooded killer! I'm just a stupid drunk!"

"Shut *up*!"

"Make me! Make me shut up!" Grant had trouble finding his breath. His vision was splotchy, and a horrible cramping seized his chest. He felt his left arm trying to lock up. The shouts faded from his throat as another sobbing fit came on. He lowered his head and bawled.

"Here," said Dennis. He tossed the shovel. It landed flush before Grant. "Bury him! Just like I buried Josh! In a few minutes, you'll bury your wife and daughter. Then we're done."

Grant stared at the shovel. Its blade looked new and probably was. Dennis must've purchased the tool just for this moment, so he could watch Grant bury his family. Grant slightly turned so he could see Bobby. His lifeless eyes gazed up, not flinching when snow landed on their marble-like surfaces. Reaching out, he put the tips of his fingers on Bobby's lids and pushed them down. When he took his hand away, they remained shut.

"Grab the shovel, Grant. Start digging…please…" Dennis sniveled. He wiped his mouth. "Just take the fucking shovel, finish it. Please…"

Grant stuck his hands under the long handle, fingers worming through the snow and appearing on the other side. They curled around the wooden bar. The solidity of the tool felt comforting, almost as reassuring as if a gun had been placed in his hand. He snorted and sucked the dripping snot back into his nose.

"What did you say about Kara?" Grant asked.

"What?"

"A minute ago."

Dennis stepped forward, wiping his eyes with his free hand. The other held the knife, though it was no longer being thrust in Grant's face. It hung by his leg, as if unaware it was supposed to be doing something. "You murdered *both* of my children, Grant. Even though my daughter was still in the womb, you still killed her."

Grant's hands squeezed the shovel.

"You killed my wife, my son, my daughter…" Dennis kicked snow at Grant. It burst when it struck his shoulder, sprinkling down the front of his coat. "You killed them *all*!"

Dennis leaned down as he shouted the last sentence just as Grant hoped he would. It made ramming the shovel into his stomach easier. Though it only just pierced him, the bowed blade still went in deep enough to shock him so Grant could scramble up. It was hard to get his shaky feet planted, but he managed to do so and reared back the shovel as if it were a baseball bat.

Grant swung.

The jolt of metal hitting skull reverberated around him and sent a numbing rush up his arms. Wobbling back a few steps, Dennis reached up to his face. Blood poured from the large gash in his forehead. Grant swung again. This time Dennis was farther away than he'd anticipated and he only caught his shoulder. But it was enough to leave a spewing gash and spin Dennis on his feet before dropping him to the ground. He landed on his back, and didn't move again.

Grant staggered to where Dennis lay motionless. He raised the shovel high above his head, extending his arms all the way. When his arm moved back far enough that it no longer blocked his view, he caught sight of Bobby in the corner of his eye. The shovel fell from his fingers, imbedding into the ground. The handle tilted stiff and peninsular.

Seeing his son brought Grant back to the situation. Before, he'd watched in the distance like a madman, twirling his fingers as his minion enacted the savagery for him. But now he was himself again. The rage had abated and the misery had returned.

Grant saw a section of hoary ground was glowing. He reached in and retrieved the flashlight. It was dusted in snow, but worked fine. Turning back to Dennis, he shined the disc of light onto his body. Eyes wide open; blood saturated his face in a crimson mask.

Grant went to Dennis, keeping the light on him. Though it didn't appear as if Dennis was in any shape to try anything, Grant wanted to be ready just in case. Squatting, he searched Dennis's pockets. He found two sets of keys. Since he had no idea which belonged to Edgar's truck, he took them all. He stuffed them in his coat pocket as he stood.

He walked to Bobby. Not wanting to see him in grisly detail, he shut off the light and tried stuffing it in the other pocket of his coat. It wouldn't fit, so he let it drop. He would need both arms anyway.

Sinking to a crouch, he pushed his arms under his son and stood with him cradled close. He felt awkward and slightly stiff in Grant's arms, but not heavy. Nothing felt as if it would be too much for him to carry at the moment.

With the sudden strength of ten, Grant started running. He entered the woods with Bobby supported over his arms, and started up the hill at a steady pace. He didn't plan on stopping until he reached the cabin.

CHAPTER THIRTY-FIVE

Sonja saw the mailbox with the M-crested flag hanging under it and, without thinking, stomped the brake. The wheels locked, but the truck kept going. The tires squelched as they skidded across the snow, making the truck quake. Shouting in panic, Sonja tried to hold the wheel in place as it fought her attempts. It jerked from her hands, spinning, which brought the back of the truck out to the left. She felt the truck turning as it scooted across the slippery road beneath her, unable to find purchase.

When she grabbed the steering wheel again, she turned it in the direction of the spin. That helped. She was able to keep the gyration as smooth as possible. Soon she was facing the way she'd come and the truck was still moving. There was a sound of crunching metal that gently shook the truck, ceasing the rotation. Now she was still.

Huffing, Sonja kept her hands gripped to the wheel. She shook the fallen hair out of her eyes. The truck's engine chugged. Through the windshield she could see snow flurries twinkling in the headlights' glow. Not as a heavy as it had been, the snow still came in a balanced course.

"Good one, Sonja."

She gulped, panted some more. What had she hit? She put the truck in park. Turning in the seat, she looked out the rear windshield. She could see the brake lights' red spill on the bushy ridge behind her. She hadn't quite reached that point, which was a positive. There was most likely a ditch that separated the road from that natural wall. With her limited expertise on trucks, she doubted she could've gotten it out.

The mailbox is missing.

Sonja took a deep breath and held it, hoping to calm her jittered nerves. The mailbox wasn't missing. It was under the truck. She'd wiped it out.

Facing forward again, Sonja lifted her hands. She held them over the steering wheel and saw how badly they trembled. Her whole body matched their tempo and style. Sonja took another deep breath and let it out through pursed lips, whistling.

"Okay," she said. Her voice sounded odd, a little hoarse and shaky. "You can do this." She glanced at Massey's handgun. It was still in the seat. Thankfully it hadn't been thrown to the floorboard and accidentally fired.

Lowering her hands to the steering wheel, her fingers curled around the ribbed circle. It felt slick and hot in her sweaty hold. Another deep breath and the drumming of her heart abated. Though it still felt as if she was being punched from the inside, the swift rate had greatly slowed.

"Come on," she told herself. "You can do it."

It took determination to remove a hand from the wheel long enough to pop the gear. Her foot felt tight and cramped when she made it move from the brake pedal to the gas. The truck remained still until she applied pressure. The engine gave a small roar. Metal grinded behind her and the truck made a lethargic thrust forward. Something broke in the rear with a scraping crack, then the truck moved easier. Slowly, she turned the wheel to the left, bringing it back onto the road. When she was parallel to the ridge, she took her foot away from the gas and let the truck roll to a stop. Holding her foot just above the gas pedal made the tendons around her ankle strain.

She looked out the windshield and could just see a dark path between white-streaked trees. The snow's weight made the limbs droop onto the drive, nearly concealing it. If it hadn't been for the mailbox, she'd have driven past.

Making such a sharp turn in these conditions would be tricky. Nibbling on her lip, she turned the wheel and applied the gas. She felt the back tires already trying to get away from her, so she straightened the wheel a tad and the truck started moving. The headlights poured into the dark ingress between the trees, shoving away the shadows and glaring off the harsh white of the snow. The front end hit the limbs and knocked them out of the way. Carefully, she got the truck in and began her ascent.

Thank God for these tires.

Her car would have never made it up the hill. Hell, it wouldn't have made it off the highway. Though she felt the snow shift underneath the wheels, yanking the steering wheel sharply at times, she held onto it and kept going up with the speedometer glued at 3mph.

A few minutes later she saw the car blocking her way. Its rear had crimped lines where the paint had been scraped off. The red casing of the brake light had been smashed. The snow behind it was trodden and led a compacted path around it. Whatever had gone around was much smaller than this truck and it still had trouble from the looks of it.

Sonja groaned.

No way was she getting around it.

Feeling somewhat defeated, Sonja lifted her foot away from the gas pedal. It took no time for the truck to stop since it was on a hill. Putting her foot onto the brake, she jerked the gear into park. Then she pushed the emergency brake.

She wasn't sure how far up the cabin was, but whatever distance was left would have to be handled on foot.

Sonja zipped her coat, put her beanie back on, and unbuckled. She grabbed the gun from beside her and was about to cut off the truck but paused. Maybe she should leave it running. It'd keep the heat going and would make it easier to leave if she needed to. Besides, after how her luck had been so far, it might not crank back up. Checking the gas gauge, she saw there was a little over a quarter of a tank left. It had been full when they'd left this morning.

She shouldered the door open and hopped out. The cold air felt wet as it swarmed her, freezing the sweat on her face and making it sting. Her eyes dried out and she blinked to make them feel less itchy. She put the gun in her coat pocket, the handle hanging out, and used both hands to throw the heavy door shut. She could smell the exhaust that billowed from the tailpipe.

After a quick look around, she started hiking against the wind, holding her beanie in place. She only gave the car beside her a quick glance in passing. The window was smashed, the inside layered in snow. She didn't know who it belonged to, but from its condition, she assumed Dennis had gotten to it.

Her chest tightened, and not just from the excursion of her walk. A combination of sadness and fear squeezed her lungs. She wanted to get to the cabin as quickly as possible.

But she was petrified of what she would find.

CHAPTER THIRTY-SIX

Kara paused to catch her breath. She jerked her head back, flinging her sweat-damp hair out of her face. Lips in a tight line, she huffed through her nose. She looked behind her and avoided Mom to check where Dad's chair was. Seemed a good bit farther away than it had been the last time she looked.

Still not getting anywhere.

Kara took slow deep breaths. The strong smell of burnt wood mixed with urine was drawn into her nostrils. The pungent odors made her eyes water. Her clothes felt glued to her, especially around her thighs. It made her skin feel as if she was being bitten by a hundred mosquitoes all at once. She wished she was wearing something dry, but there was no way she could make that happen yet.

Her original plan had been to rock side to side until the chair tipped over. She thought if she landed hard enough, it might break the wood so she could slide the ropes off. Though the plan seemed like a good one, she was too afraid to try. The chair might not break and she'd be stuck on the floor in the puddles her pee had made that now seemed to flow in all directions on the hardwood. No thanks. Or she might injure herself in the fall. Either way, there was too much risk to try it out.

The new plan was to scoot her way into the kitchen to the utensil drawer and find a knife. Preferably a steak knife. It should be sharp enough to cut through at least one of the ropes, and with a hand free, she could manually untie the rest. Now that was a better plan. It would take her a long time to get into the kitchen, but it was worth it.

If it works.

It would work, she was sure of it. Just hold the knife at angle, the blade pointing back at her, and work with her wrists. The process would be tedious and long, but eventually she'd get it to work.

Kara strained with her legs, as if trying to jump. The chair legs hopped and slid a few paces. Then she rested. Out of breath and sweaty, Kara leaned back her head. She stared at the ceiling and saw a few stains spreading across like black acne. Her back throbbed with tightness and there was an awful cramp in her neck that spread into her shoulders. She couldn't believe how exhausted she already was. She was in better shape than this. Three days a week at the gym for two hours each visit, plus the spin classes—this shouldn't be nearly as hard.

But she was sleep-deprived, mentally vanquished, hungry and very thirsty. It sickened her how much more she yearned for some water and clean clothes than the gloom over her mother and brother.

Don't start now.

The tears that had begun to make tiny bubbles in her eyes stopped. If she allowed herself to focus on that, she would stop trying altogether. No, she needed to hold off on her true emotions as long as possible. It would only infect her with woe and make her give up. Sadly, the grieving process would have to come later. Mom and Bobby would want it that way.

She threw herself against the ropes, the chair's legs groaning across the wood floor. She moved about an inch before having to stop. She was just to the doorway that led into the short hall. The next doorway led to the kitchen. She could see a square-shaped spill of light on the floor and smeared on the wall coming from the kitchen.

It wasn't very far away, but to Kara, it felt like miles. She was so weak, and the thought of keeping this mission going any longer was overwhelming. She looked at the floor and contemplated trying Plan A.

Don't. You'll regret it.

She was regretting this plan as well. Neither felt as good to her as they had when she'd first thought of them. Another glance at the floor and she could almost feel the hardness jolting her. The weight of her body coming down on her arm, a snap and tremendous pain ripping through her.

Kara shook her head. She wasn't going to tip the chair over. No matter what.

If only Dad would come back. He could get her loose.

What if he doesn't? What if Dennis comes in, more blood on his clothes.

"It's time," he'd say.

For all I know, I'm the only one left. He'll want to kill me too.

And Kara couldn't let that happen. She no longer wanted to live for her sake, at least not at the moment. Happy endings of her making it out of this cabin, getting married and starting a family of her own were detached fantasies in her mind. They felt so far away, like imaginations of a little girl.

What drove her now was Dennis. He couldn't get away with this.

Her fingers gripped the tips of the chair arms so tightly, the wood creaked. She saw him on his back, her straddling him, and punching a knife into his chest. It was the knife he'd used to cut Bobby's cheek. The blade vanished to the hilt and she kept pushing.

Kara suddenly felt as if she was recharged. The chair shot forward when she thrust with her hips. The legs hit the floor with a bang. Jerking forward, the chair scatted over the wood, tooting with each lunge. Her rump jolted her spine with hot pain.

In her mind, the knife was wrenched out, blade dripping blood. It slammed back down with a moist crunch. Dennis begged, cried, and screamed for her to stop. But she wouldn't. Each time the knife came down in her explicit image, the chair's legs came down on the floor.

Groaning and grunting, Kara moved on. She passed through the doorway into the hall. Darkness fell over her, messing with her vision. She focused on the bright entrance. It was closer now, blurred through her teary lenses. Her body's pain began to cut through her momentum, first with her feet and ankles, her buttocks, then her legs. She felt her speed dwindle.

Keep going, Kara!

The knife raked across Dennis's throat, making his eyes go wide. Gurgling sounds came from the wound as blood sluiced all over.

Kara kept going. Growl, shove, and thrust, the chair scooted. It wobbled slightly, as if off balance, but she didn't slow down. If she stopped, she wouldn't be able to start back up again. She knew this was her last shot. Her body would not allow her to try again with either plan.

The chair hobbled into the kitchen. Bright light washed over her. Her teary eyes made everything look as if she was staring at the sun from under water. She blinked to clear her eyes.

Glass shattered off to the side. Kara whipped her head around. She gazed over the table, to the doors that opened onto the deck.

And glimpsed somebody standing on the other side of the glass doors, reaching in. A gun appeared through the space.

Kara screamed.

Sonja had tried looking through the windows. Where there weren't any blinds blocking her view, heavy curtains wouldn't allow even a glimpse inside. She ran around to the front door, putting her ear close. At first, she hadn't heard anything, but slowly she began to make out what sounded like a groan. It resonated from deep inside the house. She'd tried the knob, but it was locked. Blasting the door open briefly crossed her mind, but she was afraid of stray bullets zipping through the house. Who knew what they'd hit, so she decided against it.

Sonja ran down the steps and kicked her way through the snow to the other side of the house. She saw a small deck. Light poured from the glass doors, making a rippling glow across the bed of white. As she headed to it, she saw the faint inclinations of footprints carrying in the opposite direction, as if running away.

She wondered if they belonged to Dennis. She knew he was here. That had been his van she'd spotted parked among the other vehicles.

And after a quick peek inside, she'd learned what he'd done when he visited the cemetery. Why he'd waited until now to dig up their bodies, she had no idea. Unless he was planning on dying tonight, and wanted their presence close when it happened. Even that seemed unlikely.

Why dig them up at all?

She didn't know, and figured Dennis probably didn't know either.

Sonja could've stood by the van, dwelling on the endless possibilities of his motivations, but she'd made her legs get moving again. They'd brought her to the cabin. Its shape was concealed in the darkness of the early evening, and with the windows up top throwing out dim light that wound into a breach of shadows near the bottom, it gave the impression of a grinning skull.

Sonja shivered. Everything inside of her told her to turn back, to get back in the truck and drive away. She'd pushed those warnings aside and started moving.

Back in the present, she carefully climbed the steps to the porch. The snow was piled like white planks, and her foot sank deep into each one. She reached the flat surface and padded through even higher snow to the door. A steady drone was louder now, like an engine of some kind. Sounded like a generator. If so, that would explain why the power was working.

The brightly lit room on the other side of the door was a kitchen with an attached dining area. A table was directly in front of her, with a counter all that separated it from the rest. She heard the growling right away. It sounded like somebody trying to bench press too much weight and screaming with determination to do it. Clattering followed, like logs being dropped on the floor. Movement caught her eye.

A young woman bounced into the kitchen, her face flushed red and wet as she strained. She was seated in a chair, squirming against its back. She pitched forward and was snatched back, but the chair pogoed onward a couple inches. She took a couple short breaths, then repeated.

Oh my God.

She recognized the girl as Kara Marlowe. Though she was a mess, Sonja still matched her to the photos she'd seen of the young woman.

It took her a split second to grasp what Kara was doing. Her arms, unmoving and firm on the chair, had been tied down. She saw the tan lines of rope wound around her wrists and forearms. The bulges of her neck muscles, veins swelling like cords, showed how hard she was struggling to move even a fraction.

Sonja tried the knob. Locked. Without thinking about it, she pulled the gun from her coat, held it by the barrel, and smashed it through a pane of glass in the door beside the knob. As she reached in, angling the barrel away from Kara so she could pinch the tab on the knob, the poor girl started screaming.

"It's okay," said Sonja. "I'm here to help!"

She doubted Kara had heard her over the piercing cries. The tab turned and Sonja pulled her arm back, feeling the coat snagging on glass teeth still holding on to the frame. Trying the door knob again, it turned. She threw it open and ran inside.

Kara was still shrieking when Sonja reached her. Sonja understood how it must look from Kara's point of view: A mad woman busting into her house, carrying a gun. After what Kara and her family had probably already endured, Sonja couldn't blame her.

Dropping to a crouch, Sonja placed the gun between her feet. She put her cold hands on Kara's bare arm. The young woman flinched, but didn't stop screaming.

"Kara! I'm not going to hurt you!"

Though Kara's screams softened to whines, she didn't stop.

Sonja shuffled closer, brought her hands to Kara's soaked face. She pushed the strips of hair plastered to her cheeks back. This close to the young woman, Sonja picked up the stale odor of pee. It must've been coming from Kara because she reeked of it.

"Listen to me, Kara." Sonja gave a quick look around. "Where is he? Where's Dennis?"

Kara stopped her frenzy as if a switch had been flipped. She pulled her head back from Sonja's hands, looked at her. "You know Dennis?"

"It's complicated. I tried to get here sooner. Where is he?"

"I don't know. He left with my dad."

"He's not here?" Kara shook her head. "Okay." She looked around, spotting a smashed block on the wall that she figured used to be a telephone. "Are there any other phones in the house?"

"He burned our cell phones in the fire!"

Sonja shushed her, nodded. "Okay. We have to get you out of this." She tapped the ropes binding Kara's right arm. "Where's a knife?"

"Over there," said Kara, motioning with a chin thrust. "Top drawer. Beside the sink. I was trying to get there." Kara smiled, almost laughed. "Nearly made it."

"You did fine," said Sonja. "Very fine."

Sonja squeezed the young woman's hand before standing up. Then she rushed through the kitchen, dodging the island that was in the middle. She wondered how Kara had planned to make it around this without trouble.

I'm here now. She doesn't have to worry about it.

Sonja reached the counter.

"Who are you?" Kara asked.

She opened the drawer, sifting through the utensils. There were knives, but nothing that would get the job done quickly. "Sonja Dumont." She slammed the drawer shut, turned around. On the island was a rack of knifes, much larger than what was in the drawer. She went to it, grabbed the top handle and pulled out a large chef's knife. "That's better."

"Didn't think I could reach it," said Kara. She attempted a smile that looked pained. "Figured I could pull the drawer open with my teeth."

Sonja shushed her again as she approached. She squatted in front of Kara, slipping the large blade behind the ropes. Though it was tight, the blade fit without any difficulty. She began wiggling it back and forth, sawing into the rope. "Is everybody else okay?" she asked.

When Kara didn't answer, Sonja paused and looked up. She saw the young woman's face had crumpled. Her mouth was a quivering tight line that had little beads of tears or sweat about to fall off.

Kara shook her head.

God...

Sonja swallowed. It made a wet clucking sound. "Who's…left?"

"Me…so far as I know, Dad is too. Dennis made him leave with him…" Kara's words choked into sobs.

Nodding again, Sonja started working on the rope. She'd dug a frayed gulley into the coarse line, splitting the ropes. Sprigs curled out in all directions. "Do you know where they went?"

Kara sniffled, took deep breaths. "No. He said it was time for Dad to bury his son."

"What?" Sonja paused. Her back prickled with cold taps.

"And he was covered with blood when he got back…Dennis had it all over him. I know it was Bobby's. I know he killed him. He killed Mom too, killed Aunt Georgia."

"Kara." The girl's words kept going, pushing through her tears and becoming unclear. "Kara!" Biting down on her lip, Kara sucked in her cries. "Calm down, okay. We don't have to talk about this now. We just have to get you…" The rope at Kara's left foot snapped. "Loose."

Kara groaned as she lifted her leg a tad. "Thank youuuu…" Her pleasured moan turned to a grimace. "Ow!" Her foot dropped back down. "It hurts!"

"It's going to take a minute for the blood to pump right again. Just relax. Let me get the rest."

A couple minutes later, Sonja had all the ropes cut. Kara leaned forward, rubbing her abraded wrists. Wincing, she hissed through clenched teeth as she flexed her fingers. The ammonia-like smell of urine was stronger, burning Sonja's eyes. She knew it was coming from Kara. The girl had peed in her pants. Knowing this caused Sonja to feel immense pity for the girl. How long had she been tied to the chair? Probably all day, so she had no choice but to pee herself.

There was no time for Kara to shower, but Sonja knew she wouldn't be able to handle the long drive back into town in wet clothes. And Sonja hated to admit, the smell would be almost too rank to bear.

"Why don't you run and change your clothes?" said Sonja.

She put her hand on Kara's shoulder. Kara turned to her, eyes widening before lowering. It was as if she was too ashamed to look at Sonja.

"I'll help you up," said Sonja.

Kara nodded.

Sonja stood up, her legs feeling sore and achy. The long trip here and the excursion in the snow left her muscles throbbing.

And how do you think Kara feels? She's been tied to this chair all day.

Sonja reached around Kara's back. Her hand bumped her breasts as it moved around to go under her arm on the other side. She thought about apologizing, but Kara didn't seem to notice. Squeezing Kara, she held her in place as the young woman pushed herself up. She felt Kara trembling in her arms, as if standing took every ounce of strength she had.

"Ah, my legs!" Kara groaned between her clenched mouth.

"It's okay," said Sonja. "Just give them a minute."

"I don't have a minute…"

Kara took deep breaths through her nose, stirring the strands of hair hanging in her face. Sonja felt the tremors in Kara's muscles dissipate. The limpness went away, and she felt less like a dummy and more like a statue.

"I'm good now," said Kara.

"You sure?"

"Yes!"

Sonja let go. "Sorry."

Kara closed her eyes, looking regretful. "No, I'm sorry. I didn't mean to yell."

Sonja nodded, though Kara couldn't see her. "Let's get you upstairs and changed."

"No. I'll do it. Give me two minutes."

"All right. I have a truck down the driveway. It's still running. I'll get you down there and…"

"No. We're going to look for my dad."

Before Sonja could disagree, Kara was already moving. She walked like a toddler taking her first sprint. She wobbled this way and that on her way out. It would've been funny had it not been so sad.

She heard the faint sounds of Kara's feet on the stairs.

I hope she doesn't fall.

Sonja walked out of the kitchen. Standing outside the doorway, she turned to the left. She could see the edge of the staircase across from the front door. Kara's hand clutched the rail near the top. Another moment, it disappeared on the other side of the wall. She heard the ceiling pop as Kara scurried above her.

Good job, Kara.

Sonja turned and looked down the short hall to her right. She noticed a smell that reminded her of mornings when she'd camped with her cousins. They'd awake in their tents to the odor of the snuffed campfire, almost as if water had been poured on it.

Sonja started walking toward the doorway at the end, where a light haze was curling out. Checking the pocket of her coat, she felt the hardness of the gun. The barrel bumped against her hip as she walked.

She paused in the doorway.

My God Almighty.

Sonja felt the strength in her legs go away. She slapped her hands on the door paneling, fingers gripping, to hold herself upright.

"Dennis...what did you do?"

Marion Marlowe was dead. Her plum-colored skin looked more like foam rubber than flesh. There were bruises along her arm, intercepted with cracked blue lines that ended at a nub of spiky flesh. Half her arm was gone. She spotted it on the TV stand, the meat cleaver that had most likely severed it imbedded into the wood.

Chairs had been assembled in the room like a small poetry reading. She counted three, which was odd since there were four members of the family. As her eyes scanned the room, she saw what was left of the fourth chair in a pile by the floor. Somehow, she knew that was Bobby's chair.

Kara had said Dennis took Grant to bury his son.

Tears turned the scene before her into dark smudges, like a morbid painting that was fading with age. She'd figured out what Dennis's intentions were, but she wasn't prepared for seeing the proof of his rage.

A loud bang resonated from behind.

Sonja jumped. Spinning around and screaming, she caught sight of a large figure rushing toward her. It was hard to make out who through her wet vision.

"Who are you?" a loud voice demanded.

It's not Dennis!

Must be Grant. Did that mean that Dennis…?

Big hands grabbed her shoulders, slammed her against the wall. The back of her head rebounded off the unyielding wood. Bright splotches exploded like fairy dust. She was being shaken, then slammed against the wall again and pulled back. Her knees buckled, pulling her down, but the hands jerked back up and shoved her to the wall. She was pinned there. Trying to lift her head and look at this man was impossible. Her forehead fell against his coat. It felt cold and damp against her brow.

She heard the man's deep voice yell something. It was gargled and swilled with punctuation that she couldn't decipher. Then she could hear Kara's voice, loud and shrill.

"Dad!"

The deeper voice roared like a cannon, but quickly dispelled to a softer pitch. She felt the grip that pinned her to the wall slacken, though it didn't go away completely. She was glad, because she would've fallen had they not been there to brace her.

CHAPTER THIRTY-SEVEN

D ad helped Sonja into the kitchen, assisting her as she sat in the chair Kara had been imprisoned in for the last…how many hours?

Kara looked at the stove. A digital clock was between the dials. She was surprised when she saw it wasn't even 7:00 p.m. yet. Felt like it was midnight.

"Kara, get some ice out of the freezer."

"Okay," she said, already moving. Even after pausing to get a clean dishtowel from a drawer to wrap the ice in, she reached the fridge in a blink. As she opened the door, she heard Sonja talking behind her.

"No," said Sonja. "Don't bother. We have to get going."

"You've got a nasty bump on your head," Dad said. His voice lowered with guilt. "I'm sorry about that. I didn't know who you were…"

If you would've let her explain who she was before you tried to bash her brains in.

"It's fine," said Sonja through a moan.

Inside, the freezer was mostly bare. The plastic tub underneath the icemaker was half full, and she dug her hand in and grabbed a handful. Holding the towel open on her hand, she dumped the cubes on top, then wrapped the towel around to form a white head and tail, like a ghost. She hurried back to Dad and handed it to him.

"Thanks," he said, applying it to Sonja's head. The woman winced, cried out. "Sorry."

Dad took the ice away and Kara saw the pink hillock pushing through Sonja's dark hair. This time he was much more delicate when he put the ice to it.

"Got it?" he asked.

Reaching up, Sonja held the towel and nodded. Dad took his hand away.

"All right," he said. "Now we can leave."

"She's got a truck," said Kara. "Down the driveway."

"Still running," she said. "Low on gas, but it's a big one. We can get away from here."

"There're gas cans in the shed. Edgar filled them for the generator..." Dad's eyes looked grim. "Anyway, there's extra gas in the shed. I can get it before we leave. We'll take Edgar's truck down the driveway—"

"Edgar's truck?" said Kara, cutting him off.

Dad nodded. "Yeah."

"Is he...?"

Dad nodded again.

Kara felt terrible, remembering how much she used to tease his appearance. Sometimes Bobby had her in tears from his tasteless jokes about the poor man. Making fun of Edgar for things he couldn't help.

And now he was dead.

So is Bobby...

Though Kara hadn't asked for confirmation, she assumed so since Dad was alone when he came back. She wanted to know for sure, but also wanted to spare Dad the agony of having to tell her. Informing her of Edgar seemed to almost be too much for him to handle.

Plus, she didn't want to know for sure. Not yet.

But he is. I know he is.

Kara felt her mind beginning to collapse and quickly prodded a support beam underneath to hold it up. She would have to hold it all in for now. Later, when she could finally let it out, she feared she may never be able to stop.

When she looked at Sonja, she saw Dad was no longer kneeling beside her. She spun around, finding him on his way out of the kitchen.

"Dad?" He stopped, looked back. "Where are you going?"

"To get your mother."

Kara flinched as if he'd made a swing at her. "Dad, you can't…she's…"

But he was already gone, his footfalls softening as he walked away. Kara chased after him, following him into the hall.

"Dad? Don't go in there."

"Stay back, Kara."

"Dad, please."

"Mr. Marlowe?" Sonja's voice came in the back of this weird train of survivors. "Grant? You don't want to see what Dennis—"

"I know what he did!" Dad turned back, his face a fuming red sheet. "I know!"

Kara stopped. For a brief moment, she was afraid of her father.

Sonja stepped beside her, still trying to talk him out of going back into the living room. "She's gone, Grant."

Dad stepped forward, passed Kara and stood in front of Sonja. He was at least a foot taller than her, so he glowered down into her eyes. "I'm *not* leaving her here. She's coming with us. *All* of us."

Sonja held his galled stare a moment longer before giving up. She nodded. "Okay. Whatever you want."

"We're still a damn family," he added. "We came here together and we're going to leave this fucking hellhole together. I'm going to get your mother, then Georgia, and put them in the truck with Bobby. I'll load up all the gas we have and then we will drive down to the other truck. That's the plan. No exceptions. Are we all clear?"

Nobody argued with him.

It took longer than Kara would've liked for Dad to finish. Just as he said, he moved Georgia first, leaving her inside the body bag. Finished with that, he got a blanket from the upstairs closet and used it to cover

Mom. Kara was glad he did. Seeing the condition of her mother's body was unnerving.

He carried Mom through the front door draped over his arms, just as, Kara imagined, he'd done on their wedding night. Sonja closed the door behind him. She stood next to it, back to the wall, fingers resting on the curve of the gun handle poking out from the pocket of her coat.

Coat.

Kara turned and started down the hall.

"Where are you going?" asked Sonja in a worried voice.

"To get my coat."

"Oh, right. You might need that."

Kara walked into the kitchen, squinting at the bright light. In the hallway it had been dim, but in here it glared like an operating room. She started for the coatrack across the room. It was one short. *Bobby's.* Fighting back the weeping that wanted to come, Kara kept walking.

And saw somebody move in the corner of her eye.

Oh, God!

Gasping, Kara jerked to a halt. She threw her hands up, putting one against her chest. So did the other person.

Idiot! I shouldn't have come in here alone!

Kara quickly turned, preparing to run. She noticed the intruder did the same, moving at an angle, putting one foot forward. Kara paused. Moved her head up and down, watching from the sides of her eyes as the other person mimicked her movements.

Sighing, Kara turned around. She gazed at her reflection in the glass doors. From the darkness outside, it was like a mirror that broadcasted her smirk back at her.

I really am an idiot.

Kara shook her head at herself and started walking again. As she neared the door, she felt cool air blowing through the busted pane. It brought goose bumps up on her arms. Rubbing them, she felt their lumpy texture.

She grabbed her coat, lifting it from the hook. Then she hurried out of the room.

In the hallway, she turned right. Sonja still leaned against the wall.

"Everything okay?" asked Sonja.

"Yeah. Just…yeah."

Sonja looked as if she wanted to ask more, but didn't. Kara was grateful.

She started walking toward Sonja, zipping her coat. A sudden gust of wind howled outside, pushing against the cabin. The walls creaked and popped under the heavy draught. The snow made sprinkling sounds against the windows and the door. The trees clacked like bones scraping together.

Kara put her hands in her pockets, and waited.

A couple minutes passed.

"How long's he been gone?" Kara asked.

"Too long," said Sonja.

Kara felt squirmy inside. He should've been back by now. It didn't take nearly as long with Georgia.

Something had happened.

"But," said Sonja, "he did say he was going to get the gasoline cans."

"That's right," said Kara, exhaling a relieved breath. She'd forgotten about that. "Yeah. He did say that." She felt slightly better, but knew the creeping sensation inside wouldn't go away until he was back.

More time went by.

"Now I'm getting worried," said Sonja.

"Me too."

Been worried.

Sonja pushed herself off the wall, turned around and gazed at the front door. Since there were no windows here, they were blind to what was on the other side.

"He's had time, right?" Sonja asked. "To get out there, get them…loaded, and to put the gas cans in the truck. Right?"

Kara thought so, but she didn't say anything.

"I better go check on him," said Sonja.

"No!" Kara grabbed the woman's arm. She felt the coat crush in her grip and quickly eased up on it. "I don't want to be left in here. Not anymore."

Sonja looked at her from over her shoulder. Her mouth was a crooked line of sympathy. "You're right. I wouldn't want to be left behind, either. All right. We'll both go. We'll just go out a little ways, see if we can find him."

Kara nodded. "Okay."

Sonja's hand curled around the door knob. It turned. Instead of opening the door, the woman hesitated. She looked back another time, giving Kara a look that showed her reluctance. Kara knew how she felt, because everything inside of her was screaming not to go out there.

The door opened. Cold air rushed in, throwing Sonja's tied hair back like a propeller.

Kara followed her out.

CHAPTER THIRTY-EIGHT

They didn't find Dad on the porch or in the front yard.

"Maybe he's at the truck," said Sonja, heading toward the side of the house.

Kara hurried to keep up. The wind pushed against her, making her movements difficult. Snow left stinging dots across her face, and she vigorously blinked to keep it out of her eyes. It reminded her of being at the beach on a windy day, how the sand felt like ant bites when it pelted her skin.

Looking around, Kara saw no sign of her dad. Flurries flew at an angle against the vehicles, but Kara didn't know if it was a fresh fall or if the wind was throwing around what was on the ground.

Edgar's truck was closest to them with a van in the middle and the Jeep on the far side. Sonja headed to the truck, ducking her head against the wind. Her arms were stiff at her sides as she squealed from the snow patting her face.

Kara was being left behind, so she hurried to catch up to Sonja as she reached the back of the truck. Sonja sucked in a breath and turned around. She held up her hands as Kara approached.

"Stop. You don't want to see this."

Panic fluttered through Kara. "Is it Dad?"

Sonja met her halfway. "No. Something else."

Kara looked past Sonja's shoulder, and saw just enough to know why the woman had stopped her. The tailgate was down. Bobby's shoe peeked around the edge of the truck bed. Clumps of snow had hardened around the bottom.

"Oh, God..." muttered Kara. She pulled away from Sonja and put her hands on her own cold and damp head. "Oh, *God!*"

Emotions tore through her, trying to pull her in several directions. Kara shook her head, trying to rattle them away. Dad had said something about putting everybody in the truck with Bobby. She hadn't paid attention to it then, but now she knew he'd found her brother and must've carried him all the way here. She wondered how far he'd had to go. It had to have been excruciating work. Maybe he passed out from exhaustion or had a heart...

"Come on," said Sonja. She put her arm around Kara and started to turn her. "Let's find your Dad."

Kara thought she nodded a response. She was guided away from the truck, her legs moving without her mind's consent. Kara vaguely wondered where they were going. Looking around, she noticed the cabin to her left, rising in view as they went down. When she faced forward, she realized they were heading toward the shed.

Why are we going out there?

To see if Dad was there, obviously. Inside the shed was where he kept the gas cans.

How did Sonja know that?

Didn't take her long to figure it out. That was the location most people kept gas cans.

As they approached, Kara spotted another pair of feet, toes up, that led to a dark lump inside an even darker mass. Something sleek glowed from the center of lump, angling toward the ceiling.

"Oh, damn." whispered Sonja. "Is that...?" She stopped walking.

Kara stood beside Sonja, shaking her head. "No. It's Edgar. Dad doesn't have shoes like that."

Nose wrinkled, Sonja bared her teeth. "Jesus, Dennis..." She shook her head. Sonja took a step forward.

A cranking noise disturbed the night, clacking through the wind. Sounded like a rope being yanked on a pulley. Sonja stopped, grabbed Kara's arm and jerked her close. Together they gazed at the shed.

"What the hell was that?" asked Sonja.

The whirring clack repeated, sputtering before coughing to silence once more.

"Oh, shit," Kara muttered.

Sonja's grip on her arm tightened. "Get inside, Kara."

"No."

"Go, now!"

"I'm not leaving you out here!"

The ratchet-like noise erupted again, this time catching and revving into a brattle—the loudness of a tiny motor coming to life.

"Shit," cried Sonja. She started pushing Kara. "Run! Get out of here!"

"No!"

Kara stepped in front of Sonja, holding her arm out as if trying to shield her. Sonja stopped fighting and joined Kara in staring at the shed.

The shadows parted and Dennis clambered from the darkness. He walked in a crouch, leaning forward with each step. His face was a thin red mask. A gash the width of a candy bar stretched across his forehead. His teeth looked very white, his eyes wild flickering orbs. In his left hand, he held Dad's chainsaw by the front hand guard, with his right arm reaching behind him. A trail of smoke puffed from the exhaust pipe.

The dark pulled back like a blanket, revealing Dad bit by bit. Dennis dragged her father by the collar of his coat. When his body was clear of the doorway, Dennis dropped him.

Dennis stood up straight, bringing his now free hand up to the chainsaw, sliding his fingers around the trigger guard. His index finger found the trigger and squeezed.

The chainsaw brattled as he held it above his head, the smoke now pouring out. He screamed.

Sonja also screamed. "Dennis! What are you doing?"

The chainsaw poised above his head, Dennis's eyes flicked in Sonja's direction. They glared at her, unblinking, like two balls of hate. He screamed again.

Sonja, still screaming, seemed to be trying to compete as to who could be louder. Kara pulled her, trying to make her move, but the woman wasn't budging.

"Stop, Dennis!" Sonja held up her hands, fingers flexing. *Please!*

Dennis's head trembled as his scream turned to a roar. His mouth formed a ring shape as the breaths of his rage came out in a cloud. The chainsaw spun and wailed as he squeezed the trigger.

"Come on, Sonja!" Kara jerked the woman's arm, making her turn. She pulled Sonja's face close. "Go!"

Sonja came unglued from her spot. They started to run. Kara looked back over her shoulder and saw they weren't quick enough.

Dennis was already right behind them, bringing the chainsaw up. The spinning teeth were a blur as they came at Kara's stomach.

She felt hands slap her back, throw her. On her way down, she spun around.

Sonja now stood where Kara had been, turning to face Dennis. Her arms were down.

Kara's back pounded the ground.

Dennis saw what was about to happen right before it did. His eyes widened, mouth dropping open. He shouted, "No!"

The whirring blade struck Sonja's stomach from the side, ripping open a trail across her abdomen. Her innards exploded as the chainsaw's teeth devoured them. Red sprayed out in a mist that splashed Kara, making her scream.

Dennis let the chainsaw fall and caught Sonja under her arms as she was starting to drop. The engine died when it hit the ground. "Sonja?" he said, winded. His throat made a clucking sound, then he huffed harder. "Sonja!"

Sonja stared at him through shocked eyes. Her mouth moved, but instead of words, blood was what came out. Head twitching, she looked Dennis in the eyes. In unison, they went down on their knees,

Dennis keeping his hold and Sonja still staring. She coughed up blood. Red bubbles formed between her lips as she tried to talk.

Dennis shushed her. "Oh God, I'm so sorry...I didn't mean to...God!"

Sonja's head dropped back, as if she was trying to look at the sky.

"No," said Dennis. He shook her. Sonja's head fell forward, her chin resting against her chest. He began to sob.

"*Nononononononononoooo...*"

Kara watched as Dennis lowered Sonja to the ground. He put her on her back and leaned over her as he wept. Slowly, Kara rolled onto her side. She looked toward the shed. On his back, Dad looked to be in the same position except for his legs. His knee twitched, then his leg moved a little.

Dad was waking up. He was okay.

She checked on Dennis. He hadn't moved. Leaning over Sonja, his hands gently patted her chest. She could hear him whispering apologies. Kara couldn't help feeling bad for Dennis. He hadn't wanted to hurt Sonja. But it was too late for him to take it back.

She was dead.

Because she wanted to help us.

Another one had died because of Dennis.

"Happy now?" she asked.

Dennis seemed not to have heard her. Rolling over, Kara pushed herself up to her knees. Her ribs felt sore and cold. She rubbed her hand across them, wincing at the pain it caused. Felt like one of them might have been cracked when she fell.

"See what you did?" she asked, wincing at the sharp pinch above her hip.

"I see it," said Dennis in a low voice. "This shouldn't have happened."

Kara stared at Dennis. He didn't seem to be crying now. His fingers caressed Sonja's check, rubbed down to her chin where he lightly tapped her lips.

"Shouldn't have happened," he repeated. Then he looked over his shoulder, but not at Kara. His eyes were aimed at the shed. "His fault."

Dennis stood up, bringing the chainsaw with him. Holding it by the front hand guard, his other hand grabbed the pull grip and gave it a yank. This time there were no false starts. The chainsaw revved right to life.

Dennis turned around, facing Kara.

She lurched onto her back, elbows digging into the snow. Eyes on Dennis, she dragged herself backward. Dennis stepped forward, feet sinking into the grooves her legs made in the snow. The air began to thicken with the stench of oil and gas. Her eyes watered, throat closed.

Kara dropped onto her back. She stole a quick glance of her father. He'd hardly moved since the last time she saw him. In her mind, she saw him running to her aid, saving her at the last moment. But that wasn't going to happen.

She was about to die.

Dennis stood at her feet, the chainsaw held out to the side of him, the blade angled up. The wound on his head spilled blood, another on his shoulder leaked blood onto his arm. He held her stare for a few moments before turning his head. He looked back toward Dad, then to Kara. He did this a couple times, as if trying to decide on something.

Then he turned away from her and started walking toward Dad, revving the chainsaw.

The swelling clatter of the small engine seemed to be what Dad needed to shock him awake. He rolled onto his stomach, got on all fours, and gazed up at the looming Dennis with dazed eyes.

He's out of it.

Dad wouldn't know what was occurring until Dennis was already tearing him apart. Kara couldn't let that happen.

Getting up was hard. Her ribs felt like they were shifting under her skin. Each movement caused a sharp prod inside that stole her breath. When she was upright, she immediately regained her bearings and charged at Dennis.

A few steps behind him, she jumped.

Please don't turn around!

She imagined him spinning to face her, the twirling chain pointed up. Her stomach smashed against the tip and the blade ripped through as if her body was soggy paper.

But then the vision was gone, and she was landing on Dennis's back. Her legs hooked around his waist, arms slithered around his throat and squeezed.

CHAPTER THIRTY-NINE

Grant was confused. His scattered mind was slowly floating back to reassemble a conscious thought. He'd been in the shed. Edgar was on the ground, so he'd taken a wide berth to avoid seeing him. He remembered finding two of the three gas cans before pain blasted through the back of his head.

Now he was outside in the freezing weather. Snow dotted the back of his heated neck with cold. He looked up. Dennis stood several feet away, swinging the throttling chainsaw with one hand and swatting at his back with the other. It took a moment for Grant to note the pair of legs that were crossed at the ankles above Dennis's crotch. Even from here Grant could see how red Dennis's face was. Arms constricting his throat were what caused it.

A head appeared over Dennis's shoulder. Behind the bright curtains of hair, Grant recognized his daughter's snarling face.

"Die! Die! Die!" she shrieked above the chainsaw, spit flying. "Die you fucking bastard!"

"Kuh-Kara?" Speaking made his brain feel as if a spike was hammered into it. Grant's throat retracted. His stomach gave a flip and he leaned forward and dry-heaved several times. When he looked back up, his eyes were blurry with tears. "Kara!"

Grant wiped his eyes, saw Dennis swaying. Kara screamed into the night sky, demanding Dennis to drop dead. The chainsaw fell, hitting the ground with a soft thud. Its hiccupping putter was muffled in the snow.

With both hands free, Dennis reached back. One gripped a handful of Kara's hair, the other catching her under the arm. He pulled. Kara swung over his shoulder. Screaming, she performed a complete flip and her back pounded the snow. Dennis, losing his balance, also fell.

Before Dennis hit the ground, Kara was already crawling for the chainsaw. As she reached it, Dennis's hands slapped down on the tool first. The blade spun as the engine revved. Kara screamed and flung herself away from the spinning chain thrust at her face. Where her head had been, Grant saw strands of yellow hair fluttering in the air.

"Kara!"

Finally, his daughter heard him. Her head whipped in his direction. Her hair was slightly lopsided, shorn by the chainsaw's snagging loop. Grant ignored the throbbing spikes in his head and forced himself to stand up. A trail of wetness flowed from the back of his head and moved down the nape of his neck. The skin around his skull felt as if it was being pulled taut against the forming bulge on his scalp.

He wasn't sure what to do, but knew that he had to get over there, help his daughter. She was all he had left and, no matter what, she was going to make it, whether he did or not.

Grant started jogging, unable to fully sprint.

"Dad!"

Kara's face wrinkled in pain as she got up. She held her side, bending slightly over, and ran. Grant moved toward her, the distance between them closing. He held out an arm, ready to pull her into his embrace.

But she bypassed him, heading for the shed.

Grant stopped running. He turned to watch her vanish inside the darkened doorway. The chainsaw screamed behind him.

Grant twisted, just missing Dennis's swipe. Everything seemed to slow down. He felt the air of the spinning chain, smelled the oil that kept it loose. As his head avoided being sawed off, he glimpsed Sonja's body on the ground. A wide gulley split her midriff. He kept turning, dodging Dennis as he ran by.

Motion cut back to normal. Dennis turned around, yelled and charged Grant with the chainsaw out. Grant leaped over Sonja, dashing toward the shed. Dennis skidded to a halt, spun on his heels and followed.

In Grant's vigorous line of sight, he saw Kara stooped over Edgar's body. Her arms were stiff in front of her, vanishing to her elbows in the shadows. She looked feral with her mouth opened wide, baring her teeth. The veins on her neck bulged. She suddenly stumbled back, arms rising. When she stood up, the ax was ripped free of Edgar's chest. She stepped out, holding the ax with both hands. One half of the blade was tarnished in red.

Grant headed for her, feeling the air being cut behind him. His coat pulled taut against his chest briefly before it sagged forward and hung on his shoulders. Cold air soaked his back. His shirt trembled under the chainsaw's hungry bite.

He's so close!

His coat slipped down his arms, hanging around his elbows. The tattered edges showed how close the chainsaw had come to his spine.

"Get behind me, Dad!"

Kara held the ax up, her face a pale crumpled snarl.

Grant grabbed her arm and jerked her to him. He didn't stop running.

"What are you doing?" Kara yelled from his side.

She fought him at first, but quickly matched his pace. Maybe she was beginning to understand they were no threat to Dennis as long as he had the chainsaw. If they could get to Edgar's truck, they could get out of here. That was what needed to happen. As much as he wanted to fight, Grant knew escape was the smarter option.

Grant pulled Kara to the left as they neared the felled remains of Kara's favorite tree. His daughter jerked her arm out of his hand and turned around.

Grant stopped running. "Kara!"

Dennis was already at her, swinging the chainsaw as she swung the ax. The ax and saw met with a high-pitched clang. The striking metal caused a flash of sparks. Kara was thrown back. Her rump hit a pile of sawed branches, making them tumble. She bounced down the rolling logs, crying out each time her buttocks smacked a bough.

Dennis stepped beside her, chainsaw idling.

Grant rushed Dennis. "Not her!" He slammed into Dennis just as he went for Kara. Holding him in a reversed bear hug, he pulled Dennis back. The chainsaw bumped his leg on its way to the ground. It shut off.

Breaking away from Grant, Dennis pivoted to the right. He swung out, his fist catching Grant on the jaw. It rattled his brain, making his vision turn fuzzy. He saw Dennis coming in for another and turned to avoid the next punch.

Swinging upward, Grant's fist pounded Dennis's stomach. The wind exploded out of Dennis, doubling him over as Grant brought his knee up. It smashed his chin. Dennis staggered back, turning. The tree stump caught his hip. A leg flew high, but instead of falling over the other side, he landed sideways on the flat top. His feet kicked open air as his weight came back down. His feet slapped the ground. Dennis sagged against the tree stump, braced on elbows, trying to catch his breath.

Kara rushed in from the side, the ax held above her head. She brought it down.

Dennis saw her coming and dived out of the way. The ax punched deep into the stump's rim, splitting the wood. Kara loosed an exasperated scream, started pulling the handle up. The ax didn't move.

Grant, spotting Dennis groping for the chainsaw, ran at him, preparing to kick. He shot his leg forward. And missed. His left foot skidded across the snow and left the ground. He saw it rising in front of him. Then Grant's back pulverized the ground and slid a few feet. The brutal landing blasted the air out of his lungs. It felt as if he was trying to suck air through a flattened tube.

"Stay away from him!" Kara shouted.

Grant wiggled onto his side in time to catch Kara grabbing handfuls of Dennis's hair. Dennis was just a few inches shy of Grant, his hand reaching for his ankle when Kara pulled him back. It looked as if she was trying to pull a mask off to reveal a hidden identity. Shouting, Dennis was either stretching or being tugged to his feet. Kara suddenly stumbled back. Her feet stepped on a log. It rolled out from under her and pulled her down onto the corrugated hardness of the rest. Grant noticed clumps of hair sticking out between the cracks of her fingers.

Dennis struggled to his feet, bent at the waist. His hair was prominently thinner. He looked at Grant and growled. The cavity of his forehead wound crinkled and started to bleed again.

This time, Grant didn't give him the chance and scrambled up and ran at Dennis, swinging. Some of the blows connected, others didn't. Dennis fought back, fists hammering Grant's face, punches landing on his midsection. Grant's stomach was so empty, Dennis's hands might have gone all the way through.

Grant staggered back with each strike, unable to block them. He swung around, threw back an elbow and cried out from the thunderbolt of pain that moved up his arm when it struck Dennis's head. He stayed on his feet when Dennis speared a shoulder into Grant's side. His shoes dug into the snow, burrowing ditches through the white as he slewed in reverse. Grant pounded the other man's back as he scooted backward, each blow making solid contact. He was so tired. The long trek back uphill, toting Bobby, all the walking, the trauma, lack of food and water…Grant was fading more and more.

Out of nowhere, Dennis sank down to his knees, and for a moment Grant thought he was actually overpowering his assailant.

Then pain exploded in his groin.

Heat gripped his muscles, crushing his stomach and killing his air. Grant couldn't find his breath, couldn't focus his eyes. A shape flitted low to the ground and Grant's eyes cleared long enough to see Dennis rearing back his fist and thrusting forward.

Another burst of fire filled his groin from a second dirty hit. Grant's legs folded. He dropped onto his side, making whimpering sounds as he tried to breathe.

Dennis threw back his head, gasping. Fresh blood sluiced down his face, thinning the dried, crusty sections and causing them to run. Cherry wetness poured from his jawline. He used the flat of his hand to wipe his eyes clear. Then punched the snow and shoved himself up.

Standing over Grant, Dennis swayed slightly. He held his side as he took several short breaths. "It's over…Grant."

Grant agreed. He had no fight left. His testicles felt as if they'd been forced into his lungs. His shivering body was useless and weak. There would be no getting back up for another round. He'd failed. Failed his family. Failed himself.

Clutching his crotch, Grant watched Dennis straighten his back. Ligaments and bones popped as he stretched back his shoulders. Blood ran down his face in freshets.

Grant was still crippled. He knew all that was left was surrendering. Dennis had won.

I'm sorry, Marion, Bobby, Georgia.

He turned to where Kara had landed.

I'm sorry, K…

She was gone.

His flustered grimace that had made his face tight loosened into a frown. Where was she?

Then, as if to answer him, she appeared from the side of Dennis. Her arms wrapped around the man's legs, like she used to do to Grant when she was a little girl and didn't want him to leave home.

Looking down, Dennis held his arms out for balance. "What the…?" He saw Kara. "Let go!"

Kara squeezed his legs, pushing his knees together. She looked up. Eyes screwed shut, her face stretched into a sneer. Her bright hair was glued to her cheeks and forehead. She brought a leg forward, making her knee nearly touch her chin.

Dennis tottered back. He flapped his arms. Eyes rounded, he let out a "Whoa!" With both hands, Kara thrust his calves toward Grant.

Dennis tumbled over Kara's shoulder, as if doing a backward dive into a swimming pool. His arms spun circles as he plummeted toward the tree stump.

The exposed half of the ax blade stopped his descent with a juicy crunch.

Dennis's exclamation turned to a high-pitched moan as the bowed edge of the outward blade burst through his chest.

He lay against the tree stump, the blade holding his torso up and his legs stretched across the ground. His feet kicked holes in the snow. He lifted his bobbing head and gazed down at the protruding curve of the blood-caked blade. Two crimson lines ran from the corners of his mouth. Seeing what had happened, he screamed, showing fear for the first time. He patted his shoulders. He tried to reach behind him, probably to see if he could dislodge the ax. Realizing there was no possible way to do so, he screamed some more.

Grant spotted his daughter slinking along the ground on all fours, her sopping hair blocking her face. At first, he thought she was coming to check on him, but she stopped a few feet short.

Her hands fumbled over the chainsaw.

"Kara!" Grant called. He knew what she was going to do. "Don't!"

If she'd heard him, she gave no indication. She stood up, armed with the chainsaw. She dragged her feet through the snow toward Dennis.

It's okay. She doesn't know how to work it.

Kara jerked back the cord and the chainsaw rattled to life with a burst of exhaust, proving Grant wrong. She squeezed the trigger, making the little motor wail. Wanting to stop her, Grant tried to get up, but his testicles were swollen and tender. The slightest movements made them feel as if they were being nailed to his thighs. He dropped back onto the ground, reaching out.

His screams were drowned out by the revving chainsaw.

Dennis saw her looming closer, the blade spinning as it lowered to his chest. He nodded, giving her permission to begin.

But she hesitated. The engine's power decelerated to a poppy idle. The motionless blade lowered away from Dennis's midriff. She looked at Grant from over her shoulder. Her face looked even wetter now, almost shiny in the night and cursed with despair. He knew then it would be her permanent look. She'd never recover from this and would live with the desolation this night had caused for the rest of her life.

Her lips moved, silently speaking. She mouthed: *I'm sorry.*

"No!" Grant shouted.

Kara revved the chainsaw and turned around. Without any kind of hesitation now, she brought the spinning teeth down and touched them to Dennis's stomach. It ripped through his coat, his shirt, sawing a messy line into his abdomen. Dennis's body quaked on the ax, arms bouncing, legs kicking. His fingers curled into claws that trembled. He screamed as his blood showered Kara in sticky red.

Grant spotted the sawblade sticking out of Dennis's back. Soggy chunks were flung all over, spattering the stump in a gloppy mess. The brattling blur moved upward. More wet crunches mixed with Dennis's screams as his body puked out ground-up innards. Now Dennis's body convulsed as if electrified. Blood exploded from him, dousing Kara, matting her hair to her face. Her hands were slick red gloves.

The saw moved all the way up, cutting a path through Dennis's torso before splitting him into halves. The blade came free and Kara thrust it into the sky. Gore and blood rained down on her from the chainsaw as she unleashed a warrior's scream.

A chunk of Dennis rolled onto the ground, landing on its side and facing Grant. It looked as if Dennis had been partially buried in the snow, leaving half his body exposed.

Kara shoved the saw up, screaming at the sky harder, as if she wanted God's ears to hear her pain.

CHAPTER FORTY

Kara walked into the kitchen. She had on fresh clothes and her mother's coat. Her hair was still a little damp, even though Grant had heard the hairdryer going. Her face was devoid of expression. It looked as if she wore a featureless mask of herself, one that was stained slightly pink from the blood she couldn't wash off.

She glanced at Grant and blinked as if noticing him for the first time.

"Ready to go?" he asked.

Kara nodded. "Yeah." She zipped the coat, putting her hands in the pockets. "Bet Sonja's truck's run out of gas by now."

"I loaded the gas cans. It's fine. They should get us somewhere."

"Where?"

"The hell away from here."

Kara nodded.

Grant stood up from the table, groaning. It was still hard for him to move around from Dennis's hits below the belt, but he could at least maneuver without dropping to the ground and sobbing now. His whole body was filled with pain. Stiff muscles riddled with the worst kind of soreness he'd ever felt. His head felt as if a large icy hand was trying to compact it into a ball.

"So, what's the plan?" she asked.

"We drive. That's all I know for now."

"It's going to be hard, with the weather."

"We'll make it work."

Kara nodded again, clucked her tongue. "You're mad at me, aren't you?"

"Mad at you?"

"Yeah. For what I did…to Dennis."

"No."

"Yes, you are. I can tell from how you keep looking at me like you're ashamed."

"I'm not ashamed and I'm not mad. But I didn't want you to do it."

"So you are mad."

"I just told you I wasn't mad."

Kara sighed. "Why wouldn't you want me to? You, more than anybody, should be delighted by what I did."

"Because. You made a conscious decision to kill him. At that point it wasn't an issue of self-defense. How could I be *delighted* by watching you slaughter someone?"

"Nobody would blame me for it."

"It was murder, Kara."

She shook her head. "Don't be a lawyer right now."

"I'm not. I'm being your father. You killed him in cold blood, just like…" He stopped, not wanting to compare his daughter to the monster he'd created. "You could have gone a different route, is all."

"Well, I didn't." She shrugged a shoulder. "It's done." Her bottom lip quivered, and she bit down on it. "Sorry I let you down."

"Hey," he said, hobbling toward her. He put his arms around her and pulled her to him. She didn't hug him back. "You didn't let me down. I just didn't want it on your conscience for the rest of your life."

He felt her body jerking against him. The front of his shirt felt wet from her tears. He pulled her tighter against him, and finally her arms went around his back and hugged him as well.

"What worries me…" Kara stopped, as if trying to make her voice not sound so jittery. "I don't feel bad at all for killing him. Not at all.

He killed Mom, Bobby, Aunt Georgia. He killed Edgar and Sonja..."
Her head shook against his chest. "I feel better, a little, that he's dead."

"I know," he said. "So do I."

Grant held his daughter for a long time. Eventually she stopped crying, but they remained in the kitchen, clasped in an amicable clinch of father and daughter.

Kara pulled away from the hug first, wiping her saturated eyes.

She waited for Grant by the glass doors as he got his dissected coat back on.

Then, together, they left the cabin.

Outside, the snow had finally stopped falling. From the tumult it had been for what felt like a lifetime, the night was heavy with tranquility. The only sounds were the soft crunches of their footsteps through the snow. Even the wind was still, as if Mother Nature had put a calming hand over the area in regard for them.

Grant held Kara's hand as they walked to Edgar's truck, didn't let go until he'd helped her inside. He gave one last look around before opening his door. Any moment he expected Dennis to reappear, somehow glued back together and hungry for another bout of punishment.

Dennis didn't appear. He was dead, another lost life added to so many.

Grant climbed into the truck, and knowing there was no longer any threat out there, he still locked the door. He glanced at Kara as he reached for the key. Her door was also locked. For a reason he couldn't comprehend, he smiled seeing that it was.

The truck started on the first try.

Moving slowly, they began their journey down the hill.

ABOUT THE AUTHOR

Kristopher Rufty lives in North Carolina with his three children and pets. He's written numerous books, including *Hell Departed, Anathema, Jagger, The Lurkers, The Skin Show, Pillowface,* and many more. When he's not writing, he's spending time with his kids, or obsessing over gardening and growing food.

His online presence has dwindled, but he can still be found on Facebook and Twitter.

Kristopher Rufty

Made in the USA
Las Vegas, NV
21 February 2023